Praise for *Rough Treatment*

"Harvey has a fine hand for simply drawn, beautifully realized characters (the two burglars are works of art) who seem to stumble into everyday answers to extraordinary problems. In the end, the plot gets resolved but the characters don't—and, Harvey rightly implies, that's life."—*Chicago Tribune*

"Harvey is quietly stretching the limits of the police procedural with his three-dimensional characters, his sense of humor and brisk pacing, and his understanding of what makes people—and the world—go around."—*The Miami Herald*

"What matters about *Rough Treatment* is not the crime fiction subgenre it represents, but that it's such expert storytelling. Everything contributes. Compelling characters, vigorous narrative drive, and a prose style quirky enough to be interesting but not irritating. Actually, almost everything in this book is appealing, including one of the most chivalrous burglars since Raffles."—David Delman, *The Philadelphia Inquirer*

"As in most police procedurals, *Rough Treatment* focuses on a variety of engaging cops and an intriguing line-up of crooks. So what sets Harvey apart from William J. Cunitz, John Wainwright, Mark Hebden, and all the other writers who continue to successfully mine the police procedural vein? Quite simply, the British poet and novelist is an elegant stylist as well as an accomplished storyteller: his skill adds depth to every character in the book."
—*Mostly Murder*

"A new '90's breed of British police procedural—and another winner for Harvey." —*Kirkus Reviews* (starred)

"This rough slice of English life is cut from the cold, gray industrial heart of the Midlands, the same spot frequented by Alan Sillitoe, and Harvey exposes it with Sillitoe's unflinchingly sardonic vision."—*Booklist* (boxed and starred)

Rough Treatment

Rough Treatment

John Harvey

A Marian Wood / Owl Book
Henry Holt and Company   New York

Henry Holt and Company, Inc.
Publishers since 1866
115 West 18th Street
New York, New York 10011

Henry Holt® is a registered
trademark of Henry Holt and Company, Inc.

Library of Congress Cataloging-in-Publication Data
Harvey, John, 1938–
Rough treatment / John Harvey
p.   cm.
I. Title.
PR6058.A6989R6   1990   90-32160
823'.914—dc20   CIP

ISBN 0-8050-5496-0

Henry Holt books are available for special promotions and
premiums. For details contact: Director, Special Markets.

First published in hardcover in 1990 by
Henry Holt and Company, Inc.

First Owl Book Edition—1997

A Marian Wood / Owl Book

Printed in the United States of America
All first editions are printed on acid-free paper.∞

10   9   8   7   6   5   4   3   2   1

Rough Treatment

1

'Are we going to do this?' Grice asked. Already the cold was seeping into the muscles across his back. January he hated with a vengeance.

Milder than usual days, Grabianski thought, you expected nights like these. 'A minute,' he said, and started off towards the garage. For a big man, he moved with surprising lightness.

Through an estate agent's wide-angle lens it would have been a mansion, but from there, where Grice was standing at the head of the pebbled drive, it was just another oversized house at the southern edge of the city.

Daylight would have made it easier to tell that the cream weather-proof paint had not been renewed this last or even the previous summer; the wood of the fake timbers was shedding its casing like a bad case of eczema. Miniature fir trees sat stunted in barrels at either side of the front door. Three steps up and ring the bell. Grice tried to remember the last time he had gained entrance to somebody's house by ringing the bell.

'Well?'

For reply, Grabianski shrugged, hands in pockets.

'Meaning what?' Grice said.

'Back seat, the floor, it's full of junk. Maybe they don't use it at all.'

'Junk?'

'Newspapers, magazines; tissue boxes and chocolate wrappers. Three pairs of high-heeled shoes.'

'What d'you expect? It's a woman's car.'

'Because of the shoes?' •

'The shoes, the size – look at it. It's a second car, a woman's car. What man would drive a car like that?'

They stood looking at the garage roof, half-lowered, the bonnet of the car sticking out from under the left-hand side.

'I don't like it,' Grice said.

'The list of things you like,' said Grabianski, 'you could write on a cigarette packet and still have room for the health warning.'

'I don't like the car being here.'

'I thought you wanted to get on with it.'

'One way or another I want to get out of this damned cold.'

'Then let's go.' Grabianski took three or four steps towards the house.

'The car . . .' Grice began.

'What you're saying, the car's here, it's a woman's car, therefore the woman's here. That what you're saying?'

'What if I am?'

Grabianski shook his head: instead of wasting his time watching soap operas, Grice should get himself some education. An evening class in philosophy, logic. That might teach him.

'In the dark?' Grabianski asked.

'Hm?'

'She's in there in the dark?'

'Sleeping?'

'It's too early.'

'Maybe she's got a headache.'

'What are you all of a sudden, her doctor?'

On the other side of the tall, trimmed hedges and back along the broad avenue there were lights showing; they couldn't stand there forever.

Grice shuffled his feet. 'You think we should do it?' he said.

'Yes,' Grabianski answered. 'We're going to do it.'

They began to walk along the lawn beside the drive, not trusting their feet to the pebbles. As they crossed the grass towards the rear, both men glanced up at the red, rectangular box of the burglar alarm high on the wall.

Maria Roy lay back far enough for her breasts to float amongst the scented foam which covered the surface of the water. In the pale light from the nearby nightlight they were soft-hued, satin, the darker nipples hardening beneath her gaze. Harold, she thought. It didn't help. Softly, she rubbed the tip of her finger around the mazed areolas and smiled as she sensed her nipples tense again. What kind of a marriage was it if after eleven years the only place you had ever made love was in bed? And then, not often.

2

'Never mind,' she said to her breasts softly. 'Never mind, my sad little sacks, somebody loves you. Somewhere.'

And easing herself into a sitting position she gave them a last, affectionate squeeze.

'Never mind, my sad little sacks of woe.'

'Is that a light?' Grabianski whispered.

'Where?'

'There. See? Edge of the curtain.'

'The blind. It's a blind.'

'Is it a light?'

'It's nothing.'

'It could be a candle.'

Grice looked at him. 'Maybe she's holding a seance.' He eased the edge of plastic a millimetre to the left and the patio door breathed open.

'Why else do you think I'm calling you,' Maria Roy said into the telephone, 'to tell you how much I love you?'

Underneath the robe she was wearing she smelt lightly of talc. Givenchy Gentleman: *talc parfumé*. Well, Harold had to be good for something, didn't he?

'No, Harold,' she said, interrupting him, 'I'm intending to fly there. Under my robe, this very second, I'm growing wings.'

There was a half-full glass of wine on the circular table, next to the telephone, and she picked it up, two fingers and thumb. The wine was left over from last night, or was it the night before, and it had tasted sour to begin with.

'Yes, of course I've tried doing it manually, but it won't budge.'

She turned her head and blew cigarette smoke towards the centre of the room; the receiver away from her face, she could still hear his voice. On and on.

'Harold . . .'

And on.

'Harold . . .'

And on.

'Harold, the machines are always breaking down. The time code is always disappearing. The sound is forever slipping out of synch. I don't know why they assign you the worst dubbing suite

3

in the entire studios, but they do. All of the time. Yes. It could be that they're trying to tell you something. I'm trying to tell you something. I've already taken a bath and when I've finished my drink – no, it isn't, it's only wine, and bad wine at that – when I've finished I'm going to get changed and then, since I can't get the car out of the garage and you won't drive out here and fetch me, I'm going to have to call Jerry and Stella and ask them to make a detour and pick me up.'

She let out some more smoke and sighed, loud enough to let him know that whatever arrangement they came to now she was agreeing to it under sufferance. She was in the habit of making it clear most transactions between them took place that way.

'Yes, Harold,' she said, 'I have heard of the word taxi. I also know the word goodbye.'

She looked at the receiver back in its cradle and smiled that the connection could be so easily, so instantly, broken. She moved through to the kitchen with a slight swish of silk against her legs and threw the contents of the glass down the sink. She stubbed out her cigarette, set down one glass and took up another, walking it back to the living room. The trolley of bottles stood between the TV set and the shelves of video-cassettes and magazines and paperback books. She noticed that a couple of Harold's dog-eared scripts had found their way down from the room he was using as a study and made a mental note to tell him to take them back. She twisted the top from a bottle of J & B Rare and poured herself a generous amount. Despite the stupid garage, the stupid car, the call to Harold, she was still feeling good after the bath.

She tasted the scotch, more than a sip, thought to hell with Harold and when she turned and lowered the glass she could see the man in the doorway right over the rim.

'Oh, Christ!'

Her left hand went to her mouth and she bit deep into the skin at the base of her thumb, something she hadn't done since she was a child.

Strange things were happening to the walls of her stomach and the blood was racing to her head. She leaned back against the shelves, certain that she was going to faint.

4

The man was still in the same position, almost leaning against the jamb of the door but not quite. He was a big man, nothing short of six foot and stocky, wearing a dark-blue suit with a double-breasted jacket that probably made him broader than he actually was. He didn't say anything, but continued to stare at her, something in his eyes that was, well, appreciative of what he was seeing.

'Oh, Christ,' Maria whispered. 'Oh, Christ.'

'I know what you're thinking.'

When he did speak it made her jump, his voice so startling after that silence, his man's voice so different in that room. She looked back at him, not knowing – now that she wasn't going to faint – what it was that she should do, if she should do or say anything. And if she did, would it do any good?

'I know what you're thinking.'

Maria Roy didn't know whether he had spoken again or if the same words were reverberating inside her head.

'We won't ' – a slight pause – 'hurt you.'

She moved her fingers around the glass; her mouth was so dry that her tongue seemed to be sticking to it. She knew she was meant to register the word *hurt*, but what snagged instead inside her brain and wouldn't let go was *we*.

We.

She tried to stop herself from looking away, searching; she listened for sounds but heard nothing. Perhaps it had only been something he had said, something to make her more frightened; perhaps he was on his own.

Maria swallowed a little air.

Was that better? If he was on his own?

A smile slid lopsidedly down his face as if he could tell exactly what she was thinking. She knew then that this was not new for him; he was relaxed, through a confidence that came from practice, practice and experience. Why else would he be smiling? Then she heard steps on the stairs and knew that his *we* had been no lie.

The second man was shorter but still not short; he was wearing a brown suit that was already going shiny and brown shoes that were old but well-polished. He was about the same age as the first – early to mid-forties, Maria guessed. The same age as her husband, but not afraid to show it: not for them the pretensions that sent him off to the studio in zips and coloured logos and with sixty-pound trainers on his feet instead of real shoes.

The two men exchanged glances and then the newcomer walked across the room – taking his time, sauntering almost – and eased himself down on to the leather-covered settee.

'Nice place,' he said conversationally. 'Got yourself a pretty nice place.'

Maria looked from one to the other, unable to rid herself of the idea that they had broken into her house and now they were going to make an offer to buy it: two men in suits and real shoes.

Despite herself, despite everything, Maria Roy arched back her head and began to laugh.

The three of them were sitting down now. Grabianski in the deep armchair with the Liberty-print covers and Grice back against the far corner of the settee, legs crossed and looking just this side of bored. Maria Roy sat on a straight-backed chair across the room from the pair of them, apex of the triangle. Grabianski had the same mildly amused expression in his eyes and Maria knew he was trying to look up her legs, doing his best to peer between the folds of her silk robe, all the while trying to figure out whether she was wearing anything underneath or not.

She caught herself wondering precisely which pair of knickers she had pulled from the airing cupboard and stepped into. If they were truly, you know, clean. As if she were having an accident. She took a swallow of the J & B to keep herself from laughing some more. An accident was exactly what she was having, more or less.

'You want another drink?' asked Grabianski hopefully.

'She doesn't want a drink,' Grice said, recrossing his legs.

'How do you know?'

'It isn't that kind of occasion.'

'Well, I want a drink,' Grabianski said, levering himself out of the chair. The buttons of his jacket were unfastened and Maria could see that his body was in shape for a man of his age; no belly starting to strain against his belt. Harold, he worked out three times a week, stupid little weights strapped to his ankles, and still he had a pot belly.

'No vodka,' said Grabianski, disappointed, searching amongst the bottles.

'Sorry,' Maria apologized.

'For God's sake!' Grice protested. 'What is this?'

'We're having a drink,' said Grabianski amiably.

'We're in the middle of a burglary, that's what we're doing,' Grice said, pressing the heel of one hand hard against his knee.

'We had some people round the other night,' Maria was explaining. 'We ran out of vodka and somehow we've not got around to replacing it.' What was she doing, apologizing?

'It doesn't matter,' Grabianski said, leaning towards her reassuringly. 'Scotch is fine.' He lifted the bottle. 'Scotch?'

Grice grunted and Grabianski poured three whiskies, his own no more than a splash, but still he carried it into the kitchen to dilute it with water. When he came back, neither of the others had moved.

'Can we get on with this?' Grice complained.

Grabianski gave him his drink, handed Maria hers and sat back down. 'Relax,' he said. 'We'll get it done. What's the hurry?'

He wished Grice would take a walk, go and look at the rest of the house, go and steal something for heaven's sake. He thought then it might be all right for them, himself and the woman — what had she said her name was, Maria? Legs that seemed to go on forever. He bet that if she were wearing anything under that robe at all, it was one of those skimpy pairs you could cover with the palm of one hand. Christ! He could feel himself starting to sweat. Smell it. Look at her, staring back at him, reading his mind. What he was thinking: she knew what he was thinking.

Maria Roy was thinking that at any moment the phone would ring and it would be Jerry or Cynthia wanting to know where she was, where they were. Or Harold, maybe, the great Harold himself, calling to apologize and say he'd be there to pick her up after all, drive over together.

Except, she remembered, the shorter one, the one rubbing at his knee joint as though he were getting twinges of rheumatism, arthritis, something, had disconnected the phones.

'Finish up the drink,' Grice said to his partner. 'It's time we got down to business.'

7

Grabianski nodded, sipped a little scotch and water and got to his feet.

'Let's go,' he said, smiling.

Maria knew he was looking at her.

'No,' said Grice, on his feet also and moving towards the door.

'Let her help out,' said Grabianski. 'Save wasting time turning everything upside down.'

'You think she's going to do that?'

'Sure. Why not? As long as we're going to take it anyway.'

Not for the first time Maria wondered if they were for real. Maybe it was some elaborate joke set up by one of Harold's friends: a couple of out-of-work actors offering something a shade more sophisticated than a singing telegram. What would they have called it back in the sixties? A happening. Well, it was that right enough. She stood up and for a moment the hem of her robe caught against the inside of her thigh. Grabianski's mouth fell open and he stared. She hadn't had that effect on Harold for so long she couldn't remember.

'This I don't believe,' said Grice from the doorway.

Maria Roy finished her second glass of scotch and put the glass on the seat of the chair. 'Maybe I should lead the way?'

She knew Grabianski would be close behind her and she knew how tightly her robe clung to her when she climbed the stairs.

'There's just one thing more,' Grice said. The jewellery and the cash and the credit cards had been packed into one of the set of matching soft leather cases they had bought on last summer's trip to the Virgin Islands. Her two fur coats were folded over Grabianski's left arm.

'What's that?' Maria asked, but the expression on Grice's face told her that he knew. They both knew, she could sense it. How did they know about the safe?

She had to push the pillows aside in order to kneel on the bed; she lifted away the Klimt print and handed it to Grice, who leaned it against the bed upside down. She thought she might genuinely forget the combination, but as soon as she touched the dial her fingers made all the right moves.

She swayed backwards as the door swung open.

'Empty it,' Grice told her.

There was another jewellery box, the real one with the real jewels inside, the ones that had come to her in her mother's will, those that Harold had bought when he still had the need to impress her high on his agenda. There were two sets of bearer bonds, secured with thick rubber bands. Two wills, his and hers. A video a cameraman friend of Harold's had shot when they'd spent a week on some wretched little Greek island in a foursome. Harold had got an upset stomach from all the olives he'd jammed down his throat, the cameraman had proved to be well hung but had preferred to fiddle with his lens and watch his string-bean girlfriend licking salt out of Maria's navel, and when she got back to England Maria discovered she'd contracted a mild case of hepatitis.

Grabianski had a hand stretched out towards her, waiting for the cassette to be put into it.

'That everything?' asked Grice.

Maria nodded.

'Don't worry,' said Grabianski, 'you can claim it all back on the insurance.' He grinned down at the video-cassette in his hand. 'Except this.'

'You're sure?' said Grice.

'Certain,' said Maria, getting off the bed without showing his friend any more than she had already. Now all she wanted was to get them out of the house as quickly as possible.

'Wait a good half hour before you call the police,' Grabianski was saying, the two of them on their way from the room. 'You want to do yourself a favour, think about the descriptions you give them with a lot of care.'

'A couple of blacks,' suggested Grice, right behind them.

'Leather jackets and jeans.'

'Balaclavas.'

'Ski masks.'

'They forced you to open the safe.'

'Better,' said Grabianski, 'made you tell them the combination.'

'Right,' agreed Grice. 'That is better.'

He turned back into the room.

'Where are you going?' Grabianski asked.

'Wipe her prints from the safe,' Grice replied.

Watching him, Maria felt her legs weaken. Grabianski was standing close alongside her, fingers pushing softly in and out of the softness of her best fur coat.

Grice was standing on the bed, leaning towards the safe. Maria watched him as he used his gloves to smear whatever prints she'd left and continued to watch him as he reached into the rear of the safe.

'Uh-oh,' he said, turning back towards the pair of them, looking straight at Maria, 'you lied.'

2

Resnick had despised estate agents ever since one of them ran off with his wife. Before that he had merely found them distasteful, on a par with the young men who worked in car showrooms, forever eager to hustle forward from their desks, breath smelling of too many cigarettes, hands moist at the centre of the palm.

Anxious to get them in place but slow to take them away, three agencies had kept their 'For Sale' boards lined up against the dark stone of Resnick's garden wall for much of the past month. Finally he had fetched a spade from the cupboard beneath the stairs and removed two himself, leaving the third – a small concern, lacking forty-eight offices all over the East Midlands, but having on its staff at least one man Resnick felt he could talk to. It had been this man who had phoned Resnick and urged him to be present when he showed round some prospective buyers, 8.30 that morning.

'Busy people,' the agent had explained, 'a couple, looking to start a family, professionals, it's the only time they can both get there. I think you'll take to them,' he had added hopefully. As if that really mattered.

The house had been on the market now for twelve weeks and no one had as much as made an offer. It was a difficult size, the right property in the wrong location, the mortgage rate was up, the mortgage rate was down, prices were escalating, stabilizing – Resnick simply wanted to get out of the house. Lock the door and hand over the key. There.

So Resnick had arranged for his sergeant, Graham Millington, to go through the night's messages with the officer who had drawn the early shift, conduct the morning's briefing and then, along with the uniformed inspector in charge, report to the station superintendent.

'All right, Graham?' Resnick had said.

Millington had stood there, moustache shining, like a man whose birthday has come as a surprise.

* * *

When the couple arrived in their separate cars it was 8.43 precisely. The man got out of a shiny black Ford Sierra that had so many aerodynamic modifications that if he ever strayed in to the runway at Heathrow he would be sure to take off. His wife's preference was for a simple white Volkswagen GT convertible. They were both wearing light-grey suits and both checked their watches as they locked their cars and turned on the pavement.

A minute or so later a green Morris Minor drew into the curb and a woman Resnick had never seen before got out while the engine was still coughing. Her black sweater was loose and large and had the sleeves pushed up to the elbows; a short skirt – dark blue with white polka-dots – flared softly above thick ribbed tights and low red boots, which folded back in deep creases over her ankles. She had a clipboard bearing the details of the house in her left hand and she used the other to shake hands with her prospective clients.

'Mr and Mrs Lurie . . . good morning to you. I hope I haven't kept you waiting.'

She steered them towards where Resnick was standing, amongst the flat grass and dark unflowering bushes of a winter garden.

'Mr Resnick, right?'

Her smile was slightly lopsided as she touched his hand; the accent like a brisk but clipped Australian.

'Ought I say detective inspector? That'd be more proper.' She stepped ahead of him towards the front door. 'Shall we go inside?'

'What happened to Mr Albertson?' Resnick asked, low-voiced, as they passed through the hallway.

'He's left to go into the ministry.'

'He rang me only yesterday. About this.'

'I know. But isn't that the way it always is? Sudden. Look at Saul. Paul.'

Ahead of them Mr and Mrs Lurie were discussing the potential expense of ripping out the kitchen units and replacing them with natural oak.

'I'm Claire Millinder,' she said to Resnick, smiling quickly with her eyes. She moved past him into the kitchen. 'This is a perfect room in the mornings because of the light. You could easily fit a nice circular table over there and have it as a breakfast bay.'

The Luries looked at their watches.

'Shall we take a look at the reception rooms?' Claire Millinder said breezily.

Resnick didn't have the heart to follow them. One of his cats, Miles, came out of the living room as the visitors walked in and now rubbed the crown of his head against the side of Resnick's sensible shoe.

I hope they don't run into Dizzy, Resnick thought. If Dizzy took a mind to it, he might just bite either Mr or Mrs Lurie through the expensive material of their trouser legs.

They came out of the living room and Claire shepherded them in the direction of the stairs.

'You have to look at the master bedroom. It's really airy and you won't believe the amount of storage space.'

Resnick continued to stand there, a stranger in his own house.

When they came back down again, Resnick was letting Miles out through the back door. How were his cats going to make the adjustment to somewhere new when after all this time one of them still couldn't operate the cat flap that had been there for years?

'Inspector?'

He closed the door and moved back towards the hall.

'Darling, do you realize what a new bathroom suite would cost?' Mrs Lurie was asking her husband. 'To say nothing of the redecoration. And that poky little room at the back, I can't imagine what it could be used for, apart from storing things in boxes. What else could you get in there?'

'A cot,' Resnick said quietly.

'Sorry?'

'Nothing.'

Claire was looking at him from over the end of the banister rail.

'Darling,' said Mr Lurie, pushing back the sleeves of his suit and shirt to show the face of his watch.

'Yes, of course. We have to dash.'

'Work, you see.'

'Work.'

13

They stood in the doorway, arms almost touching. 'We'll be in touch.'

'Of course,' Claire said.

'Thank you for letting us see the house.'

Resnick was on the point of telling them it had been a pleasure, but stopped himself with little difficulty.

The heavy door fitted solidly back against the frame.

'Has he really joined the ministry?' Resnick asked. 'Albertson.'

'Anglican, I believe.'

For some moments they stood there, Resnick in the hallway close to the low table bearing a hat he almost never wore and a pile of old newspapers he'd been meaning to throw away, Claire with one hand on the dark-brown banister while the other held the clipboard close along her thigh.

'I don't know what makes people do things like that, do you?' she said.

'No.'

'D'you think they hear, you know, bells, voices?'

'The Sound of Music.'

'Running away.'

'Perhaps.'

She looked at him, considering. 'Why do we do anything? Why, for instance, do you want to move from this house?'

'That's difficult.'

'To explain or understand?'

'To explain.'

'But you do know?'

'Yes, I think so.'

'Well,' moving down the stairs, past him along the hall, 'that's all right then.'

At the door, she turned.

'They didn't think much of it, did they?' Resnick said with the beginnings of a smile.

'They hated it.' Grinning.

'You think it's saleable?'

She fingered the paper close by the door frame where it was coming unstuck from the wall. 'Yes, I guess so. You might have to drop the price a little.'

'I already did.'

'I'm sure we can sell it.'

Resnick nodded, pushed his hands down into his trouser pockets and pulled them out again. A skinny cat, dove grey with a white tip beside its nose and another on the end of its tail, wound between the edge of the now open door and Claire's boots.

'Is that yours too?'

'That's Bud.'

'There was a tabby with a chewed-up ear asleep in the bowl inside the sink.'

'Pepper.'

'Three cats.'

'Four.'

She glanced down for a moment towards her clipboard, shifted the balance of her weight from one foot to the other. 'Got to go.'

'There's a set of keys at your office.'

'I suppose there is.'

'Any time . . .'

'Right.'

'As long as you come with them.'

She looked up at him, almost sharply.

'I mean, I don't want you just doling out the keys and letting people wander around.'

'No, no. Understood. We wouldn't do that.'

Resnick nodded to show that he understood also.

Claire opened the door wide and went through on to the first step. 'I'll do what I can, inspector.'

'Of course.'

'You just might need to be patient, that's all.' Another step and then she swung her head back with a final grin. It wasn't only that her smile was off-centre, Resnick realized, she had a couple of teeth near the front that overlapped. 'But you're good at that, I'll bet,' she laughed. 'Being patient.'

It would have been easy to have stood in the doorway and watched her walk the length of the slightly meandering path, out through the gate and all the way to the car. Instead, Resnick went back inside, into the kitchen: one more cup of coffee for him to enjoy and Graham Millington to be thankful for.

* * *

The station at which Resnick was based was in the inner-city, far enough from the centre to feel its own identity, not so distant that it was like being in the sticks. North-east, between the fan of arterial roads, were turn-of-the-century terraced houses, infilled here and there with modest new municipal buildings and earlier, less successful, blocks of flats with linked walkways waiting to be demolished. Most of those living there were working-class poor, which meant they were lucky to be working at all: Afro-Caribbean, Asian, whites who had clocked in at the factories producing bicycles or cigarettes or hosiery, before those factories had been torn down to make way for superstores or turned into museums celebrating a lace-and-legend heritage. To the west was an enclave of Victorian mansions and tennis courts, tree-lined hilly streets and grounds big enough to build an architect-designed bungalow below the shrubbery and still have room for badminton. Once a year these people opened up their gardens to one another and served weak lemonade they'd made themselves, a small charge, of course, for charity. The only black face ever glimpsed belonged to someone cutting through or lost.

There was blood on the floor in the reception area, bright enough to be recent. A uniformed constable slid back the reinforced-glass panel as Resnick entered.

'Nosebleed?' Resnick asked, nodding towards the floor.

'Not exactly, sir.'

He pushed open the off-white door and at once he could hear the slow clip of a typewriter, several typewriters, the bright hiccup of telephones breaking into life, the low, persistent swearing of a man who knew four words and used them, without connection, over and over.

Resnick nodded at a WPC who went past with a woman leaning on her arm, a traveller of sorts, a few weeks here begging door-to-door and then, somehow, she would hitch a lift to another city, twenty miles distant, and do the same. Gone and then back. Today there was a dark swelling below her left eye, purple shading into black; the upper corner of the other eye was ridged with scabs that broke to leak a little pus. The policewoman walked her slowly, patting the back of her hand.

Resnick walked along the corridor towards the cells, turning into the first room, where the custody sergeant, crisp white shirt, neat dark tie, was entering an admission in his book.

At first it was difficult to tell whether the young PC or his prisoner was injured. A knife, its blade broken off an inch or so from the point, lay on the custody sergeant's desk.

'Anything I can do for you, sir?' the sergeant inquired, continuing with his entry.

Resnick shook his head.

He could see now that most of the blood had come from the prisoner, a gash to the side of his head, another wound high beneath the soiled shirt that stuck to him like a bandage.

'He was brandishing a knife and making threats, sir,' the young constable said. He didn't need to explain himself to Resnick, but he did need to talk. His face was bleached unnaturally pale. 'I told him to calm down, put down the weapon, but he refused. Carried on shouting and swearing. Offering to cut me open.'

The man was swearing still, less loudly, the intervals between each of his four words growing, so that just when it seemed he had stopped, run out of breath altogether, the next one would topple into place.

'Argument over the day's cider supply,' put in the sergeant.

'It couldn't have been much after nine o'clock,' Resnick said.

'Early risers, this crew.'

'While the rest of the world is polishing off its Shreddies.'

'I called for assistance,' the PC said, his voice less than level, 'but I didn't know how long I could wait.'

'Chummy'd already marked one of his friends' cards for the hospital. He's there now, getting a piece of his nose sewn back on. With any luck.' The custody sergeant looked round at Resnick. 'This young man did well.'

'I took the knife off him, sir, only he got . . . he injured himself in the process.'

Resnick looked at the man, whose eyes were now closed, though his mouth kept opening at still lengthening intervals. 'You don't think he should be over at casualty, too?'

'Just as soon as the doctor's had a look at him, Charlie. It's all in hand.' Resnick turned towards Len Lawrence, the chief inspector, a man who'd once read a novel full of earthy Midlands grit and had believed it.

'Anything special, was it, Charlie?'

Resnick shook his head. 'Common or garden interest. Following the trail of blood. You know how it is. Instinct.'

'Thought maybe you were seeing how the other half lives.'

'Pounding the streets, you mean? Out amongst the real folk.'

'Something like that.'

'We get our fair share, you know.'

'CID. Thought it was all white-collar crime for you lot. New technology. Voice prints and visual identification courtesy of the nearest VDU.'

Resnick stepped past the chief inspector, out into the corridor. From one of the cells came a sudden, startled shout, as if someone had woken out of a dream, not knowing where he was.

'My sergeant acquit himself all right this morning?' Resnick asked.

'Loved every minute of it, didn't he? Had his shoes shining so bright, could've trimmed his moustache in them.'

Probably had, Resnick thought on his way up the stairs. Somewhere early in his career, someone influential had told Millington that a smart appearance at all times was the one sure way to the top. In the drawer of his desk he kept, alongside the necessary forms and a copy of the Police and Criminal Evidence Act, 1984, a zip-up bag containing shoe-cleaning gear, a needle and thread for sewing back on stray buttons and a pair of nail scissors in a crocodile case. Resnick presumed it was those Millington had been using when he went to the gents and found tiny trimmings of hair trapped against the porcelain of the sink.

It was Graham Millington, too, and not Resnick, who was interested in the uses of computer-based technology. Aside from the superintendent's, his had been the only name signed up for a weekend seminar at the Home Office Scientific Research and Development Branch down in sunny Hertfordshire.

The door to the CID room was ajar and through the glass panel Resnick could see Mark Divine single-fingering his way through a scene-of-crime report as though the typewriter had only been invented the day before yesterday.

So much for the new technology!

Lynn Kellogg and Kevin Naylor were talking energetically

about something urgent, over towards the rear of the room. None of them as much as noticed his arrival.

His own office was a partitioned section, a quarter of the room immediately to the right of the main door. He would have taken bets on Millington being behind his desk and he would have won.

'All right for size, Graham?'

Millington flushed, banged his knee on the edge of the desk trying to get up, juggled with the telephone but clung on to it at the third attempt.

'It's for you, sir,' he said, handing the receiver towards Resnick.

'Thought it might be.'

'Yes, sir.'

Resnick took the phone, making no attempt to speak into it. Millington hesitated by the door.

'Spare me five minutes, Graham, fill me in.'

'Yes, sir.'

'Later.'

Millington drew in air, nodded, closed the office door behind him.

'Hallo,' Resnick said into the phone, moving aside some papers so that he could sit on the corner of his desk. 'DI Resnick.'

'Tom Parker, Charlie.'

'Morning, sir.' Tom Parker was the detective chief inspector based at the central station and each morning that Resnick was on duty he would call through and discuss what was happening on his patch.

'Thought you were taking time off?'

'An hour, sir. Personal.'

'The house?'

'Yes, sir.'

'They're buggers, Charlie. Never find the one you want and if you do, you can never get shot of it.'

Thanks! Resnick thought. He said nothing.

'You remember that little spate of break-ins, a year back, Charlie? Late spring, was it?'

'March, sir.'

March the second: Resnick had gone to a club in the city to hear Red Rodney, a jazz trumpeter who had worked with Charlie

19

Parker. In his sixties, three months after having surgery on his mouth, Rodney had played long, elastic lines, spluttering sets of notes that cut across the changes; for the final number he had torn through the high-speed unison passages at the start of Parker's 'Shaw 'Nuff' with a British alto player, unrehearsed, inch perfect.

Resnick had gone into the station the following morning, the sounds still replaying inside his head, to be greeted by Patel with a mug of tea and news of another burglary. Five in a row and that had been the last. Big houses, all of them. Alarms. Neighbourhood watch. Money and jewellery and traveller's cheques. Credit cards. Heavy with insurance.

'Out at Edwalton, Charlie. Reported this morning. Same MO. Thought it might be worth your while taking a drive out. Might give us a chance to see if those suspicions of yours were correct.'

Resnick said he'd get on to it first thing, just as soon as he'd had a briefing from his sergeant.

Come on, come on, Graham Millington was thinking, half an eye on his superior through the glass. Don't make a meal out of it. There's some of us with a day's work ahead of us. Himself and young Divine had a Chinaman to talk to concerning an overturned five-gallon container of cooking oil and an inadvertently struck match.

When Resnick opened the door from his office, Millington swung his leg off his desk and stood up.

3

Jerzy Grabianski had been born within sight of the white cliffs of Dover, but that was never quite enough to make him feel truly English. His family – those of them lacking the scruples or sentiment that would have prohibited them from grabbing an overcoat and a length of smoked sausage and leaving everything else behind – had quit Poland in 1939. Variously, they had walked, run, bicycled (his grandmother and his elder sister sharing a crossbar in front of his father's strong, pumping legs), clung to sides of already overcrowded cattle trucks, hid beneath the tarpaulin of coal barges, again walked, until the leather of their boots wore through to their socks which wore through to their feet, which bled and blistered and finally hardened but never enough.

They had a strong imperative.

On 1 September of that year, Hitler invaded Poland on three fronts; on the 17th, Russia came through the fourth. By the 28th Warsaw had fallen and on the following day Germany and Russia sat down to divide the country between them.

The Grabianskis left Lodz, where most of them had worked in textile factories, and made their trek west. By way of Czechoslovakia, Austria and Switzerland, they crossed the border into France at La Chaux de Fonds, at the bridge over the Doubs River. Most of them. Waking that last morning, they had realized that Krystyna, Jerzy's sister, was not huddled beneath her grandmother's greatcoat, ready to rub the sleep from her eyes.

It took them several hours of circling and retracing their steps before they found her, floating face down near the western shore of Lake Neuchâtel, one arm hooked around the broken oar that someone had thrown adrift. They pulled her on to the land and pressed and pummelled at her thin, breastless chest, but all that happened was that she got colder and stiffer. The broken oar was the shovel with which they dug the shallow grave in which to bury her. She had been eleven years old.

Her father – Jerzy's father – unclasped the string of wooden beads from around Krystyna's neck and kept it close until it was lost one black night when he parachuted out over the English Channel. But that was 1944.

The remaining family had split up, some to stay in what soon became Vichy France, others to head for England where they lived as close to the Polish government-in-exile of General Sikorski as was possible. Battersea: Clapham Common: Lambeth. Jerzy's father had joined the air force in France, utilizing his skills as a navigator; when France fell he flew bomber campaigns over Germany with the RAF until the war ended. He was not a man easily deflected from a course once he had set his mind to it, and being spilled into the freezing Channel only made him more determined.

He had vowed to get his family out of Poland and, for the most part, he'd succeeded. He had sworn to help defeat the Nazis and so he had. Somewhere inside himself he had made an agreement to make up for Krystyna's death with another child but the strain of the last five years had rendered his wife an old woman. She died at thirty-seven, looking fifty-seven, lay on her front in the upstairs back bedroom of a terraced house between Clapham and Balham and simply stopped breathing. When they found her she had one arm curled out from the bed and was clinging to the bedside table as her daughter had clung to that broken oar. And she was almost as cold.

She was buried on a day of slant rain and keen wind, in a walled cemetery within sight of St George's Hospital. Walking home afterwards, temporarily lost in the maze of streets, Jerzy's father bumped – literally bumped – into a nurse on her way home from duty. She took one look at his father's face and thought that he might be in shock, insisted that he came along the street to her rented room and sit down a while. Probably because of her uniform, Jerzy's father did as he was told; sat in a small room that smelt of camphor and accepted cup after cup of strong sweet tea.

The nurse was to become Jerzy's mother.

Jerzy.

It had been years since anyone had called him anything other than Jerry.

Many years.

He walked to the window and looked down on the hotel car park, out over the college and the other small hotels, over the bowling green, the tennis courts, the stretch of worn grass and the edge of the cemetery on the hill – the first cluster of marble and sculpted stone, graves, one of them his father's. He would have to take a walk there later, when the light was beginning to fade and the bell soon to be rung to announce closing. Long enough to read the inscription but not too long. He wondered, maybe, should he take flowers?

He knew that kids climbed over the wall and stole them, went from house to house and sold them, wrapped in discarded newspaper.

There was a bottle of Bass and a can of Diet Pepsi in the courtesy fridge, tea bags and a small jar of instant coffee alongside the electric kettle, containers of UHT milk. From the wall behind the television set a reproduction of Van Gogh's *Sunflowers* stubbornly refused to bloom. He lifted his watch from the dressing table and strapped it to his wrist: Grice was already twenty minutes late.

Resnick had two clear memories of Jeff Harrison. One was a league match at the County ground, Notts against Manchester City, and City needed three points to win the division. The normal crowd, three to five thousand, was swollen by at least as many Manchester supporters. Not only a special train, but coaches, convoys of them, had come across the Pennines and down the M1. Notts had little enough to play for, save pride, and the Manchester celebrations were underway before the match began. Banners, flags, most striking of all, faces painted sky-blue and grey; so many raucous clowns shrieking their team towards promotion.

Police presence had been increased: never by enough.

Resnick had been there as a spectator, his usual place midway along the terraces flooded for the occasion with unfamiliar bodies. All that good humour was bound to bring a negative response, spill over into ugliness. When it happened, half time, Jeff Harrison, in uniform, waded into a dozen youths who had climbed the barrier on to the pitch. He was in the midst of them when the bottle struck his face. Resnick had tried to push a way through to him, but there hadn't been the time, and in the end there wasn't the need. Harrison had hurled two of the supporters back against the wire, caught hold of a third and thrust his arm up behind his back; the rest had scattered, except for a big lad with a shaved head daubed the same colours as his face. The lad had a Stanley knife in his hand. Likely he'd been drinking since early that morning; he'd pulled the knife from his pocket without thinking and now that he was fast against a uniformed officer with the crowd roaring at his back, the worst possibility was that he would panic.

Jeff Harrison, blood streaming from the bridge of his nose, blocking out one eye, had stared him down with the other. Half a minute, more or less, and the weapon had been laid on the turf, its blade retracted. There were four youths waiting between the touchline and the barrier when reinforcements arrived.

The second occasion was later, after Harrison had transferred into CID. He and Resnick had been involved in a raid on a warehouse on the canal that was suspected of housing stolen goods. They picked up a known thief running clear, a villain, real dyed-in-the-wool, regional crime squad had had him targeted for months. Try as they might, nothing would tie him in, nothing that would stand up as evidence.

'Bend the rules a little, Charlie,' Harrison had said. It was one in the morning, in a drinking club off Bridlesmith Gate. 'In a good cause. That confession I heard him make, you heard it too.'

'No, Jeff,' Resnick had said, 'I did not.'

Two memories, clear as daylight.

'Good to see you, Charlie.'

'Jeff.'

They shook hands and Harrison offered Resnick a seat, a cup of tea, a cigarette. Resnick sat down, shook his head to the rest.

'Course, you don't, do you?' Harrison emptied the ashtray into the metal waste bin and lit up again. He was still in CID, like Resnick now an inspector.

'Tom Parker says you're interested in this break-in.'

Resnick sat forward, shrugged. 'Might fit, might not.'

'I've had a copy of the report done for you. Young DC went out there, Featherstone. He's not in as of now, or you could have talked to him yourself.'

Resnick pushed the manilla envelope into his side pocket. 'You didn't go out there?'

'Couldn't see any point. Pretty straightforward. Run of the mill.'

'You'll not mind if I do?'

Harrison tapped ash from his cigarette and leaned his chair back on to its hind legs. 'Help yourself.'

Resnick got to his feet. 'Thanks, Jeff.'

'Any time. Charlie,' the chair came down on all fours, 'we must have a drink or two. Been a while.'

'Yes.' Resnick was heading for the door.

'You do come up with anything,' Harrison said, 'you'll keep me posted.'

'Depend on it.'

After Resnick had gone, Jeff Harrison sat where he was until he'd smoked down that cigarette and then another. What was it about Charlie Resnick that made him so special? With his shirt still crumpled from the wash and his tie knotted arse-about-face.

Grabianski tried to imagine how Grice spent his afternoons. He pictured him sitting in the auditoriums of mostly empty cinemas, eating popcorn and doing his best to ignore the snores and shuffles from the semi-darkness around him. The last film Grabianski had seen had been *Catch 22*, and he had barely lasted the opening sequence: the promise of blood and bowels spilled across the airplane fuselage had brought back memories of his father's wartime stories, too keen for Grabianski's own stomach. He had thrown up, quietly, into a toilet-bowl in the gents, fluttered his half-ticket down into the flushing water and left.

'Jerry!'

Grice was standing near the hotel entrance beneath a sign that promised colour TVs and en-suite showers in every room. His fists were stuffed into the pockets of a sheepskin car-coat and his thinning hair had been combed sideways over the broad curve of his head.

'Come on. Let's go.'

Grabianski climbed into the front of a nearly new cherry-red Vauxhall that was parked at the curb.

'You changed your car,' he said as Grice pulled out into the slow stream of traffic.

'Observant today,' Grice said sharply. He jabbed the palm of his hand at the horn and found the indicator, swore, tried again and swerved around one vehicle and cut across another to make the roundabout.

'What's pissing you off?' Grabianski asked.

Grice depressed the accelerator and laughed. 'This is pissed off?'

'You tell me.'

'Eleven thirty this morning, that was pissed off.'

'Your day got better?'

'Better beyond belief.'

'I'm glad.'

Grice measured the distance between a milk truck and the central bollard almost to perfection.

'Whatever it is,' said Grabianski, both hands tight against the dash, arms tensed, 'do you have to celebrate this enthusiastically?'

''S'he doing delivering milk this time of day, anyway? Gone three in the afternoon. He early or late or what?' He glanced over at Grabianski, who was just easing back in his seat and starting to breathe more freely. 'You know that's the best way to break your arms, don't you? We hit anything, seat belt's not going to do your arms one bit of good, you got them braced like that. Snap!'

Grice lifted his hands from the steering-wheel long enough to clap them together loudly in front of his face.

'How far are we going?' Grabianski asked. Unless he sat well down in the seat, the upholstery of the roof touched against his head.

'Relax,' Grice said, 'we're almost there.'

Grabianski nodded and looked through the side window. Supersave Furnishings were offering a 40 per cent discount on all beds, settees and three-piece suites, free delivery: green-and-blue plaid moquette or dimpled red plastic with a fur trim seemed to be the popular styles.

* * *

26

They found a parking space between a Porsche and a gleaming red Ferrari with personalized number plates. The house was four storeys, broad and glowering Victorian gothic. High above the arched front doorway, panes of stained-glass caught at what was already late-afternoon light.

'I didn't know we were working,' Grabianski said, looking up towards a pair of circular turrets at either end of the roof.

'We're not.'

Grice slipped off his glove, took a ring of keys from his pocket and used one to open the front door.

The entrance hall was harlequin-tiled and marble-edged; the stairs broad and thickly carpeted, and there were dying pot plants on each landing. Outside one of the doors two bottles of milk were turning to a creamy green. Grice fingered a second key into the lock of flat number seven, top floor.

'We'll have to get that changed,' he said, pushing the door open over a collection of free newspapers and amazing offers from *Readers' Digest*. 'Anyone who fancied it could get through there easy as breathing.'

He walked along a short corridor and into a long room with high windows on one side and a slanting roof on the other.

'Servants' quarters,' he said, pointing towards the windows. 'Never wanted them to see the light of day, did they?'

Grabianski poked at a dark ridge in the carpet with the toe of his shoe. 'What are we doing?' he said.

'Moving in.'

Resnick had tried the number three times without getting a response. He had driven out to the house and knocked on the door, rung the bell. For twenty minutes he had parked on the opposite side of the road, leaning back with a copy of the local paper spread across the wheel. A woman with a shopping basket on wheels walked past him, slowly, twice; up along the opposite pavement, back down this one. Finally, a man in his sixties, wearing a blue track suit and leading a small Yorkshire terrier, tapped on the window.

Resnick folded his paper, wound the window midway down and smiled.

'I don't like to bother you, but . . .'

'Mrs Roy,' said Resnick, nodding in the direction of the detached house across the road.

'Yes, I believe she's . . .'

'She's out.'

'Yes.'

The man stood there, gazing in. The dog was probably cocking its leg at the wheels of Resnick's car.

'I think she left at lunchtime,' the man offered. 'When I took Alice for her midday walk the car was there in the drive – the Mini, that's hers – but then as we came back I couldn't help noticing that it was gone.' He paused, gave a short tug on the lead. 'I've no idea when she might be back.'

Resnick took his warrant card from his pocket and opened it under the man's nose.

'Oh. Oh. Of course, there was a burglary. Just the other day.' He shook his head. 'It still happens, doesn't seem to matter how vigilant you are, they still get away with it. I mean, I know you do your best, but, then, there's only so much you can do. I suppose that's it, isn't it? More of them than there are of you. A measure of the way things have changed. That and other things.' He leaned a little closer. 'Do you know they were three weeks after the last bank holiday before they came and emptied our dustbins and only then after I'd telephoned each morning at eight sharp; four mornings on the trot, that's what it took. And, of course, when they did finally come, it was the usual torrent of bad language and litter and such left scattered the length of the drive.'

Resnick rewound the window, switched on the ignition and put the car in gear; if he waited until the good neighbour got to his conclusion about the way the country was going to rack and ruin, he might have felt obliged to ask him which way he'd voted at the last couple of elections.

He would call in at Jeff Harrison's station on the way back and see if the PC who'd spoken to Maria Roy had returned. If not, there was plenty to attend to back on his own patch, and little about this to suggest it was urgent.

As he turned the car around and headed back the way he had come, he was wondering why the alarm system at the Roy house had apparently failed to function.

* * *

28

'Took me till twelve o'clock to screw an extra hundred out of this imbecile in the showroom and even then, God is my witness, I had to walk almost to the door twice. So, by a little after 12.30 I've had a couple of halves and a scotch and without really knowing why, I'm inside this estate agent's, pretending to look at properties between forty and sixty thousand, when what I'm really doing is looking round the edge of the desk at this woman in red boots.'

Grice was sitting on a reversed wooden chair, with his heels tucked into the rungs at the side. He had a can of Swan Light in his hands and the rest of the six-pack was behind him on the table. 'Get something non-alcoholic,' he'd told Grabianski. 'One thing I can't stand, falling asleep in the middle of the day.' It was somewhere between four and five and Grabianski, who wasn't drinking anything, was in the only easy chair in the room, staring back at Grice and trying hard to seem interested.

'She comes over and asks if she can help and I point at a few things and joke about mortgages and so on and then I'm telling her I'm probably only going to be in the city for a few months and buying anything's really out of order. "Work?" she asked and I nod. "Short-term contract?" I nod again and mumble something and I don't know if she mishears me or guesses or what, but she says, "Oh, you're working out at the television studio," and I say, "Yes, that's right," and she gets this bright little look in her eye and asks me if I'd mind waiting there a minute, which, of course, I don't, so she goes off and when she comes back five minutes later she's got these papers fastened to her clipboard and she asks if I'd be interested in renting somewhere on an agreed temporary basis.'

Grice swallowed some 1 per cent lager and belched.

'I sit down at her desk and she explains they've had this flat on the market for over a year and no way can they sell it. Half the people who look at it say it's too dark, and the ones that don't care about that all pull out when their surveys show them there's damp coming through from the roof above the kitchen and the bathroom, and half a dozen attempts to patch it up haven't done a scrap of good. Seems the only answer is to take off the whole roof and have it renewed and there's no way of that happening because it would need all the other flat owners

29

to kick in with five hundred and they're not listening. "Why don't you take over the tenancy for three months? That way, at least we're getting something back for the owner." I can see she's on a hiding to nothing and it takes me less than ten minutes to knock fifty a month off the rent.'

He pointed the can at Grabianski. 'I knew you'd be chuffed. Knew you wanted to get clear of that poxy hotel.'

Grice unhooked his heels and stood up.

'For tonight, there's an old z-bed you can make up in here and I'll have the bedroom. Tomorrow we'll go into the city and buy you a proper bed.'

Before then, Grabianski hoped, they would figure out what they were going to do with the kilo of cocaine they had taken from the back of Maria Roy's bedroom safe.

4

He couldn't see the clock face from where he was sitting, but he guessed it was somewhere between half-two and three. Low, from the stereo, the song of Johnny Hodges' saxophone, the note held, rising, while the rhythm pulsed beneath it. On the label he was using an alias, but his was the perfect print, the impossibility of disguise. 'You'd Be So Nice to Come Home To'. Resnick shifted in the chair and, implanted half-way up his chest, Bud complained, somewhere between a hiss and a whimper. *Why, for instance, do you want to move from this house?* 'Come on, sweetheart,' said Resnick, 'time to go.' He cupped both hands beneath the cat's body and lifted him to the floor; felt against his thumbs, the ends of his fingers, the animal's bones were like the spars of a model mast, matchwood and hope. *Why?*

His feet were bare against the fibre of the carpet. Mr Albertson had surveyed it with a slow shake of the head: you could try for a couple of hundred, curtains as well, but in the end . . . Now Albertson had got him to a nunnery or wherever and Resnick's affairs were in fresh hands. *You're good at that, I'll bet. Being patient.* He measured dark coffee into the percolator, tamping it down. At first, when he had ceased being able to sleep through, he had made himself cut back on caffeine, less throughout the day, none after the fall of light. All that happened, his team had suffered. Half a sentence out of their mouths before he had shot them down. On and on until Lynn Kellogg had cornered him in his office and asked, direct, soft burr of her Norfolk voice at odds with the anxiety of her eyes, sir, what's wrong?

He had restored his usual ten cups a day or more, tried tempering them before bed with Horlicks and the like, warm milk and whisky. If he managed three to four hours, unbroken, he counted his blessings. Better than sheep. Bud purred encouragingly and Resnick opened the fridge for the tin of cat food: one gain from these sleepless middle nights he and the runt of his litter had shared together – free to eat alone and unpestered, Bud was at last beginning to put on a little weight.

31

Whereas himself . . . he pressed the flesh where it swelled beneath his shirt and thought of Claire Millinder looking at him from the doorway of his house. In the other room the record had come to an end and all he could hear was the thin scrape of the cat's collar against the edge of its bowl and the slow drip of the coffee falling through.

It was not the way Rachel had looked at him: neither the first time she set eyes on him, nor when she said goodbye. *Charlie, I'll be in touch, I promise. I just need time on my own, to think things through. All right?* Her mouth had been warm for a moment against the cold of his winter cheek and they had both known, although she was not lying, that she would never speak to him again. Nor write. He saw her then, clearly, not that last time but the one before, standing in the garden at the front of this house, so still, and Bud cradled in her arms. When her eyes closed on his, they had been opaque with fear.

That poky little room, Mrs Lurie had said, what else could you get in there?

As both Resnick and Rachel knew, if you hacked at it enough, you could squeeze in, just, the body of a man, full-grown.

And just as his brush had never succeeded in covering from sight the nursery animals that once had danced across the wallpaper, so his memory – and hers – could not remove the sight, the smell of so much blood.

Why do you want to move from this house?

Resnick poured coffee and padded back into the other room, cat at his feet.

After the burglary, Maria Roy had been standing by the reconnected telephone, willing it to ring. She had changed out of her robe into a plain black dress, rust-coloured tights and low-heeled black shoes. There was almost no make-up on her face, no polish on her nails. Although she was waiting for the phone to ring, she jumped when it did.

'Harold?'

'I know where I am, which is at Jerry and Stella's. I'm halfway through my second vodka martini; Stella says there's a good chance of the veal spoiling, you never rang them to ask for a lift, where the hell are you?'

'Come home, Harold.'

'What?'

'Home. Come. Now.'

'You crazy? You know how good Stella's veal is. The way she does it with the capers and the chopped green olives . . .'

'Harold, come home. I promise you'll lose every shred of appetite.'

'You know what that canteen's like at the studio. All I had all day was salad and a little smoked mackerel.'

'I thought we should talk before I called the police.'

'The police? What are you . . . Someone's stolen your lingerie from the garden again; you want them to force open the garage door? What?'

Maria gave a short-tempered sigh. 'Before I can contact the insurance company about making a claim, I have to notify the police of the burglary.'

'Which burglary?' Harold Roy asked without thinking. Six seconds later, without waiting for an answer, he thought he knew.

While waiting for her husband to arrive, Maria had carefully washed out the glasses her two visitors had used and restored them to their usual place. She had wiped Grabianski's prints from the trolley and the scotch bottle. It was going to be difficult enough, without needing to explain the how and why of sitting round, all three of them, old acquaintances having an early-evening drink.

Unbelievable!

She hadn't believed it had happened. Even after she had made herself sit down, calm as she was able, and take the events through, step by step, in her mind. Three times she had returned to the bedroom to check, but each time the jewellery, the money – all of it – was missing. Gone. He had really sat there, that man, tall and broad and looking at her as if she'd stepped out of an advertisement for French perfume. Wanting her but afraid to do more than look. Which was why, she supposed, after that first rush of cold fear, she had not been afraid. If anything, he had been in awe of her.

She heard Harold's car turn too fast into the drive and moved to the living room so that she would be standing there when he came in, the central light dimmed just enough, her hands loose at her sides, perfectly still.

God! thought Harold, stopped in his haste. She looks awful!

'Maria?'

Unnervingly, she stared right back at him, not answering.

'Maria?'

So pale.

Her eyes, dark and large, widened.

'The cocaine – did they find it?'

She bit her teeth down into the flesh of her lower lip and nodded.

'Shit!'

He brushed past her and banged his leg against the side of the drinks trolley, hands steadying himself and the shaking bottles.

'I suppose they stole the vodka, too?'

'We're out of vodka.'

Harold grabbed a bottle of gin and locked himself in the bathroom, refusing to open the door until almost an hour later. By then the bottle was a third empty and he was sitting on the floor with his back against the side of the bath, one foot resting on the bidet. Talcum powder dusted the grooves of his cream cords.

Maria hitched her skirt up by some inches and sat on the bath, one arm around his shoulders. She was in danger of feeling genuinely sorry for him, but it passed.

'I suppose it wasn't such a good idea,' she said after a while, choosing her words with care.

Harold drank some more gin before offering her the bottle.

'It seemed OK at the time,' she said. 'All we had to do was keep it locked away safely.' She sighed. 'It was a favour.'

'He was taking advantage.'

'He wasn't expecting us to help him out for nothing.'

'A couple of weeks' free supply.'

'That's not to be sneezed at.'

Harold glanced up at her to see if she was making a joke; he ought to have known better.

'What are you going to tell him?' she asked.

'I don't know.'

'Do you think he'll believe the truth?'

'Do you?'

Maria reached down for the bottle. 'You think we ought to phone the police?'

'And report a missing kilo of cocaine?'

'Is that how much there was?'

'That's what the man said.'

Maria wriggled her skirt a little higher and pushed her knees out sideways. 'Let me have another drink and then I'll call them.'

Harold gave her back the bottle and grunted.

'Is it still 999?'

Harold didn't know: neither did he know how long he could stall the man for whom he was taking temporary care of a sizeable quantity of illicit drugs nor what he would tell him when he could do that no longer.

The police officer who finally came to the house was polite and spoke with a West Country accent; he was wearing a sports coat from British Home Stores and printed his notes quickly in black biro. 'Easier to read back in court,' he had explained. Maria had felt one of her rare flushes of maternal feeling: the constable looked all of seventeen.

He had looked all over the house, paying particular attention to the main bedroom and the rear patio where the burglars had gained entry; the loose wires from the alarm, no longer attached to anything.

'You will be careful not to touch things,' he had said. 'We'll have someone round in the morning to dust for prints. Not that I suppose we'll find any that will be of much use.'

Wonderful! thought Harold. 'Shouldn't that be done tonight?' he asked.

The constable had shaken his head: scene-of-crime wouldn't be available until the next day. He asked them to make a complete list of everything they thought was missing, especially anything they thought might be traced. Good-night.

For the first time in years, Maria came into the bathroom as her husband was getting out of the bath and towelled his back. She made cups of Milo and brought them to the bedroom. With the light out, she turned on to her side and stroked his shoulder, his chest, the muscle at the side of his neck.

35

'Maria?'

'Mmm?'

'These two . . . they didn't, you know, touch you at all, did they? I mean, if they had, if anything funny had gone on, you'd have told me about it, wouldn't you?'

'Of course I would.' Maria's voice was muffled by the duvet cover.

'Yes,' said Harold, 'of course.'

Beneath the bedding, her face pressed against the slack of her husband's pot belly, Maria was thinking about the tall Grabianski, the way he had looked at her when she'd been wearing her robe. It had been enough to make her feel, well, damp.

'Maria?'

'Mmm?'

Harold's fingers slid through her hair.

After some moments he closed his eyes. Out of sight, Maria waited for the change in his breathing that would tell her Harold was asleep.

Maria sat with her half-grapefruit and her cup of weak tea and jostled the pages of the *Daily Mail*. At the opposite side of the table, Harold looked away from *Screen International* for long enough to shake bran flakes on to his muesli. Since his last birthday he'd been troubled by constipation; since that and starting work on his present series for Midlands TV.

'Would you believe this?' he said, chewing steadfastly.

'What's that?'

'The forty-fifth version of Jekyll and Hyde.'

One for each year of your life, Maria said to herself.

'Anthony Perkins,' Harold said.

'Which part?' asked Maria, reaching for the teapot.

'Huh?'

'Which one's he playing?'

Harold set his spoon down in the bowl and pushed it aside.

'You're not going to leave that?' said Maria, glancing up.

'Why not?'

'You'll suffer.'

'I'm suffering enough already.'

36

She watched him lift his camera script from the table and snap open his briefcase.

'It's not going any better?' she asked.

'Worse.'

'What's the problem?'

Harold stood between the table and the sink and stared at her. Maria turned a page of her newspaper. 'I haven't got the time,' he said. 'And anyway, you're not interested.'

'Harold, that simply isn't true.'

He switched the case to his other hand as he walked through to collect his coat. Thirty-six hours since the burglary and still she hadn't reverted to her old ways. If she wasn't exactly slavering all over him (thank God!), she wasn't moaning on at him either. The other night he was sure she was about to go down on him and he'd had to pretend to be asleep to put her off. He tucked a scarf inside the collar of his padded blouson and opened the front door.

''Bye,' he called before pulling the door to behind him.

''Bye!'

What niggled Harold was that he couldn't work out what she had to be feeling so guilty about – unless she'd faked the break-in and taken all the stuff herself. He smiled at the thought and turned out of the drive so fast that the rear wheels spun on the pebbles and he nearly ran into that nosy old bastard with the track suit and the yappy bloody dog that was always hanging about. Probably him, Harold thought, who was pilfering Maria's best knickers.

There was no reason for him to have recognized Resnick driving along in the opposite direction.

5

Resnick was not the only officer in CID whose sleep patterns were disturbed. Not in the station for half an hour, Kevin Naylor had rounded on Patel and torn him off several highly coloured strips for allegedly taking a pen from his desk and not returning it. Even for a gold-nibbed Mont Blanc, it would have been inappropriate. And for Kevin Naylor . . .

His colleagues had stared on in disbelief, as if Bambi had turned without warning on the nearest rabbit and savaged it for nibbling at the wrong blade of grass. Anyone other than Patel would have taken it less calmly; but he had not survived in the force without developing a certain stoicism towards the insults a darker skin is sadly heir to.

Naylor had finished his tirade with a poorly aimed kick at the nearest filing cabinet and headed for the door.

'Kevin . . .' Lynn Kellogg had moved to intercept him, but he swept past her and out.

'Stupid tosser!' Divine's voice had risen from the silence. 'Serves him bloody right!'

'What's that mean?' said Lynn, with enough of an edge to get Divine going.

He pushed aside a bundle of papers and sat on the corner of a desk, preparing to enjoy his audience. 'What it means is if our Kevin weren't so keen on playing martyr to that prissy wife of his . . .'

'That prissy wife, as you put it, has had a bad time.'

'Oh, so that's why she's playing Lady Muck, while Kev runs around after her like a skivvy, is it?'

'Now you're just being stupid.' Lynn turned away, aware that she was playing into Divine's hands. But she had been upset by Kevin's outburst and hurt by his refusal to talk to her afterwards.

'It's stupid right enough,' Divine taunted. 'Him having to get up in the night when the kid cries, change its nappies, all that Mr Perfect crap.'

Lynn couldn't stop herself. 'I suppose you think that should be Debbie's job?'

'Why not? She's the mother, isn't she? It's her kid.'

'Theirs.'

'She's still the mother.'

'And she's ill.'

'Aaah!'

'You're a callous bastard.'

'Facts. Not callous to look at the facts, is it? She knew what it was all about, didn't she? What it meant. If she didn't like it, she should've kept swallowing her pill.' Divine pushed himself off the desk. 'That's what it's for, isn't it?' He moved towards her, a leer on his face. 'Then, since lover boy took to his bike and scarpered, you wouldn't be bothered with that. Unless you keep swallowing them on the off-chance that some dark night . . .'

Lynn's feet were perfectly set, her weight balanced, the backward dip of her shoulder exactly right; the open hand that cracked across Divine's face spun him sideways, jarred him backwards.

Four fingers, red, slightly parted, glowed on the suddenly pale skin of Divine's cheek.

'You . . . !'

'No!' Resnick's shout came from the door to his office.

'That bitch, she's not . . .'

Resnick moved with surprising speed, placing himself between the pair of them. The flat of one hand was set firmly against Divine's chest. He had seen the DC battling through the ruck of the rugby field on more than one occasion and had no illusions about the damage he could do if he found the opportunity.

Patel was close by Divine on his right side, ready to grab his arm if necessary. Hurt anger showed in the tightness of Divine's eyes, the unsteadiness of the breathing through his open mouth.

'Let it be,' Resnick said.

'No . . .' The pressure against Resnick's hand showed no sign of diminishing.

'Leave it there.'

Divine took an awkward step sideways, colliding with Patel. Resnick moved with him.

'You saw what the stupid cow . . .'

'Divine!'

'What?'

Resnick looked him full in the face, five, ten, fifteen seconds; slowly he lowered his hand, slowly stepped a pace back. Divine glared back at him, staring him out. His face was stinging and what he wanted to do was place his own fingers against it, tentatively, but he wasn't going to give Resnick that satisfaction. Not Resnick, nor any of them.

'Over,' Resnick said. 'All right?'

Divine couldn't keep it up. He looked away, allowed his head to fall, pushed one hand up through his hair and let his shoulders slump.

'My office,' Resnick said, almost an invitation.

'Sir . . .'

'Now, OK?'

'Yes, sir.'

To be sure, Resnick kept himself between Divine and Lynn until his office door had opened and then closed, Divine on the other side of it. For the first time he could see that Lynn was almost as pale as Divine himself, certainly as shaken by what she had done.

'Five minutes,' he said.

'Right, sir.'

He wasn't sure at which point Kevin Naylor had come back into the room, only that he was standing close by the main door, bemused, tired, doing his best to stifle another yawn.

'With respect, sir, he's a pig.'

'That doesn't sound like respect.'

'I meant for you, sir, not Divine.'

'In many ways he's a good detective.'

'Yes, sir. If you say so.'

'His arrest record says so, not me.'

'Is that all there is to it, sir, arrests?'

'The public would say so.'

'And you, sir?'

'He is a detective, you all are detectives. Your job is to detect crime, detain perpetrators. If you want something else, maybe you should go back into uniform, community policing.'

'Is that what you want, sir? From me, I mean?'

'No.'

They sat there for some moments, Resnick and Lynn Kellogg, silence between them.

'How about you, Lynn? Needing a change?'

'No, sir.'

'Good.'

Resnick stood up, Lynn following suit. The last thing he wanted was to lose her, especially to Divine's crass arrogance: Divine, Naylor, Patel, she was the brightest of them, lacking Patel's diligence, but her sensibilities were the most finely tuned.

'There shouldn't be any repetition,' he said, moving with her towards the door. 'I've made it quite clear what will happen if there's any retaliation.'

He had left Divine in no doubt that the least false move would result in the carpet being whipped from beneath his feet so fast he would think he was in the Co-op's Christmas version of *Aladdin*.

'How's it coming along at the centre?' Resnick asked.

Lynn was submerging herself daily among the shoppers who coursed through the shopping centre, on the look-out for a gang of thieves who were getting away with over a thousand pounds' worth of goods a week. It wasn't casual, wasn't kids, though they could be a part of it: it was planned, highly organized, profitable – except for the shopkeepers.

'I suppose there's no chance of some extra bodies, sir? You know how many shops there are in that place. And these people, whoever they are, they know what they're doing. Otherwise the store security would have nabbed them by now.'

Resnick held open the office door. 'I'll have a word. See if we can't liberate a few WPCs out of uniform.'

Lynn Kellogg walked past him with a smile. 'Men go shopping as well, you know, sir.'

It had all been, Resnick thought, one hell of a way to start the day. If Lynn Kellogg had kept her fist closed, he thought, chances are that Divine would have gone down for an eight count. He allowed himself a smile at the thought; then frowned again over when he had heard about young Kevin Naylor. First chance he got, he would have him in for a word.

Ahead of him, a top-of-the-range red Citroën came out on to the road too fast, narrowly avoiding a pedestrian exercising his dog. Resnick glimpsed the driver's tense face as he went past; heard, even through the reinforced glass, the bass reverberating through the car's four speakers.

Pebbles scattered across the pavement from the drive confirmed Resnick's identification. Either Harold Roy was late for work or else he was glad to be out of the house. He braked with care outside the double garage, shut the car door firmly but not loudly and turned the key to set the lock.

Maria Roy had abandoned any thoughts of driving into the city and spending some more of Harold's money. In the nine months they had lived there, she felt she had exhausted the best of its possibilities. Those dress shops with a tendency towards the exclusive she had become bored with, and the prospect of buying more tights from John Lewis or another lampshade from Habitat gave her a cold tightening wherever she kept her heart. Maybe she would lounge around this morning, phone a few friends, go in this afternoon and have her hair done, pick up some mussels from Marks and pop them in the microwave when she returned.

For now it was enough to have Harold out of the house.

She flipped back through the pages of the paper, undecided between making a fresh pot of tea or going upstairs to run her bath. That she did neither was due to the ringing of the doorbell.

Through the window she glimpsed the sleeve of an overcoat, white-and-grey herringbone. Only in those last seconds before she opened the door did Maria think it might be her burglar, returned.

What she saw was a man, tall and bare-headed, a brown scarf pushed haphazardly inside the collar of his coat. To Resnick, there was no disguising the surprise, the hint of disappointment in her eyes.

'I'm sorry,' Resnick said with something of a smile.

She looked up at him, uncomprehending, one hand holding tight to the folds of her robe. 'Sorry?'

'Not who you were expecting?'

'Expecting?' For God's sake, Maria thought, you sound like a ventriloquist's parrot.

'You looked as if you were expecting somebody . . .'

'Oh, well, my husband, he left in a hurry . . .'

'I think I saw him.'

'Driving too fast, that was him. Four times out of five he's back, swearing because he's left a script behind.'

Resnick nodded. 'I see.' For several moments he said nothing and then: 'Don't you want to know who I am?'

Maria Roy drew in rather too much air, and nodded.

Resnick took out his wallet and showed her his identification.

'Resnick?' Maria said.

'Detective inspector.'

She looked at his face: his eyes were dark and a little hooded and there were too many lines of tiredness surrounding them. He had shaved that morning, but not too closely or too well. There was a trail of dried blood speckling the skin below his left ear, dark like old tears.

'The last time,' she said, 'it was only a constable.'

Resnick smiled again, closer to the full works.

'I was just about to make some more tea,' Maria said, holding back the door as she stood aside to let him in.

He would have preferred coffee but accepted tea anyway, black with a slice of lemon. He watched with a sense of strange familiarity a woman moving around her own kitchen, wearing a robe that reached down to her calves and occasionally opened itself at her thigh. Was it really silk, he wondered, or pale imitation? By the time she had set a selection of biscuits on a plate before him and sat down herself, across the table which still held breakfast things, he had concluded that it was real.

'Is the tea all right?'

'Fine.'

She was well enough into her forties to need more flattering lighting if she were to pass for less. That didn't matter to Resnick one scrap, but he sensed that it did to her.

He pushed the plate out of easy reach and caught her smiling, understanding why.

43

'When you thought I might have been your husband, you said something about a script. Is he a writer?'

'Writer?' Maria shook her head. 'D'you think we could afford to rent a place like this if he were a writer?'

'Harold Robbins,' Resnick said, 'Jackie Collins.'

'Oh, sure. But then we'd be out in LA, not here in the Midlands.'

Resnick lifted his cup from its saucer. 'What does he do?'

'Harold? Rumour has it he's a director.'

'In the theatre?'

'Not any more. Television.' She tapped a cigarette out into her fingers, lit it, inhaled and, averting her head, released a film of fine smoke. 'He's here on a twelve-month contract. The series to end all other series.'

'Why here?'

'A good question. Everyone thinks the business is all in London, but that's only where they take one another out to lunch.' She waved away more smoke with a flap of her hand. 'Since I became Harold's camp follower, I've really seen the world. Birmingham. Manchester. Southampton. Belfast – I couldn't go to the supermarket for Tampax there without being searched twice.' She looked around for an ashtray, couldn't see one within reach and deposited a neat quarter-inch of ash against the rim of her saucer. 'Now here.'

Resnick drank some more tea. It was a mixture of Earl Grey and something he couldn't identify, but it was too weak.

'I've never been really sure what a director does,' he said.

'That's Harold's problem, too.' She stubbed out the remaining two-thirds of her cigarette and stood up. 'Anyway, why all this interest in Harold?'

'Making conversation,' said Resnick pleasantly.

'I'm surprised you can find the time.'

'Actually, I think what I'm doing is trying to put you at ease.'

'Then the last thing you should be talking about is my husband.'

'I'm sorry.'

'Don't be.'

'A sticky patch?' suggested Resnick helpfully.

'A quagmire.'

44

'Oh.'

Maria continued to look at him: the tie he was wearing – red-and-blue diagonals – failed to hide the fact that the top button of his shirt was hanging on by a thread of the wrong colour.

'Perhaps we should change the subject,' Resnick said.

'Perhaps we should.'

'You said the house was rented, it's not yours.'

'We have a year's lease. I believe the family who own it are in Canada.'

'But the insurance is yours?'

'We had our names put on the policy, to cover the contents.'

'What I can remember of your inventory, quite a lot of money was involved. Several items of jewellery valued in the high hundreds. More.'

'Harold checked with the company after we moved in. They sent somebody round to make sure the house was secure. I suppose he was satisfied.'

'By a disconnected burglar alarm?'

Maria's eyes tightened. 'We were asked to have it properly reinstalled.'

'Why didn't you?'

'We were getting it done. I think one man came out, but Harold said his quotation was outrageous. He was getting in touch with somebody else. I suppose he just hadn't got around to it.'

'The man who came? You don't happen to remember his name?'

Maria shook her head. He had been wearing red-and-white running shoes and a pale leather jacket and his breath had reminded her of her parents' ageing cocker spaniel.

'Would your husband remember?'

'I dare say he might. Why? Is it important?'

Resnick shook his head. 'I doubt it.'

Maria clicked her lighter. Detective inspectors came in more promising packages. True, this one was a little too much on the slobby side to be seen with in public, but once you got your head around that he wasn't a bad looking man. Big, she would have to grant him that. He was a big man. For a moment cold rippled her stomach and she was back in the living room, staring at

Grabianski over her glass of scotch, the way he had stood easy in the doorway, watching her. A big man.

'These burglars,' said Resnick, changing tack, 'you've not had any more thoughts about what they looked like? The one you saw first, for instance.'

Without thinking, Maria answered: 'As a matter of fact, he looked a bit like you.'

'But black,' Resnick said.

'Sorry?'

'Like me, but black. You told the officer . . .'

'Oh, yes, of course.'

'He was black, then?'

'Yes.'

'Both of them?'

'That's right. Absolutely.'

'No doubt?'

'Well, there couldn't be, could there?'

'But like me? One of them.'

'I suppose . . .'

'It was what you said.'

'I know.'

'You said, as a matter of fact . . .'

'Yes, I know. I meant . . .' She gestured vaguely with her hands. 'His size, height, you know, he was . . .'

'He was about my size?'

'That's right.'

'Six foot, a little more?'

Maria nodded.

'Fourteen stone?'

'I suppose so, if that's what . . .'

'Big?'

'Yes,' she said, clasping and unclasping her hands. 'Big.'

Resnick flipped open his notebook. 'In the descriptions you gave to the detective constable, you said that both men were medium height or less. Skinny hipped, I think you said that as well. Tight blue jeans, leather jackets, tight curly hair.' He eased himself back in his chair. The electric clock, narrow hands on a blank face, clicked as it reached the hour. 'Not very much there

46

which suggests either man was anything approaching the large size. Is there, Mrs Roy?'

'No.'

'How do you account for that?'

Bastard! she thought. You've caught me out and you're loving it.

'I suppose I must have made a mistake,' she said.

'This time or last time?'

'Last time.'

'You're sure?'

'Yes.'

'Time to reconsider.'

Maria's mouth was dry and she wanted to go to the fridge for some fresh juice but she knew that she couldn't, shouldn't move. 'I've had more time to think about it clearly, everything that happened. I'm less confused.'

'There's nothing else that's clearer now? With the benefit of time.'

Slowly she shook her head. 'I don't think so.'

'Nothing to do with the safe, for instance?'

'What about the safe?'

'You didn't tell them it was there?'

'Of course I didn't. What kind of a stupid . . .?'

'Just opened it for them.'

'No.'

'No?'

'I told them the combination. One of them opened it.'

'The one who looked like me, or the one who didn't?'

'I don't remember.'

'Think about it, Mrs Roy. Take all the time you need.'

She sighed. 'It was the other one.'

'The one who didn't look like me?'

'Yes.'

'Skinny hips?'

'Yes.'

'And you hadn't said anything, you hadn't given them any hint that might have led them to believe there was a safe in the bedroom?'

'No. I've told you.'

47

'I think that's what you claimed, yes.'

'I told all of this to your, whatever you call him, constable.'

'Since when you've had a change of mind.'

'Not about that.'

'All right,' said Resnick, leaning forward, 'let me put it another way. Did you get the impression that the burglars knew about the safe when they broke in? Take your time.'

She did. 'I'm not sure,' she said finally.

'They didn't go straight to it?'

'No. I don't know. I don't think so. I wasn't there, I mean I wasn't with them all the time, not both of them.'

'Not when they found the safe?'

'No. That's right.'

Resnick surprised her by getting to his feet. He picked up his cup and saucer and carried them to the draining board. For a moment, Maria thought he was going to wash them up.

'Is that all?' she asked.

He turned to face her. There was, she thought, something unrelenting in his eyes: not when she had first let him in, made him tea, but now, there when he needed it. When he sensed he'd caught the smell of something.

'Unless there's something else you've remembered?'

'I don't think so.'

'If I may,' said Resnick, on his way to the front door, 'I'll ask someone to call round and go over your account with you. Just to set the record straight.' He paused. 'Some time, I'll have a word with your husband.'

'Harold? What on earth for? He wasn't here.'

The corners of Resnick's mouth wrinkled into a smile. 'Try to convince him to do something about that alarm. You don't want to run the same risks twice. After all – ' he turned the catch to open the front door – 'suppose they took it into their heads to come back?'

6

'See this?'

Grabianski glanced up from his position at the window. Even standing on an oak dining chair, he was having to crane his neck to get the right angle for the binoculars.

Grice was standing a few paces into the room, newspaper folding back over one hand, bacon sandwich – white bread and brown sauce – in the other.

'You read this yet?'

Grabianski shook his head.

'This report, right, according to this, you know how many burglaries there were in this country last year?'

Grabianski didn't know; that is, he knew for certain about seventeen, but, those apart, his knowledge was vague.

'Seventy-three thousand,' Grice informed him. 'Seventy-three.'

Grabianski didn't know if that was a lot or not: it sounded a lot.

'That's less than the year before. Eight per cent down.' Grice held the sandwich to his mouth while he righted the paper. '"Welcoming this reduction,"' he read, '"the Home Secretary stressed that effective action against crime required a commitment from every responsible citizen."' Brown sauce blobbed downwards and settled into the newsprint.

'Neighbourhood watch,' said Grabianski.

'Personal security.'

'Alarm systems.'

Grice shook his head. 'Eight per cent reduction at the same time as, get this, assaults and muggings have risen to the level of 420 a day. Now how many's that in a year?'

Grabianski was working it out in his head. 'Leaving out Christmas and bank holidays, about 150,000.'

'Right!' said Grice vehemently. 'Over twice the number of burglaries.' He waved the remains of his bacon sandwich in Grabianski's direction. 'And if that doesn't tell you something about the state this country's got itself into, I don't know what does.'

Nodding slowly, Grabianski turned back to the window.

Resnick stood in front of his superintendent's desk, fighting the feeling that, although Jack Skelton wasn't even in the room, he should be at attention. It was something about Skelton himself, of course, always so straight-backed, each greying hair of his head brushed into formation, shine of his shoes fresh and unblemished. Something, also, to do with the way everything on the surface of his desk was arranged in carefully regimented order: three pens angled against the blotter, black, blue and red; papers pinned inside their appropriate trays, notes in Skelton's precise hand attached; the diary, black and padded, a marker of red ribbon in place at the day; inside three matching silver frames, Jack Skelton's wife and daughter beamed perfect contentment from between matching hair-styles and almost matching dresses.

'Charlie.'

'Sir.'

Turning, Resnick saw the cuffs of his superior's crisp grey shirt had been turned back once, then once again. His tie was held in place by a discreet silver-and-blue clip. The jacket to his charcoal-grey suit was already hanging behind the door. It was Jack Skelton's way of showing that he was still a working copper.

'Sit down, Charlie.'

'Sir.'

Seated himself, Skelton flipped his diary open and then closed. 'This break-in over on Harrison's patch, there's some suggestion our old friends might be paying us another visit?'

'It's possible, sir.'

'Likely?'

Resnick leaned one elbow on the edge of the desk, only to remove it quickly. A mistake. 'They were professionals, no two ways about that. About as careful with the inside of the house as Pickfords. No reason they had to know what they were going to find, but they could have had a good idea they wouldn't be wasting their time.'

'Unlikely out that way, eh, Charlie? Put in a thumb and pull out a plum every time.'

Or find the silver threepenny bit in each slice of the pudding, thought Resnick. 'Could say the same here, sir. Big, old houses, expensive property. Unless it's all going on the mortgage and keeping the kids in private school, there's likely to be something around worth taking.'

'Jewellery, money, furs, the occasional negotiable bond – not interested in video recorders and stereo as I recall.'

'That's right, sir. None of the stuff recovered. Each place they went into, either no security system had been installed or it conveniently failed to function. There was an alarm box on the wall at the Roy house, but it doesn't look as though any attempt was made to neutralize it. That wasn't because they were being sloppy, so what does that leave? Luck?'

'Not a great believer in luck, as I recall, Charlie.'

Resnick shook his head.

'We checked out the security firms,' said Skelton. 'Last time around.'

'And double-checked. One lead, an engineer who'd been sacked and seemed to bear a grudge, we liked him for it for some little time, but in the end we couldn't prove any connection.'

'Do we know if he's still around?'

'We can find out.'

Jack Skelton set the palms of his hands against his desk and eased his chair back six inches. 'Harrison's not going to be happy at you meddling around down there without more than your sixth sense by way of justification.'

'It was the DCI put me on to it, sir. He'll smooth Harrison over.'

'For now, Charlie. For now.' Skelton took hold of the ribbon end and opened his diary; this time it remained open. Appointments had been entered in either red or blue ink and Resnick wondered what the significance of that might be. 'If this proves to be no more than a one off, if there's nothing else to link it to us, don't get involved. Seventy-three thousand burglaries last year, Charlie. What do you think the clear-up rate on that lot was?'

Having to stand up on his toes for so much of the time was giving Grabianski a lot of trouble with the muscles at the back of his thighs. Hambones? Hamstrings? He moved the binoculars away from his eyes and eased himself back down on to his heels.

Best part of twenty minutes he'd been watching it now and still he couldn't be certain.

First off, he marked it down as a wren, tiny brown bird with its tilted tail. Marvellous the way it crept between the branches and under wisps of dried grass the wind had lifted there and spread. Calling no attention to itself, like the best of thieves. Except, of course, when it sang. Then the sound it made was loud and clear, surprisingly penetrating for such a tiny bird. Which, of course, was what made him think that it was not a wren.

The song, when finally it came, was short and not so sweet. Grabianski had refocused, watched more closely. The tail – the tail was wrong; instead of tilting up it followed the curve of the back, spreading wide instead of moving to a point. And the underside – wasn't that a show of white?

When it climbed, without faltering, straight up the sheer trunk of tree, he knew: it was *certhia familaris*. A tree-creeper.

Grabianski went back up on to his toes and scanned along the branches, this way, then that. Ah! There! Finger and thumb turning a fraction, he honed in. Yes. Look at the way the beak curves down so it can get at insects buried in the bark.

'Grabianski!'

The shout surprised him and he had to grab the back of the chair to prevent himself from toppling off.

'You want to watch out. There's a law against that sort of thing, you know.'

The entrance to the station was chock-a-block with Chinese. It was enough to make Resnick, as he made his way through with his lunch, guilty for not having sweet-and-sour pork, a couple of spring rolls at least. What he had was pastrami and horseradish on black bread, Jarlsberg and parma ham on caraway with rye, two fat gherkins wrapped in shiny white paper.

'What's going on?' he asked the nearest constable once he was inside the door.

The PC gestured towards the stairs. 'Your sergeant, sir. Got one of them in interrogation.'

Resnick nodded and continued on his way. When he knocked on the door of the interview room and peered around it, Graham Millington was face to face with a bespectacled Chinaman wearing a red tuxedo with dark velvet lapels. There was a tape recorder on the desk between them and it seemed to be recording a lot of silence.

Resnick closed the door softly and went along the corridor to the CID room. Patel was trying to reach the boiling kettle with one hand without losing his grasp of the telephone into which he was talking.

'Yes, madam,' he said with exquisite politeness, although Resnick sensed that he was saying it for the umpteenth time. 'Yes, madam. Yes.'

Resnick stepped around him and lifted the kettle clear. He made a sign at Patel that suggested tea.

Patel smiled and nodded.

'Yes, madam,' he said. 'I really think the best thing for me to do is transfer you to the duty sergeant. Yes, I am sure he will take care of the matter. Promptly, yes. Yes. Good day.'

Resnick dropped tea bags into the pot while the DC transferred the call.

'Anything interesting?' he asked when Patel had set down the phone.

'Peeping Tom,' said Patel. He seemed to find the idea mildly amusing.

'Bring me through a cup when it's had time to mash.'

'Yes, sir.'

Before Resnick could retreat inside his office the phones had rung twice more. He slit the brown paper bag down one side with his biro and opened it out, an improvised tablecloth. It was either that or get vinegar all over his team's reports. Well, today it would be vinegar: most usually, a mixture of mustard and mayonnaise.

He was biting into his first gherkin when Patel came through with his tea; savouring the second when Millington knocked and entered, his face a picture of grief.

'I don't want to be racist, but that bugger's bleeding inscrutable.'

'You don't need an interpreter?'

'Bloody mind-reader, more like.'

'Want me to have a go at him?'

'No disrespect, sir, but I was wondering if Lynn might have any luck?'

'Feminine wiles, Graham?'

'Not exactly, sir. Thought he might not find it so easy to stare at her and play dumb. Respect women in their culture, don't they?'

What they did, Resnick thought, was bind their feet.

'Mean taking her out of the centre,' Resnick said.

'No more than an hour, sir.'

'OK.'

Millington nodded and rose to go.

'Fire officer's report, Graham – got that now, have we?'

'Came through earlier, sir.'

Resnick made a point of looking at his desk. 'Not to me.'

'I'll pass it through, sir.'

'Good.'

Jesus! Millington thought as he shuffled papers around on his desk, I've just got to leave him one loophole and he gets me through it every time. Straightening with the report, he saw Patel smiling gently at him from across the room. You're the one I should let loose on him, Millington said to himself, turning away, then you could have a high old time being sly and devious to one another. In for a racist penny, in for a pound.

The jewellery was sent Red Star to a highly respectable Glasgow silversmith, who, some short time later, made a transfer of funds under an assumed name, equally into two accounts. These accounts, needless to say, were also held under pseudonyms. At intervals which coincided with the determining of interest, money from these accounts was filtered through to the Isle of Man.

It was Grice's idea and his particular pleasure, annually, to fly over to Douglas, ostensibly to check on their financial affairs; in reality his cherished ambition, so far in vain, was to be present when one of the TT riders came off his bike going into a hairpin bend.

Once a year, Grice and Grabianski had what Grice liked to call a financial summit. Aside from those periods when they were 'working', this was the only occasion the two men met. They took their equal share of any proceeds and used it only in such ways as would not compromise the operation or increase the risk of discovery. Grice had purchased a small villa in the north of Portugal, well clear of any riff-raff (by which he meant the British or German varieties), and occasionally indulged himself on a flight to visit an old friend in Australia, via a number of Far Eastern brothels and massage parlours.

Grabianski had a time-share in a Forestry Commission cabin in the Scottish Highlands and one of the smaller houses in Macclesfield, a location that put him within easy reach of both the Peaks and the Pennines. Each year he travelled overseas with the Ramblers Association – so far, he had walked Turkey, Crete, the Himalayas, New Zealand and was working himself up to Peru.

They were two men with little or nothing in common, aside from a shared trade or craft. They didn't like one another, but then they didn't have to. What they both were was careful. Contacts they cultivated assiduously; usually Grabianski softened them up and then Grice took over and kept their spirits keen and their pockets never quite full enough. Cities they treated as provident farmers did their fields – every so often, they were left to lie fallow.

'I've been thinking about this kilo,' Grice said.

'Mn?'

'I think we'll give them the chance to buy it back.'

Resnick ate his last piece of pastrami and washed it down with a mouthful of cold tea. He could see Naylor moving around in the outer office and knew he should call him in and have a talk – trouble with sleeping? Debbie still experiencing difficulties? Not to worry, happens to the best regulated of families. But if you'd like to talk about it . . .

Resnick knew that that was just about the last thing, right then, he wanted to do. He picked up Millington's preliminary report and scanned it through. The man he was interviewing owned several restaurants and had a controlling share in others. His youngest son had incurred his wrath by marrying into a local family, non-Chinese, and opening his own restaurant and takeaway.

That had been three weeks ago. Since then there had been broken windows and worse. The fire officer seemed in no doubt that when the son's new premises had flared up it had been arson. A large container of cooking oil had been manoeuvred into the cellar and set alight; the result had been charred girders and melted chopsticks. Only because the place had been closed and the residents of the upstairs flat on their way back from a party had there been no fatalities.

Resnick hoped the young man had had time to obtain sufficient insurance.

Insurance.

He screwed paper and crumbs into a ball and bounced them off the rim of the waste bin on to the floor.

'Patel,' he called from the door.

'Sir?'

'Here a minute.'

There was Naylor, glancing across at him from above his typewriter, adding to the guilt.

'Patel,' Resnick said, 'get yourself down to Jeff Harrison's nick. Have a word with a young PC, Featherstone. He went out to investigate a burglary, Harold and Maria Roy. In through the back, out the front. Professional job.'

'Yes, sir.'

'I had a word with the woman; what she told me and what she told Featherstone don't seem to tie up. Shake the inconsistencies around a little, talk to her. See if you think she's just confused or if she's lying.'

'This will be all right, sir? With Inspector Harrison?'

'Help ourselves, he said. Well, in as many words. It's been okayed from on high, so we're covered. Which brings me to the other thing – find out some more about her insurance. Who's the policy with? Were they recommended? She suggested they took over the insurance from the house owners, but that may not be accurate. If she wants to show you papers, let her. And perhaps you can encourage her to remember who it was came around and gave them a quotation to get their security updated.'

'That's all, sir?'

With some of the others, Resnick might have pegged it as facetiousness. 'For the present,' he said and then, because there was no way of avoiding it, he invited Naylor into his office.

The two men looked at one another with less than ease. Resnick had a strong sense of Naylor wanting to talk to someone, needing to, but sensed that it wasn't himself.

'How's Debbie?' Resnick asked.

'Oh,' Naylor shifted his feet awkwardly, 'fine. She's fine. She . . .'

'Lot of broken nights.'

'Yes, sir.'

'Strain on both of you.'

Naylor stood and shuffled his feet; the collar of his shirt was suddenly too tight. One hundred and one places you would rather be than here.

'You're getting some help?'

Naylor's eyes panicked.

'There must be somebody . . . I don't know, district nurse . . .'

'Health visitor. Yes, sir. She comes round every so often, though Debbie says she doesn't know what for.' Three times out of four, Debbie kept the door locked and pretended there was nobody home, but he wasn't telling Resnick that.

'How about the doctor? Any use?'

'Not a lot, sir. Debbie says . . .'

Resnick switched off. What was that old game he'd played at school? Simon says this, Simon says that, whatever it might be, no matter how daft, that was what you did and fast. No questions asked. He glanced up at Naylor, who seemed to have finished.

'You know, we could arrange some counselling, from this end. If it's interfering with your work.' Resnick could see from the look in the young DC's eyes that he'd as well have suggested something bizarre in the way of sexual practices. 'If you wanted to talk things through, the pair of you, with some professional – it's available, OK?'

'Yes, sir.' Anxious to be away.

'All right, Kevin.'

Out of there like the proverbial clockwork rabbit. Resnick shook his head, gave himself a few moments to ponder whether

57

he should have taken a place on that course in man-management, then picked up the phone and dialled Midlands TV.

'Mr Roy is out on location,' announced a voice like high-gloss make-up. 'I can put you through to the production secretary if you wish.'

Resnick wished.

'Engaged, will you hold?'

Resnick held.

7

Harold Roy's father had named him after a bandleader who specialized in comic songs and second-rate, searing clarinet. After thirteen years of alternately bullying or buying young Harold into spending his evenings and weekends practising a number of instruments – piano, violin, clarinet (of course), even, for a particularly uncomfortable three months, the tuba – he had given in. His son would never emulate his namesake: he would not be a musician. Even Harold's one attempt at a comic song – wearing a gingham tablecloth to entertain a Christmas gathering with 'I'm Just a Girl who Can't Say No' – had ended in failure. There had been muted applause and an aunt saying loudly, 'Can't carry a tune for his life, bless him!'

Aware of disappointing his parents and seeking to make amends, Harold had shown an interest in drama school. Sure enough, they had clapped their hands and given him all the encouragement he had needed. That is to say, money in his bank account and a tilting end-terraced house on the borders of Lewisham and New Cross.

Almost from the first, Howard knew that he had made a mistake. Classes in improvisation reduced him to a stuttering wreck; movement and dance brought back all those afternoons wasted with the metronome, only this time it was his feet and not his fingers that refused to obey the rhythm. A one-line part as an attendant lord in *Macbeth* made it clear to him that the only person who survived the entire experience without humiliation was the director.

So a career was born.

Harold knew he could ill afford to be proud and he espoused those projects no one else considered. A black comedy involving a legless man trapped in a cellar with twelve radios, each tuned to different stations; an autobiographical piece by a fiery working-class lad whose mother was a drudge, whose father was dying from pneumoconiosis and whose sister was selling herself on the streets of Cardiff; a wordless epic, thirteen hours with intervals, about Vietnamese peasants, for which the props included twenty-seven hoes and a gallon bucket of pigs' blood nightly.

Well, this was the sixties and Harold Roy knew better than to look back. Before the bubble burst he went into rep. Salisbury, Lancaster, Derby: *Lady Windermere's Fan, The Importance of Being Earnest, Charley's Aunt*. For every four Agatha Christies he put on a John Osborne revival.

This was how he met Maria. Hard-bitten, attractive, opinionated, coldly sexy, Maria was perfect as the best friend who encouraged Jimmy Porter's wife to leave him and then stays on to share his bed and do his ironing. When the curtain rises for the second act, she is in her slip at the ironing board and Harold took to secreting little notes between the folds of the creased shirts. Maria found this charming; she was at a loose end and, in Chester, Harold seemed the acme of sophistication. She hitched her wagon to someone she thought was going to make her a star and all he did was make her pregnant.

All right, Maria thought, coming round from the anaesthetic, the least you can do is make money.

Harold's first work in television was directing live drama for Granada. He waved his arms a lot, called actors of any sex 'love'; most importantly, he got on first-name terms with the crew and saw to it that the cameramen were never in need of a drink after the unit had wrapped. He hung an expensive lens from his neck and was forever squinting through it, always looking for angles. He said yes to everything, no to nothing, he was always in work. His agent put him up for the latest Dennis Potter, the new John Mortimer; what he got was another *Emmerdale Farm*, an *East-Enders*, a *Grange Hill*.

Now he was working on a series for Midlands Television about a working-class family who win a fortune on the pools.

Dividends.

Resnick parked his car in the forecourt of the pub, hoping that his cats would forgive him for not calling home first to feed them. But he didn't think this would take very long. A double-decker bus, fitted out with narrow tables between the seats, stood alongside the location catering van. The remnants of the evening's salads clung to the edges of large bowls; trays of fruit and cheese stood close to urns of tea and coffee. Jam roly-poly said the board by the serving hatch, bread-and-butter pudding. There was the unmistakable smell of chip fat over everything.

Resnick tapped on the window of a transit van bearing the Midlands TV logo. The driver lifted the open pages of the *Sun* from his face and wound the window down.

'Harold Roy,' Resnick said. 'I'm looking for him.'

There was something familiar about the driver, but he couldn't place what it was.

The man squinted out towards the close streets of the Broxtowe Estate. 'In there.'

'Thanks,' said Resnick and waited while the window was raised and the newspaper returned to its previous position. He stepped over the low fencing and across the main road. The constable in his uniform overcoat, diverting traffic, recognized Resnick by sight and stepped clear of the four or five small children who were hanging round him.

'Evening, sir. Didn't know you were out this way.'

'I'm not.'

'Right, sir.'

'Hope they're paying your overtime for this.'

'Yes, sir.'

Resnick left him entertaining his kindergarten. The oldest of them wasn't more than ten and most would be there until the pubs had closed.

Two more vans were parked at the curb, inside which the artists played cards, filled in crosswords, read, waited their calls. Thick cables ran to and from a third van, close to the corner. Arc lights had been set up on stands and just outside their beam, groups of men stood around in donkey jackets, rubbing their gloved hands together, smoking. Resnick was reminded of photographs he'd seen of the general strike.

A young woman wearing a harassed expression and a violent blue bomber jacket bounced past Resnick in red baseball boots with white stars at their sides. Embroidered on to the centre of the jacket's back was a fist with the middle finger thrusting skywards.

'Naomi!' she spat in the walkie-talkie in her hand. 'I want Laurence here and I want him now!'

There was a squawked reply that Resnick failed to understand.

'You!' she said, pointing hard at Resnick. Each finger of her glove was a different, bright colour. 'Get back behind the van. Back!'

'I'm looking for . . .'

'Back!'

Resnick raised an eyebrow and turned towards the van. As he did so, the man he had seen earlier behind the wheel of the red Citroën threw back the sliding door and jumped out. Harold Roy was wearing a waist-length blue jacket and brown leather boots beneath his designer jeans. A white scarf spiralled round the collar of a red wool shirt.

'Chris, would you mind telling me what in God's name we're waiting for? This shot's been lit and ready for the last fifteen minutes.'

'Laurence,' said the girl, the evenness of her voice scarcely disguising her antagonism.

'What about him?'

'He's changing his costume.'

'Now? Now he's changing his costume? Half an hour after he's been called?'

'We didn't have any choice. Continuity.'

'Well, if costume didn't spend the entire day with their heads up each other's arses, they might have noticed that sooner.'

'It's being taken care of, Harold. It's in hand.'

'I don't want him in hand, I want him here, now.'

'On his way.'

'Now?'

'Now.'

Harold Roy took a couple of steps back and looked around; some of the crew and the extras had been watching the exchange, most were carrying on with their conversations or simply standing motionless, leaning against something, bored.

'Next thing we know, Harold announced to everyone and no one, 'Mackenzie's going to be asked why we're behind schedule again. And I'm going to make sure the blame for that goes where it belongs.'

Chris turned her back on him and walked away, letting her embroidered finger make her reply.

She came back towards the lights a few moments later with an actor Resnick recognized from a coffee commercial. A slim man with a ponytail, wearing a shiny black jumpsuit, bustled behind them, pulling stray threads from the back of the actor's jacket.

'All right everybody, positions please.'

Harold Roy slid the van door shut behind him. Resnick didn't think it was the best moment to go and talk to him about his house being burgled.

'Hallo,' said the voice at the other end of the phone.

'Hallo.' Maria was watching *Dallas* on TV. Why didn't her precious Harold ever get anything like that to work on?

'Hallo,' the voice repeated.

'Who is this?' Maria asked. The voice was familiar and she wondered if it was somebody from the studio, maybe even the producer. 'Is that Mac?' she asked. Theodore James Mackenzie was the producer and originator of *Dividends*; when he was in a good mood he liked to be called Mac.

'No.' A pause. 'You know who this is.'

Then she did. She spun around and leaned her head back against the wall. 'You'll never keep John Ross from me!' Sue Ellen was screaming at JR from the heart of their rented twenty-four-inch FST Sony.

'You do know, don't you?'

Her hand less than steady, Maria set down the receiver.

Laurence had to walk ten yards along the pavement, look at his watch under the streetlight, walk another five yards, look up towards the bedroom windows of the semi-detached brick house and say: 'Cheryl, you're going to wish you'd never turned me out of your bed, so help me!'

It wasn't *Dallas*, but it was trying, just not very hard.

He seemed to be required to repeat this a great many times and after the first few, Resnick wandered back to have a word with the constable on traffic duty.

'How much longer?' Resnick asked.

63

The officer checked his watch. 'Won't be above an hour, sir, you can be pretty sure of that.'

'Work to time, do they?'

'On the dot. Five, four, three, two, one, someone pulls the plug.'

'Not like some then,' said Resnick with a faint smile. 'In need of a little time and half to ease the mortgage payments.'

'Bought a caravan with mine, sir — miners' strike. Over at Ingoldmells. Get up in the morning and pull back the curtain and the only thing in view is the sea. Unless there's a mist.'

'But not here?' Resnick persisted.

'Don't think it's so much the cash, sir. More a case of good will.'

'Good will?'

'Doesn't seem to be a lot of it about.'

Resnick nodded and took a couple of paces away. Two of the undernourished kids who'd been tugging at the constable's uniform trousers and trying to dribble spittle down on to his boots without him noticing, were shifting their attention.

'You on telly?' one of them asked Resnick. He had a bright, liverish flare on one cheek, burn or birth mark, it was impossible to tell which.

Resnick shook his head.

'Told you!' said his friend, whose hair had been cropped so short it was possible to see the scabs across his scalp.

'He's lying! You're lying, aren't you, mister? I've seen you.'

'No,' said Resnick, turning away.

'Go on,' shouted the boy with the blemish, 'tell us.'

'I should watch out if I were you,' said the constable. 'He's a police officer. Detective inspector.'

Resnick gave him a quick look that said, thanks very much.

'He your boss, is he?'

'Not exactly.'

'Bet he is. Hey, mister, order him about, tell him what to do.'

'I'll tell you what to do and that's clear off from here. Scram.' The constable shooed the lads away with his hands and they skipped out of his reach, off to where the crew were standing around, to scrounge cigarettes.

'I suppose it's naïve to ask where their parents are,' said Resnick, 'why they're letting them run the streets.'

'Better here in sight,' said the constable, 'than nicking the radio from somebody's car or shinning up the drainpipe and in through some old dear's bathroom window.'

Which was when Resnick knew why the driver asleep under the *Sun* was familiar.

Maria Roy had drunk the first whisky too quickly, the second she had forced herself to sip slowly. Not that that was such a good idea. Hadn't she read somewhere that sipping alcohol only made you drunker faster? Or was that only if you sipped it through a straw?

She paced the downstairs of the house from room to room, telling herself that when he rang back she was going to be ready, she was going to be calm. This time she would be reasonable, ask him what he thought he was playing at, what he wanted.

There were three telephones in the house and none of them would ring.

'Alf?'

He was no longer catching forty winks in the van. Instead, he was standing by the rear of the catering vehicle, talking to a man in a white apron who was slicing open four dozen soft bread rolls.

'Alfie?'

He was built like a whippet on two legs; so much so that it was difficult not to keep peering behind him, looking for the curled end of skinny tail that should have been poking out from beneath his coat.

'Sergeant.'

'Inspector.' Resnick corrected him.

'Didn't think you'd made me.'

'Wasn't sure at first.' Resnick stepped back and refocused. 'It was the hair.'

'How about it?'

'You didn't used to have any.'

Alf Levin brushed a hand across his head. 'Wonderful, isn't it? Modern technology.'

65

'You're not telling me that's all the result of a transplant?'

'No. False as evidence, isn't it? Wig job. Toupee. It's since I've been working for Midlands. Got to know a few of the boys in make-up. Measured me up, colour samples, the works; I must be the only driver working for this company with a hundred per cent guaranteed, architect-designed head of hair. Stand in front of a force-nine gale in this and all that'll happen is it flicks up a bit at the ends.'

'Let's talk, Alfie,' said Resnick, with a glance towards the caterer, who was now severing the links between large numbers of sausages.

'I thought that's what we were doing.'

'Over there,' said Resnick.

Alf Levin only hesitated for long enough to light a cigarette and toss the used match out across the forecourt. 'If I'm not back for my sausage cob,' he said, 'call my brief for me.'

Maria was sitting on the lavatory in the downstairs bathroom: the seat was down and her skirt was spread wide across her legs. The empty glass was being slowly rolled between the fingers of both hands, back and forth.

'Come on, you bastard,' she said aloud. 'Pick up the phone.'

8

'Your DI not still around, I suppose?'

Millington jumped at the sound of the superintendent's voice; his knee caught the edge of the table and, though he held on to the mug at the second attempt, most of its contents splashed over his hands, the magazine he'd been reading, the floor.

'No, sir. Not seen him since this afternoon.'

Skelton nodded and surveyed the room: halfway between a grammar school staffroom and the men's locker facilities at the private squash club where he was due on court in twenty minutes.

'Any message, sir?'

A curt shake of the head, dismissive. "Night, sergeant.'

Graham Millington forced out his polite reply, watching the super turn back through the doors, sports bag in his hand. Five games with some sweaty barrister and then a couple of G and Ts before he drives home to whatever his wife's keeping warm for him. All right for some. Millington's own wife would be at her second-year Russian class and he'd stop off at the chippy on the way back, either that or a toasted ham-and-cheese in the pub, couple of quick halves.

He pulled a handkerchief from his pocket and dabbed at the desk top, wiped between his fingers. That the superintendent should find him the only one left in the office, working late, was fine – but why did he have to come in when Millington was drinking half-stewed tea and browsing through the copy of *Penthouse* he'd found in Divine's in-tray?

'Know about your form, do they?'

'Midlands,' said Alf Levin, 'they're an equal-opportunity employer.'

They were sitting at a corner table in the lounge, keeping as much distance as possible between themselves and a bunch of extras who were boasting about how many times they'd worked with Michael Caine and Bob Hoskins.

'How long?'

'Eighteen months, no, getting on two years, must be.'

'Sounds like a sentence.'

Levin lifted his pint, flicked away the beer mat that had stuck to the underside of the glass. 'That was a twelve.'

'Out in nine.'

'Less.'

'Good behaviour.'

'Overcrowding.'

Resnick leaned forward, one elbow resting close to his Guinness, largely untouched. 'Nice to see that it works sometimes. Sets you back on the straight and narrow.'

'Wasn't the nick.'

'You're not going to tell me you found religion?'

'No. A good probation officer.'

'Needle in a haystack.'

'Sharp as one. Found me a place to live, made sure I kept the appointments, even got me along to a couple of meetings, counselling sessions.' His thin face wrinkled brightly; with that wig he looked a lot less than his forty-odd years. 'Me, counselling sessions!'

'Useful, were they?'

'No,' Levin scoffed, 'but that's not the point. Point is, she put me up for this. First time I've been clean since I left school and headed north with nothing but my native wit and GCE Metalwork.'

'You make it sound like the Wizard of Oz.'

'More Dick Whittington, I like to think.'

'Wasn't he heading for London?'

'Ah, only after he got turned around. Sound of Bow Bells. Remember?'

'And are you really turned around, Alfie?'

Levin clapped a hand to his breast. 'God is my witness.'

Resnick set down his Guinness and looked round the bar. 'Don't think he's in tonight, Alfie.'

'I thought he was everywhere.'

'Ah,' said Resnick, 'so you did get religion.'

'Bought an LP by that Cliff Richard,' Alf Levin said. 'Does that count?'

*   *   *

'Are you alone?' Grabianski asked.

'Yes,' said Maria, so quietly he hardly heard.

'Sorry?'

'Yes.'

At the other end of the line, she could imagine his smile.

'We've got to meet.'

'No.'

'We have to.'

'Why?'

'Why are you pretending?'

She didn't know: she didn't try to say.

'How about now?' he asked.

'No. You can't. It's impossible.'

'Nothing's that impossible.'

'Harold . . .'

'Your husband?'

'My husband.'

'What about him?'

'He'll be home soon.

'Get out before he does. Meet me.'

'No.'

'Then I'll come to you.'

'No!' Too hasty, a shout.

She heard him laugh, and then: 'All right, then. Meet me tomorrow. And don't say you can't.'

Maria could feel the sweat along the palm of the hand which was holding the receiver, knew without needing to see that it was trickling down towards the curve of the mouthpiece. Knew that she was just as damp in other places, damper.

'All right,' she said, eyes closed tight.

Alf Levin decided that since they'd started bringing out all those curry flavours, poppadums and the like, crisp-eating had become a part of international cuisine.

'What it is,' he said to Resnick, who shook his head when Levin offered him the packet, 'is you're asking me to grass.'

'Not in so many words,' said Resnick, wondering how he might put it better.

'Inform on my previous associates, if such they were.'

69

'Assist. Assist, Alfie. Your duty as a citizen.'

'A reformed citizen.'

'Exactly.'

Alf Levin tipped back his head and shook what was left in the packet down into his mouth; trouble with crisps was, all the buggers did was make you hungry. And thirsty. No matter what the flavour.

'Another, Mr Resnick?'

'I'd rather have an answer.'

When he pulled back his upper lip, Levin revealed two remarkably long front teeth; strong, as if they could break a weasel's back with a single bite.

'It's not as if I mix in those sort of circles.'

'But you could.'

'I could do a lot of things.'

'For the right reasons.'

'How many of them?'

'Righteousness breeds its own rewards.'

Alf Levin screwed up the spent crisp packet and got to his feet. Across the bar, the extras were starting to move, noisily, towards the exit.

'Come on, Mr Resnick,' Alf Levin said, 'before I have to drive that lot back I want a couple of those sausage cobs.' He winked down at Resnick. 'Hot snack on wrap.'

Harold Roy stood off on his own, not eating, turning his back with an automatic gesture when he unscrewed the top of his small silver flask and tipped it over into his polystyrene cup of coffee. Resnick, watching, found it easy to sympathize. The director looked like a man with anxieties aplenty; besides which, the coffee was dreadful.

Harold bunched up the empty cup in his hand and dropped it into the refuse sack as he walked past, heading for the lounge. Fair enough, thought Resnick, taking a seat at the bar, three stools along.

Resnick heard Harold order a large vodka and tonic and smiled. That should be me, he thought: every night for supper his grandfather had sat down to a plate of pickled herrings, raw red onion thinly sliced across the top, thick yellow mayonnaise at the side. Black bread. Vodka. Every night.

'Yes, duck?' asked the woman behind the bar.

'Guinness,' said Resnick.

'Pint?'

'Half.'

He took the first sip, the flavour rich and the temperature pleasingly cool beneath the creaminess of the head. From outside came the sound of engines starting up, but not everyone was leaving. Clusters of people came in, their voices shriller than usual, the occasional 'fuck' for emphasis beautifully articulated. Close to Resnick's right shoulder a young man with a gold stud in his ear and a leather jacket artistically dabbled with paint asked for a St Clements and got a hard look.

'Cheer up, Harold!' Someone clapped him on the shoulder. 'Could be a lot worse.'

Evidently Harold didn't think so; he didn't acknowledge the remark at all. Coins had found the jukebox and for the first eight bars a few voices sang along with Tom Jones. For some little time Resnick had been aware that he wasn't the only one with an interest in Harold Roy. Leaning back against the wall, between the cigarette machine and a large plastic yucca, a prematurely balding man wearing a loose-fitting leather jacket was talking to a pretty, dark-haired girl in moon boots, every now and then sneaking a look over the top of her head towards the bar. If he doesn't want a word with me, thought Resnick, it must be Harold. Advice or condolences, either way he was being polite, waiting for the perfect moment, biding his time.

Some people were not so restrained.

The producer of *Dividends* was in a hurry to get to his director, but he still managed to shake a few hands, squeeze a few shoulders, smile a few smiles between the entrance and where Harold was sitting, slump-shouldered, on his stool.

'What went wrong?' he asked, slipping on to the seat alongside Harold. 'This time.'

'Don't start, Mac,' Harold replied, not looking up from his glass.

'No one's starting, Harold.'

'Good.'

71

'No one's starting anything.'

Harold nodded wearily, pushed his glass along the counter towards the barmaid, gesturing that he wanted another.

'Nobody seems to be getting close to finishing, either.'

'I thought you weren't . . .'

'I'm doing my job, Harold. It's a pity you don't seem capable any longer of even pretending to do the same.'

Those of the crew and cast who had come into the bar were very quiet now; from the other bar there was the persistent, irregular click of balls from three pool tables. Tom Jones had become Elvis Presley: he wished.

Harold Roy's eyes were heavy and red, an amalgam of alcohol and anger, a strong leavening of shame. There was a moment when Resnick thought Harold might have shouted, thrown a punch, the fresh contents of his glass. It passed. As he looked away, twenty people seemed to take a breath.

'How many scenes were we down, Harold?'

Harold shook his head. 'Can't we talk about this in the morning? In the office?'

'How many?'

Mackenzie's voice was relentless; Resnick couldn't see his face, didn't need to know how much he was enjoying the act of humiliation.

'One? Only two this time? What was it?'

'Four.'

'What was that?'

'Four.'

'How many?'

'Four!'

Harold caught his heel against the stool as he tried to jump to his feet; it swayed for a moment and fell heavily. He stumbled awkwardly, glass in hand, vodka splashed across his clothes.

'It's a wonder,' said Mackenzie, 'the booze and all the other junk you use to pickle what once might have been a brain, it's a wonder you can stand at all.' Mackenzie moved until he was close to Harold, close enough for Harold to have taken a swing at him, taunting him, maybe, to do exactly that. 'In case it's slipped your memory, we have a programme we're supposed to be getting ready for transmission. You let any more fall off the back end of the schedule and we'll be down to fifteen-minute episodes. Instead of an hour.' The look he gave Harold was all contempt, no pity. 'In the office,' he said. 'Eight-thirty. We'll get it sorted.'

Mackenzie left with the same speed as he'd come in and this time there were no handshakes, no good words. Just a direct stride and a hand that came out fast as he stiff-armed one side of the door. A lot of people began to talk at once. Resnick finished his Guinness and denied himself the scotch he really wanted. Harold was back at the bar, back at his stool, waiting for another large vodka. I wonder what are the chances, thought Resnick, of him leaving his car here and calling a cab?

In the excitement, he hadn't noticed the man who'd been rolling his cigarette slipping away. Whatever he had wanted to say to Harold, he'd made up his mind it could wait until a better time. Resnick checked his watch and agreed: apart from anything else there were four cats at home anxiously waiting to be fed. Anxious save for Dizzy, who, by now, would have scavenged off and found his own.

''Night,' he said, turning away.

''Night, duck.'

Harold Roy's head moved sideways, his eyes passed over Resnick but they didn't really see him. The booze and all the other junk, Mackenzie had said. Resnick thought about that as he unlocked his car and slid behind the wheel. He also thought about Mackenzie and what it was that made men like that relish wielding the power they enjoyed so publicly. He had come across officers like that in the force, enough to have realized they were more than an odd phenomenon. For three years, back when he'd been in uniform, he had served under one; never happier than finding an excuse to give you a bollocking in front of the other officers, wipe his feet all over you and then expect you to smile and hold the door. Christ! thought Resnick. If I ever found myself getting that way I'd jack it in. No question.

He changed up into second and turned on to the main road. In less than ten minutes he would be back in the centre of the city.

The problem is, he thought, you probably don't know that you're doing it. Although – he grinned at his reflection in the driving mirror – between young Lynn Kellogg and Jack Skelton, there's no shortage of folk to tap me on the shoulder, steer me back towards the straight and narrow.

Straight and narrow, straight certainly, that was the superintendent: if Resnick ever found out Skelton's parents had made him wear a brace on his back through his formative years, he'd be less than surprised.

Jack Skelton sat in the armchair, forward, his back to the curtained window. The traffic on the road seemed distant, quiet. He hadn't bothered to get up and switch on the light. He could see the outline of his sports bag where he had left it, smell the faint sweat of his squash clothes. This time he had lasted eighteen minutes without looking at the ticking clock.

9

Miles met Resnick the instant his feet touched the pavement; the cat had recognized the sound of the car's engine from the end of the street and come running. Now he made his welcoming cry from the irregular stones atop the wall, strutting, tail hoisted high as he presented, turn upon turn, his fine backside. Resnick reached up a hand and stroked the smooth fur of the cat's head, behind and below the ear.

'Come on,' said Resnick. 'Let's get something to eat.'

Miles ran along the wall before jumping to the ground, wriggling between the bars of the gate even as Resnick was opening it.

Before he reached the front door, Resnick was aware that Dizzy was there, too; as usual, silent and seemingly from nowhere, he had materialized at the crucial moment. Right now he was nudging Miles out of the way, laying claim to be the first through into the house.

Resnick switched on the light and bent to scoop the post from the carpet. Four envelopes and a business card. He set the chain and slid the bolt.

It struck cold walking through the hallway, and Resnick tried to remember when he had last bled the radiators; maybe it was later than he'd thought and the system had closed itself down for the night.

Pepper had wedged himself between bread-bin and coffee maker, two paws protruding. The tip of Bud's tail showed, a muted white, curling past a leg of the kitchen table.

Miles and Dizzy nudged against either side of Resnick, miaowing shrilly.

'Hush,' he said, knowing that it would do no good.

Tin opened, he forked some into each of the bowls, green, blue, yellow, red, then sprinkled a shower of dried heaven-knows-what over the top. The full-fat milk he gave them, keeping the semi-skimmed for himself. What time was it? Once he'd ground two handfuls of dark beans and poured in the water, he felt relaxed enough to remove his coat, loosen his already loose tie, unfasten and ease off his shoes. In the living room he selected some Lester Young from the shelf and switched the stereo on low. New York City with Johnny Guarnieri: three days past Christmas '43 and just shy of New Year, shining and plump like a fat, silver apple. Back when everything must have still seemed possible. 'I Never Knew'. 'Sometimes I'm Happy'.

Back in the kitchen Resnick lifted Dizzy away from Bud's bowl before slicing bread, rye with caraway. He scooped the contents from a tin of sardines in soya oil, sliced a small onion and spread the rings across the fish; there was a large enough piece of feta cheese to be worth grating. He picked up the business card and took it, with his sandwich, towards the music.

Claire Millinder's signature, diagonally across the bottom of the card, red felt-tip, was rounded and neat. *Tried contacting you, work and home*, it read. *Why don't you get yourself an answerphone?*

'A microwave, that's the answer,' Graham Millington had told him. 'That way, you wouldn't have to eat those sandwiches all the time.'

'Never quite understood, Charlie,' Jack Skelton had said one strangely slack afternoon, 'what it is you've got against CD. Exactly.'

'The way Debbie sees it,' he had heard Naylor explaining to Lynn Kellogg, 'if we invest in a dishwasher now, the extent to which we're going to find use for it, well, it's going to get more instead of less.' Resnick couldn't remember if that was before she'd had the baby, or after.

Lester was bouncing through 'Just You, Just Me', the first chorus almost straight, a trio of those trademark honks marking his place near the end of the middle eight, perfectly placed, perfectly spaced, rivets driven in a perfect line. Intake of breath, smooth and quick, over the flick of brushes against Sid Catlett's snare, and then, with relaxed confidence and the ease of a man with perfect trust both of fingers and mind, he made from that same sequence another song, another tune, tied to the first and utterly his own.

> *What are these arms for?*
> *What are these charms for?*
> *Use your imagination.*

76

The reason Resnick didn't get an answerphone: how else to keep bad news at bay? The messages that you didn't want to hear.

He had seen a photograph of Lester Young taken in 1959. He is in a recording studio, holding his horn, not playing. The suit he is wearing, even for those days' fashions, seems overlarge, as though, perhaps, he has shrunk within it. His head is down, his cheeks have sunk in on his jaw; whatever he is looking at in those eyes, soft, brown, is not there in the room. His left hand holds the shield with which he will cover the mouthpiece, as if, maybe, he is thinking he will slip it into place, not play again. It is possible that the veins in his oesophagus have already ruptured and he is bleeding inside.

The coffee would be ready. In the kitchen Resnick picked up the envelope that was not brown, the address on which had not been printed via computer. He was trying to work out how long it had been since he had seen that writing. How many years. He wanted to tear it, two and four and six and eight, all the multiples until it was like confetti.

'Here.'

He lifted Bud with one hand and set him back in his lap. The cup of coffee was balanced on the arm of the chair. The first take of 'I Never Knew' ended abruptly; some saxophone, a piano phrase never finished. Lester is standing there, tenor close to his mouth, but now he is looking away. As if something has slipped suddenly through that door in 1943, unbidden, out of time. A premonition. A ghost.

10

The call came through, as they tended to do, a little shy of seven o'clock. More often than not it was couched in tones of sleepy bewilderment, the voice of a householder who had found, before the day's first cup of tea, the rear window forced, the front door wide open, either, both. Usually it took a while for the anger to seep through. Rees Stanley had been angry already. The snow at Obergurgl had been piss-poor: ten centimetres on the lower slopes (ten!) and only fifty centimetres of shallow powder higher up. His wife and teenage daughter had wallowed in exorbitant après-ski at his own great expense, his younger son had contrived to break all the toes on his left foot and the ruse of taking the au pair along had been a complete waste of time and money.

The drive from Gatwick had been, for Rees, a silent vigil, a struggle to keep awake and in the outer lane, while those around him slept and stirred and snored.

And then this . . .

The duty sergeant wrote down the details laboriously, editing out the expletives. 'Here, Mark,' he said, holding out the sheet of paper towards Divine as the DC passed through, 'one for you.'

'Cheers.'

Divine glanced at it as he took the stairs two or three at a time. Why was it that sensible people kept so much indoors instead of in the bank? If it'd been some old-age pensioner, fifty quid stuffed under the mattress, he could have understood it, poor old sod. But this . . .

Divine dropped his topcoat over the back of a chair and headed for the kettle. There was work enough to do before Resnick and Millington came nosing around. Details of the night's other burglaries, movement of prisoners in the police cells, messages received; all had to be sorted and filed and ready to be placed on the inspector's desk, together with his mug of tea, strong, no sugar.

Back page, front page, page three: what he'd really like was ten minutes to put his feet up, relax with the paper.

Some chance.

'Ideas?' said Resnick, looking round.

Millington, Divine, Naylor, Kellogg, Patel – none of them seemed eager to offer an opinion.

'Family away for its winter fun and high-jinks and all there is by way of security is an alarm box on the wall which hasn't functioned these last eighteen months. Much the same as the Roy job. What d'you make of that?'

'Luck?' offered Divine, shifting his chair a shade further from the inspector's desk.

'Whose?' said Resnick.

'Lucky they didn't get turned over before now,' said Millington. 'What's the point of an alarm that's not wired up?'

'The appearance, sir,' Patel said, sliding his fingers together. 'That is the deterrent.'

Millington turned his face aside, ignoring him.

'Didn't work that way this time, did it?' said Divine.

Resnick drummed a two-fingered pattern on the underside of his desk.

'If it wasn't fortuitous, sir,' Lynn Kellogg began.

'Wasn't what?' interrupted Divine.

'Fortuitous. You know, like you said, luck. A lucky chance.'

'Don't they have that word in the *Sun*?' asked Naylor, a smile crossing his face, rare these days.

'Only in the crossword,' said Millington, a *Mail* man through and through.

'Well, if it wasn't, sir,' said Lynn, looking at Resnick, getting back to the point, 'I mean, if whoever did it was working on some kind of information, why did they leave it till the last minute?'

'Maybe they came back early,' said Divine. 'The Stanleys.'

'Right,' said Resnick positively. 'Good point. Maybe they did. Make sure you find that out when you're there.'

Good God! Mark Divine was thinking, he actually agreed with something I said.

79

'Ask about that duff alarm. Who fitted it in the first place, who disconnected it, why?'

'Sir,' said Graham Millington, 'wasn't there a . . .'

'Lloyd Fossey.'

'Yes, Lloyd. Expected him to be black with a name like that.'

'Or Welsh,' said Divine.

'Wasn't either. Sutton-in-Ashfield, born and bred. Shifty little bugger. Something wrong with one eye.'

'Fossey worked for one of the local security firms until he was sacked,' Resnick explained. 'We thought he might have been working out a grudge . . .'

'Using what he knew to supplement his dole money,' chipped in Millington.

'But we couldn't ever tie him in to anything.'

'Slippery bastard.'

'Better luck this time, Graham,' Resnick said.

'Do what I can, sir,' said Millington, 'after I've got this Chinese business sorted.'

'Another lot of slippery bastards,' said Divine, low-voiced.

'Why do you say that?' asked Patel.

'Nothing,' said Divine.

'But you said . . .'

'Forget it.'

'No, I should like . . .'

'Not now,' Resnick said evenly. 'I'm due to see the superintendent in ten minutes and that doesn't leave us enough time to offer Mark guidance in avoiding the pitfalls of racial prejudice.'

'What prejudice?' asked Divine, aggrieved. 'All I said was . . .'

Resnick gave him a hard look and he didn't say any more.

'I could try and fit it in this afternoon,' Millington said.

'Good. If there's a problem, see that it's handled by someone else.' Resnick checked his watch. 'Mark, make the Stanley house your first call. Anything that seems important, phone it back in before you move on. Kevin, it would be interesting to know if this place and the one the Roys are renting are insured by the same company. Check back on that last outbreak of similar break-ins, see if there's any connection there. They'd have access to a lot of information any self-respecting burglar would give a great deal for. See if you can find out who, if anyone, came out to check the properties before insurance cover was agreed. If this is the same team as last time and if they are working on inside knowledge, we won't be satisfied just catching them, we want the source as well. All right?'

Resnick stood up, signalling a shuffling of feet and scraping of chairs.

'Lynn,' he said, as the officers were filing out, 'are you back in the shopping centre?'

'Yes, sir.' She sounded less than enthusiastic.

'I might pass through later. I'll let you buy me a coffee.'

'Right, sir.'

Resnick touched Patel on the arm and the young DC jumped. 'You were right to pick up Divine,' he said. 'Not that I suppose he understood.'

'No, sir.'

'Perhaps I should have let you try to explain.'

Patel looked back at him without responding.

'Maria Roy,' Resnick said. 'How did you find her story?'

'Shaky, sir.'

'Inconsistent?'

'Absolutely.'

'The two men who broke in – she's still maintaining they were short and black?'

'Tall, sir. Tall and black. They were growing taller all the time I was with her.'

'But still black?'

'Oh, yes, sir.'

Resnick winked at him. 'Maybe she's colour-blind?'

'I don't think so, sir. Not so many people are. In my experience.'

Resnick nodded. 'Then I wonder why she's lying.'

My God! thought Maria Roy. What is it that's the matter with me? I should be seeing some kind of doctor, some psychiatrist, not standing here, hiding in doorways, waiting to meet a man I don't know. A criminal. She thought her breath was coming so quickly, so loudly, that the other women moving past her, in and out of Debenhams, could surely hear. She took her hands from her pockets, pulled off her gloves, finger by finger, returned her hands to the pockets, gloves bunched inside them. What had she chosen this coat for? It didn't even look smart. She put up the collar and then pulled it down again; it made her look like a spy and besides, it didn't do a thing for her colour. The hands on the clock high above the Council House were taking forever to reach eleven. And even then she had no way of knowing for certain that he would come. No: that she knew.

She was refastening the top button on her coat when she saw him, Grabianski, threading his way between shifting grey clusters of pigeons in the square.

Resnick liked to sit on the end stool, either that or the one next to it. That would be the side of the stall that placed him close to the perspex container of orange juice and the milkshake maker, not the heating unit that kept sausage rolls and pasties lukewarm.

'Ten minutes,' said Sarah, one of the two girls who worked there. 'All right?'

Resnick gestured with the upturned palm of his hand, all right. The espresso machine was like an old-fashioned train; every so often you had to wait for it to get up steam.

Two ladies in their late fifties sat down and dumped their bags of shopping, ordering cups of tea as they lit their cigarettes. Most of the other customers were stallholders in the indoor market, drinking from their own mugs which were kept beneath the counter, making jokes.

Resnick was thinking about what Skelton had said as he was leaving the superintendent's office: 'The source of this information, Charlie, if there is a source – you don't suppose it could be closer to home?'

'Stop it,' Maria said.
  'Stop what?'
  'You know what.'
  'What?'
  'Staring.'

They were upstairs above a card shop, a place that called itself a tearooms, though neither of them was drinking tea. They had the window seat and a view down across the city centre, the square with its latter-day punks and its alcoholics sharing the spray from the fountains, the splendid grey stone of the Council House at the far end, the municipal mosaic and the carved lions at either end of broad steps. A bus, green and two-thirds empty, slid by, turning up the sloped street that would lift it towards the columns of the renovated theatre. A news vendor shouted the arrival of the first edition. A flotilla of truant kids sailed by on roller-skates. Couples paused beside a rail of leather coats, reduced. Young men in shirt-sleeves, moustaches and tattoos. Ordinary people doing ordinary things.

'Don't!'

It was only whispered, an exclamation all the same, sudden, like a hiss of brakes.

Still, heads turned. Grabianski only smiled the same eager, sure smile. His hand rested on her knee, the hem of her skirt where he had pushed it high, not moving, only the thumb moving, the soft ball of it making soft circles against her leg, the slight catch of her tights, round and round below her knee, the meeting place of calf and thigh.

'Is everything all right?' asked the waitress, showing bored concern.

Maria could only narrow her eyes, arch back her head and sigh.

'Why don't you go away?' Grabianski said pleasantly enough. 'We want anything, we'll call.'

'What are we doing?' asked Maria. It was minutes later and Grabianski's thumb was still and she could speak.

'Morning coffee,' he smiled. 'Elevenses — isn't that what it's called?'

It's some kind of torture, Maria thought, that's what it is. He started to pry with his thumb again and she caught at it, leaving her fingers meshed in his. He brought the outside of his left leg inside her right and pressed so forcefully she had to push back or be turned around in her chair.

'People are watching us.'

'You only think that.'

'They can see.'

'What?'

'What you're . . . doing.'

'What am I doing?'

Driving me crazy, Maria thought.

'They're spreading butter on their teacakes,' Grabianski said, 'making neat little ticks on their shopping lists, wondering if they should go for a pee. They're not watching us.'

'Look,' she started.

'Yes?'

'You still . . .'

'Yes?'

'You haven't told me . . .'

'What?'

'You said, on the phone, you said . . . there was something you wanted.'

Grabianski laughed deep in his throat and Maria was surprised by the sound, almost a growl, and she imagined him in bed beside her – well, not beside her, quite. He laughed again and squeezed her leg. How does he know, Maria worried, whatever it is I'm thinking?

'Excuse me,' said Grabianski. The waitress had her black-uniformed back towards him, taking someone else's order. 'Excuse me.'

'Yes?' She was tired and young and there was a dull wedding ring on her finger; at the front of the shiny black dress was a frilly white apron of the kind Maria thought were only worn in the pornographic videos her husband sometimes found exciting after just enough cocaine.

'The bill.'

'In just a moment, sir, I'm . . .'

'We're leaving.'

'I'll be with you in . . .'

'Now.'

The waitress looked down at the pad that hung from her waist, made a fuss of fumbling back and forth, snatched at a sheet and ripped it down the middle, tore away the rest and set both parts on the table alongside Grabianski's second, untouched, cup of coffee.

'Thank you,' he said, placing a five-pound note into her hand and steering Maria around her and towards the stairs. 'We'll be sure to come back again.'

84

'Are you always like this?' Maria asked once they were out on the street.

'Like what?'

'I don't know. Excited. Full of yourself.'

'No,' he replied, 'I don't think so.' He was heading her towards the taxi rank on the south side of the square. 'No.'

'You're not on anything, are you?'

'On?'

'Yes, you know.'

Grabianski shook his head. The Asian taxi-driver broke away from the conversation with his friend and helped open the door of his cab. 'Never seen the need,' Grabianski said, climbing in after her.

They sat there for several seconds, the driver looking at them over his shoulder.

'Go on, then,' said Grabianski.

Maria turned to him, uncertain.

'Give him your address.'

Resnick had finished his two espressos, skimmed the local paper, exchanged with Sarah their ritual sentences. A glance at his watch told him there was no time to wait for Lynn, still feigning interest in the coming fashions at Miss Selfridge or Next. He stopped at the first delicatessen for a pound of smoked sausage, a quarter of dried mushrooms (an extravagance that went a long way), two ounces of dill and a slice of poppy-seed cake; from the greengrocery stall adjacent to the fish market he bought a January King cabbage and half a cucumber; at the cheese stall he chose feta, Jarlsberg and a strong cheddar; finally he bought pickled herring, horseradish and sour cream from the delicatessen near the exit. Here, as at the first, the saleswoman spoke to him in Polish, knowing that he understood, and Resnick answered in English.

There were idle moments when he thought he should do more than sell the house, sell up altogether, apply for a transfer to another city, another town.

He knew he could never do it: this was his life.

Here.

Beyond the other end of the market, close by the escalator and the Emmett clock, a dozen or so Poles stood in overcoats and checked caps, cigarettes cupped inside their hands, talking of the past. Medals and military campaigns: bortsch and cold winters. The airfields or the mines had brought them here and they had stayed. Vodka for these men would always carry the taste and scent of tarragon or bison grass, cherry or wild honey.

When Resnick had been a young man the only vodka he had known had been made in Warrington.

He pressed the button for the lift, descending to the car park. Ten minutes would see him at Midlands Television, hopefully speaking to Harold Roy.

11

Mackenzie had been up since five to six. Two freshly squeezed orange juices, cereal sprinkled with wheatgerm and bran – before that he had swum lengths of the pool for twenty minutes, up and down, thinking his way through the day. Now he was on his feet in the production office, crease in his trousers, gold clip attached to his tie; in the smoked glass of the partition window he saw himself reflected, a straight-shouldered man in a blue wool blazer, double-breasted. Not a day over thirty-five: ten years less than truth.

He sat at his desk, swivelling the chair towards the television monitor and leaning forward to slot a cassette into the VCR. The first scene from the previous day's shooting appeared on the screen.

Mackenzie pulled a stiff-backed book towards him, uncapped his pen and began to make notes. He was hoping that Harold would remember their 8.30 appointment – if it was necessary to come down on him heavily, he would prefer that it happened before the others arrived. Not that he would find their presence off-putting; merely, experience told him that rumour made legends faster than fact.

He grimaced at a scene on the screen and wondered how many viewers would pick up the slight flinch, the moment of hesitation before the leading man went into a fierce clinch with his leading lady. Even then, they might put it down to her bad breath rather than his sexual preference.

'Mac . . .'

Mackenzie depressed the pause button as he turned.

'Mac, I wanted to catch you . . .'

'In early this morning, Robert.'

'This scene, I wanted you to take a look at it.'

'Ah, Robert, I would if there were any chance.'

'It's not a lot, only a few changes.'

Mackenzie shrugged. 'I've got to review what we shot yesterday before the others come in. Meeting at 9.15.' He treated Robert Deleval to a dismissive smile. 'You know how it is.'

Deleval glanced down at the green script pages in his hand. 'Maybe I should have a word with Harold, then?'

'Don't you think he's got enough on his plate already?'

Deleval shook his head. 'But Mac, these lines, they just don't stand up as they are. I'm not sure they even make sense.'

'Little late to decide that now, isn't it?'

'I didn't even see them till yesterday. Somebody's changed them since the run-through.'

'Somebody?'

'Yes.'

'Any idea who?'

Robert Deleval looked at the producer for some seconds before replying. 'No,' he said.

'I'll talk to Harold about it, don't worry. Leave it to me. We'll get something sorted.'

'It'll need a rewrite.'

'Leave it to me.' Mackenzie held out his hand and waited for Deleval to give him the half-dozen pages. He waited until Deleval had left the room and walked along the corridor before tearing the pages into two, then two again and dropping them into the nearest bin.

'Writers!' he announced to the empty office. 'The world would be a better place without them.'

Harold Roy had forgotten the arrangement with his producer. He had woken up late, sweating and appalled by the smell of his own sheets. Maria was swanning around in that housecoat of hers, looking abstracted, except when she was gazing at herself in mirrors. There was still a missing kilo of close-to-pure cocaine hanging over Harold's head, and each time he turned a corner or went through a door he was expecting to come face to face with its owner.

'Come on, Harold,' the man had argued. 'What have you got to lose? I'll tell you – nothing. But on the other hand, what have you got to gain? Huh? To gain. A percentage, free, more or less free, call it a little storage charge, holding charge. I just can't look after it at the moment. I've got problems, you know how it is. I've got to move out, this woman I've been staying with, hey, that's what happens, right? This and that. I'll find somewhere else, a flat, a room, move into a hotel if I have to. All I want you to do is keep this safe. No touching, no sneaking off the top. You'll get your share. That I promise. A couple of weeks', no, a month's supply. Look, Harold, it's good stuff. You know it's good stuff. You should remember that, huh? Look, you don't, over here, try that, there, one, two, a couple of lines. Hey! Isn't that just amazing!'

And Harold had left with the kilo in his case, wedged between his Filofax and camera scripts. If only to stop the man talking: once he'd got wound up, once he'd had a snort himself, he was like a creature with three mouths.

Couldn't shut him up.

'You're late, Harold.'

'I know, Mac, I'm sorry.'

'OK, don't worry.' Mackenzie threw an arm across Harold Roy's shoulders. 'Let's go and get some breakfast.'

'I already had it.'

'So did I. Let's get some coffee.'

'I thought we had a meeting?'

'So we have.'

'Then why are we going off for coffee?'

'We can talk there more easily.'

'What's wrong with here?'

'Nothing.'

The production associate and the production secretary stared at the green screens of their VDUs, fingers poised over the keyboards, not moving.

'This is the production office, isn't it?'

'What's that supposed to mean? You know it is.'

'And that's what we're going to talk about?'

'What else?'

'Then let's do it here.'

Mackenzie drew a breath. What had got into the little snot this morning? 'You want witnesses, is that what you're saying?'

'I'm saying, this discussion, this meeting, I want it to be here. There's something wrong with that?'

'Nothing.'

'Fine.'

'You don't think coffee would be a better idea? The canteen.'

'Mac.'

'Yes.'

'Whatever you're going to say, say it.'

'I'm bringing in another director.'

'What?'

'I'm bringing in . . .'

'You're doing what?'

'Bringing in another . . .'

'You can't.'

'Harold . . .'

'There's no way you can do that.'

'Look, Harold, if you'll give me a chance to explain.'

'Explain, shit. This is my series.'

'No, Harold, you're the director.'

'Exactly.'

'It's *my* series.'

'You hired me.'

'I know that.'

'I have a contract.'

'I know that also.'

'Then you know damn well there's no way you can bring in another director.'

Mackenzie shook his head. Why hadn't he realized it would be like this? 'Harold, it's done.'

'What do you mean, it's done? What's done? Nothing can be done. There's nothing to fucking do!'

'We have to sit down and talk about it. Work . . .'

'There's nothing to talk about.'

'Work it out.'

'Nothing to work out.'

'Harold, he's starting this morning.'

'Who is? Who's starting this morning? Who?'

'Freeman Davis.'

'Freeman Davis?'

'He's flying into East Midlands from Glasgow. Eleven-oh-five. I'm sending a car to meet him.'

'Freeman Davis can't direct traffic.'

'He won an award at BAFTA.'

'The skill is not to win an award at BAFTA.'

'Cheap shot, Howard.'

'He's a cheap director.'

'No, Harold,' Mackenzie sneered, 'you were cheap. How else did you swing this job in the first place? What is it? Fifteen years or more of credits and you're still cheaper than a Clapham Common scrubber on a slow Saturday afternoon. Davis has cost this production money it can ill afford.'

'Then instead of sending a chauffeur, send a message. Go back to Glasgow. The Scots need you.'

'We need him. Which is why, however expensive he is, hiring him is cheaper than seeing the whole series go under.'

'That's absurd. There's no way that could happen. Not this far along.'

Mackenzie took an envelope from his pocket. 'The company had a special meeting in London yesterday. If we go as much as a half-day behind they'll cancel and cut their losses.' He tapped the envelope. 'This was faxed up to me at the hotel last night.'

He offered the envelope to Harold, who shook his head and stared at the ground.

'We're not firing you, Harold.'

Slowly, Harold raised his eyes.

'Don't think that. No way. You couldn't have imagined that. No. You'll work together. Freeman and yourself. One of you can be rehearsing the actors, stay down on the floor while the other's in the control room. Freeman can do editing, not the fine cut, nothing like, just an assembly so that we can see where we are, how much we need. Your supervision, of course. You're the senior partner, Harold, Freeman understands that. I wouldn't have offered him the job if he hadn't agreed to that. I think that's the main reason he accepted, the chance to work with an experienced director like yourself.'

Harold knew that they were looking at him, all of them, waiting for him to speak, but he no longer knew what to say. He'd stood his ground, argued his case, no one could say he'd done less than that. Now the inside of his body felt hollow and if he did open his mouth he was afraid that whatever sound came out would be too faint for anyone else to hear.

After some moments he turned around and quietly left the room.

Mackenzie tossed the envelope he'd pulled from his pocket across to the production secretary. 'Better file that. Never know when we might be needing it again.'

When the secretary slid the folded piece of paper from inside the envelope it was blank.

It was a red VW with a soft top, and a green sticker on the side window proclaiming the use of unleaded fuel. The driver was tall, five eight or nine, and the shoes that she wore added an inch of their own. She grabbed a creamy white three-quarter-length coat from the back seat and slipped it over her shoulders; the doors locked, she dropped the keys down into the leather case she was carrying, dark and soft and with a strap that swung low as she walked with it tucked beneath her arm.

'Do I know you?' she said, barely breaking her stride.

'No, no, I don't . . .'

'The way you were staring at me.'

'Sorry.'

'As if you thought you might know me from somewhere.'

'I'm afraid not.'

She stopped then and looked at him, the broadness some pounds short of overweight, the suit with more shine than his shoes.

'I was going to ask for directions.'

She nodded. 'To?'

'I've got an appointment.'

'Reception's around the corner from that white building over there.'

'Harold Roy.'

'Ah.'

'You know him?'

'Yes. We're working together, the same show.'

'Perhaps you could take me to him.'

'I think, maybe, you should still go via reception.'

'Wouldn't this be quicker?'

She began to walk and Resnick fell into step alongside her; if they had a long way to go, he thought he'd have trouble keeping up.

'What are you seeing Harold about?'

'I probably shouldn't say.'

'You're not his agent?'

'No.'

She stopped by a single door marked *No Entry*. 'He does know you're coming, I suppose? I mean, what I don't want to do is steer you past security and find you've come to deliver a writ or something.'

'I can promise you it's not that. And, yes, I did phone ahead to say I was coming.'

'Fine,' she pushed the door open and held it as Resnick walked through.

'You're not the police, are you?'

'Why do you say that?'

'Oh, I don't know.'

'Do I look like a policeman?'

'No.'

They were walking down a long corridor, narrow, with walls that had been painted a muted shade of lime green. For no apparent reason, a typist's swivel chair sat midway along, unoccupied. Resnick allowed her to gain half a pace on him so that he could look again at her hair, the way it shifted slightly as she walked, dark and then darker shades of red.

'You're not expecting Mr Roy to be arrested?'

She turned her face towards him. 'Only on grounds of taste.'

'His clothes?'

She stopped. They were almost at the end of the corridor. 'Have you seen any of his work? Anything he's made?'

'Not that I know of.'

'If you had . . .' Her mouth moved into a smile and for an instant the tip of her tongue pressed against the underside of her lip. 'Forget it. Forget I ever said it. I never said that, OK?'

'Right.'

'Not a word.'

Resnick nodded his agreement. Her eyes were green and they were brown and although she was no longer smiling there was still amusement in those eyes.

The first corridor opened out on to a second, broader, photographs and posters from programmes framed along both walls.

'You go down here and take the first right. The *Dividends* production office is at the end.'

'*Dividends*?'

'The show Harold's directing.' Resnick moved away, not too far. 'If he's not there, he's already in the studio. That's Studio Three. Back on to this corridor and keep going, you'll see the signs.'

'Thanks.'

'Diane Woolf,' she said. 'In case we're ever in another car park.'

Resnick wanted to offer her his hand, but wasn't sure if it was the right thing to do. Before he could make up his mind, she was making her way through the door into the ladies: he hadn't as much as told her his name.

There were two people in the production office and neither of them was Harold Roy. Resnick found him close to the studio entrance, slamming down the receiver to end a call with his agent. His late agent. Who'd be stupid enough to carry on shelling out 10 per cent to a mealy-mouthed former child star with a receding hairline, whose idea of doing business was sitting around the Groucho Club half the day, reading *Screen International*. Especially when the only advice he was prepared to give in a situation like this was to keep talking and watch your back.

'Mr Roy . . .'

'Harold . . .'

'Harold . . .'

Resnick had arrived at the same time as Robert Deleval, now waving another few pages of script, and Chris, the first assistant, still in star-spangled baseball boots.

'Mr Roy, I wonder if . . .'

'Harold, we've got to do something about this dialogue.'

'Five minutes, Harold, and we'll be ready to go.'

Harold Roy slapped both hands against his ears, closed his eyes, opened his mouth and let out an almost soundless scream. When he looked again, Chris had hunched her shoulders and bounced away, leaving Resnick and Robert Deleval as they were.

94

'You heard what she said, five minutes.'

'Not with this script, Harold.'

'What's wrong with the script? Aside from the fact that you wrote it.'

'Not this one, I didn't.' Deleval fanned Harold Roy's face with the page. 'Not this load of crap.'

Harold snatched them from his hand. '*This* load of crap exists because what you delivered in the first place was a *real* load of crap. And I now have four minutes and a few seconds to turn this crap into television.'

He pushed the script back at the writer as he turned towards the outer studio door. Resnick placed himself so that the door would open no more than six inches.

'I phoned,' he said.

'Four minutes,' said Harold, 'and counting.'

'That might be enough,' said Resnick, 'though I can't promise.'

'I don't know what you're talking about.'

'Burglary, sir.'

'Burglary? What . . .' And then he remembered. 'You're, em . . .'

'Resnick. Detective inspector.'

'Oh, shit!' Harold looked at his watch, at the green light above the studio door. If Mackenzie was really intending to produce Freeman Davis, Harold certainly intended to have things in hand when he arrived. Two scenes wrapped, at least, and another ready to go this side of lunch.

'I can see you've got a lot on,' said Resnick, 'but there are one or two things I need to check.'

'My wife . . .'

'I know. It's a matter of verification, really. It needn't take long.'

In his mind's eye, Harold Roy could see himself kneeling up on the bed and pushing the packet containing the cocaine to the back of the safe.

'As soon as it's sorted,' Resnick said, 'we can get out of your hair for good. Shouldn't be any need to trouble you again.'

Harold leaned back against the wall alongside the door. 'Inspector, bear with me. Let me get this first scene finished. It's not complicated. An hour at most. While they're setting up for the next, we can talk.' He eased himself off the wall. 'It's the best I can do.'

'All right,' agreed Resnick. 'If I could make a couple of calls from your office . . .'

'Help yourself.'

Harold Roy walked through into the studio and when Resnick started back along the corridor he found that he had Robert Deleval at his side.

'You're a detective?'

'Inspector. Yes, that's right.'

'Murder – you deal with murders?'

'Sometimes.'

'In that case I might be seeing you again.'

Resnick looked at him. 'How's that?'

'Because,' said Deleval with feeling, 'if that bastard continues to murder my scripts the way he has up to now, I might end up by killing him.'

12

All the way in the taxi he hadn't touched her: not then, nor down the pebble drive, nor on the step behind her while she nervously fitted her key into the lock. Which was why, when he set his hand, spread flat and wide, against the small of her back, the shock nearly jolted her off her feet.

'Wait,' she said. Maria. 'Wait.'

Her head was being pressed awkwardly back against the wall; a table, low and spilling with circulars and misdirected post, cut into the backs of her legs.

'Let's go upstairs.'

But already his thumbs were moving against her nipples, his head bending towards her breasts.

'What's your name? I don't even know your name.'

'Grabianski.'

'No, your other name.'

'Jerzy.'

'What . . . ?'

'Jerry.'

'But you said . . .'

'It's what I was christened, baptized. Jerzy.'

'When did you change it?'

'When I stopped going to confession.'

'When was that?'

'When I couldn't go on embarrassing the priest any longer.'

She looked across at him, waiting for his smile. She was propped against pillows, little make-up left on her face. She had not bothered to collect her other things from the foot of the bed, the carpet, the stairs; had slid, instead, inside a half-slip, creamy silk.

'Jerzy,' she said quietly.

'OK,' he grinned, 'now are you going to give me absolution?'

She moved so as to stroke the skin inside his upper arm, soft and surprisingly smooth. So much of him was like that, the

97

smoothness of a younger man, never slack. She wriggled some more and rested her face against his shoulder, one of her breasts squeezed against his ribs. She said something else that he couldn't hear. Grabianski knew that if they stayed in that position for long, he would begin to get cramp. Already he was wanting to pee.

'Maybe she's not the brightest woman in the world,' Harold Roy was saying, 'but on a good day she can tell black from white. Smoked salmon she might forget, come home with mineral water and some fancy new knickers instead, but that's not what we're talking about, is it?'

He offered Resnick an extra-strong mint, placed one in his own mouth and, almost at once, crunched it with his teeth. Always a disappointment, preferring them to last till they were wafer thin, a sacrament. Jewish father, Catholic mother, the nearest he got nowadays to religion and ritual was this: communion with a plainclothes officer while balancing fragments of peppermint on the back of his tongue.

'She would have been frightened, Mr Roy.'

'Terrified. Out of her wits. Any woman would be.'

'In the circumstances, she might easily have panicked.'

'It's an awful situation.'

'It could have been worse.'

'I suppose so.'

'For your wife, I mean.'

Harold Roy closed his eyes for several seconds. 'I don't like to think about it,' he said.

'Even so,' Resnick continued, 'when she spoke to the constable, it's possible she was still in a state of shock.'

'Confused, you mean?'

'Exactly.

Resnick watched as Harold Roy popped another mint. *The booze and all the other junk you use to pickle what once might have been a brain.* He didn't suppose that Mackenzie had been alluding to Trebor Extra-Strong.

Harold knew the time without looking at his watch; he was ahead and needed to stay that way, had to be back in the studio inside ten minutes, less.

98

'Inspector, if . . .'

'Sometimes, once people have made a statement, even the most innocent of people, they feel worried about changing it – as though, in some way, it might incriminate them.' Resnick waited until Harold's eyes were focused upon him. 'You understand what I'm saying?'

'Yes.'

'If your wife wanted to change her statement, for whatever reason – if, with time to think more clearly, calmly, she had reconsidered – she would let us know?'

'Of course she would. I mean . . . of course.'

'Nothing she said, to you, nothing she's said, suggests she might be having – what shall we call it? – second thoughts?'

'Nothing.'

Through a succession of glass-panelled walls he could see people working at keyboards, speaking into telephones, drinking coffee. Should any of them glance up they would see me, Harold thought, closeted here with a shabby police officer when I should be getting on with the job.

'Inspector . . .' Harold Roy began to rise.

'Of course,' said Resnick, 'I understand.'

They stood for a while longer, facing each other across the small, anonymous room.

'Maybe you'd speak with your wife; if there is anything, encourage her to get in touch.'

Harold Roy nodded, opening the door.

'Whoever it was broke into your house, the sooner we can put them out of business, better for all concerned. Especially while there's still a chance of recovering your property, some of it, at least; whatever they might not have been able to dispose of right away.'

In some indeterminate way, Harold felt he was being almost accused of something, without understanding what. 'Back past reception, inspector . . . you can find your own way out?'

'No need to keep you, Mr Roy. Thanks for giving up your time.'

Designer clothes, expensive haircut, Resnick watched him move through a maze of rooms, stride lengthening with each one until he had gone from sight. For the present. Though he didn't know exactly why, Resnick felt certain that he would need to talk to Harold Roy again.

From the heaviness of her body, the change in her breathing, Grabianski knew that Maria had drifted into sleep. If he angled his head, he could read the time on the clock-radio beside the bed. No wonder his stomach was beginning, gently, to complain. He should have had something to eat in the tearooms, that waitress trying to come on, all airs and graces. Grabianski smiled: how he'd enjoyed sitting there the way they had, feeling her up under the table and those others knowing it, trying hard not to look, trying their damnedest to look without making it obvious.

Saliva spooled on to his chest from the corner of Maria's mouth.

It had been good, Grabianski thought, better than good, better even than he'd imagined. It was possible to go for months, years, believing sex was overvalued; sometimes, in the soiled beds of strange towns, overpriced: a quick loss of joy. Then this.

Maria groaned and rolled her head away, a trail of spittle stretching from her mouth like translucent gum until it bubbled and broke.

'I'm sorry. I must have fallen asleep.'

'That's OK.'

He took hold of an edge of sheet and dabbed carefully at the side of her mouth.

'What have you been doing?' she asked.

'While you were sleeping? There wasn't an awful lot I could. do.' He smiled at her and she thought, God, here is this man seeing me like this, no make-up, bleary-eyed and slobbering, and he can smile like that. 'Watching you,' he said.

'Is that all?'

'Thinking.'

'About what?'

The smile broadened. His hand started its move back towards her breasts.

'Is that all?' Maria said again.

Grabianski quickly pushed back the covers and didn't miss the sharp look of disappointment in her eyes, concern. 'If I don't pee,' he said, 'I'll burst.'

'Second on the left,' she called after his disappearing buttocks.

But then as she lay back down she remembered that he already knew the house quite well.

Resnick walked back along the narrow corridor by which he had entered the studio, remembering Diane Woolf and regretting he had come up with no good reason for seeking her out, other than to get caught staring.

Again.

'Drooling at the mouth, inspector?' He could hear her voice inside his head, imagine the expression on her face as she said it.

Resnick walked through into the car park and was face to face with Alfie Levin.

'Mr Resnick.'

'Alfie.'

Born again or simply biding his time, Alf Levin was unable to disguise the alarm he felt at Resnick's sudden presence: the old enemy.

'Still looking for Harold Roy?'

'This time I found him.'

'Not the most popular round here.'

'So I'm beginning to realize.'

'You're not the only one looking for him, neither.'

Resnick stepped aside to leave room for two men in overalls carrying a fifteen-foot ladder between them, smelling of cigarette smoke and paint. 'Are you about to tell me something, Alfie?'

'Not in the way you mean, Mr Resnick.'

'Which way's that, Alfie?'

'Merely passing on a bit of information, the kind that crops up in conversation. Not informing. Not that.'

Resnick nodded, waited.

'Skinny bloke, thin on top . . .' Without meaning to, Resnick found himself looking at Alf Levin's toupee, searching for the join. '. . . hanging around when I parked the van. Did I know when they'd be through for the day, *Dividends*?'

'Did you?'

'Yes, but I wasn't going to tell him.'

'Why not?'

'Kosher, he'd go through reception, wouldn't he? Same as anybody else.'

'What did you think he was after, then?'

Alf Levin shook his head, took one hand from his trouser pocket and offered it towards Resnick, palm up. 'Way I see it, that poor sod's got troubles enough. He doesn't want some feller who can't afford decent shoes . . .'

'Shoes?'

'Yes, he was wearing them trainer things, filthy too. Hanging round to put the squeeze on him, if you ask me. Tap him for a loan or something like that. Probably some actor, down on his luck.'

'Have you seen him around before?'

'Maybe, once or twice.'

'Talking to Harold Roy, looking for him?'

Alf Levin thought about that. 'Can't say, Mr Resnick. But I can say when I saw him last.'

'Yes,' said Resnick, 'so can I. I was there that night, remember?'

'Can I forget?'

'Then you won't forget what we were talking about?'

'You were talking about.'

'You've been thinking it over.'

'I told you . . .'

'I'm not asking you to grass on anyone you know, Alfie. What I'm after – a little occasional conversation. Much like this one. Nothing more than that.'

'I don't believe you, Mr Resnick.'

'Might be better if you did.'

'Who for? For you, yes, OK. But me . . . ?'

Resnick laid a hand on Alf Levin's shoulder, aware of the memories it would bring rushing back. 'Insurance, Alfie. Now you're going straight that's the kind of thing you ought to be thinking about, a little insurance.'

Resnick walked round him and headed towards his car, keeping his eyes open for Harold Roy's Citroën on the way. It wasn't impossible that a lean man, prematurely ageing, would be skulking close by, rolling one of his own. I should have checked his description through records before, Resnick thought, I shouldn't have been so sloppy. If it were Divine or Naylor, I'd have given him a bollocking.

He wondered, as he drove past the security guard at the gate, whether Kevin Naylor had fetched up with anything that would point them in a new direction, if Graham Millington had found the time to renew acquaintances with Lloyd Fossey. Something, somewhere had better move soon, or it would be like last time, over and gone before they even got close.

Maria Roy was wearing little enough and even that was a whole lot more than Jerry Grabianski. She stood against the couch and it was impossible to stop her legs from trembling.

'I see you bought some more vodka,' he said, the same old smile (that's what it was to her now, already). 'I thought you might.'

There it was, the quiet cockiness about him that she liked. Not like his partner, the one he'd been talking about, Grice. That was different: harsh, totally without humour. The only kind of jokes she could picture Grice laughing at were those in which people suffered indignity or pain.

'Want one?'

Maria shook her head; it was light enough already.

This is where I first saw him, she was thinking, this room, the way he stepped through the doorway and made me shake as much as now. Just look at him, standing there so naturally, naked, as if he belonged. A man who knew he still had a good body and had no need to be ashamed of it; what it felt; what it did; the way it looked. Moving back towards her, he deposited his glass on the table so that both hands were free.

They were like kids who'd that day discovered what it was all about; couples sneaking into a borrowed bed after weeks of cars and cinemas. Maria recalled the first time she'd been away with a man, a boy – well, seventeen and straddled in between – she had lied to her mother, brazened out her father, caught the early evening train to Weymouth and met him on the front, close by the pier as planned. Two nights in a hotel with measured cornflakes and weak tea and she'd been so sore she could scarcely walk her way back to the station.

'We've got to talk,' Grabianski said.

'Not now.'

'Good a time as any.'

She looked down at him. 'You sure about that?'

103

He grinned. 'Well, maybe in a little while.'

'Yes,' said Maria, touching him, closing her eyes.

As he'd told both his mother and his father, separately and together and seemingly forever throughout his adolescence, he didn't believe in God. Neither version. Not unless (he had loved the abrupt downturning of the mouth that signalled his father's disapproval, the frisson of horror that had juddered like a migraine across his mother's eyes) he had announced, He was born again in Tupelo, Mississippi, in a two-room country shack. But, the way things had started to turn around today, Harold Roy might be persuaded to believe in miracles. Even Jesus in blue-suede shoes.

Once he'd got that policeman out of his hair, shut Deleval in a room with a typewriter and a ream of paper to do some more rewrites he had no intention of using, he had got on top of things. Costume and make-up had got their collective finger out, there had been a surprising absence of boom shadows, those artists who had forgotten their lines had covered with others just as good. When they finally wrapped, all of the scheduled scenes had been shot, along with one held in reserve, and they'd run through the first scene from tomorrow's order.

Freeman Davis, when he arrived, had been tanned from a week filming a chocolate commercial in Morocco and was affably on his best behaviour. Keen to take the chance of working with one of the real pros in the business: when he said that he showed a line of perfectly capped teeth. Harold had shaken his hand with equally feigned enthusiasm before Mackenzie had whisked Freeman away to look at the material they'd shot so far.

Poor bastard! Harold had thought.

He was in such a good mood when he left the studio that, for the first time in ages, he actually felt like getting laid. Even by Maria. After dinner they could start in on a second bottle of wine, and he would find one of those videos he'd bought in Streatham High Street.

He was in such a good mood he didn't spot Stafford until it was almost too late.

* * *

Hands in the pockets of his parka, one leg crossed behind the other and balanced on the toe of his trainers, Alan Stafford was leaning against the side of a transit van and waiting. Harold slewed to a halt even as Stafford's head turned. He ducked back fast between a pair of matching Volvos, uncertain if he'd been fast enough. He wanted to wait, peer round the car and check, but instead he was walking fast, faster, running now, making a wide curve through the rows of parked cars, working his way round to where his own Citroën waited. Hasty glances over his shoulder told him that Stafford was not following; maybe his reactions had been quick enough and Stafford hadn't seen him at all. By now it was dark, getting darker, he would have been little more than a shape, nothing to mark him out, register.

Jesus! thought Harold. I oughtn't to be carrying this much weight. Last week, was it? The week before? A designer he'd worked with on a couple of previous shows, he'd reached across the table for a cigarette and dropped face down into the linguine. Forty-seven years of age. Tragic!

'Harold.'

At the sound of the voice, Harold Roy's mouth opened, his eyes closed, adrenalin raced through his body. Alan Stafford stepped out from alongside the Citroën, the dull orange of the overhead light shining oddly off his angular face inside the hood of the parka.

'What's the matter, Harold?'

'Nothing. I . . .'

'You didn't want to meet me.'

'No, I . . .'

'Avoiding me.'

'Alan, no, I didn't know you were . . . I didn't see you.'

'You didn't *see* me?'

'No.'

'Just ran fifty yards to keep out of my way.'

'That's not true.'

'You always go back to your car that way.'

'Yes. No. I . . .'

'Exercise for you, Harold. Jogging.' He reached out and caught hold of Harold with forefinger and thumb, a roll of flesh through the fine denim of his shirt. 'No more than you need, Harold.

Dangerous to be carrying so much weight, a man of your years . . .' he gave the flesh a sudden tweak, '. . . your appetites.'

'Yes, I, I know, funnily enough, I was just thinking . . .'

'What, Harold?'

'The same.'

'Huh?'

'The same, same as you're saying, I ought to . . . do . . . some . . . exercise.'

Stafford brought his thumb and finger even closer and more painfully together before releasing his grip and letting his arm swing back down to his side.

'How's our secret?' Stafford asked, smiling; edging closer. Two men, walking close to one another, talking excitedly, passed within fifteen yards of them; Harold almost called out.

'Still safe?' Stafford persisted.

Harold nodded.

'Safe and sound.'

'Of course.'

'Inside your safe.'

'Yes. Where else . . . ?'

'Nothing. Nothing, Harold. Don't sound so worried. It's just that I'll be needing it.'

'Soon?'

'Tomorrow. The day after. I'm not certain yet, but soon. Good news, eh, Harold? You can get your share of the investment. Five per cent, wasn't that what we . . . ?'

'Ten.'

'Oh, yes,' Stafford laughed. 'Of course, ten. Ten per cent interest on one kilo, you're looking at . . . £1,200, Harold. That's a lot of money to be made just for storage. A solid profit, even if you take it out in kind.'

'I know,' said Harold. His mouth was dry, like ashes gone cold. He prayed he didn't sound as nervous as he felt. Not for the first time in his life, he wished that he could act with a degree of conviction.

'A good enough deal for you not to get greedy.'

'Course it is.'

'That's good, Harold.'

'Yes.'

'Good to hear.'

'This much to be made, there's no call, that or anything else.'

He was close enough now for Harold to feel his breath on his face; smell – what? – cheese, cheap aftershave and, beneath that, what might be gin. Something pressed, hard, against the side of Harold's leg, hard and metallic. Flinching, he wanted to look down but stopped himself, looking instead into Stafford's face, searching for reason or meaning.

'The pub the other night,' Stafford said, 'location. The bloke you were drinking with at the bar.'

'No one. I wasn't. I talked to Mackenzie, a few minutes, nothing more.'

'In here again today. Seeing you.'

'That inspector . . .?'

'Resnick.'

'I never spoke to him before today.'

'Coincidence that he was in the pub, just a few stools away?'

'Must have been. I didn't know, didn't remember . . .'

Whatever was pressing against him pressed harder so that Harold had to choke back a shout of pain. Around them car doors were slamming, engines starting up. First one set of headlights then another swept over them and past.

'If I find you've been setting me up . . .'

'What reason could I have for doing that? Alan, listen . . .'

'That I don't know yet. But I'm not taking chances.'

'Alan, look, I've told you before. This business with the police, it's nothing to do with you, with . . . you know . . .'

A man with a heavy blue duffle coat stopped at the car immediately to Stafford's left and unlocked his boot. He was whistling Butterfly's first love song from Act One: Harold wished he were on a hillside overlooking Nagasaki, anywhere other than where he was.

Turning, the man nodded at Harold, who recognized his face but not his name. 'Anything wrong?' the man said.

'No,' Harold said. 'Nothing.'

'Uh-huh.' The man glanced sideways at Stafford, who had backed off beyond arm's length. 'I thought perhaps you had a flat battery, some problem like that.'

107

Harold's tongue dampened his lower lip. 'I'm fine,' he said. 'The car's fine.'

'Good.' The man nodded, turned and climbed into his car. Before he began to pull away, the sounds of an operatic overture filtered out into the dampening air.

'Eight o'clock, Harold. I'll phone you. Tell you where to bring the stuff.'

'a.m.?'

'Bright and early. And, Harold . . .' Stafford patted the side pocket of his parka, '. . . if, for any reason, you don't show up with what's due to me, if anything's out of line, I hope I don't need to spell out what's liable to happen.'

When Harold Roy ran the events through later in his mind, he could never clearly see Alan Stafford picking his way between the still-parked cars. What he could feel, with absolute recall, was the sharpness of the blade that moved upwards along the inside of his leg until it had been pressing against the heart of his groin.

13

Grabianski's first thought was that the woman on the bed looked strangely familiar; his second told him it was Maria. The third, panic rising till he could taste it like bile at the back of his mouth, was that there had been a camera hidden in the Roys' bedroom.

'Will you look at this?' Grice was sprawled across an easy chair, a large pack of salted peanuts, honeyed popcorn, a can of Diet Pepsi all within easy reach. 'I've seen hotter things at the bottom of the freezer.'

'Where did you . . .?'

'Hey, come on now . . .'

'What the fuck . . .?'

'Grabianski, take it easy!'

On his feet, Grice watched as his partner's fingers fumbled for the proper control, found it at the third or fourth attempt and all three out-of-focus figures flicked from sight.

Grabianski stared at him, legs braced before the silenced television, the VCR. It wasn't often Grice thought about the twenty pounds or so by which Grabianski outweighed him, the extra fitness, the speed: wasn't often that he'd felt the need.

'Look . . .' Grice began.

'No!'

'Look . . .'

'No. That's you. Looking. You're the looker here. You're the fucking, what d'you call it? – yes – you're the voyeur. No wonder this place already smells the way it does. Sitting round all day stuffing yourself with that junk, jerking off over . . .'

Grabianski came close: came close to catching Grice by the shoulders, hurling him back across the partly furnished room. Grice knew it. Knew, also, when the moment had passed, anger falling back across his partner's eyes.

'Where did you get this anyway?'

'The set? I went out and hired it. Rent them both together, it's as cheap as pissing.'

'The video – the tape.'

'You know where we got that.'

Grabianski's hands fell away to his sides. 'Shit!' He turned away and walked towards the window, hesitated, moved towards the door.

'Jerry,' Grice said, following after him, 'let me get you a drink. Here, look, while you were busy I did a little stocking up.'

In the middle of the kitchen floor a cardboard box held half a dozen bottles of spirits, two four-packs of beer. Tins of soup and sardines, two loaves of wrapped, sliced bread stood on the work surface, close by the gas hob.

Grice bent towards the box. 'Scotch? Vodka? I got vodka, two kinds. I can never remember which it is you like best.'

'Forget it.'

'I just bought it.'

'Forget it.'

'OK.'

Grice shrugged his shoulders, gave a little shake of the head. He had brought through his Diet Pepsi with him and now he poured what was left into a glass and added a finger of scotch.

'It's the tape from the safe, right?' Grabianski said.

'Right.'

'Jesus!'

'If it's any consolation, she didn't look as if she was having a lot of fun.' In fact, Grice thought, she looked as though she had the hump. He kept the thought to himself; right then, he didn't think Grabianski would appreciate the joke.

'Anyway, Jerry,' Grice said after a couple of moments, 'how was it? How'd it go?'

Grabianski stared back at him stonily.

'No, I mean when you made her the proposition, how did it go down?'

'Lloyd Fossey, sir.' Millington had met Resnick in the small, sloping car park and was walking close alongside him, into the station. 'Last time I saw him, he was living in the middle of a terraced street out in Sutton, stone-cladding on the front wall and a van parked out front with his own name misspelt on the side panel. Now he's got a detached house out towards Burton

Joyce and, according to the bloke across the road, he's driving an F-reg. Audi.'

'Come on in the world,' said Resnick, starting up the stairs.

'Moved into this place nine months back, not far short of three hundred thousand.'

I wish someone would offer that for mine, thought Resnick. Half of that. Anything.

'No matter if he's mortgaged up the wazoo,' Millington pushed open the door to the CID office and stood aside to let Resnick pass through, 'he's got to have found a lot of cash from somewhere.'

'And you don't think he acquired it servicing security systems?'

'Electronic surveillance consultant, that's what Fossey introduced himself as when he moved in. Looks as though he's using his own place for demonstrations. Lift a crocus out of the flower bed and you'll be up to your ears in alarm bells.'

'Crocus?' said Resnick.

'Unnatural this year, sir, the weather. False spring.'

Right, thought Resnick, I've known a few of those too. At the back of the room, Patel had paused in typing up a report and was trying to catch his eye. Divine, chair tilted back on to its rear legs, was listening with the telephone to his ear, a bored expression on his face.

'And Fossey?' Resnick asked.

'Honeymoon, sir. Expected back the day after tomorrow.'

'Canary Islands?' suggested Resnick. 'Turkey?'

Millington shook his head. 'Benidorm.'

'At least it's not Skegness.'

'Close your eyes, sir, difficult to tell the difference. So they say.'

Resnick knew that Millington drove his wife and kids each summer to Devon, each autumn a week with his wife's parents somewhere north of Aberdeen. The Christmas she had gone off on a three-city tour of Russia, Millington had stayed home and dressed the tree.

'Sir,' said Patel.

'A minute,' said Resnick, holding up a hand, fingers spread wide.

'I got in touch with a few of the security firms,' Millington

111

continued, 'to see if anyone knew what Fossey was into. Sounds as if what he does is chat people up, goes round their homes, makes a lot of fuss about the need for a personalized system and more often than not brings in someone else to fit it up.'

'Taking his fee off the top.'

'Naturally.'

'Nice work if you can get it. And if the systems you've recommended don't keep the bad boys out, more work is what you won't get.'

'Agreed,' said Millington. 'But what about the places he gets a good look at and where he isn't taken on as consultant afterwards?'

'Can we check that out?'

'Difficult until I can get hold of Fossey, find a way of looking through his records. Supposing he keeps them.'

'Worth checking all the security firms, see what contact he's had with them?'

Millington nodded. 'I'll get someone on it, sir. It's 137 to 143 in Yellow Pages. Maybe Naylor when he's through collating the stuff from the insurance companies.'

'And you'll arrange to greet Fossey on his return?'

'Flight BA435. I'll make sure he's welcomed back.'

Millington turned away. Patel was still hovering; Resnick pointed towards Divine, still half-listening to an interminable call. 'Rees Stanley?'

'Right pissed off, sir. No snow. Came back two days early, like we said.'

Resnick acknowledged the information, beckoned Patel.

'I ran into the PC who went out to the Roy house, sir, the one who took Maria Roy's statement.'

'Ran into him?'

'I made it seem that way, sir. I thought it was best.'

'And?'

'He thought there was something not quite right at the time. Tried to tell Inspector Harrison, but the inspector wasn't interested. Told him to write up Mrs Roy's statement and forget about it.'

*   *   *

Grabianski had ejected the Roys' holiday movie and removed it from Grice's sight. Not that Grice would have bothered watching it a second time: all those goose pimples, all that sagging flesh was enough to give him the heaves. It was common knowledge that where sexual attraction was concerned, one man's meat was another man's poison, but what Grice had seen was enough to turn him vegetarian.

Grabianski, who had left that morning like the original good-humour man, was as sullen as a lovesick calf. Sapped. So much for the exchange of bodily fluids. He'd always known that Samson getting his hair cut was a symbol for something else.

'What did she think of the idea? I mean, d'you think she went for it?'

Grabianski really was in a bad way. He hadn't as much as opened his bird book in hours.

'You pointed out to her the disadvantages of not paying up?'

'Yes,' said Grabianski without conviction.

'You had to be doing something all that time apart from . . . All right, OK, no offence. No need to get on a spike about it. I just need to be certain.'

'So be certain. I laid it out.' (Grice suppressed a snigger.) 'As we planned. Street value of a kilo of cocaine is 24,000 and rising. Back in their hands for twenty, no questions either way.'

'What did she say?'

'I told you.'

'Tell me again.'

'They've got as much chance of raising 20,000 in forty-eight hours as England has of winning the next World Cup.'

'She's a soccer fan?'

'All right, she didn't say that, not exactly. It was what she meant.'

'Stick to what she said.'

'What she said was, I could sit here till hell freezes over before we could come up with that much money.'

'And what was your response to that? Aside from crossing yourself.'

'I didn't cross myself.'

'Get to the point.'

'She reckons her husband is stupid for agreeing to hold the stuff in the first place. She says, right now he's scared out of his wits, looking over his shoulder all the time, terrified the guy's going to think he's been double-crossed and come after him. Her Harold's frightened this dealer's going to cut his face, break both his legs, you name it, kill him.'

'How's she feel about this?'

'Maria? She thinks it's terrific. Especially the latter.'

'She wants her old man killed?'

'Slowly for preference, but she'd settle for a bullet in the back of the head.'

'Christ! What's he done to her?'

'Recently? Not a lot.'

'Great! She wants him dead so's you and her can waltz off into the sunset.'

Grabianski got up from where he was sitting and picked up his binoculars, walked to the living-room windows.

'Put those down and listen to me. It's dark out there. All you can see are street lights and bathroom windows.' He touched Grabianski on the arm. 'That's it, isn't it? An afternoon of shimi-sha-wobble and she's packing a suitcase. ' He pointed at Grabian-ski's crotch. 'What you got down there, anyway? A guided missile?'

'It's not what you've got . . .' Grabianski began.

'I know,' finished Grice, 'it's what you do with it. Lectures on the joy of sex I can do without. Where I get most of mine, I just lay back and leave it all to massage lotion number nine. Like the masseuse, I'm more interested in the money.'

'She'll tell him, try and get him to go along. She promised me that.'

'I'll bet. Crossed her heart and hoped her beloved Harold would die.'

'No, she'll tell him straight.'

'You think he'll make an offer?'

'Wouldn't you?'

'I'd offer twelve, wait for you to come back seventeen and a half, hope against hope to settle for fifteen. Then start to worry about finding it.'

'He can sell the car, talk to his bank manager, cash in an

insurance policy, that's what he can do,' Grabianski said. 'I think he can find the fifteen.'

'I hope so. Sitting here with a kilo of cocaine isn't good for my nerves.'

'You don't have any.'

'Correction: didn't.'

'Don't worry. He's half as scared as she says he is, he'll pay up.'

Grice's stomach made a low rumbling sound, like a bowling ball being rolled slowly along wooden boards.

Grabianski glanced over at the soup and sardines. 'We going out to eat?'

'Later.'

'What's wrong with now?'

'You're not the only one with things to do.'

'Where this time? Studio Heaven or the Restless Palms?'

'I've got to see a man about some property.'

'Renting or buying?'

'Burgling.'

'Want me to come along?'

'Suit yourself.'

'I'll leave it to you. Take a bath.'

'OK. Why don't you meet me in the Albany bar? We can have a couple of drinks, go up to the Carvery.'

'The drinks are fine. Let's eat somewhere else.'

Grice shrugged: OK.

'What I really fancy,' said Grabianski, 'is a good Chinese.'

14

There were two tramps who roamed the city, both of them big, belligerent men whose clothing flapped away in shreds and patches. When they cursed, most people looked the other way and laughed or tutted. Scarce a day he was on duty, Resnick didn't pass either of them, both: so visible it was easy to think they were the only ones. Never mind the centres for the homeless, the hostels, bed-and-breakfast families in the disinfected smell of small hotels, the squats; the city council's plans to build no council houses in the coming year. He tried to remember when he had first been stopped by a young man, hand outthrust, begging – 343 jobs in today's paper, the placards had read. Why don't you clean yourself up a bit, Resnick had thought, get yourself one of those? 'Spare change,' the man had said. 'Cup of tea.' Resnick had made the mistake of looking at his face, the eyes; he doubted if he had been eighteen. 'Here.' A pound coin, small, into the cold of the young man's palm. Now there were more of them, more each day. And still 343 jobs in the paper: audio-typists, VDU skills, computer operators, clerical assistants, lockstitch machinists (part-time).

He indicated, slowed, locked the car and left it at the curb. How many security firms had Millington said there were? Enough to fill half a dozen yellow pages. A lot of people with a lot to lock away, defend. Every Englishman's right. Put it in bricks and mortar, wasn't that the saying? Every Englishman's home his castle. Lloyd Fossey with his electronic moats and drawbridges, television scanners, remote-control.

Safe as houses: another saying.

He turned the key in the lock and as he did so his breath caught and held. Someone was already inside the house.

Resnick stepped into the hall, soft; eased the door back against the jamb, not closed; the keys he slipped into his side pocket. Listening, he wondered what had alerted him, wondered if he had been wrong, imagination conjuring games for him to play. No. Water dripping on to plastic, the bowl in the kitchen sink, the washer he was always meaning to renew. Not that. Where were the cats who should have padded out to greet him, pushing their heads against his feet?

They were in the kitchen, four of them, heads dipped towards their bowls, feeding. What else would have kept them so occupied? Claire Millinder was wearing a different sweater, blue-grey with puffy white sheep grazing across it, the same short skirt over today's mauve tights, same red boots. She stood watching the cats, can-opener in her hand.

'Hallo.'

The opener flew from her fingers as she turned, one bowl was kicked against another, milk spilt; Pepper jumped inside the nearest saucepan, Miles hissed and sprang on to the tiles beside the oven, Bud cowered in a corner while Dizzy, undeterred, finished his own portion and started on another.

'I didn't hear you come in.'

'That was the idea.'

Claire stared at him, waiting for her breathing to steady back to normal. Give me his measurements and several hundred pounds, she thought, there's a lot I could do for the way he looks.

'You thought I was a burglar,' she said.

'I thought you were my wife.'

Resnick coaxed Pepper out of hiding, nuzzled the scrawny Bud behind the ears, the animal's heart still pumping against its delicate ribs; he dropped handfuls of beans into the coffee-grinder, shiny and dark.

'You're at home here, aren't you?'

'This house?'

'The kitchen.'

Resnick took two-thirds of a rye loaf from inside a plastic bag, margarine from the refrigerator. 'How about a sandwich?'

'Most men I've come across, even the ones who are good at it, good cooks, they never seem really comfortable with what they're doing. Like it's some kind of challenge. All those ingredients lined up in order to use; lists of times stuck over the cooker like something from an organization-and-methods seminar.' Claire shook her head dismissively. 'It's not natural.'

117

'A sandwich?'

'Sure.'

Sandwiches, in Claire Millinder's experience, were neat slices of wholemeal bread pressed around cheese rectangles or turkey breast, augmentations of tasteless salad and a smear of low-calorie mayonnaise. For Resnick, they were more satisfying on every level: two major ingredients whose flavours were contrasting but complementary, sharp and soft, sweet and sour, a mustard or chutney to bind them, but with the taste all its own, finally a fruit, unforced tomato, thin slices of Cox or Granny Smith.

'May I use your phone?'

'Through there and on the left, help yourself.'

She was finishing the call when Resnick came into the room, two mugs in one hand, plates balanced on the other.

'God! When you said a sandwich, I wasn't expecting . . .'

'Here, can you take one of these?'

'OK, got it.'

'You don't have to eat it all, you know.'

'No, that's all right. It looks wonderful.' She eased back into the armchair. 'Good job I just cancelled my dinner date.'

Resnick looked at her curiously. Tarragon mustard was about to drip over the edge of the plate and automatically he caught it on his finger and placed it on his tongue.

'Steak or scampi with a feller from a building society. All he'll want to do is talk mortgages and try and smile his way inside my pants. I'm glad for an excuse to be out of it. But not them.'

That's what I am, thought Resnick: an excuse.

'Sorry.' She tried the coffee. 'I didn't shock you?'

'No.'

'A lot of men, they don't like women to be outspoken.'

'The same men who cook by numbers?'

She gave him a warm, crooked-toothed smile. 'I've been mixing with the wrong types, obviously. It's the job that I do. Everyone expects a commission on everything. It's all a hustle. No percentage: no sale.'

A car alarm went off somewhere down the street. Miles came across the carpet to sniff the leather of Claire Millinder's boots and went on his way, disapprovingly. When Rachel had sat

118

there, Resnick remembered, the cats had jumped up into her lap and purred.

'Look, you didn't mind? I mean, it's a bit of a cheek, I know . . .'

'As long as you were here . . .'

'Not feeding your cats, I didn't mean that. I meant my still being here when you came home. I should have left with my clients, made sure the house was locked behind me.' She set down her plate on the arm of the chair, crossed one leg over another. 'I wanted to snatch some time to myself. I don't know, it felt good here, sort of . . . the place I'm living, three or four years old, one of those studio apartments where the bed folds back into the wall and there isn't room to swing . . . well, you know what I mean. This is different, a bit shabby, but it's large, lived-in. You feel that things have happened here.'

With the outside of his shoe, he pushed at the nursery door. Something stopped it and it would open no further.

'That's it,' Claire repeated, 'lived-in.'

Resnick glanced at the phone, willing it to ring. One half of Claire's sandwich remained untouched. He got up and moved towards the stacks of records. 'I'll put on some music.'

'No. No, don't.'

'Sorry, I thought . . .'

'I'd rather talk.'

He looked down at her, the crossing and re-crossing of legs, the smile, a little uncertain now. 'I think I'd rather not.'

Claire drew a slow breath, lowered her head. For some moments neither of them moved and then, with a nervous laugh, she got to her feet.

'Funny, isn't it?'

'Funny?'

'Strange. I feel so comfortable here, comfortable with you. All right, I thought, I'll sit here, talk, relax, get to know him, know you better.' She pressed the palms of her hands together, once, twice. 'That's not what you want.'

'I'm sorry.'

'Yes, well . . .' Claire picked up the plate and her mug and set them on a table. 'Best thing is . . .' She was reaching into her bag. '. . . I should give you your keys back.'

Resnick shook his head. 'No.'

119

'Someone else from the office . . .'

'No.' His hand closed over hers, over the keys. 'You like the house, you said so. You can sell it.'

'You're sure?'

'Yes.'

When he drew his hand away, a splodge of yellow remained near the knuckle of her little finger, mustard.

'Look,' she said at the front door, 'you may not want to act on them, but there are some things you could do. To make the place seem a better buy.' Resnick waited. 'First off, shift the timer on your heating, waste a little money, leave it on right through the day. People come to a place like this and as soon as they see the size of it, they've got these huge bills flashing in front of their eyes – gas, electricity, lined curtains, double glazing. They assume it's going to be difficult to heat, cold. Surprise them.'

'Second?'

'More money, I'm afraid. Nip into British Home Stores and splash out on a few more lamps. That'll help to make it look warm, too. Brighter.'

'There's more?'

'Get a good cleaning person. A professional. I'm not saying regularly, just once, a whole day, two days.'

'I'll think about it.'

'All of it?'

Resnick held the door for her as she stepped out on to the path. The street lamp elongated her shadow across the patchy grass. The repeated whine of a car alarm, the same as before, different.

'If I'm showing people round, I'll make sure and phone first.'

'Leave a message at the station.'

'Of course.'

Now that she was outside the house, neither of them really wanted her to go.

'You still think I should drop the price?'

'Maybe not. Not yet, anyway.'

'All right. Good-night.'

''Night. And, listen . . .'

'No, it's all right.'

''Night.'

"Night.'

He heard Claire Millinder's footsteps, heard the door of her Morris Minor open and close. The car alarm was still sounding and he wondered how long it would be before someone came to attend to it, the owner or a passing policeman. Claire's headlights cut a moving arc across the opposite wall and he caught a glimpse of her face before it was gone from sight.

Back in the living room, Dizzy and Pepper were picking their way fastidiously through the remains of her sandwich. Resnick looked at his records, thought about Johnny Hodges, thought about Lester Young, finally couldn't decide. He walked into the kitchen and opened a drawer and removed the unopened letter from his former wife. Postmark: Abergavenny. He lifted the bowl from the sink, turned to the cooker and lit the gas. The flame licked along one edge of the envelope and held. When it was truly alight, Resnick dropped it into the sink and poked at it with the end of a knife, watching it burn.

The ashes he flushed away until nothing remained.

15

'Harold!' the voice had said, authentic as spaghetti sauce just-like-mamma-makes (Mfr. Rotherham, Yorks.). 'Freeman and I are at the Royal, the Penthouse Bar, be great if you joined us for a couple of drinks. Loosen up. Limber down. Give us all a chance to talk things through.'

'Screw,' said Harold, 'you.'

He sounded as though he meant it.

'Who was that?' Maria had called from the stairs. Beneath her robe her legs were still shiny from her bath. The amount of time she spends slopping around in that thing, thought Harold, the rest of her wardrobe might go for junk.

'Nobody.'

'It must have been somebody.'

'That's what he'd like us to believe.'

Harold left his wife to her own conjectures and his talcum powder and went off in search of solace. What he could have done with, right then and there, were a couple of lines of coke, let the linings of his nose know who was boss. Pow! Was it true, he wondered, opening a bottle of the next best thing, all those rock stars of the seventies, having their nostrils rebuilt from the inside? Harold shuddered: silver plate.

He looked at the depth of alcohol in his glass and decided to double it.

'Harold! Pour me a drink and bring it up here.'

He went over to the door and closed it on her screeching. 'Screw you,' he said quietly, careful lest she hear and think he was being serious.

'Look at that, over there. Look at those.'

Grabianski peered around a giant pot plant, a decorated column. 'Where?'

'There. Jesus, how can you miss them? The table in the corner, past the piano.'

Grabianski saw two women, mid-twenties, black dresses

slashed low, enough gold to affect the commodities index. 'What about them?'

'Let's go over.'

'Go over?'

'Join them.'

'Together?'

'What d'you mean, together?'

'At the hip?'

'Jerry, you're not on something, are you?'

'Just hungry.'

'You'd prefer food to that?'

'Infinitely.'

Grice shook his head in near despair.

'Besides,' said Grabianski, 'they're probably waiting for somebody.'

'Sure. The first man to dangle a room key in front of them and ask them to feel his wallet.'

'We don't have a room key.'

'We have better. A flat five minutes' walk away.'

Grabianski stood up.

'That's more like it,' Grice said. 'Only mine's the one on the left. OK?'

Grabianski couldn't see any difference. 'That's not where I'm going,' he said.

'You're going to take another piss?'

'Going to eat. You stay here and catch an expensive sexually-transmitted disease.'

Grice grabbed hold of Grabianski's jacket. They were both wearing their best suits, the ones they had worn to burgle both the Roy and the Stanley houses. It had been Grabianski's idea: he had been brought up on stories of Raffles, the gentleman burglar. His favourite movie was Hitchcock's *To Catch a Thief*. When he looked in the mirror he was always disappointed not to see Cary Grant.

'We've left it too late,' said Grice, disgruntled.

'To eat?'

'Look.'

A couple of men had sat at the women's table and were talking animatedly, craning their necks towards the display of cleavage, thinking already of the lies they would tell to their wives.

'Let's go,' said Grabianski.

'Still Chinese?'

'Chinese.'

Maria Roy changed what she was wearing three times before coming downstairs. It would have helped had she been able to recall which of her outfits Harold had last expressed an interest in, even noticed. Finally she settled for a silky suit, high at the neck, loose-fitting trousers, the colour of tangerine. Perfume at the wrists, behind the ears, a dab or two between her breasts before raising the zip to the raised collar.

When she walked into the lounge Harold was so far into the bottle she might as well have wrapped herself in yesterday's bin liners.

He was stretched out on the settee, one leg on, one off; there were three glasses arranged along the floor, each of them partly full. 'That was Mackenzie,' he said. 'On the phone, earlier. The shit wanted me to go to and slime around this fucking Freeman Davis, fucking little asshole, fucking little pervert.'

Who? Maria thought: Mackenzie or Davis? And who was Davis anyway?

'Ease me out, that's what they think they're going to do. Little by little, little by fucking step. Freeman can handle this, why don't you let Freeman take care of that? Relax, Harold, learn to let go a little. Keep your eye on the overall picture, let Freeman cope with the day to day. Yes, fucking Freeman.'

He leaned on one elbow, reached down towards the glasses and missed all three of them.

'Fuck him! Fuck them all. Only reason they want me up in that fucking Penthouse Bar is so they can stand me by the window and push me out.'

Harold leaned too far and rolled, slow-motion, on to the carpet and was still.

'Fuck,' he said.

There was a glass panel between the sections of the restaurant, a screen, and somehow sculpted on it, in relief, the largest king prawn Grabianski had ever seen.

'Imagine that with garlic,' Grabianski said.

'Not while we're sharing the same bathroom, I can't.'

They walked through the lobby, low black tables holding thickly padded menus, a party of four enjoying a polite G and T or two before moving to their table. A tall Chinese wearing a dinner jacket asked them if they would like a drink and they ignored him, up two steps past the end of the screen and into the body of the restaurant. The waitress moved confidently on high heels, in a skirt that was tight and split well above her right knee. 'This way, gentlemen, please.' Her accent was almost pure Suzie Wong, with only a trace of the Notts–Derbyshire border.

Grabianski smiled as he shook his head and pointed off into the corner.

Grice nearly fell over his own feet staring at her leg.

'This place going to be good?'

'Rumour has it,' said Grabianski.

'Either way,' said Grice, looking round, 'we're going to pay for it.'

It never ceased to surprise Grabianski that a man who would blow £40 on fifteen minutes of massage relief could gripe continuously about a meal that went into double figures.

'May I get you gentlemen a drink?'

'Lager,' said Grice. 'Pint.'

'I'm sorry, sir, we do not serve pints.'

'No lager?'

'We have only half pints.'

'Bring me two. Right?'

'Of course, sir.' She smiled a weary smile towards Grabianski. 'For you, sir?'

'Tea. Please.'

'Chinese tea?'

'Yes.'

Deftly, she removed the pair of long-stemmed wine glasses, opened menus before each of them and moved off towards the bar.

'We'll have the set meal for two.' Grice slapped the menu closed.

Grabianski shook his head.

'You know what your trouble is, don't you?' said Grice.

'I expect you're going to tell me.'

'Used to be, all you wanted out of life was another species to check off in your bird book and another sodding mountain to climb. Now it's poncey restaurants and other men's wives.'

'I think,' said Grabianski evenly, 'I'm going to have the chicken and cashew nuts and the sizzling monkfish with spring onions and ginger. Oh, and the monk's vegetables. Special fried rice, what d'you think?'

The waitress arrived with two glasses of lager, Grabianski's tea and a decorated cup with a gold rim.

'May I take your order now?'

Grice jabbed his finger down the menu, ordering by the numbers; the waitress seemed to have transposed them on to her pad almost before he read them out. From Grabianski she got the words and an encouraging smile.

'And bring me a knife and fork,' said Grice to her back as she walked away.

Maria Roy made a perfect O with her lips and released a near-perfect smoke ring. Across the room, Harold had crawled back on to the couch and was snoring lightly. The television picture was on, the sound no more than a murmur. Maria was sitting in a deep armchair, legs tucked beneath her, ashtray and glass on either arm, reading. The trouble with shopping-and-fucking books was once you'd read one you'd read them all. And she distrusted all those female managing editors or PR directors who could reach orgasm at the touch of a button, enjoy oral sex between ground and eleventh floors in the executive lift, then step into a full meeting of the board, dabbing their lips with a scented tissue.

Even so, it made her aware of a certain itch; brought back the pressure of Jerry Grabianski's thumbs at the centre of her breasts, the weight of him on top of her. The care with which he had loved her.

Harold jumped in his sleep, threw out an arm and snorted loudly.

'Jesus, Harold!' shouted Maria. 'Why don't you shrivel up and die!'

Six hundred and forty-eight pages of wish fulfilment missed

his sleeping head by inches. Why don't I keep quiet about Jerry's offer, Maria thought? Let him think the cocaine's gone for good and wait until his dealer cuts him into four-inch squares. Serves the sorry bastard right!

She stubbed out her half-finished cigarette and lit another. Standing over her husband of more than twenty years, she saw the wisps of hair that curled from his ears, no longer grey but white, worry lines spreading from the edges of his mouth, the way his eyelid twitched compulsively, another in a succession of bad dreams. The rug was pulled out from under his career and, through no real fault of his own, it was likely his life was in danger.

She hated him.

'How's your pork?'

'It's OK.'

'Better than usual?'

'OK.'

'Because if it's anywhere near as good as this chicken . . .'

'Jerry.'

'Yes.'

'The pork is pork, all right?'

'Mm.'

'So can we get back to business?'

'Go ahead.'

'Two places and then we're out.'

'Out?'

'As in, over and.'

Grabianski lifted a piece of green pepper with his chopsticks, dipped it into black-bean sauce, then bit into it, thoughtfully. 'How come?'

'Sources,' said Grice.

Grabianski looked at his bowl, the dishes resting on hotplates. 'What's wrong with them?'

'Drag your mind from your stomach a minute. Up to now they've been – what d'you call it?'

'Impeccable.'

'Now I'm not so sure. I think a couple more at most.'

Laughter rose from the round table near the centre of the

room, coarse and loud, and echoed, one diner to another. Voices raised, the clatter of dishes as a hand came slamming extravagantly down. From the corner of his eye, Grabianski saw the manager appear at the far end of the screen.

'And then?'

'What d'you mean, and then? Like always, we scarper.'

Grabianski sipped jasmine tea. 'How about this flat? Didn't you tell her three months minimum?'

'I told her what she wanted to hear.'

A black woman walked in with a white escort, guided by the waitress towards their table. From the middle of the restaurant rose the unmistakable chant of the British football fan, the repeated sound of supposed chimpanzees.

'Banana fritters for that one!'

The laughter was raucous and harsh. The couple pretended not to hear.

'You know what I feel about unnecessary risks,' said Grice. 'What we've always felt. It's why we've kept clear of the law for as long as we have.'

'I know,' said Grabianski. He was thinking about something Maria had whispered into the side of his neck, the tip of her tongue moving over his skin: 'Jerry, if I could have one thing in the world, it'd be to be able to do this, with you, forever.' Grabianski didn't believe in forever, not even in the afterglow of good sex, but he did believe in a year, nine months.

'What are you thinking about?' asked Grice.

'Nothing.'

They both knew it was a lie.

The largest of the group around the middle table got to his feet. Like them he was white and male, but older than the rest. Forties, even. The others were not so many years out of school, a few of them still on YTS.

'Feeding time,' called the man. He had a short, square haircut, a black bomber jacket with red-and-green bands around the sleeves. He lifted one of the dishes from the table in front of him and tossed the entire contents high through the air, towards the couple who had just entered.

'Please . . .' The dinner-jacketed manager started towards them.

The black woman wiped rice from her shoulder, the sleeve of her dress. The man with her was on his feet and glaring; all of the blood seemed to have drained from his face.

'Come on, then, sunshine!'

'What's the matter, nigger-lover? Don't like the service?'

The waitress moved in front of the shaking customer, placing both hands on his chest. 'Sit down, sir,' she said. 'Pay no attention.'

Another plate of food struck her back, caught in her hair.

'Please . . .' urged the manager.

One of the men swung a fist from where he was sitting and punched him low in the stomach and he sank to his knees, groaning.

'Fetch the police,' called one of the other customers.

'Shut your fucking mouth!'

Two, then three Chinese appeared from the kitchen, wearing short white jackets, white aprons; one of them carrying a carving knife, another a broom handle.

Grice watched Grabianski go tense, straighten his arms against the edge of the table.

'Jerry, stay out of this.'

The waitress ran diagonally across the room; maybe she was heading for the phone, maybe she simply wanted to get away. She tripped over an outstretched leg and lost her footing, arms flailing until she collided with the metal edge of the screen. Spinning away before she fell, the blood was already pumping from a cut over her eye.

'Jerry!'

The leader of the gang reached down into a sports bag by his feet and flourished an axe.

'Keep out of this,' hissed Grice.

Grabianski didn't look back at him; he was watching the blade of the axe. 'How?' he said. The man wielding the axe lifted it high over his head before bringing it crashing through the table. Three of his friends took hold of the manager, arms and legs, and tossed him head first against the glass screen, cracking it across.

Grabianski had hung his suit jacket over the back of his chair;

now he slipped his watch from his wrist and set it down between the chopsticks and his cup of jasmine tea.

The youth who'd tripped the waitress was twisting an arm up behind her back and trying to tear away the top of her dress. Grabianski began to move through the mêlée towards them, three coins tight between the knuckles of his fist.

Harold Roy gripped the sides of the toilet bowl and slowly lowered his forehead until it was resting on the cool of the porcelain. How could they say there was something wrong with cocaine when, whatever it left you feeling, it was never like this? He knew, just knew, that come morning he was going to feel like death.

Maria pushed open the bathroom door, took one look, made a retching sound and went away. Life without Harold: devoutly to be wished. She went into the bedroom, laughing. What was she doing, remembering that? Chester Playhouse – or was it Salisbury? – and her one and only Ophelia. Well, to be honest, she had been an ASM, understudying Ophelia and the Queen both. Twice she got to sing those childish chants and wander round the stage with fake flowers threaded through her hair. Afternoon matinees with schoolkids pelting each other with peanuts and Maltesers and the noise so great it wouldn't have mattered if she hadn't remembered a single line.

The rest of the time she helped the dresser, shifted scenery, made sure the swords were in the right place for the duel and learned everybody else's words as well as her own.

Not alone my inky cloak, good madam, nor customary suit of solemn black.

How many people, she wondered, would bother to turn out for Harold's funeral? They'd probably get Mackenzie to write two paragraphs for *The Stage*.

That the funeral – how did it go? – the funeral, dum-di-dum, sweetmeats, bakemeats make up the marriage feast.

Jerzy Grabianski.

Jerry.

Harold came to the doorway and leaned against it, sagging. His eyes found Maria and tried to focus. No, you don't, you bastard! Maria thought. I won't pity you. I'm damned if I will!

He lurched three paces into the bedroom and stopped.

'Harold,' she said.

'Hmm?'

'There's something I'd better tell you.'

16

Resnick pushed at the door. Something stopped it and it would open no further. He had tried to sleep twice already, the downstairs settee, the shores of his own double bed. All of the usual strategies: the whisky and milk, the music, what he imagined at third remove to be relaxation exercises, stillness that cleared the brain. As possible as removing each last trace of blood from the boards, worked and worried into the grain. Inside the room, his fingers touched the walls, the paper's slight give, layer upon layer, sheet upon sheet. If he stood there long enough he would be able to smell it, stubborn as fragments caught beneath a nail. He looked at his hands. *What seemed like pieces of him.* During his marriage this room had meant babies: the possibility of life. Later, when his relationship with Rachel had ended, it had given birth to something else. Always a bloody business.

Why, for instance, do you want to move?

Oh, Christ!

Resnick closed the door behind him; there was a lock, he needed the key. Rachel. What had she called it? *A womb with a view.* Hadn't she been coming there that day to say to him, hold on, back down, goodbye? It had been a simple enough story: a murderer who had visited his house to what? Confess? Exact a little penance? Five Hail Marys and a blade with a blunt, serrated edge. There were those, Resnick believed, for whom life was a matter of steps, delicate and small. Along the corridor, up and down the stairs, the rest of the house awaited him.

Jack Skelton picked up his cup and stretched his limbs. When they had moved into this house out in the suburbs there had been something good about its proportions. Suitable. He and his wife had looked at his superintendent's salary, the entries in their building society accounts, his and hers. The proper calculations. It would be, they both agreed, their last move. Even after the children had left home, they would want somewhere large enough for them to visit, bring their husbands, wives, grandchildren.

The clock stood between small framed photographs above the wide fireplace. Twenty past one. Alice had already come down and asked him to go back to bed. 'She won't have a thing to say when she does get in.' Skelton had quit pacing the L-shaped room, lounge and dining-space combined; he had looked back at his wife and raised his eyebrows, an annoying gesture he had been trying to cure himself of since a cadet; raised his eyebrows and nodded. 'In a while.'

Alice had turned back to the stairs, gone to their bed alone.

Skelton walked now past the dining table, through the sliding door into the kitchen; his hand against the side of the kettle showed it to be still warm. Instant coffee was in a jar above the fitted hob. There were no longer buses running and he wondered how his daughter would be getting home. He did not allow himself to consider she might not return, that night, at all.

'Kate.'

Skelton woke to the sound of the key turning in the lock. He had fallen asleep in the chair and there was an after-memory, recent, the muffled noise of a car drawing up and pulling away.

'Katie.'

She turned to face him from the foot of the stairs. Her hair had been hacked short for some months now and tonight it was greased into abrupt, frozen spikes. Her face was pale, save for lips painted black. She wore a black T-shirt over skin-tight black trousers; a black leather jacket dripping with crosses and gothic impedimenta. A cartridge belt, empty, hung loose over one hip; white socks led to black winkle-picker shoes that were beginning to crease upwards at the tips.

One foot on the bottom tread of the stairs, a hand to the banister, she glared at him, head erect, the epitome of tough.

'I fell asleep,' Skelton said.

'Down here?'

'I was waiting . . .'

'I know what you were doing.'

'I was worried.'

'Yeah.'

133

'We were worried, your mother . . .'

'Don't.'

'Don't what?'

'What you were going to say, don't say it.'

'You're being very unfair . . .'

'And she doesn't give a shit about me, so don't you pretend that she does.'

'Katie!'

He moved towards her fast, one arm raised: hit her or hold her?

The girl narrowed her eyes and stared him down: two months past sixteen.

'Coffee,' said Skelton, stepping back.

'What?'

'Coffee. I could make us some coffee.'

She looked at him, incredulous, and laughed.

'We could talk.'

Kate shook her head.

'All right, then, just sit.'

She snorted, bitter. 'A bit late for that, isn't it?'

'I don't see why.'

'Late, I thought that was the point.'

'Of what?'

'All this.'

Skelton sighed and turned away, but now she wasn't prepared to let him go.

'This welcoming committee,' she sneered. 'The long-suffering looks. The way you're being so bloody careful not to ask me if I know what time it is.'

He didn't know what to do with her hostility: smother it, deflect it; impossible to ignore it. There were silver rings in both her ears and even in the subdued suburban lighting they shone. What use was anger when every thought he had of her was something other than that? Sentimental, that's what Kate would call him: sentimental old fool.

'I'm going to have some coffee anyway,' he said.

He was sitting on a stool, elbows on the fitted surface, cup held between both hands, when she came into the kitchen. She pulled out one of the other stools, but didn't sit on it; stood less than easily, instead, examining the floor.

'Sure you don't want some?'

Kate shook her head.

Skelton wished he didn't think like a policeman, didn't think like a father. Silence settled uneasily between them. Kate showed no sign of wanting to move. Shut up, said Skelton to himself, shut up and wait.

'How did you . . . ?' he began.

'I got a lift.'

'Who from?' The question out before he could stop it.

'Nobody I knew.'

He looked at her sharply, not knowing if it were true or if she was saying it to shock him, hurt. Her response as automatic as his.

'I stood in the road and stuck my thumb out. These two blokes pulled over. I don't know who they were, do I?'

'You could have phoned.'

'Yeah? Where?'

'Here. Phoned me. I would have . . .'

'Come to meet me, my father the superintendent of police. No thanks.'

'Then you should have left earlier.'

'I couldn't.'

'Got a taxi.'

'What with?'

'Money. You had money.'

'I spent it.'

'Katie.' Skelton turned on the stool, reached out his hands towards her. 'Don't do this?'

'Do what?'

He withdrew his hands as he stood. 'Look,' he said, 'if you're going out at night and you think you're going to be this late back, tell me.'

'And you'll say, don't go.'

'I'll give you the money for a taxi.'

'Every time?'

'Yes, every time.'

'No,' she said.

'Why ever not?'

'Because it'd get spent before it was time to come home.'

She pushed her way past the sliding door and left him to listen to her footsteps, rising up the stairs above his head. In the morning she would come down with all the gel rinsed from her hair, the earrings, all save one, replaced by studs, neat and small. Blouse, jumper and skirt: no make-up. Half a dozen halting words and she would be gone.

Katie.

When the phone rang, the cats stirred before Resnick. He had finally fallen asleep with a pillow jammed over his head, arms and legs stretched diagonally across the bed.

'Hallo,' he said, lifting the receiver, dropping it. 'Hallo, who is this?'

'Sir? Sorry to disturb you, sir. It's Millington. Something like the Tong wars, sir. I thought maybe you'd want to come in.'

Resnick rubbed at his eyes and groaned. 'Ten minutes, Graham,' he said. 'Quarter of an hour.'

'What on earth,' he said aloud, addressing three cats, searching for his trousers, 'does Millington know about Tong wars?' He stepped into one leg, manoeuvred towards the other. 'Must have been another evening class his wife took.'

17

'Kevin,' Resnick called across the room.

'Yes, sir.' Naylor looked up from what he was doing, the shaft of a pencil pushed through the sprocket hole of an audio cassette, carefully winding back the loop of overflowed tape. What was the use of recording interviews if the technology let you down?

'Finished checking those insurance companies?'

'Sir. It's all typed up, I had it . . .' He set down cassette and pencil and started to shuffle papers across his overcrowded desk. The phone close behind him burst to life and, instinctively, he turned towards it, stopped, went back to his search.

'Later, Kevin, later. Just tell me – anything worth following up? Any clear connections?'

Naylor shook his head. Abruptly the ringing tone shut off, to begin again when he was in mid-sentence. 'Five different companies, four of them national, no more than two homes insured with the same people.'

Disappointment evident momentarily in the set of his mouth, Resnick moved away.

'But, sir . . .' Naylor was on his feet, one arm extended.

'Can't somebody answer that?'

Patel and Divine started up from different sides of the office.

'A couple of them did use the same broker . . . might be something there, sir?'

'Check it out,' said Resnick without enthusiasm.

'Oh, and sir . . .'

'Go on.'

'When the insurance people did an examination, wanted security brought up to scratch, the broker, he recommended Fossey.'

There wasn't a lot that morning with a chance of making Resnick smile, but that little titbit came close. 'You're on your way to see this broker?'

'Right after I've sorted this, sir.'

Resnick nodded. 'Good.'

'Sir,' Divine had his fingers over the mouthpiece, 'something about a peeping Tom.'

'Downstairs. Uniform.'

'They transferred the call up here, sir.'

'Transfer it back down again.'

Divine shrugged, did as he was told.

Before Resnick could retreat into his office, Millington had wearied his way through the main door. Cold coffee was slopping over the sides of the polystyrene cup in his hand. The skin below his eyes resembled washing left too long in the rain.

'Kevin might have turned up something new on friend Fossey,' Resnick told him.

Right then it wasn't what the sergeant wanted to hear. He wanted a change in the rota that would give him instant forty-eight-hour leave; he welcomed dreams of featherweight duvets and mattresses that both supported yet absorbed body weight; the repatriation of all citizens of Chinese extraction, effective as from two months previous; hot coffee in a real cup.

'Thought you'd be interested,' said Resnick.

'Right now . . .' began Millington, but thought better of it.

'Enough on your plate,' suggested Resnick and Millington looked at him sharply, suspicious it was a joke in bad taste.

'Half of them boxing clever, the others too thick to be worth a shovel load of horseshit!'

'Graham?'

'My grandad – every time a horse and cart appeared in the street, he used to go rushing out with his dustpan and brush. Marvellous for the garden, so he said.'

'Excuse me, sir.' It was Patel, politely at Resnick's shoulder. 'The duty officer says there's a Miss Olds in the lobby, wanting to see you.'

'Ms Olds,' Resnick said, rearranging the first syllable. 'Get that right and she might not gobble you up for breakfast.'

Patel flushed, embarrassed. Mark Divine, just within earshot, grinned and looked interested.

'This anything to do with your investigation, d'you think, Graham?'

Millington sighed. 'Very likely, sir.'

Resnick signalled towards his office door. 'Make sure I'm up to date, then.' To Patel he said. 'Apologize to Ms Olds, see if she wants tea or anything. Stall her for ten minutes. OK?'

Patel didn't have a lot of choice.

'Anything you can't handle . . .' Divine called after him, and then, to the room in general, 'Way that boy blushes, what's the betting he's still a bleedin' virgin!'

It was still short of 8.30. Millington and a team of six officers had been interviewing customers and staff from the Chinese restaurant since the early hours of that morning. Eight people had been taken to casualty by ambulance, three detained, one of those undergoing surgery to stop serious bleeding and sew back into place several fingers that had been severed by an axe. Until an hour ago, Patel and Naylor had been at the hospital.

So far, the leader of the gang that had been responsible for most of the injuries, to say nothing of hundreds of pounds' worth of damage, was sticking to his story. Paid him to go in there and make trouble? No one had paid him anything, not so much as a couple of luncheon vouchers. The axe? Happened to have it with him, didn't he? Back that day from a friend, borrowed it to take down this old plum tree in his garden, sour as old maid's piss. Wielding a dangerous weapon? What would you do, half the sodding Red Guard coming at you waving meat cleavers? Turn the other fucking cheek?

The lads that had been with him were either too much in his thrall or didn't know anything anyway. For half of them, it hadn't been so much different from the end of any Saturday night.

The manager was chain-smoking French cigarettes, butterfly stitches over one eye, left arm resting in a broad-arm sling. He knew nothing about a family feud. Nothing. The last time he had seen Mr Chao and his son they had been sitting together, a family occasion, very pleasant, smiling; Mr Chao had taken his son's arm as they talked.

The witnesses mostly confirmed that it had been the men, rowdy and loud, who had started the trouble. As to what had been said, who had actually threatened whom, they were more vague. Except for one, the kind of witness Millington wished he could get in the dock a sight more often. Big fellow, took a couple of knocks himself, but not the sort to bruise easily. Odd sort of name, Czech, Polish, one of those.

'This bloke, sir, the one I was telling you about . . .'

'Customer who went wading in?'

'Polish, I think.'

'Local?'

Millington didn't know. 'Name's Grabianski. You don't know him, I suppose?'

Resnick shook his head.

'Wondered if you'd be interested in having a few words. Expressing thanks, as it were. Not often you get a member of the public chiming in when there's that sort of shindig going on.'

'Maybe later,' Resnick said. 'Keeping Suzanne Olds off your back ought to be a first priority. There's no suggestion we're charging Chao for anything? I assume that's why she's here this hour of the morning.'

'Wish I could say we were, sir.'

'Bringing him in for questioning?'

Millington looked doubtful. 'Without one of these laddies breaks down, points a finger . . .'

Resnick got to his feet. 'All right, Graham. Time to invite Ms Olds to share the mysteries of the breakfast canteen.'

Millington's head turned at the door. 'If it's down to a triple-decker egg-and-bacon sandwich, sir, brown sauce, think of me.'

Suzanne Olds had once treasured dreams of a career as an internationally fêted ice-skater: ice-dance champion of the world, the tears engendered by the national anthem not yet dry on her cheeks as she signed the forms that would turn her into a professional sensation. She had been at the rink every evening after school. Saturday mornings, Sundays; her parents had paid for her to visit Austria, Colorado; coaching bills had rivalled their mortgage. Sacrifices they had made for her: no second cottage in the south of France, no winter family holidays, all those mornings driving her to practice, collecting her. For what? A fantasy, but whose? Sunday afternoons in front of the television, old black-and-white films in which Sonja Henie shook her Shirley Temple curls, laced up her skates and danced into the arms of Tyrone Power, applause, the final credits, more of a fortune than ever she could dream.

At fifteen, at Streatham, Suzanne Olds went for a triple axle and never made it.

Simple as that.

After three operations on her knee, the consultant had said, enough. Suzanne went on to university, history and economics. By twenty-eight she was driving a company car, had a first-floor flat off Fulham Broadway; she was confident and articulate and looked good in a tailored suit, she did her homework, knew statistics; Suzanne Olds and market research were made for one another.

In the aftermath of her thirtieth birthday, she turned down a serious proposal of marriage and dictated her resignation. The following morning she applied to read law at LSE.

'Why are you bringing me here?'

'All the interview rooms are full.'

'What's wrong with your office?'

'I thought you'd like some breakfast.'

She looked at Resnick from beneath lowered lashes. 'Coffee,' she said. 'Black.'

He grinned and shuffled a few places along the queue. Neither salmonella nor listeria had quenched the police appetite for endless fried eggs, bacon, sausages, brittle toast or fried bread mired in fat.

'Here,' said Resnick. 'In the corner, a bit of peace.'

She still knew how to wear a suit and most eyes followed her like magnets.

'Lucky sod!' said one officer too loudly as Resnick went by. The look he received was enough to make his sausage cob stick in his throat.

'I presume this isn't social?' Resnick said, sitting down.

'I gave up on that front long ago.' She tried the coffee; it wasn't as bad as she had feared. 'Where you are concerned.'

In truth, she'd never really started. Nothing beyond a few polite inquiries as to the inspector's marital status, a handful of chance meetings, once an invitation to a legal dinner that Resnick had turned down.

'It's Mr Chao, then, is it?'

'Naturally, he's concerned about what happened last night. Also, any implications that might, incorrectly, be drawn.'

Resnick smiled. Suzanne Olds was an elegant woman; when the cards lay that way, an intelligent adversary. He was only a little older than she, only a few inches taller. She leaned back in her chair and balanced her cup across the fingers of one hand. Her hair had been swept back and pinned in place; she was wearing a crisp white blouse with a loose black bow at the throat, a charcoal-grey suit with a slight flare to the skirt and black brogue shoes with solid heels.

'Implications,' Resnick teased.

'Let's not waste time being naïve, inspector. Your officers have already expended a great deal of energy and man-hours attempting to prove my client's involvement with that unfortunate fire in his son's premises.'

'Your client?'

'Mr Chao has a retainer on my services.'

'To cover any eventuality.'

'Exactly.'

'And the service you're performing for him on this occasion?'

'To express his regret that such a thing should happen at all, even though, of course, he was in no way culpable. Neither Mr Chao nor his staff. To promise you that he has instructed those working for him to give the police their fullest cooperation.'

'And the cooperation of Mr Chao himself?'

'Inspector, my client simply happens to be the owner of the premises where this fracas took place. He was not present at the time and neither he nor his immediate family are in any way involved. Why should Mr Chao make himself available to the police in this matter?'

Resnick took his time; when he had finished talking to Suzanne Olds there were others waiting who were less stimulating. 'If what you say is true, Ms Olds, why should he call you so early in the morning and prioritize your expensive time?'

'Shall we say,' she replied, leaving her coffee far from finished, brushing an imaginary speck from her suit skirt before standing, 'Mr Chao achieved his considerable position in the business community by being both far-sighted and cautious.'

All right, thought Resnick, OK: for now, let's leave it at that.

* * *

There were three messages waiting on Resnick's desk: Rees Stanley had phoned to discuss what progress had been made regarding the burglary of his house and would call back at eleven; the superintendent was due at Central Police Station this side of lunch and he wanted to talk to Resnick before leaving; Jeff Harrison had rung through twice and would be ringing back.

Resnick pushed open the door of the main office. 'This message from DI Harrison . . .'

'Came through to me, sir.'

'Any idea what he was after, Lynn?'

'Didn't say, sir.' Her round face was rounder when she smiled. 'A pint of Mansfield?'

Hmm. From what he remembered, Jeff was strictly a spirits man. Doubles, at that. The occasional chaser. Coppers' tables in the back room of some bar or other.

Stanley, Skelton, Harrison: Resnick decided he would go and talk to – what was his name? – Grabianski. One of the newer members of the Polish community, perhaps.

18

When the phone rang, Harold Roy was sitting with a tomato juice, trying to concentrate on his camera script. If it wasn't going to take them half the morning to take out that flat, it was worth putting in a third camera to get the reverse close-ups. At least that would give the vision mixer something else to do, aside from the *Independent* crossword and buffing her nails.

'Yes,' he said into the receiver, responding to Alan Stafford's voice. 'Yes, of course I'm listening.'

So, from beyond the doorway, was Maria, though there was little enough for her to hear. What she could see was her husband wiping away the sweat that formed on his hands, dabbing along his trouser leg. Within less than two minutes, the conversation was over and all Harold had said had been 'Yes', another four times.

'Harold . . . ?'

Maria stepped in front of him, blocking his path to the front door. The look he gave her was harder, more strained than she could recall seeing before. Maybe this, all of this, was pushing him too far.

'Harold . . .'

'What?'

'When you, go, I mean, to talk to him . . . It is going to be all right?'

'Are you going to stand there in that thing all day?' he asked. 'Or is there a chance you might get as far as the bathroom and swab down?'

'Milton Keynes,' Grabianski was saying, 'the kind of deals they were offering, it would have been stupid to stay put. Brand new premises, low rates, corporation grants, credits – as against that there was this factory in Leicester, ventilation problems, heating, it would have taken us so far into the red putting it right, I doubt we'd ever have got out again.'

'So you relocated?'

'Lock, stock and machinery. Down to the land of the concrete cows.'

'Regrets?'

Grabianski shook his head. 'The walking's not what it was, but aside from that . . .'

'Walking?'

Grabianski settled back in the chair the inspector had offered him; relaxing into this, enjoying it. Another fifteen minutes or so and he would be in the car and on his way out to see Maria. Less than an hour and they'd be in bed. 'Rambling, I suppose you'd call it. Hiking. Up the M1 from Leicester and you'd be in Monsal Dale before the mist had burnt off the hills.'

'That's not what you're here for now, here in the city?'

Grabianski smiled. 'Wish it was. No: business, I'm afraid.' He sat forward again, an elbow resting on his knee. 'We've still got connections up here, outlets. Sheffield, Manchester. Every so often I have to make the trip.'

'You do it all yourself? The travelling?'

'My partner or myself, depending.'

'You've got a partner?'

'Since I started, more or less.'

'Not the man you were with in the restaurant?'

'Last night? Yes.'

'You were both here, then? This time.'

'Yes.'

'I thought you said . . .'

'It depends. There was a lot to do, people to see.'

'Wholesalers.'

'That's right. Sometimes it's easier to spread the load.'

'While the factory runs itself in sunny Milton Keynes.'

'Like silk. Well, more like cotton. To be accurate.'

'Look,' said Resnick, 'I mustn't keep you.'

'No problem,' smiled Grabianski. 'It's good to talk.'

'Not many people,' said Resnick, standing, showing Grabianski towards the door, 'would have got involved.'

'To be honest,' Grabianski had turned again, one shoulder almost resting against the door's edge as he held it open, 'if I'd thought about it, neither would I. But I suppose, I don't know, something triggers you off and before you know it . . .' His smile broadened and he stepped out of the room, Resnick following.

'What d'you think it was?' Resnick asked, side by side in the corridor. 'The trigger?'

'Oh, the girl, I suppose.'

'The waitress?'

'Yes.'

Resnick paused at the head of the stairs. 'Nice to know the age of chivalry is being nurtured in the industrial heart of Milton Keynes.'

'Ah,' said Grabianski, 'I've always been too much of a romantic. Friends say it'll be my downfall.'

'Part of our national heritage,' Resnick suggested. 'Yours and mine.'

'Facing up to invading tanks with the cavalry.'

'Something like that.'

They descended to the ground floor and Resnick turned the lock on the door that would let them into the entrance. Traffic sounded heavy on the road outside, the last build-up of the morning.

'I suppose it's a hotel when you're making these trips?' Resnick said. They were outside, on the top step.

'Afraid so.'

'Any one better than another?'

'King's Court – at least the service is good.'

'If not the restaurant.'

'Sorry?'

'I meant, not so good it stops you eating out.'

Grabianski offered Resnick his hand. Two big men, standing together, wearing suits; tired, when you saw them close, around the eyes; they were both tired. For both of them it had been a long night: an early morning.

'This business,' Grabianski said, 'I hope you get it sorted out.'

'Oh, we will. Eventually.'

'Take care.'

'You, too.'

Resnick watched as Grabianski walked along the pavement, turning left at the pedestrian lights and then right again opposite the entrance to the cemetery and what had once been a gents' urinal.

'Patel,' he said, as soon as he was back into the CID room, 'get on to the King's Court Hotel. Mansfield Road, somewhere. A copy of their guest list, the last ten days.'

Harold Roy sat at the centre of the control panel, the production secretary at his left, Diane Woolf, the vision mixer, on his right.

The bank of monitors in front of them showed three cameras at the ready, three different angles on a living room decorated in lavish bad taste, the house the *Dividends* family had moved to after their stroke of fortune. One of the cameras swung suddenly sideways, following a make-up girl's tightly jeaned gear.

'Eye on the job in hand, John,' said Diane into the microphone.

'It was,' came the reply over talk-back.

'Can we go for this?' asked Harold of the floor.

'You don't want to rehearse?'

'What was that we just did?'

There was a pause, squeaks of static and then: 'Once more for sound, Harold, please.'

'Shit!' said Harold.

'You won't say that if we get a boom shadow,' commented the sound engineer from the adjacent booth.

'It's exactly what I'll say.'

'We could be rehearsing this while we're arguing,' said the floor manager.

Harold jammed both hands over his ears. 'Do it,' he said. 'Do it!'

The first actor made his entrance and immediately there was a gigantic boom shadow, smack across the back wall.

'Don't anyone dare say I told you so.' Harold glared through the glass panel to where the sound engineer was busy relaying instructions to his operators.

'Lighting's coming down, Harold.'

'In God's name, what for now?'

'Just a tweak,' came the lighting man's voice through one of the mikes.

'Jesus!' whispered Harold and looked at the clock.

'Here.' Diane Woolf prised back the silver paper from another roll of extra-strong mints and passed them towards him. Harold took two and crunched them both.

'Would you like some aspirin?' asked the production secretary, a manicured hand on his arm.

'I'd like to get something, just something, recorded before we break for lunch.'

'Harold?' It was Robert Deleval, querulous from the doorway. 'Since we've stopped anyway, I was wondering if we could just change a couple of these lines?'

'Robert.'

'Yes?'

'Die!'

Resnick's interview with the superintendent had been brief and strangely inconclusive; Skelton had seemed abstracted, his mind on other things.

'Chao's not without friends in the city, Charlie. Wouldn't hurt to bear that in mind.'

'Member of the golf club, is he, sir?'

'Charlie?'

'Sorry, sir.'

'Only you know what Millington can be like if he feels stymied. If they're all sitting there, playing stum. Might be a red rag to a bull.'

Red flag, Resnick thought.

'I'll see he keeps the lid on it, sir.'

'Do that, Charlie.'

Skelton had sat there, looking up at him; Resnick thinking, there are other people I have to see, things to do. 'Anything else, sir?' said Resnick. 'Only . . .'

'No. No, Charlie.' A deft sideways movement of the head; Lawton deflecting the ball into the net. 'That's all.'

Resnick had already passed Rees Stanley on to Divine, with instructions to his DC to pacify the man, find out whether any of his neighbours knew of the family's plans to return early, suggest that he joined his local neighbourhood watch. Jeff Harrison had phoned a third time and Resnick shuffled it to the back of his mind. Somehow he wasn't anxious to talk to Jeff – especially if it were about what he feared it might be.

148

'Sir?'

Patel was waiting outside Resnick's office, shoulders straightening a little more as the inspector approached. The constable was wearing a jacket with a fine check, slacks that had been staprest when they were last cleaned.

'King's Court, sir. All their records are kept on computer.'

'And?'

Patel shook his head. 'Some problem with it, apparently. Won't print out.'

Resnick sighed. 'I'll drop by.'

The Barry Manilow record that Maria had put on when she went to the bathroom was little more than a muffled noise, a subdued thunk of amplified bass beneath occasional piano. Cigarette smoke smudged the light, surprisingly bright through the decorated lace at the bedroom window.

'You like that stuff?'

'Mmm. Don't you?'

Grabianski didn't know. He felt about music the way his partner felt about birds, large ones and small ones; with music it was slow ones and fast ones. Mostly these were slow ones.

'Hey!' cried Maria.

'Yes?'

'That.'

'What?'

'What you're doing.'

'That?'

'Yes.'

'What about it?'

'Where did you learn to do that?'

Grabianski managed to manoeuvre himself on to his side without disturbing his right arm, the fingers of his right hand. He flicked his tongue a couple of times against the auricle of her ear and Maria seemed to shiver without moving. He did it some more and this time she moaned. He could remember clearly where he had learned to do that: and when. He had been fifteen and she had been the daughter of the caretaker, a skinny sixteen-year-old who wore spectacles and thick cotton knickers. There was a doorway, recessed into the rear wall of the building, deep

149

enough to take both of their bodies, pressed close together. Aside from the girl's parents, her aunts at Christmas and on her birthday, Grabianski didn't think anyone had ever kissed her before. Not anywhere. Not with their tongue: certainly not against, around, inside her ear.

'Jerry.'

'That's my name.'

'No, it's not. Not really.'

'It's close.'

'I know.'

'Close enough?'

'Mmm,' crooned Maria. 'Mmmm.'

'After all,' Grabianski grinned, 'what's in a name?'

The King's Court Hotel had been converted from a double-fronted family house with cellars and attics for the menials and menial tasks and out-buildings for the coach and horses. Now it catered for a new generation of computer-software salesmen, parents up for the weekend to visit their student offspring, Americans or Germans on thirty-day tours anxious to be photographed by the statue of Robin Hood. The receptionist assured Resnick there were no vacancies, pursed her lips at the sight of his warrant card and pushed at the edges of her perm with one hand, hoping there was a camera somewhere and they were on *Crimewatch*.

She was in her indeterminate thirties, wearing a tight-fitting black jacket with significant shoulder pads and a badge that read Lezli. Not, Resnick guessed, the way it had been spelt on her baptismal certificate. Unless they had been blessed with a dyslexic vicar.

'You're having problems with your computer,' Resnick said.

'I thought you were from the police?'

'That's right.'

'Then what are you doing, coming out to service our computer?'

'I'm not.'

'Moonlighting, that's what it's called, isn't it?'

'Something like that.'

But Lezli was having a quick fantasy about Bruce Willis, easy enough to slip into when you did the kind of job that kept her sitting hours on end, either talking to the wrong end of the telephone or talking to idiots. What on earth that Maddie reckoned she was doing keeping him at arm's length for a couple of series, she couldn't imagine. Her, she would have taken him down on the executive carpet before the first episode was halfway over. But then, that would have been real life, not television.

'Hello,' Resnick said.

'Yes?'

'About this computer I haven't come to service.'

'What about it?'

'I don't suppose there's any chance it's working yet?'

Lezli shook her head and bit the end of her pencil. Five calls she'd made that morning and each time the same snot-nosed voice had promised her somebody would be out within the hour. Which hour, that was what she'd like to know.

Resnick decided to try another line – anything less and he'd lose her again. 'How long ago did you make the switch?' he asked.

'Switch?'

'Putting all of your records on to disc.'

'Oh, let me see, that'd be about a year ago. Yes, somewhere around there. A year.'

'Then anything prior to that . . .'

'Those little cards.'

'And you threw them out, once they'd been transferred.'

'You're joking. That's what I wanted to do, would have done if I'd had my way, but, no, the manager he said five years you've got to keep them, five years.' She leaned across the desk towards him and Resnick could clearly see the hard edges of the contact lenses on her pupils. 'That's not a law, is it? Five years?'

'Not as far as I know.'

'See. I told him. Not that he listens to anything I say, apart from no and even that I have to shout.'

'They're accessible?' Resnick asked.

'What?'

'If it was important, you could get at them easily?'

'Is it important?'

'Very.'

She blinked at Resnick, not wanting to go scrabbling about in the office, manager staring at her backside, dragging out a lot of old filing cabinets, dust up her nose and under her fingernails.

'It would be a great help,' Resnick said encouragingly.

Lezli made a show of sighing and went away, returning over five minutes later with three six-by-four card cabinets, balanced uneasily one on top of another. She set them on the counter and went in search of some tissues to dust them down with.

'That's not all five years?' Resnick asked.

'Three,' she said as if defying him to demand the rest.

Resnick wasn't one to push his luck unless he was sure it was likely to pay off. He leafed through a tourist brochure for the county while Lezli shuffled the cards. The information came to hand with surprising ease.

'You want me to write this all down?'

'If you don't mind.'

Grabianski had given as his address the registered offices of G & G Textiles and Leisurewear, Milton Keynes; he had stayed at the hotel twice before in the last three years, several weeks each time and only on this current occasion had he cut short his visit.

Resnick looked at the receptionist with renewed interest. 'He checked out today?'

She shook her head. 'I could have told you that without going through all this palaver. Three days ago. Something urgent had cropped up. He didn't say, but I reckon it was at home, wife taken ill or something.'

'He's married then?'

Lezli nodded emphatically. 'He's never said, but you can always tell. I can.' To my cost, she thought.

Resnick took the sheet of hotel notepaper with the dates; he was pretty certain that one period coincided with the previous run of break-ins they were investigating, overlapped at least.

'Thanks,' he said. 'You've been very helpful.'

Lezli watched him go with some interest; she still couldn't get it out of her head there might be a camera hidden somewhere. That was how they did it, wasn't it? Those programmes. Through the glass of the doors she saw Resnick climbing into his car. She didn't think it could have been for the telly, otherwise they'd have made him smarten himself up a bit, surely? Done something about the heavy creases in his clothes, that dreadful tie.

One thing she was certain of – unlike that Mr Grabianski, Inspector Resnick didn't have a wife at home looking after him.

19

It was the key scene of the episode. Having won in excess of a million pounds and taped expensive sticking plaster over his festering marriage, the principal male character is returning from a board meeting of the pizza chain he has set up with part of his new fortune. His fellow directors have turned on him and taken control of everything from his expense-account BMW to his plans to launch a new fruit-and-salami takeaway special. Distressed and close to violence, he arrives home at the mock-gothic paradise in which he has installed his family to find his wife *in flagrante delicto* in the swimming pool with the newspaper delivery boy. It was a tense and marvellous dramatic moment and Harold couldn't seem to get it right.

'I'm coming down!' he screamed into his microphone and leaped from his control-room chair.

'Harold's coming on to the floor,' relayed the floor manager.

'Oh, shit,' came a voice over somebody's talk-back, resigned.

The actress playing the wife was having the straps at the back of her bikini top retied and a little more body cosmetic applied to tone down the goose-bumps. The husband was pacing the studio floor, trying to retain the mood, remember the awful lines he had been given. The delivery boy, a youthful twenty-year-old with a gold earring and the residue of serious acne, was feeling up one of the make-up girls beneath her shiny blue overall.

'Trouble, Harold?' Mackenzie strolled on to the set with all the natural instincts of a shark sensing blood.

'Nothing that can't be sorted.'

Mackenzie wasn't about to be easily convinced. Harold threw an arm around the leading actor's shoulders and drew him further to one side. 'Listen, love, what you're doing, it's working beautifully for me, only it's just the tiniest bit too — what can I say? — internalized.'

The actor looked at him in disbelief.

'You come home, you've been shafted, you feel shattered, you're seeking consolation and what do you find instead? I know

154

all that rage you're feeling, the shock, absolute desolation; it's there for me, but I think you've got to give us a little more. Outside. Show it.'

'What you mean, Harold, is you want ham, three inches thick.'

'Energy, that's what I want.' Harold gave the actor's shoulders an encouraging squeeze. 'Think what's happening here. You see her, dripping water from the pool you bought her, the pool she's been cuckolding you in, and you want to kill her. I don't just want to see that, I want to feel it, smell it. OK?'

'Yes, Harold. Understood.'

'Great! Terrific!' Harold spun away and clapped his hands. 'OK,' he called to the floor manager. 'Soon as I get back upstairs.'

'Ready to go again, everyone,' cried the floor manager. Today her baseball boots were emerald green with blue numbers over the ankles; her sweatshirt expressed faded support for the Washington Redskins. 'Quiet, please! Be still!'

'Right,' said Harold, flinging himself at his chair and turning back the pages of his camera script to the top of the scene. 'This is the one!'

'All I'm saying is,' said Robert Deleval with hushed urgency, 'if this scene isn't made to work, the whole thing falls apart.'

Sitting next to the writer in the glass-panelled box behind the control room, the trainee design assistant switched her gum from one side of her mouth to the other and feigned interest.

'Without this,' hissed the writer, 'nothing else really makes sense.'

'Nothing?'

'Exactly. It's central to an understanding of what the piece is about.'

'Well, I suppose I can see it's . . .'

'No, it *is* the script. The core.' Robert Deleval had one knee on the upholstered bench seat, both hands waving in the trainee's face. 'This is where the whole narrative comes together.' He jumped to his feet and carried on waving his arms. 'The primary drive of the story, the themes of money and betrayal, all that stuff that's been swimming around in the subtext, this is where it all comes to the surface. Right there in that confrontation by the pool. Don't you see?'

She was staring up at him, slowly shaking her head. In about half an hour they should be breaking for lunch.

Deleval punched his fists against his thighs. 'On one level, it's pool as in football pools, on the other, pool as in undercurrent. If fucking Howard can't make this work . . .'

'Yes?'

'We're sunk.'

'Ready?' Harold asked.

Alongside him, Diane Woolf ran her tongue across her lower lip, hands over the buttons of the console; somehow she was managing to look at the coloured annotations she had made to her script at the same time as all three camera monitors before her.

'Now or never,' she replied.

'Before we go,' Harold said into his mike.

'Oh, Christ!' whispered the production secretary, 'all this fucking foreplay.'

'Remind Laurence of what I told him,' Harold told the floor manager.

'Will do, Harold. All right, everyone, silence on the floor, if you please. I can still hear somebody talking. Quiet, please! OK. Forty-seven, take five. Action.'

Laurence pushed his way through the door and into the set of his horrendously decorated living room, just as a cry and a loud splashing sound came from beyond the partly opened French windows. The actress playing his wife, hair and body freshly sprayed by make-up, ran into the room, a towel clutched to her micro-bikini.

'Oh my God!' she screamed.

Another splash and her toy-boy lover was right behind her, looking concerned, looking beautiful in an obvious kind of way, looking hungrily for the camera.

'So this is what I splashed out all that money for, is it?' emoted Laurence. 'So that you could turn our home into some suburban Sodom and Gomorrah!'

'You've got it all wrong,' pleaded his wife. He had, she thought, desperately struggling to improvise a reply. There was nothing about Sodom and Gomorrah in the sodding script!

156

Upstairs, Harold Roy let out a constricted cry of anguish.

Robert Deleval pounded both hands against the glass.

'Now I can see at last what a petty bourgeoise little Whore of Babylon you've always been!' roared Laurence, declaiming in a style that would have taken the RSC back at least a decade.

'Oh, Christ,' moaned Harold, 'he's giving us his Othello.'

'Strumpet!' howled Laurence, flinging out an arm and tearing away the top half of the bewildered actress's bikini.

'Cut!'

'Shit!'

'Bastard!'

'Bitch!'

Harold's head slammed forward hard against the end of his microphone; not once, but twice. Diane Woolf closed her eyes; the production secretary held her breath.

Suddenly Mackenzie was there in the control room, face shining. 'Fine, Harold. Terrific job. You really did the business this time.'

Harold swivelled his chair, propelled himself to his feet and punched Mackenzie smack in the mouth.

'You know,' said Maria. 'Harold and I never do this.'

'Never?'

'Nuh-uh.'

'Never now or not ever?'

'Once, maybe. A long time ago. Even then it was a mistake.'

'How come?'

'He was out of his head and lost his footing. Fell in.'

Grabianski laughed. He had, Maria thought and not for the first time, a wonderful laugh. Loud and open, like a man who isn't afraid to let go. So different to Harold in this as in all other things. Whatever her Harold was about, it wasn't letting go. A shelf or more in the medicine cabinet stacked with laxatives, and still he was as constipated as a church mouse.

'Poor fool doesn't know what he's missing,' said Grabianski, scooping almond-scented lather into his hands and sliding them between Maria's arms and over her breasts.

'I know.' Maria leaned back against him, twisting her neck until she could kiss him. Grabianski's legs were wrapped around her, knees above her knees, calves resting inside her own. Oh God, tongue in his mouth, she could feel him stiffening again against her buttocks. His age, how did he do it?

'Maria,' he said gently.

'I know.'

'Harold – is he going to say what we want him to say?'

She pulled her head clear until they were both facing the taps. 'What else?'

'I don't know.'

'What then?'

'Sometimes, when they're pushed into a corner, men'll do strange things.'

'Harold?' Maria scoffed, laughing.

Grabianski loved the way her hair clung dark to the nape of her neck; he loved having his arms, his legs, full of this woman.

'When's he meeting this dealer?'

'I told you, I don't know. For sure. Tonight, some time. After the studio. It must be.' She leaned forward just far enough to allow her hand to slip back between them. 'Don't worry. You're not worried about it, are you?'

'No,' Grabianski shook his head. Honestly, there was no reason for him to worry, little enough.

'You think the water's starting to get cold?' Maria asked.

'A little.'

'Maybe we should move back to the bed?'

'In a few minutes,' said Grabianski. 'In a while. Relax.'

Mackenzie had still been stemming the blood from his split lip when Harold Roy drove his Citroën out of the car park at a speed that made the wheels spin. The production secretary was gently applying a plaster to the cut as Harold overtook a brewery lorry and then swung in front of it and almost immediately skidded left into his own road. 'Listen,' Mackenzie said into the telephone, 'that solicitor we use, give me his name and number.' The Citroën came to a halt half on the gravel, half on the grass.

'What was that?' asked Grabianski.

Maria, facing him now, straddled above him, head thrown back, failed to reply.

It was only with the slam of the front door that Grabianski was certain.

'Maria! Up!'

'Yes!' yelled Maria. 'Oh, yes!'

A voice rose like a muffled echo from below and then there were footsteps hurrying up the stairs.

'Maria?'

Grabianski seized hold of her arms and held her as he levered himself backwards, leaving her to splash through the lukewarm water as he pushed himself to his feet and swung one leg over her astonished head, jumping from the bath as fast as he was able.

'Who . . .?' gasped Harold, clinging to the handle of the bathroom door. 'Who the fuck are you?'

He was staring at a naked man, a few sad bubbles of foam hanging desolately from his erection. Behind him his wife was trying to submerge herself below the level of the water.

Harold wasn't tempted to have any truck with Sodom or Gomorrah, never mind Babylon. 'Go to it, you bitch!' he encouraged. 'Drown your fucking self!'

'Harold Roy,' said Grabianski, extending a soapy hand. 'Jerry Grabianski. Let's go outside,' he said, grabbing at a towel. 'We've got a lot to talk about.'

20

Resnick pushed pieces of paper around his desk: Grabianski's visits to the King's Court, burglaries following the same MO – there was no denying the overlap. A call to Milton Keynes had established that while the industrial estate Grabianski had given as a business address existed, there was no textile factory on the site, nobody had heard of any Grabianski.

Resnick laughed. Even now he couldn't be certain what it was that had alerted him. A man steps into a fight when he could easily turn away; not a tearaway, some youngster looking for a buzz. This was a man close to Resnick's age, choosing to go up against a violent gang and an axe and why? Because he liked the way the waitress had taken his order, brought his tea? Did Resnick believe that? *Ah, I've always been too much of a romantic.* And did it mean that any time a citizen did what the police encouraged citizens to do, their duty, they immediately came under suspicion? *Friends say it'll be my downfall.* No, it had been something about Grabianski's plausibility that had started a nerve somewhere beneath Resnick's skull tapping. A man so used to dancing on thin ice, he'd long since ceased to look down and see how black and cold the water was beneath, how close.

'Naylor!'

The young DC was sitting at the computer keyboard, worrying away at the inside of his lip with his teeth. He knew there was a way of getting from one file to another so as to transfer information between them, but he was damned if he could remember the command. Last night he'd taken home the manual intending to work his way through it, but last night had been no better than the rest.

'Naylor, are you wedded to that thing, or what?'

'Sorry, sir.' He executed the command for save and hurried towards the inspector's office.

'How's it going?' Resnick was back behind his desk, one leg crossed over the other.

'OK, sir.'

'Supposed to save us time, those things.'

'Oh they do, sir. No doubt about that. Just a matter of getting the hang of them.'

'Sergeant Millington, he's your man.'

'Yes, sir.'

'Took a course.'

Naylor nodded. He'd heard all about it in the canteen: the drinking, the lecturer from Stirling University, all five-syllable words and nancy gestures, the detective inspector who went knocking on a woman sergeant's door at two in the morning and found his superintendent had beaten him to it.

'Here.' Resnick pushed the first of his pieces of paper in Naylor's direction. 'This man. Grabianski. He was at the King's Court Hotel during the periods these' – another piece of paper – 'burglaries were committed.'

Naylor looked expectant.

'I've had him checked through CRO, nothing. When I interviewed him about something else altogether, he spoke of having a partner, a business partner. Implied they travelled together, but it doesn't look as if they stayed at the same hotel. According to Millington, this other man's name is Grice.'

Naylor groaned inwardly, seeing what was coming. 'Right, sir. So check all hotels and guest houses, those dates, any man booking in alone.'

'They arrived on the same dates, left on the same dates; this last time, they pulled out early, after three days.'

'Right, sir.' It was fine; a whole lot better than he'd feared. Naylor left and went back into the main office. He wondered whether he should phone Debbie and what the chances were that he'd catch her at the wrong moment, in the middle of changing the baby, mixing her feed, even – blissfully – sleeping. He sat back at the keyboard and pushed the disc into place; the odds of finding this particular needle in a haystack were more in his favour.

Strange, Resnick was thinking, waiting at the sandwich counter, the way bits and pieces drifted into your mind, no clear reason. What he was recalling then, an afternoon, would have been late fifties, he'd been pally with this lad, family had friends with a

161

place in the country. Rare back then, not a second home exactly, above an hour's drive from London, north-west. It had been a farm, the name on the gate still, Lower Brook Farm, white letters fading into greying wood that was mottled over with moss. God! He'd been shy then. A group of village girls, chalking on the wall beside the local shop, hanging from the ends of open gates. 'Charlie! C'm here, Charlie!' This time, walking down the lane alone, his friend off somewhere else, running errands, one girl had fallen into step beside him. Pat. Patricia. She was taller than him, looked older, but that didn't mean she was. 'Can you, you know, do it yet?' He could still remember how his ears had burned, how he had wanted to run away. Sitting on the chipped white railing round the bridge, she had leaned her face into his and kissed him; rested, so sparingly he still wondered if it had been true, her hand between his legs. 'Come on, then, Charlie,' she had laughed, mockingly. 'Half a crown over the hedge!'

'Sorry to keep you waiting,' said the young man behind the counter.

'That's OK.'

Resnick passed over a five-pound note and waited for his change. Brown bag in hand, he left the deli and cut back left, past a row of fireplaces stripped from torn-down houses and about to be rehabilitated into the homes of the tastefully well-to-do. Waiting for the lights to change at the main road, he saw Skelton, smart in track suit, blue-and-white Reeboks on his feet, jog down the station steps and begin his run away from the city, stride already beginning to lengthen.

In the lobby he recognized Mackenzie's face straight off, although it took him a few moments to remember where from. What was Harold Roy's producer doing there? Come to that, who had given him a thick lip?

'You might be better off going to central station,' the uniformed officer at reception was saying.

'I don't have time for that. This is the nearest to the studio. This is where I am. OK?'

'Everything all right?' Resnick asked, leaning his head towards the reinforced glass.

'This gentleman wishes to lodge a complaint, sir. Assault.'

'You were mugged?' Resnick said to Mackenzie.

The producer scowled. 'More like a dispute at his place of employment, sir,' said the officer.

'Not Harold Roy?' said Resnick.

Mackenzie assumed the expression of someone who'd been punched a second time, this one from behind. 'You know that bastard?'

'In a manner of speaking.'

'He's blown his marbles. Utterly. Punched me in the face in the middle of a perfectly normal conversation, not the least provocation, and then walks out of the studio in the middle of a scene. I'm telling you, that man wants psychiatric help; that man needs hospitalization; that man needs locking up.'

'Carry on,' said Resnick to the officer. 'You might let me see a copy when you're through.'

He hadn't got his sandwich out from its white waxed paper before Millington was knocking on his door. 'Don't let me interrupt you, sir.'

Resnick had no such intention. Millington watched the inspector push several wayward slices of dill pickle back between the salad and the chopped liver before taking the first bite.

'Graham?'

'That Olds woman, sir, never thought I'd be grateful to have her around.' Resnick knew the feeling. 'Don't know how she's done it, but somehow Chao and his lad are in there shaking hands, lot of bowing and smiling, sorry things became a little heated, so sorry. Like the end of a Charlie Chan movie, sir.'

Quite often, when Millington had been on early shift, he had found himself sitting down with one or other of his kids, eating crisps while they drank tea and watched the late afternoon film on TV. *Charlie Chan in the City of Darkness*, *Charlie Chan's Murder Cruise* (they'd seen that one at least twice), *Charlie Chan at the Wax Museum*. Twenty-seven of them there were, all told; his son had looked it up in the library down on Angel Row.

'No charges, Graham?'

'Only that bunch of yobos. Affray, aggravated assault, carrying a dangerous weapon with intent. He must have paid them a lot, cause they're not budging from their story.'

'Frustrating,' Resnick suggested.

163

'Not really, sir,' Millington shook his head. 'Glad to see the back of them.'

Resnick bit into his sandwich again and a blob of grey-brown chicken liver landed on his blotter. If I ate like that, Millington thought, the wife would make me sit out in the garage.

'This man Grice,' Resnick said.

'The one from the restaurant? Grabianski's mate.'

'Didn't get involved in the fighting, did he?'

'Didn't even hold his coat.'

'Careful, then?'

'More than that, sir, now you mention it. More – cagey, I'd say.'

Resnick was regretting not bringing back a slice of treacle tart. Sugar highs might be artificial, but when you were still eating your lunch and it was tea-time, anything that did the trick was a bonus.

'You haven't forgotten Fossey, Graham?'

'Tomorrow, sir. Now this other business is sorted.'

Resnick nodded dismissively; Millington turned to go. 'Let's see about pulling Lynn out of the shopping centre, shall we? Aside from what it's likely doing to her mind, she hangs around there much longer she's going to be spotted for what she is.'

'OK, sir.'

The door had hardly closed when the phone rang. Picking it up, Resnick thought, damn, it's Jeff Harrison, why haven't I taken him up on that drink? But the accent was from the other side of the world.

'It isn't exactly good news, I'm afraid,' said Claire Millinder.

Resnick made a face and listened.

'I nearly, so very nearly, came close to a sale this morning. That family I told you about. Loved the size of the rooms, the garden, everything.'

'What didn't they like?'

'It was on the wrong side of the city.'

'Jesus, what are the buses for? Haven't they got a car?'

'Schools, that's the thing. One kid in secondary, another in the last year of primary, little girl about to graduate from the infants come September. Not that she's got anything against ethnic minorities, the mother said, but if her sweetheart was outnumbered by Asians eight to one, what sort of a start was she going to get?'

'I hope you told her,' Resnick said with more than a trace of anger.

'I smiled my nice professional smile and told her, should they reconsider, be sure to call me.'

'But she won't.'

A pause. 'No.'

Resnick glanced at his watch. 'OK. Thanks for keeping me in the picture.'

'No problem. Look . . . it may be nothing, I mean, you may not like it, but I've got this idea.'

'About the house.'

'Of course.'

'Go ahead.'

'See, I'd rather talk to you about it, you know, face to face so to speak.'

Resnick didn't say a thing.

'You're not in this evening, I suppose?'

Charlie. Oh, Charlie! 'Yes,' he said, 'later.'

'Around nine?'

'Fine.'

'Great. Red or white? I'll bring a bottle.'

'I thought this was . . .'

'Some propositions, they're best made when you're not quite sober.'

'Look . . .'

'Joke. Joke. Hey, I was joking, OK?'

'Yes. Sure.'

'But I will bring the wine. It's good to unwind after a long day, don't you think?'

When Lynn Kellogg finally got back to the station and wrote up her report of another largely wasted day, her stomach was beginning to send warning signals that must have been audible twenty yards away.

She was halfway along the canteen queue when she noticed Kevin Naylor. He was sitting at a corner table, close against the far wall. He was slumped well forward, one arm hanging down towards the floor; his face was in his bread and butter and a lock of his hair curling into his soup.

165

21

Lynn Kellogg's flat was in the old Lace Market area of the city: finely proportioned Victorian factories built by philanthropic entrepreneurs who thoughtfully provided chapels on the premises. A little uplift for the soul before a sixteen-hour day. Most of these tall brick buildings were still in existence and were gradually being restored, at least to a state of better repair. There were also a number of car parks and, angled between three of these, the housing-association development where Lynn lived.

She led Naylor across the interior courtyard and up the stairs towards the first floor. The post inside the door was the usual collection of unwanted solicitations, glossy offers to lend her money; the usual letter from her mother, Thetford postmark, Tuesdays and Thursdays, the days she went shopping.

'Take off your coat, Kevin. I'll put the kettle on.'

The living room was small, not poky, a haven for pot plants and paperback books left face down and open, a uniform shirt and a towel draped over the radiator.

'Tea or coffee?'

'Whatever's easiest.'

'Kevin.'

'Tea.'

'Coffee might keep you awake better.'

'OK, then. Coffee.'

By the time she carried the mugs through from the kitchen, he was keeled over in the high-backed armchair she had bought at the auction by Sneinton Market, asleep.

The best part of an hour to fill, Harold Roy had wandered into a wine bar in Hockley. All he knew was that he wanted somewhere quiet to sit, a couple more drinks, something, maybe, to eat; think things through. What he was going to say.

It wasn't the place.

The lighting was right, subdued enough to give the table

candles relevance; neither was it crowded. But the music was amplified to the point of rendering conversation difficult, meditation impossible. He made a brief pretence of looking for somebody who wasn't there and left. In – what? – he checked his watch – fifty minutes now he would be face to face with Alan Stafford.

'Look, Alan, Alan, the way I see it is this . . .'

He went into a corner pub, ordered a large vodka and tonic, yes, thanks, ice and lemon (there didn't seem to be any point in asking for fresh lime), and sat on a long bench-seat towards the fire. There was a smattering of other drinkers, a few kids who looked like they might be students, a man in a brown three-piece suit talking earnestly to somebody else's wife, a dog roaming from table to table in search of crisps. Retriever, labrador, he could never tell the difference.

His first reactions to Maria's infidelity had been expected and unthinking: anger, disillusion, shock, rage. Hours later he was beginning to see it in a different light. After all, if someone else wanted to get his jollies humping that tired old body, where did that leave him except off that particular hook? And what was so great about what they had going for them that it was worth keeping together, even regretting? The way to go, the light at the end of what had seemed an infinitesimally long tunnel, let him take her off his hands, see what waking up with the back of that pushed up against you every morning did for romance. Let him. This guy. This Grabianski.

Extraordinary.

Extraordinary fellow.

Like his suggestion about what Harold now realized was a mutual problem. Knowing that, somehow, made Harold feel stronger; gave him a sense of, almost, solidarity. He'd been worried about meeting Stafford, afraid the whole situation might turn against him, turn nasty. Whatever else, Harold hadn't forgotten the knife that had been in Stafford's hand. But, as Grabianski had pointed out, when it came down to it, what Alan Stafford was was a businessman. And this was business. Nothing personal. Business.

He looked at his glass, surprised to find it empty.

On the way back to the bar he stooped down and patted the

dog. He hadn't as much as stroked a cat since he didn't know when. He was feeling good: liberated. He bought another large vodka and a packet of cheese-and-onion crisps to share with his new-found friend.

Lynn couldn't put it off any longer. Kevin was still sleeping and she had already ironed her shirt, sorted through the next day's washing, cleaned the top of the gas cooker, dusted – what was she doing? – the spaces on the kitchen shelves. *Dear Lynnie*, it would start, *the last thing I want to do is moan, it isn't as though you haven't enough on your own plate, I realize that . . .*

But . . .

But since her aunt had moved to Diss, it wasn't as though there was anyone close she could talk to; since that last time at the doctor's nothing she did or took seemed to rid her of those pains at the top of her head which came and went, *some of them, Lynnie, love, like a red-hot poker pressing against the inside of my skull, you wouldn't believe*, and there wasn't anything she could do other than go and sit in the dark until they were over.

Lynn used the handle of a spoon to tear along the top of the envelope, her mother's less-than-steady writing, blue Bic biro on Woolworth paper.

Dear Lynnie . . .

She cast a glance at Kevin Naylor, possibly the longest undisturbed sleep he'd had in weeks. It was, she realized, the first time a man had been in her flat since the one she had lived with had up and pedalled away. Somewhere in the back of a drawer there was a puncture outfit he'd left in his haste and which she had been meaning to throw out with the rubbish, but somehow had failed to get round to.

Lynnie, it's your father. Ever since he had to slaughter all those birds, the whole twelve hundred . . .

She could picture him, a brittle-boned man in a plastic raincoat and wellington boots, back and forth between hen houses, pushing at the ground with his stick.

Christ, Kevin! she thought, wake up!

Harold Roy was feeling so good he was late for his appointment. Negotiating his way to the rendezvous as Alan Stafford had described, his head swam with ideas of liberation. Fuck the business! Fuck Maria! (Well, no, let Grabianski do that – him being so great at it anyhow.) He would invest his money in something solid, buy a cottage in the Forest of Dean, write a book, maybe; get a dog.

'Where the hell have you been?'

'Hey!' Harold waved his hands around in a display of intemperate good humour. 'What's a little time between friends?'

'Are you drunk?' Stafford glowered.

'Merry.' Harold pulled his chair closer. Another pub, out-of-date enough to advertise a public bar. There was music, but it was quieter, older. Harold thought he recognized Neil Sedaka. The radio was tuned to Gem–AM. 'That's what I am, merry.'

'You're fucking drunk.'

'No, no. Not at all.' He poked a finger towards Stafford's glass. 'What'll it be?'

Stafford straight-armed himself back from the table. They were alone in the bar. He had to hold himself back from punching out at the ludicrous, grinning face in front of him.

'Lager?' asked Harold, lifting Stafford's glass.

'Forget it.'

Harold was rising to his feet. 'I'll have a vodka.'

'Like hell you will!' Stafford hauled him back down, his face jammed smack up against Harold's, the bitter odour of those paper-thin cigarettes that he rolled. Pipe tobacco.

'You're supposed to have things to tell me. Business we've got to sort out.'

'That's right,' Harold beamed. 'Just let me . . .'

Stafford dragged him back a second time. 'You make a move towards that bar once more . . .'

'OK, OK. You want to get them that badly, go ahead. Large vodka tonic. Ice and lemon.'

It was like stepping into the London Dungeon and discovering you were in Disneyland. Stafford got up and called the barman through from the lounge: vodka and a pint of lager. Jesus! This had better be good.

'Is that . . .?' Harold began, uncertainly.

'What?'

169

'Is that . . .'

'Is that what?'

'Is that Connie Francis or Brenda Lee?'

In the end she had to nudge him gently, wait while he stretched and yawned then stretched some more, embarrassed. Twenty-what? Five going on seventeen? She put a mug into his hands and he was surprised it was still warm.

'I thought I'd been asleep for longer.'

'You had. I poured the first lot away and made fresh.'

'How long . . .?' He looked at the time and sat bolt upright. 'Debbie, she'll . . .'

'It's all right.' Her hand across his arm, easing him back. 'I called her.'

Naylor's eyes moved around the small room, startled. What on earth was Debbie going to be thinking? If ever he was going to be late off shift he always made a point of letting her know. And that was only work, duty; whereas this . . .

'Don't worry. She doesn't think we're having an affair.' Said it without thinking she would or should; one of those phrases that jumps from your mouth unbidden, a soap-opera cliché. *Neighbours*. *EastEnders*. What kids watched with their tea where ten, fifteen years back it would have been making a life-sized model of the *Titanic* from cornflake packets, how to adopt a tree in the Kalahari Desert.

Naylor was on his feet, mug between both hands, his eyes still restless.

'Kevin.' She took the mug from him, the soft outside of her hand, there below the littlest finger, brushing his knuckles. Had she meant that and, anyway, what did intention have to do with this? 'Kevin, I told her you fell asleep in your tomato soup. I wouldn't have rung to say you'd fallen asleep again here if there was anything she might suspect.'

Except that you might, Lynn thought; if you were clever enough, if anything had happened, that might just about have covered it.

'I'd better call her,' he said, turning towards the phone.

Her hand again, stopping him; the second time. He was losing what colour he had from his face. 'Don't you want to talk?' she said.

Naylor reached out his hand. 'Yes,' he said. 'Another time.'

'Let me get this straight, Harold.' What was he doing? An hour here, watching this media-type in poncey clothes down vodka like it was going out of style; listening to him, taking him seriously for God's sake, and now calling him Harold. Like they were friends, or something. Partners. What did he think he was doing? He knew what he was doing. Waiting to find the best way of getting his hands back around a kilo of cocaine. The real thing. Serve him right for thinking stupid in the first place. Look, Harold — no, he hadn't called him that, not back then; he was just another over-age yuppie who'd started in because it was smart, because if it was that expensive, well, it had to be good. Dipped his nose a little too far a little too often and got hooked. Look, Stafford had said, I've got this problem, why don't you earn yourself a bonus, help me out, keep the supply flowing? Free-market economy, that's what we're all in favour of, isn't it? Crest of the wave we're all riding home on.

And he had handed Harold the bundle and said keep it safe.

Now he was getting a lot of pressure from people to deliver, pressure to come up with more cash, keep his end of several bargains, ripples that were noticed way back down the line.

You don't stay in there, Alan, a lot of other guys watching for the break. Not only them. Already he'd had to move his stash, switch his place of operations. Three times in as many weeks. Two steps ahead of the drug squad, one wasn't enough.

'Harold . . .'

'Hum?'

'What you're saying is this. The package I left with you for safe-keeping was ripped off and now the guy who ripped it off wants to meet with me and sell it back.'

'At a discount.'

'You don't say!'

'Two-thirds of what it's worth.'

'Two-thirds, shit!'

'How much then?'

'Ten thousand.'

Harold laughed in Stafford's face; actually, it was more of a giggle. In the background Dion was singing about being a lonely teenager in love. Was that with or without the Belmonts? Harold could never remember.

'Twelve.'

'I have it on good authority,' Harold said pompously, 'this merchandise is worth exactly double that.'

'Keep your voice down.'

'Sorry.' Quietly, 'Double that.'

'Maybe that's what it's worth to me. Maybe. To you and this dickhead friend, it's worth nothing but a serious spell behind bars.'

'Aha,' said Harold, 'you're trying to frighten me.'

I'd like to take you outside and kick the shit out of you, Stafford thought. 'Fourteen thousand,' he said. 'That's it. Beginning and end.'

'Fifteen.'

Alan Stafford snapped shut his tobacco tin, drew on his cigarette. 'Bye, Harold,' he said, beginning to walk away.

'All right.'

'All right what?' Turning back, but taking his time about it.

'What you said. Fourteen.'

Stafford sat back down. 'Couple of days. I'll need that to raise the money. I'll phone you.'

'No,' said Harold hastily.

'What d'you expect me to do? Advertise?'

'It's just that . . .'

'What?'

Harold had a hazy idea that he might not be around that long. Hell, he'd have to be. Sitting downstairs waiting for the phone to ring while Maria and her Polish burglar were up above humping.

'Phone me,' he said.

'That's what I said I'd do.'

'Two days?'

'Somewhere around there.'

'You want another drink?'

'No,' from close to the door, 'I don't want another drink, Harold.'

* * *

Fine, who cares? Buy myself a drink. Vodka. That's the stuff. He wished he had some of that kilo back in the bedroom, but that had gone. He laughed. Stolen. What was lost has now been found: rejoice! 'Hey,' he said to the barman, 'you know the parable of the prodigal kilo?'

'Vodka?' asked the barman.

Harold nodded, pushed across another five-pound note. 'Great music,' he said.

'Gets on my tits,' said the barman.

Harold shrugged and stood there at the bar, leaning against it, alone and thinking about what kind of dog he might choose. Had that been Patti Page or Lita Roza? He never could decide.

22

Lennie Lawrence had been born in St Anne's. Before the buggers knocked it all down and modernized the guts out of the place. Resnick had never quite grasped what was so wrong about giving folk bathrooms, indoor toilets; besides, buying a detached house in Wollaton didn't smack of a hankering for the good old days of back-to-backs.

'What's your interest in this assault then, Charlie? Not desperate to break into the media, are you? Television pundit.'

'Harold Roy,' said Resnick. 'I'd like a chance to have another crack at him. Something fishy about a burglary out at his place. Wife's statement, it didn't gel.'

'Out to rook the insurance, are they?'

Resnick shrugged. It was one of several possibilities, though it didn't explain Maria Roy's blatant misidentification.

'Good luck to 'em, eh, Charlie?'

'Maybe, sir.'

'God, you're a cautious bugger! Never mind you've this reputation for setting your track the wrong road up one-way streets, you don't like to put yourself closer to the wind than the rest of us. Not where rules are concerned; regulations, right and wrong. Bit of a bloody puritan, that's you, Charlie Resnick.'

'Maybe, sir.'

'Maybe, sir.' Lennie Lawrence mimicked him. 'Not a man to give a lot away, either, are you?'

'Is it all right, then, this complaint? Can we handle it? Keep your lads in the picture.'

'You better, Charlie.'

'Yes, sir.'

Resnick was at the chief inspector's door when Lawrence called him back. 'The old man . . .'

'Skelton?'

'Any idea what's getting his bollocks knotted?'

Resnick shook his head. 'No, sir.'

'Lost his temper the other morning. Nothing in particular. Just went. Not like him at all. Most likely male – what d'you call it? – menopause. Hot flushes. All right, Charlie. Keep me posted.'

'Sir.'

Resnick walked past the door to Jack Skelton's office, half wondering whether he should knock, ask the superintendent what was the matter. He didn't, of course; would have been too much like going up to the Queen at one of her garden parties and making a polite inquiry about the state of her bowels.

The Midlands minibus was parked across the street, between two of the regulation plane trees that rose slowly up the hill, curving to the right. Alf Levin saw Resnick's approach in his wing mirror, stubbed out his cigarette and tossed it towards the gutter.

'Known worse weather in May,' he said, coming diagonally towards the gate.

Dizzy was parading his backside up and down the stone wall, making imperious noises.

'Selling up, then?' Alf Levin gestured towards the sign.

'Trying.'

'Talking to this bloke back at the studio. Come up from Elstree when they closed it down. Like a lot of them, he bought this place out in Lincolnshire. Small village, like. Couldn't believe it at the time, how cheap it was. Wouldn't have got a kennel, back south. Anyway, right pissed off he's got with living out there. Local pub doesn't do a decent drop of bitter and when the wind's in the east there's not a lot between him and Siberia. Old lady and electric blanket, you're still cold at nights. Even this weather.'

'Is there a point to this, Alfie?'

'Only that he's had it on the market eighteen months. Can't shift it, love nor money.'

'Thanks. You've made a good day feel a lot better.'

Levin lit another cigarette, automatically cupping it inside his hand after the first drag. 'This might, Mr Resnick.'

Resnick eased the end of his forefinger through the short fur behind Dizzy's ear and waited.

'It's not that I've changed my mind, grassing. Not that I know anything you'd want, break-ins. Anyone who might be on a bit of work, I know less about it than you lot.'

175

'What is it then, Alfie?'

'That feller you was interested in, the one hanging around.'

'Thin on top. You didn't care for his footwear.'

'Name's Stafford. Drugs, that's his mark. And not just the funny cigarettes.'

'You're sure?'

'God is my witness.'

'You wouldn't like to . . .'

'No, Mr Resnick. I never said nothing, never saw you. Haul me up in court and I'll play stum. But that sort of thing, the thought of him, the Lord knows what it leads to, needles, all this HIV business. Locking away, that's what he wants.'

Dizzy jumped down impatiently and headed for the front door.

'I owe you, Alfie.'

Levin shook his head.

'Cup of tea, at least.'

Alf Levin looked towards the house. 'Some other time, Mr Resnick. Studio canteen. Not here.' He edged away, shoulders hunched. 'Don't mind me asking, you married?'

'Not any more.'

'Just you, eh.' He glanced again at the house. 'Must rattle around in there like a pea in a drum.'

'Thanks, Alfie.'

'Nothing of it.'

Resnick was already thinking about Norman Mann, the sergeant he knew with the local drug squad: wondering if he had Mann's number, if it was unlisted or whether it would be in the book?

Don't mind me asking . . .

For some moments, no longer than it took him to lay three slices of smoked ham across toasted bread, mustard, slivers of Jarlsberg cheese, Resnick regretted that he had torn up his wife's letter, his ex-wife's letter, he still assumed it to have been hers, before reading it.

. . . you married?

If he moved from here, where would he go? Somewhere her letters wouldn't find him. Not that they were many. The first, this, in several years. Before that there had been three, close together. One threatening to take him to court for more money; another apologizing, claiming a bout of nerves, despondency, a job that had been pulled out from under her – sorry, Charlie, I won't bother you again. A gap of three months before she sent an oddly distant description of the house she shared with her estate-agent husband, views of Snowdon through the upstairs bedroom window. As if she were writing to a second cousin once removed. Resnick had no sense of why she had sent that, what she had been thinking. That they might, perhaps, be absent friends, nods and glances across a hundred and more miles by courtesy of the postal services. Whatever her reasons, they had not been followed through. Years was a long time between letters, even for absent friends.

Not any more.

There were two signs Resnick had grown to recognize, markers of his mood: one when he couldn't drink coffee, the other, when his fingers ran back and forth along the spines of his record collection without pulling anything out.

A man who is sick of jazz is sick of life. Has somebody said that? And if they had, would that make it any more or less true? Charlie, he said to himself, I don't like you so much when you're like this.

He found Norman Mann's number and left a message asking that the detective call him back. Ground some coffee anyway, Colombian dark, and sat while it dripped through the machine, Miles and Bud curled on his lap, eating the last half of his sandwich. When the doorbell rang he had almost forgotten about Claire Millinder, her self-invitation to call.

'I took a chance on the red.' She was standing just a little way back from the door, a smile brightening her face and a long wool coat, dark blue, open over a short black skirt, broad striped tights. The top was beige, loose around the softness of her shoulders; except that she didn't seem the type, she could have knitted it herself. 'I tried to find some New Zealand' – walking past him into the broad hallway – 'but I had to settle for this. Murray Valley. Aussie Shiraz.' She swivelled to face him. 'It's not plonk. Good stuff.' Now she was holding the bottle out towards him. 'I've been keeping it warm on the journey.'

177

Resnick accepted it from her; at the door through into the kitchen, he stood aside to let her by. There was a high flush to her cheeks, a definite shine to her eyes; her shoulder brushed him as she passed.

'Good day?' Claire squatted close to the floor, stroking the diminutive Bud. It was difficult for Resnick not to look up her skirt.

'So-so.'

'Tired, I'll bet?'

Resnick didn't answer. He uncorked the bottle and set it down; there was some etiquette about waiting for it to breathe, but he had never been certain for how long or why.

'You're not a wine drinker, are you?'

'I've got a corkscrew.'

'I've got a tennis racket, but I'm not going to make Wimbledon.' Bud scampered away from her feet as she moved. 'What I meant was,' glancing at his waistline, 'I see you as more of a beer drinker.'

'D'you want to leave this for a while?'

Claire smiled, her mouth broadening with amusement, 'Now would be just about fine.'

He sat and cradled the glass between his fingers, watching her as she toured slowly around the room. The records, his books; haphazard, a pile of local newspapers waiting to be thrown out; the absence of anything hanging from his walls.

'You've no pictures of her, have you?'

'Who?'

'Whoever you bought this house with. Your wife.'

'You said something about a proposition.'

'That could mean,' she went on, choosing to ignore his interruption, 'remembering still hurts. Either that or you've wiped her from your mind. Altogether.' She looked at him, sitting there, uneasy in the easy chair, doubting now why she'd come, the wisdom of an hour spent in a wine bar first, knowing that brashness was never what would attract him, turn him on. But when the recklessness was there, what did you do to calm it down?

'How about some music?' She sat opposite him, perching herself on the arm of the settee, tasting the wine.

'What do you fancy?'

'You choose.'

When last he had been in this situation, with Rachel, it had been easy; he had known what it seemed important for her to hear, wanted to impress her with songs that would send their own little messages like trip hammers along the vein.

Claire watched him stooping forward, hesitant; imagined, for a moment, getting up and standing close behind him, hands pressing hard against those shoulders, faint scrape of the day's stubble as his face glanced against hers.

The stylus settled on to Ellington, 'Jack the Bear', 1940. Clipped phrases from the muted brass with their high reed responses. Jimmy Blanton's bass carrying the melody into the first rocking notes from the piano.

'Charlie,' Claire said. 'Is that what they call you?'

'Some of them.'

'It's an old-fashioned sort of name, don't you think?'

'Maybe it is.'

'I like it. Sort of makes you approachable.'

Resnick drank some wine, trying not to swallow it down as if it were Czech Budweiser, Guinness in the pub. It seemed hours since he had eaten that sandwich, probably was. There she was, this attractive young woman, right across from him, bored with what she was doing day-to-day, the people, the men that ordinarily she met. Your British policemen, they're wonderful. No: you didn't hear that any more, only in the reruns of old movies, between the snooker and the racing on slow afternoons. Still, there was something about what he did; the way, maybe, it merged with the illicit, illegal, somewhere one step over the line.

She was pretty, Claire Millinder, attractive and knowing it didn't spoil her. You got the sense she dressed to please herself and if that didn't suit, too bad. She was confident, a brashness about her that, almost reluctantly, Resnick admired. Why couldn't all that be enough?

She was saying something now about growing up on a farm back on North Island, the beaches, playing possum. The wine

179

was going down the glass too fast, going to Resnick's head. But when she approached him with the bottle he let her pour more.

'I'm sorry I haven't been able to find a buyer for your house.'

'That's all right.' She was sitting on the side of his chair, the wine bottle at her feet. 'I'm sure you've tried your best.'

'I have.'

Her fingers laid along the ridge of his upper arm, close against his neck. As he angled his face towards hers, the ends of her nails touched his cheek.

'D'you know why you're such an attractive man, Charlie? Because I don't.'

'Then maybe I'm not.'

She grinned. 'I think that's it. You're not.'

Her tongue slithered either way along his teeth before exploring his mouth, warm and never still. The insides of her lips were soft and, of course, she tasted of the wine. What was it? Black currant? His hand found her breast by accident and jumped away as if shocked.

'Charlie, I can't kiss you and laugh at the same time.'

'Which would you rather do?'

Johnny Hodges was insinuating his way through Ellington's 'Warm Valley'. As they slid to the floor, Claire managed to kick clear her shoes and catch the over-balancing remains of the Shiraz at about the same time. Whatever was gently tickling her toes was probably one of the cats. Resnick rocked on to his side, not wishing to pinion her with his weight. 'Ko-Ko' and the brass and saxes were back into their exchanges, call and response, come and then go. Claire's fingers unbuttoned his shirt. 'As your estate agent,' she said, 'I think a viewing of the master bedroom is pretty essential.'

Resnick rolled away.

'Don't,' Claire said.

'What?'

'Sigh. You were about to give out with that great, heavy sigh, and then close your eyes, shake your head a bit. You know? It isn't necessary. It's OK.' She was on her feet, smoothing down her skirt, straightening the stripes of her tights. 'It's happened before.' She grinned. 'Just not that often.'

180

Resnick felt stupid sitting on the floor of his own living room, cross-legged.

She reached out a hand and helped him to his feet.

'What does it have to be with you, Charlie? True love?'

Embarrassed, he looked away. 'Probably.'

'Oh, Charlie!' She squeezed his arm, prodded his stomach, quickly kissed the side of his neck. 'Come on,' she said, dragging him back towards the kitchen. 'I'm feeling famished and you're going to have to come up with something, if it's only Rice Krispies. Besides, if we finish that bottle on an empty stomach, we're going to be falling asleep in one another's company and that would never do.'

'Is this all you ever eat?' Claire said, looking at her plate. 'Sandwiches?'

'Most often.'

'But you're not having one now?'

'I've already eaten.'

'One of these?'

'Something like.'

'Then I can understand why you're not up for another.'

'You don't like it?'

'Oh, it's great. I just won't want to eat for another week, that's all.'

'We still didn't get round to your proposition,' said Resnick. 'At least, I don't think we did.'

Claire laughed and waited until she had chewed her way to speech. 'What we've been doing, properties that have got badly stuck – not that I'm saying that's the position here, not yet, far from it – but what we've been discussing with owners is the possibility of a short let. Three months, six at most. It means there's some income coming in, part of the deal is that we can still show clients round. If people have already found somewhere else to move on to, sometimes they have to on account of their job, whatever, it suits all round.'

'I think I can hang on here.'

'Like I said, I'm not talking right now. Just thinking, if nobody's nibbled by spring . . .'

'And if I happen to find the bachelor flat of my dreams . . .'

'Precisely.'

'I don't know.'

'There'd be safeguards.'

'I don't know if I'd be happy about strangers . . .'

'Charlie, who did you think you were going to sell the place to? Friends?'

'Selling and letting, they're not the same. Suppose it just didn't sell . . .'

'Not ever?'

'Not ever.'

'You can sell everything, sooner or later.'

'But if I moved out and then for whatever reason had to move back . . .'

'Charlie,' Coming up to him, close, but nothing sexual now; physical, yes, but different, that passion had evaporated. 'You don't want to move, do you? This is your house; you're at home here.'

His eyes were focused past her head, seeing other things. 'Maybe that's the problem.'

She kissed him deftly on the cheek and stepped back. 'Are we friends, Charlie Resnick?'

Now he was the one smiling. 'Maybe.'

'Charlie,' she said with mock sternness, 'we're not talking major commitment here.'

'Look,' Resnick said, 'now that wine's gone, I've got a couple of beers in the fridge.'

Back in the main room he played her Mose Alison, Ben Webster with Art Tatum; early, carefree Lester Young. She told him about waitressing her way through university, summers picking kiwi fruit before that crop became cheaper to grow elsewhere. Resnick listened, nodded, asked questions here and there; all the time, pecking at the back of his mind, something she had said earlier.

'Claire.'

'Yes?' She looked up at him, curling her lower lip against the tip of her tongue. The tall beer glass was balanced between the fingers of both hands. That was the moment at which he could have moved towards her, kissed her on the mouth.

'The kind of rental you were talking about before,' Resnick

said, 'you wouldn't have set one up for someone called Grabianski?'

'Male or female?'

'Male.'

She shook her head. 'It's not such a usual name. I'd have remembered.'

If Grabianski had moved out of his hotel, Resnick thought, he might have had reason enough to use a pseudonym. He tried describing him to Claire instead.

'He sounds a lot like you,' Claire said.

'You haven't seen him?'

Smiling, she held her head to one side. 'I'd have remembered,' she said.

When the record came to an end, she finished her beer and got to her feet. 'I should go,' she said.

At the door she paused, the hum of traffic rising along the Mansfield Road to her left. 'Some men,' she said, 'they can only see women as something to patronize or screw. With most of them it's both within the same five minutes. Ten, if you're lucky. You're not like that.'

Resnick wanted to say thank you, but didn't; he wasn't sure it was that simple.

'Good night, Charlie.'

'Night.'

I'll bet, Resnick was thinking, heading for the kitchen, we're still only checking the agencies that specialize in rented property; firms like Claire's, I doubt if we even gave them a call.

At the start of office hours the following morning, that was set right. The rental Resnick was interested in was a top-floor flat, unsold for too long and in this market unsaleable at a decent profit. The man who signed the lease had paid in cash, moved in right away, a short let exactly what he wanted, long enough to finish up his business, nothing more.

Of course, it hadn't been Grabianski who had seen about finding them alternative accommodation. It had been Grice, Trevor Grice, whose business address was in Milton Keynes.

23

Lloyd Fossey had grown up in a small mining town north of the city, in a street where four families out of five were known to the probation service, receiving social security or both. He had left school at sixteen, skirted around trouble, fallen for a girl who had talked him into enrolling for further education. The girl had soon gone, but the qualifications had stayed; Fossey had surprised everyone by getting a job and holding it down. He found – this lad who'd never spoken in the house for fear of his dad clouting him, who'd said little all through school lest he be mocked – that he had a way with words. Nothing too flash, never seeming – back then – too full of himself, Lloyd Fossey had discovered that people could be impressed by him; they trusted him. Most of them: at first meeting.

It was while working for his first security firm that Fossey had allowed his plausibility to run away with him. Little extras that were offered unofficially, private arrangements to make installations in his own time. It was all suggestions from the side of the mouth, money from the back of the hand. His employers suspected him of more than cowboy activity on the side – alarms, wiring, whole systems that had disappeared somehow found their way back on to the open market, into people's homes.

Fossey was sacked and the police called in. Graham Millington interviewed him on four separate occasions and each time he found Fossey more elusive than before. He knew all the answers, anticipated half of the questions; wore his best clothes and smoked ratty little cigars. His nose was too long, his cheeks had that sunken appearance that sometimes comes with poverty and never quite goes away.

Millington would have loved to have made him: for anything. More than the theft from his employer's, he wanted to tie him into that run of burglaries. If anyone was better placed to pass on information and expect to profit from it, the sergeant didn't know who was. But Fossey had continued to sit there in his expensive ill-fitting clothes, lighting one after another of those objectionable cigars. Where most suspects talked themselves into trouble, Fossey talked his interrogators into a stupor.

When Millington told him he could go, finally walk free, Fossey had shaken his hand and offered to fit his house with a burglar alarm at 40 per cent discount, estimates free of charge.

Now he was here in the kind of place Millington and his wife would only dream about after a Saturday-night bottle of Chianti and a cuddle in front of the TV.

'Lloyd Fossey?'

'Yes.'

'Remember me?'

One thing Fossey had learned from those paperbacks he'd read about succeeding in business, never forget a face. He offered his hand and a welcoming smile. 'Inspector.'

'Sergeant.'

'Sorry, thought you might have been promoted by now.'

Bastard, Millington thought.

'You're lucky to catch me,' Fossey said, 'only got back last night . . .'

'From your honeymoon. Yes, I know.'

Fossey's left eye twitched. What was going on here? 'Right now, I'm on my way to a client.' He glanced at his watch, pushing back the sleeve of his dark-blue blazer. 'Late as it is.'

'Phone.'

'Sorry?'

'Phone and tell him you'll be later still.'

'I can't do that, I . . .'

'Tell them the flight was delayed, jet lag, tell them something.'

'What is it, Lloyd?' The new Mrs Fossey was still rubbing sleep from her eyes and the remains of yesterday's eye-shadow along with it. She was wearing what was certainly Fossey's dressing-gown over what was probably one of his shirts. Millington wondered if he'd buy her some clothes of her own some day. Probably when she grew up. With that puppy fat still clinging to her, Millington didn't put her at much over eighteen; she made Fossey, who was all of twenty-five, look touched by age.

'Make us some coffee, love. This gentleman and I have got to have a chat.'

'It'll have to be instant, I can't work that machine.'

'It doesn't exactly need a degree in physics.'

'If it's as easy for you,' said Millington, 'I'd rather have tea.'

She gave him a thankful smile, pulled the dressing-gown closed and went off towards the kitchen. She'd learn, Millington thought, learn or leave him and most likely the latter.

Fossey left the sergeant in a room with a studded white-leather suite, black ash and glass tables and enough spotlights to stage a floodlit Scrabble tournament. In one corner there was a bar, stacked along which Millington counted five different malts and three brandies while Fossey was outside in the hall making a quick, apologetic phone call.

Millington waited for him to come back into the room and then sat facing him. The jacket looked as expensive as before, but now it fitted; the pale-grey trousers had creases only in the right places and his shoes looked as if they'd just come out of the box. To Millington, he was still a weasel; now he was a well-dressed one.

'Come on in the world,' he remarked, echoing his superior.

'What it's about, isn't it?'

'How d'you mean?'

'This country.'

'Is it?'

'All thanks to her, isn't it?'

Millington didn't think Fossey meant his young wife, coming into the lounge now with the tea-tray. She obviously did have clothes of her own – a pink-and-blue cotton top and tight white jeans – but that didn't prevent her from looking out of place in her own home.

'Thanks, love.'

There were three cups on the tray, but Fossey's tone made it clear that she was being dismissed. When she didn't quite close the door after her, he jumped up and pulled it to.

Millington started to pour and then stopped; it needed time to brew.

'So private enterprise really works?' Millington said.

'Course it does. How else would I have got all this? How else?' Fossey leaned back against the leather of the easy-chair. 'Ambition, that's all it needs; ambition, a bit of know-how, a lot of drive. Listen, any man' – he repeated it, hammering out the key words with two fingers in the palm of his hand – 'any man who wants to succeed in this country, can do it. And don't waste your breath telling me about unemployment and high interest rates, industries closing down, cause I don't want to know. Me, look at me. Ten – what? – fifteen years ago I'd've been out of school and down the pit like a whippet.' (Like a weasel, Millington thought.) 'Now they're shutting down those places 'cause they don't pay, throwing up nuclear power stations, putting money where it works, where it makes more money. Listen, anyone who wants to get started in business, they can do it. Start-up schemes, bank loans, Enterprise Allowance, the Prince's Trust, they're bloody throwing money at you and the trouble with all those moaning whingers is they'd rather sit round miserable and collect their dole than do something for themselves. Now, that's a fact.' He swung forward, elbows on knees. 'Right?'

'Rees Stanley,' said Millington, choosing not to look at Fossey directly, pouring his tea now it had stood long enough. 'Harold Roy.' No point in side-stepping with you, sunshine. A little something to go with your cuppa, sharper than sugar. Any luck, take his breath away, shut him up a few moments. Millington found himself wishing Fossey still smoked cigars.

By the time Millington had sat back, saucer balanced on one hand, cup in the other, Fossey still hadn't thought of the right answer.

Got you, you bugger!

'You advised them on security, burglar alarms, stuff like that.'

For the first time since the sergeant had knocked at the door, Fossey dropped eye contact.

'Don't get too worried,' said Millington, a smile in his voice. 'Not surprising you don't remember. All the business you must be turning over. Not to be expected.'

'No,' sighed Fossey, grasping at the straw. 'No, I suppose not.'

'It's why you keep records, after all.'

Lloyd Fossey set down his tea and stood close by the fireplace, before a gas fire with simulated coal and a variflame jet. Right then, it was burning low.

'I think you better come out with what you want.'

'I told you.'

'All you said, something about a . . .'

'A Rees Stanley, that's right. Harold Roy.'

'That doesn't tell me a thing.'

'Right. It's you supposed to be telling me.'

Fossey shook his head, moved on, this time towards the double-glazed windows. There were three cherry trees set into the downward slope of the garden and they were threatening to break into blossom. Still January: it was absurd.

'Confidential,' Fossey said.

Millington laughed.

'Clients invite me into their homes, they expect confidentiality . . .'

Millington moved his head from side to side, still smiling. When he got to his feet and started to walk towards Fossey he knew that, physically, he could intimidate him. Less than six foot, but square-shouldered and heavy-chested, all Millington had to do was to keep on track and, unless he jumped clear, Fossey would disappear backwards on to his lawn.

In the event, the sergeant stopped six inches short. He hoped Fossey's aftershave wasn't as expensive as everything else, because if it was he'd been duped. Or maybe it was only the familiar smell of rising sweat.

'Records,' said Millington smoothly. 'We were talking about records.'

'The office . . .'

'You don't have an office; you work from home.'

'In the city. I'm opening an office in the city.'

'That's not now, is it? Not yet.'

'Everything, all the files, they're in transit.'

'In a pig's ear!'

'Look . . .' He raised his hands, saw Millington's expression, lowered them again.

'Yes?'

'Why don't you let me get back to you? Before the end of the day. This, em, Stanley. The other feller. I'll check them through. Phone. You got my word.'

'Your word?'

'Yes.'

Millington's face made it clear he'd as soon Fossey offered him a contagious disease. He stepped far enough back to give Fossey room to move.

'Most of your business,' Millington said, as Fossey was on his way back to the safety of his armchair, 'where'd you say it comes from?'

'Advertising; Yellow Pages. Surprising the response from door-to-door shots.' He thought it was safe to go back to his tea. 'What most of it is, word of mouth, personal recommendation.'

'Except for the ones who get turned over.'

'Sorry?'

'But, then, they're not likely to be the ones that hire you anyway.'

'I don't see what you're getting at.'

'Of course you don't.'

'Look . . .'

'You said that before.'

'So?'

'What I want to look at, you won't show me.'

'I explained. I can't.'

'Course not. In transit. Temporarily.'

'It's not just that.'

'There's the whole issue of confidentiality.'

'It's all very well for you to make fun . . .'

'I'm not. No, I'm not. Professional man, professional help, like you say, privacy of their own homes. Puts you in a special position.'

'That's right.'

'Delicate.'

Fossey's hands were like moths against the sides of the chair, china of his cup, knife-edge crease of his pants.

'Makes you like a doctor, I suppose. Diagnosis. Confessional. A priest almost. All their little treasures; where they keep them safe.'

From beyond the door came the voice of Fossey's wife, asking if everything was all right, did they want more water for the pot? Nobody answered.

'Let's get back to recommendations,' said Millington. 'That of your fellow professionals. Like-minded individuals. With the safety of the community at heart. There must be some useful contacts, you grease my palm, I'll grease yours.'

'There's no law . . .'

'Against it, no, there isn't,' said Millington, fingers, as it were, tightly crossed behind his back.

'Of course,' said Fossey, careful now, 'it happens from time to time.'

'Of course,' agreed Millington. And then, several silent moments later: 'But nothing regular? No regular arrangements of that nature?'

Fossey's hands slithered against each other; were he to lift cup from saucer now it would likely slip back through his fingers. 'You get so's you see someone doing a good job, given the chance, you tell people about it. Hope they'll do the same for you.'

Millington nodded; waited.

'VG Security – I've done quite a bit with them. Obviously they've put in a good word for me, number of times. Can't think of any . . . oh, yes, stupid, there's this broker. Insurance.'

'Name?'

'Savage.'

'Put a lot of business your way, has he?'

'Quite a lot, yes.'

'Pay him for it?'

'Sorry?'

'You keep saying that, too.'

'I didn't understand.'

'Yes, you did. What do you pay him? All these referrals.'

'I don't . . . it depends. You know, whether it comes to anything. Sometimes, people, they just want to find out how to make their places more secure, then sort it out for themselves. Either that, or, minute they hear what it's likely to cost, they don't want to know.'

'Rees Stanley one of those, was he?'

'I told you, I don't . . .'

'Wanted to increase his insurance, went to his broker for advice, broker makes suggestions, everyone demands improved security. All he's got, let's say, a box on the wall that says alarm but doesn't connect to anything. You go along, suss it out, start

190

talking electronic rays, video cameras, the whole works. Stanley's got his winter holiday to think of, backs off sharpish, he's been taking the risk for so long, why not a bit longer? So the burglar alarm he's got doesn't work, but lots of them are like that, who's to know?'

'OK,' said Fossey, back on his feet. 'Out.'

'Don't do it, Fossey,' said Millington, pushing himself up.

'I'm not wasting any more of my time and I'm not answering another question.'

'You mean without your solicitor.'

'I mean, I'm not answering another sodding question.' He jerked the lounge door open wide and stood away from it.

'Oh dear,' said Millington, smiling. 'Oh dear, oh dear.'

'You're not coming into my house, making snide insinuations . . .'

Millington was passing close enough to shoot out a hand and seize Fossey where his blazer was buttoned together. 'Come a long way since Sutton-in-Ashfield, eh, Lloyd? Big house: big words. You're right though; no more insinuations. Next time, the real thing.' He released his grip and deftly flicked the tip of Fossey's nose. 'Make those files available, do yourself a favour. Don't make us go through all the performance of getting a warrant. Only makes us short-tempered.'

Mrs Fossey was dusting something in the hall. It seemed ludicrous to Millington to call her Mrs anything. She was still a kid, a child playing grown-up games, playing house. Not so much older than his own. He wondered if there'd been an aisle, if her father had walked her down it, leaning on his arm.

'Thanks for the tea, love,' Millington said, opening the front door.

'Oh, that's all right.' Her eyes were bright for a moment, then dulled as they turned away to where Lloyd Fossey stood at the entrance to the lounge.

''Bye,' the sergeant said and closed the door behind him, eager to be in his motor and away. Sensing that he would be back.

24

Mark Divine tore the edge from the free holiday offer that had been folded inside his morning paper and eased it between his teeth, high on the right side. Trouble with sodding muesli was you spent till lunch time getting the bits out of your mouth and spitting them through the window. He turned up the car radio a notch as the Four Tops came on – still making it after all those years. Doing the same dances, too. He'd seen them on *Top of the Pops*: four portly, middle-aged men finger-clicking and spinning in circles. What would he be doing when he was the far side of forty? Living out somewhere like this, perhaps. Christ, no! All that gentility, all those lawn sprinklers and dogs with German brand names. Better another city altogether. Simon Mayo, now, he'd been a DJ on local radio and there he was, doing the breakfast show from London, Radio One, chatting away with whoever was reading the news and that girl, real sexy voice, the one who did the weather. What was her name? Roscoe? No, that was the Emperor, back when he'd been at primary school. Not Roscoe. Ruscoe. That was it. Sybil. Some mornings Divine wished it was television, so that he could see exactly what was going on in the studio; what it was that made her giggle like that.

A car started up and he turned down the volume again, but it wasn't anything to get concerned about.

Maybe in five years, Divine thought, still poking soggy paper at his mouth, I'll have my stripes and be down in the smoke. The Met. Flying Squad. That'd be the thing. Him and Simon Mayo, both. High flyers.

Another car and this time it was the Citroën. Divine's fingers flicked the key in the ignition and he moved off from the curb with a speed that left burn marks on the asphalt.

Harold Roy hadn't cleared his drive before the unmarked police vehicle swung across in front of him and braked sharply, blocking his exit. If Harold hadn't broken the habit of a lifetime and slotted the end of his seat-belt into place before turning on to the road, no way his head wouldn't have smacked through the windscreen.

Divine was out of his seat and round by the Citroën before Harold Roy had stopped shaking. Standing there in his light-grey suit, pale-blue shirt, imitation-silk tie, making the sign with his fingers – wind down your window.

'What the hell . . .?'

Divine let his wallet fall open before the director's eyes, someone doing a card trick. 'DC Divine, sir. Just a few questions.'

'Questions? Is that any . . .?'

'Would you mind stepping out of the car, sir?'

'I don't see . . .'

'Out of the car, sir.'

'I'll get out when you've told me . . .'

Divine reached in and flipped up the lock, swung the door back fast. 'Out!'

Come down a little hard, the boss had said; not often he encouraged Divine with that sort of leeway. Better make the most of it. Look at this one now, doesn't know whether to be angry or humble. Puffy eyes, not enough sleep; wouldn't take much to leave him in tears, shouldn't wonder.

'Yes, officer,' said Harold, pressed back against the side of his car, guts turning somersaults like a set without vertical hold.

That's it, sunshine, smiled Divine to himself, grovel a little. 'You're aware a complaint's been laid against you, sir? Assault.'

Maria had gone running to the window as soon as she'd heard the double wrench of brakes. Now there was Harold flapping his hands and talking nineteen to the dozen to some identikit policeman. She didn't know why they bothered with plain clothes. At least the last one they'd sent out to her had been different, Asian, manners like bone china. Nice skin, she remembered that. Surprisingly slim fingers. Almost too shy to hold her stare. Little more than a boy, really.

Not like Grabianski.

The way he'd been when Harold had burst in on them, as if they had been talking about fitting double glazing instead of sharing a bath together in the middle of the afternoon.

We've got a lot to talk about.

He hadn't meant himself and Maria, adultery, the temperature of the bathwater: he had meant business. Maria hoped that whatever was going on at the head of the drive, right then, had nothing to do with it. She tightened the belt of her robe and padded back to the kitchen; one glance at the clock and she was wondering when Grabianski, as he had promised, would call.

What was the attraction, Lynn Kellogg was thinking, and not for the first, not even the first dozen times, of buying a sweatshirt that featured an advertisement for something, somewhere you'd neither use nor see? Dorfmann's Steel Tubing, the Best in the Midwest. University of Michigan at Ypsilanti. Ma Baker's Peach Pies – baked with her own hungry hands. A little logo that read Levis, Pepe, Wrangler, that was enough. That was OK. Personally, though, she drew the line at Hard Core. The remarks that had followed her up the escalator in C&A, it wasn't worth the hassle.

She picked up a striped collarless shirt and wondered what there was about it that made it worth £29.99. Caught a glimpse of herself in the mirror, cheeks almost always redder than she'd have liked. The girl with the built-in blusher. If that young assistant didn't take the smirk off his face, she might wander over and give him something to think about. A kid! Nineteen if he was a day. Gel on his hair, Paco Rabanne, the last of last summer's duty-free, clinging to his neck and armpits, and dandruff on his shoulders.

Hey!

There was that girl again, moving fast, left to right close to the railing on the far side of the balcony, heading past Miss Selfridge and into Boots.

The assistant moved between two display stands, partly blocking her way. 'Anything I can do?' he said sarcastically.

'Yes,' said Lynn, brushing past.

'Go on, then.'

'Grow up.'

Patel had become bored with counting the Porsches and Ferraris parked along the two roads that right-angled away from where he was standing. He had paced a couple of hundred yards in either direction, turning smartly to return, never letting the main door to the building out of his sight for long enough for anyone to walk out unnoticed. Keep well back, the inspector had said, don't get yourself seen. For now, enough to establish that they're on the premises; a good description of one, sketchy of the other.

He wasn't certain how to play it if they came out together, even separately. If they've got bags, cases, if they look as if they're pulling out altogether, Resnick had told him, call for back-up and don't lose them. Otherwise . . . play it by ear, use that initiative of yours.

If there'd been more natural cover, it might have been easier. When he wasn't on the move, Patel kept behind a bank of tall green dustbins, close to the wall dividing a block of modern flats from yet another rambling old house with turrets and deep bay-windows.

A lot of joggers round here, Patel thought, as yet another went painfully past him, sweat pants sagging round his hips, spectacles held in place with a broad white band of elastic. True to the stereotype, he himself played squash and was good at it. Divine had seen him with his gear one time and challenged him; after twenty minutes of losing 9–0, 9–2, 9–1, Divine had faked a pulled calf muscle and limped off to the changing room. 'What d'you expect?' he'd heard Divine expounding in the CID room the next day. 'Game for bloody poofs!'

There it goes, bottle of perfume hidden for a moment beneath the over-long sleeve of her coat, and then lost in that capacious pocket. Keep out of sight, well back. That's it, show an interest in some eyebrow pencil, fifteen shades of purple. Now move, move it!

The girl drifted around the end of the counter and at first Lynn didn't think she had taken anything, but when she looked again Lynn was ready to take bets there had been more silk scarves than that on display.

Where to now? Out beyond the store and the danger was she'd do a runner and that was the last Lynn would see of her, until the next time. But if her suspicions were correct, the girl wouldn't be satisfied with so small a haul. Lynn doubled back on herself, feigning a sudden enthusiasm for a cherry red beret. Put that on her head and walk out into the street, people would mistake her for beetroot soup on legs.

Without hesitation, the girl walked up the shallow steps and back into the centre, only this time Lynn was keeping with her.

'Mrs Roy?'

'What is it now?'

'I was just talking to your husband . . .'

'Congratulations.'

'You may know, a complaint's been filed against him . . .'

'For punching that Mackenzie in the mouth. Not before time. I can't imagine what got into him, but it's the best thing Harold's done for years.'

'What I wanted to talk to you about, though, was something different.'

'I have an appointment. I have to get ready.'

'You don't think I could step inside?'

'No.'

'It might be easier.'

'I told you, I've things to do.'

'The neighbours . . .'

'D'you think I care about the neighbours?'

Divine didn't suppose she did. He was wondering what it must be like, married to an overweight woman with a voice like a handsaw and a temper to match.

Maria Roy glanced down at the opening at the top of her robe, but did nothing about it. 'Well,' she said, 'are you going to stand there gawping at my tits all morning, or can we get this over with?'

Divine could take that kind of language from the girls who scurried and giggled their way from pub to pub, bar to bar every Friday evening, but when the woman was old enough to be his mother, he had problems.

'Well?' Maria repeated, making a show of shutting the door in the DC's face.

'This statement you made about the burglary,' Divine said. 'We have reason to believe you identified the wrong men.'

* * *

Sometimes when he was bored, Patel worked his way through the counties of England, with their county towns, the states of the American union, the capitals of the Eastern bloc countries, the winners of the world squash championship since 1965, the year in which he had been born. At others, he struggled to clear his mind of all such ephemera, facts and figures, empty it of everything save the rhythm of his own breathing and the sounds around him. Here, close to the heart of the city, it was amazing how many different natural sounds there were. Bird calls, for instance.

'Young man.'

Patel jumped, despite himself. Turning, he was face to face with a shrunken woman with tightly-curled white hair. She was wearing a thick coat that might once have fitted her, but was now several sizes too large, heavy brown wool with an astrakhan collar. On her feet were gym shoes, murky white.

'Are you the police?'

She spoke like a schoolmistress of the old-fashioned kind; Patel had read of them in books, smelling of camphor and with pear-drop breath; when they asked for silence you could, of course, hear the imperial pin drop. For himself, back in Bradford, most of his teachers had worn jeans and ill-fitting sweaters held together with badges for Anti-Apartheid, Ban the Bomb.

'Because you're either from the police or the public health department. You haven't come about that rat I reported, have you?'

Patel smiled and shook his head; showed her his warrant card.

'Good,' she said emphatically. 'Then you've come about that awful man.'

'Which man is this?'

'That man. The one who lives up there.' She was looking past Patel towards the house he had been detailed to watch. 'That pervert. That dreadful peeping Tom!'

'Excuse me,' said Lynn, fingers on the girl's sleeve, 'I've reason to believe . . .'

The girl twisted fast, kicking her heel hard against Lynn's shin and then jabbing a knee towards her groin. She flailed her arms and screamed in Lynn's startled face.

'Lemmego! Lemmego! Lemmego!'

Lynn clung on as nails clawed at her face.

'Just look,' said a passer-by to her friend, both carrying boxes of cream cakes from Bird's, neatly tied around with a bow at the top.

'All right,' said Lynn, fending off the blows. 'This isn't getting you anywhere.'

The girl ducked low and swivelled hard and the next thing Lynn was standing there with the coat in her hands and the girl was legging it away as fast as she could along the upper aisle.

Lynn hooked her left hand firmly inside the collar of the coat and gave chase. Suddenly the passage between the railings and the shop fronts seemed to be full of elderly shoppers, moving slowly, dragging carriers or pushing wicker trolleys before them.

'Excuse me, police!' Lynn called out. 'Keep back, police!'

The girl was thirty yards ahead of her, weaving in and out, tossing stolen goods this way and that; the surprised shoppers must have thought they were in the middle of a TV commercial, another episode of *Hard Cases*.

'Stop that girl!' shouted Lynn. 'Stop her!'

The girl pushed herself off one of the pillars, swinging sharp left as if to go down the stairs, breaking right again, sprinting along a clear patch of the opposite aisle, the direction that would take her to the bus station, out on to the street.

Lynn, the coat streaming out behind her like a grey flag, dug into her reserves and gained ground. A bunch of youths, lounging against a music shop window, clapped and cheered sarcastically. Ahead the girl changed direction again, making for the escalators. She was barging her way past people standing on the moving stairs as Lynn jumped past an astonished woman and baby and leaped down the up escalator. Plunging on, shouts ringing around her, close enough to reach across and grab at the girl's jumper, but the jumper tore at the neck and they were both running still, almost at the bottom.

'Hey! Watch where you're going!'

Lynn ducked under a man's angry arm and dived for the back of the girl's legs. They struck the hard polished floor and started to slide. A foot kicked Lynn alongside the head, numbing her ear. She tugged at the waistband of the girl's skirt, ignoring the blows to her own head, the clamour all round.

'Lemmego, you bitch, you fucking cow!'

Lynn took hold of the girl's hair and yanked it back, dragging her to her knees. A gold bracelet tumbled away from somewhere inside the girl's clothing and rolled in a slow curve before wobbling to a halt.

'You're under arrest,' Lynn said.

The girl spat in her face.

25

Whoever had started to redecorate the room had run out of paint or enthusiasm a third of the way down the end wall. Elsewhere more than one shade of blue had been rolled on to chipboard paper, fading blue fingerprints attached to floor and ceiling. Three sections of unmatched carpet had been interlocked across the floor. One man, overweight by as much as fifteen pounds, leaned back against the end of a moquette settee, watching a programme about mathematics for eleven to fourteen year olds. Another, cross-legged on the floor near the window, was reading Leon Uris. Norman Mann was close against the lowered blinds, binoculars in hand.

Resnick nodded briefly towards the two other officers as he came into the room.

'Not too early for you, Charlie?' asked Norman Mann pleasantly.

Resnick shook his head. He'd been awake since 4.25, Dizzy marauding underneath his bedroom window; gone back to bed but known it for a waste of time, finally up around half five, waiting for the sky to clear, the watery sun to rise.

He walked over to the window and Norman Mann obliged him by easing down one of the blinds. Resnick found himself looking out on another low block of flats, similar to the one he was in now. A curving walkway, its once-white wooden sides scattered with graffiti, led down to a paved area rich in dog shit and takeaway cartons from last night's homeward trawl from the pubs along Alfreton Road.

Mann handed Resnick the glasses and pointed to one particular door. 'Not exactly Crack City, but it's our own little contribution.' Traces of his Edinburgh accent still clung to the back of his voice like shadows on a X-ray.

'Factory?' Resnick asked.

Mann shook his head. 'Doubtful. More your outworkers. Cottage industries of old come back to haunt us. Cut the cocaine with baking powder, mix in a little water, bang it in the oven and then leave to dry. Easy as making a pie. Except what you get is a rock of crack that'll change hands for twenty-five, thirty, forty pounds.'

'You're not going in?'

'Not till we've got a better idea who's inside. No.' Moving away from the window, he offered the glasses to the officer watching the TV. 'You know how it is in this lark, Charlie, awful amount of waiting around, filling in time. Still . . .' he nodded towards the other officers, '. . . makes for a more cultured class of chaps.'

The two men laughed; one took his sergeant's place at the window, the other turning a page of his book, then turning back again, couldn't remember whether he'd read that page or not.

Norman Mann steered Resnick into the tiny oblong kitchen. The gas cooker looked as if it had been wrenched away from the wall and then left, blocking access to the sink. Something sat mouldering in the corner, wrapped in damp newspaper. Better not to ask.

'Someone living here?' Resnick asked.

'Not any more. It was squatters last. Better here than out on the streets. Still, someone flushed them out a week or so back. Uniforms probably, doing the council a favour. Useful for us though.' He shook out a packet of cigarettes and, when Resnick declined, lit one with the lighter from his back jeans pocket. 'So, Charlie, something urgent.'

'Alan Stafford.'

Norman Mann angled his head back slowly, smoke easing from the edges of his mouth. 'Bit higher class than this.'

'How high?'

'Connections all over. Newcastle, Southampton, Dover, Liverpool. Middle-man mostly, biggest profit for the lowest risk. By my reckoning he keeps some clients for himself, probably likes to keep the feel of the streets in his feet. Besides, gives him the chance to break and shake with the *hoi polloi*.'

'Television,' said Resnick, helpfully.

'Those wankers!' snorted Mann. 'All they need is a few cans of Red Stripe to be falling arse-over-tip into each other's Filofaxes. I'm talking money here, Charlie, real money. Power and influence. They don't call cocaine your champagne drug for nothing.'

'You've got a watch on him, then?'

Norman Mann looked at him archly. 'Now and again.'

'If he's so important . . .'

'He's as like got himself a bit of protection, all salted away against the inevitable rainy day. Oh, we'd like him, right enough. I'd love the bastard. But this lot here, peddling two-minute highs to schoolkids who hustle for it on the Forest, let's face it, Charlie, we're more likely to fetch up with one of them, more likely to get a result.'

'Which doesn't mean you're not interested?'

'It does not.'

Resnick nodded, wafted away the smoke that was collecting under the low ceiling in a blue-grey cloud. 'He's hanging round the edges of something pretty strange. A few things that won't stay still long enough yet to tie down, see how they all fit. But he's in there somewhere. I'll bank on that.'

'Boss,' called one of the officers from the other room, 'something's moving.'

Norman Mann made his hand into a fist and set it against Resnick's upper arm, tapping punches. 'Anything we can do, Charlie.'

'Right. I'll keep you up to the mark.'

Mann was back by the window, peering out. 'Do that. Oh, and Charlie . . . check him out with NDIU, Stafford, they'll have him pretty up to date.'

Resnick raised an arm. 'Thanks.'

'Careful on your way out,' Norman Mann warned. 'No one's going to mistake you for your average squatter.' Grinning. 'Not at second glance, anyway.'

Back inside his car, Resnick checked with the station, nothing to prevent him from moving on. He'd already had words with the DCI that morning, the request for information from the National Drugs Intelligence Unit would be on its way.

'One other thing,' Tom Parker had said. 'Jeff Harrison, I thought the pair of you had some history together?'

'Not too much,' Resnick had replied.

'Only something's ruffling his feathers and he seems to think you're back of it.' Resnick had said nothing and waited. 'Says he's tried to talk to you, but you won't answer his calls. Says you've had a couple of your lads over there, leaning on his men, ferreting around behind his back.'

'I came to you first, sir,' Resnick reminded him.

'Maybe it wasn't clear to me what you were getting up to.'

'Like I said. Trying to fit that burglary in with our other inquiries. Nothing more than that.'

'If it was nothing more than that, d'you really think Harrison would be hopping like a blue-assed fly?'

'Maybe not, sir.'

'Your favourite word, isn't it, Charlie? Maybe.'

Saying maybe inside his head, Resnick smiled.

'He's been a bit naughty, that's what you're angling for, eh? That's your suspicion. And don't, don't say maybe. Don't say anything. Not till you're this side of ready. And then I want it, Charlie. All of it. It'll be out of your hands then. You know that, don't you?'

Resnick had nodded. 'Yes, sir,' he said.

That had been first thing, before his meeting with Norman Mann. Now Resnick was slowing to turn in past the gate at Midlands TV, identify himself to the security guard on duty.

Suzanne Olds was easing her beige Honda out of the visitors' car park. Seeing Resnick, she stopped.

'Your client,' Resnick said, braking, leaning across towards her. 'You did us a favour.'

'Buy me dinner.'

'Anything but Chinese.'

'Polish, then. Isn't there supposed to be a good Polish restaurant in the city?'

They dressed up in traditional costume and each meal began with a full glass of vodka. 'Yes, there is.'

'I'll hold you to it.'

'What are you doing here?' Resnick asked. 'Another client?'

Suzanne Olds removed her glasses for a moment, the kind with lenses that are sensitive to changes in the level of light. 'Mackenzie's an impatient man. He was worried you weren't taking his alleged assault seriously. Now that you're here, I can see his fears were groundless.'

'I'm surprised the company are letting him proceed. I'd have thought they'd have preferred the whole thing hushed up.'

Suzanne Olds considered before speaking, tapped one end of the spectacle frame against the dip of her upper lip. 'I didn't say this, but I don't think a punch on the nose . . .'

'The mouth.'

'Wherever. I don't think that's the concern. I think they're using it.'

'What for?'

'To lean on Harold Roy. Exert pressure? I'm only guessing.'

'Sounds as if he should be your client, not Mackenzie.'

She slipped her glasses back into place, the car into gear. 'Don't forget,' she said, 'Gotabki, isn't it?'

'Gotabki,' corrected Resnick, stuffed cabbage in a garlic-and-tomato sauce, but she was already passing the gate and signalling right.

Mr Mackenzie was in the editing suite with Mr Freeman Davis and had left a clear message that he was not to be disturbed. As far as the receptionist knew, Mr Roy was not in the building. Miss Woolf? He could try the canteen.

Diane Woolf didn't appear to be there, but Resnick recognized somebody who was. Robert Deleval was sitting alone in a corner, staring out through the glass and watching the grass grow.

Perhaps, thought Resnick, he was searching for inspiration. Wasn't that what writers did?

'Mind if I join you?'

Deleval flapped a hand vaguely in the direction of the empty chairs. He looked like a man who had just written *The Great Gatsby* and discovered that his only copy of the manuscript had been lost in the post.

'Seen better days?'

Deleval cut one corner from a solid-looking portion of cheesecake; then another, and another. Don't play with your food, Resnick's mother had told him. It's not a toy that you should play with.

'You know what they used to say,' Deleval began, still dismembering the cheesecake, 'anything vaguely gynaecological, anything below the feminine belt. Women's problems. What's wrong with Aunt Sophie? Women's problems. OK, so that's what it is with me.'

Resnick looked at him with new interest. 'Women's problems?'

'Writers' problems.'

'They're the same?'

'No, just equally inexplicable to anyone who isn't suffering from the same things.'

It was going to be, Resnick realized, one of those less than fascinating conversations. Why had he always assumed that writers must be interesting people to talk to?

'So have you come to arrest him?'

'Arrest who?' Resnick said. At the back of his mind, something was nagging at him – shouldn't that have been arrest whom? What it was, you sat down with a writer for five minutes, miserable bugger or not, and that was enough to have you questioning your own grammar.

Either way, Deleval didn't seem to have noticed. 'Our esteemed director, of course.'

'For taking a swing at Mackenzie?'

'Bang on the button. Bust that mouth of his wide open.' Deleval seemed to have cheered up. 'Butterfly stitches, pain killers, the whole works.' His expression soured again. 'Only thing, he should have hit him harder. More. What was missing from that little scenario, a couple of good low blows.'

'Last time we spoke,' Resnick reminded him, 'you were issuing death threats to Harold Roy, not Mackenzie.'

'That was before Harold became a hero of the unofficial confederation of shafted screenwriters.'

'He was ruining your script.'

Deleval made the final incision into the cheesecake. 'Better than stealing it.' He let the knife fall against the edge of the plate. 'A couple of years ago I approached Mackenzie with this idea, a series about an ordinary family that wins a lot of money, gambling, lottery, football pools, it didn't matter. Mackenzie's interested, excited even. We work our way through the whole gamut of lunches, breakfasts, afternoons in leather armchairs that become the first of several drinks before the taxi home. Ideas are jotted down on serviettes and menus, backs of cigarette packets. Let me have an outline, Mackenzie says, we'll talk it up.

Another month and I'm working on a rough treatment. Channel 4 are interested, Mackenzie and I, we're forming our own company, the funding's promised. Do it that way, he says, we get to keep control. You, he says, you develop that treatment the way you see it. Your baby.'

Deleval glanced around, suddenly aware that the level of his voice had risen and that others were beginning to pay attention.

'Almost a year along the line,' he went on, more subdued, 'Channel 4 are out the window, the Beeb are interested, really interested. If there was some way I could restructure the treatment so it could be shown to Felicity Kendal, they'd be positively slavering. So, fine. There's still no money around, nothing up front, but I do it anyway. After all, like the man said, it's my baby and you don't let your baby starve for lack of effort, right? At this point the entire series and serials department of the BBC gets sucked down one end of the corporation vacuum-cleaner and blown out the other. Nobody seems to know if they're on their heads or their heels. That treatment's out, Felicity Kendal's out, Mackenzie's bringing our cherished, now slightly ageing infant here into the heartland of independent television drama. Suddenly my idea has become something else, someone else's idea. Ideas. Now it's some many-headed hydra, trying to run in half a dozen directions at once, desperate to be all things to all people and almost none of those things that I had in mind in the first place.'

'But,' said Resnick, 'it was your idea.'

Robert Deleval threw back his head and laughed. 'Signed, sealed and delivered, sold along the dotted line to the highest bidder. Hey, even writers have to eat. Your baby? Here's the adoption papers. Of course we'll bring him up right. Oh, we might need to slap him around a little, bring him into line. A little rough treatment, but then, who did that ever hurt?'

Resnick was looking around the canteen for signs of Diane Woolf. What had begun as interesting had degenerated into a mixture of spleen and self-pity.

'You know what a writer needs to succeed in this business?' Deleval demanded.

Resnick shook his head; it was time he made his excuses and left.

206

'You know?'

Deleval was almost roaring now and the occupants of all the adjacent tables had dropped their indifference and were openly staring.

'What he needs,' Deleval was on his feet, turned towards the interior of the canteen, 'aside from the skin of a rhinoceros and a permanently nodding head, is an extra-long tongue that won't go brown at the edges.'

He seized the plate from his table and held it close to his face. 'What any self-respecting writer has to be able to do . . .' he was pawing his hand into the pieces of cheesecake and pushing them inside his mouth, shouting through the ensuing spray, '. . . is eat shit and look as though he's enjoying it.'

After that, Resnick nearly didn't notice Diane Woolf at all. She tapped him on the shoulder as he backed past her, standing near the head of the queue balancing a plate of salad, a low-fat banana yoghurt and a black coffee.

'Shall we take this somewhere else?'

'Please.'

He followed her out through the doors and along the broad corridor, up a flight of stairs and into a small room that overlooked a section of the car park. There were several pieces of editing equipment, two television monitors and a double stack of VHS cassettes that Resnick eased back along the table so that Diane could set down her lunch. He assumed it was lunch.

'Here,' she said, pushing the coffee towards him. 'It's black. Is that all right?'

'It's yours.'

She shook her glorious head of red hair. 'I drink too much of the stuff. It's just easier to buy it and pour it away than walk past the coffee point. Besides, if you drink it, I won't have to go on murdering the house plants the company so thoughtfully provides.'

Resnick was staring at her.

'Well, what they don't provide are receptacles for unwanted coffee.'

That wasn't why he was looking at her. She knew it. Delicately between forefinger and thumb, she lifted some alfalfa sprouts towards her mouth. She had one of her long legs crossed over the other; the white dungarees that she was wearing were loose across the hips, less so where the bib was strapped over a satiny blouse, electric blue.

'I take it Robert was having another of his little fits.'

'It's happened before?'

'Like clockwork. Robert's more pre-menstrual than me and any dozen of my friends put together. He just doesn't bleed, that's all.'

'Not like Mackenzie.'

'Ah, so this isn't merely a social call.'

Wishing that it were, Resnick shook his head. 'Did you see what happened? Clearly, I mean.'

'Ringside seat.'

'And was there provocation?'

'When the wind's in the right direction, Mac could provoke the Buddha into going ten rounds.'

'How was the wind on this occasion?'

'North-north-westerly.'

'Force nine?'

'All cones hoisted.'

'He asked for it, then?'

'Doesn't he always?'

'You'd make a statement to that effect? If it came to it.'

Diane made a little moue with her mouth. 'There's my salary to think of. An expensive shoe obsession to support.' Today they were white Nikes with a yellow stripe; perhaps she kept the rest under glass, lock and key.

'It probably won't come to that.'

'You won't charge him?'

'It's a little early to say, but . . .'

'That isn't the point of it, you know.'

Resnick lifted the coffee mug but didn't drink any. 'What is?'

'Mac wants him out.'

'Of the job?'

'The job, the building, everything.'

'Didn't he hire him?'

'Hire 'em and fire 'em, that's the name of the game. Harold's been at it long enough to know the risks. They'll pay him what he's due, slip him a few promises to keep him sweet. His name stays on the credits, he won't lose his residuals.'

'His what?'

'Oh, repeats, overseas sales. They'll love this in Australia.'

Resnick, in his mind, was loving her mouth, the lower lip that looked as if it were just slightly swollen.

She ate a piece of celery, taking her time about it. 'Do you always ogle your witnesses?'

Resnick almost fell for saying something sticky and smart like, only when they look like you. Thankfully, he didn't. He had the grace to blush a little instead.

'You want some of this?' she asked, sliding the plate towards him.

Resnick shook his head.

'You should.' She smiled. 'You really should think about your carbohydrates.'

Before Resnick could suck in his stomach and straighten his back they were interrupted by a loud shouting from outside.

At the end of the short corridor, Harold Roy had Mackenzie backed up against a door and was threatening to deafen him with accusations. The most frequent amongst those seemed to concern what was going on at the other side of the door.

'If I've got it wrong,' screamed Harold, 'get the fuck out of my way and let me see what's going on in there.'

'What's being done in there is none of your business, Harold.'

'Like hell it isn't!'

'Harold . . .'

'Out of the way, you chicken shit . . .'

'Harold . . .'

Harold caught Mackenzie by the forearm and managed to swing him far enough aside to make a grab at the door handle possible. It budged, but not by more than an inch.

'It's locked.'

'Of course it's locked. With you running amok, what d'you expect? You shouldn't even be in the building.'

'You shouldn't be producing the God-slot for five-year-olds.'

'Harold, now you're being petty and vindictive.'

'When it comes to being vindictive . . .'

209

'I know, I know,' said Mackenzie, showing every sign of becoming bored, 'I wrote the book.'

'No, Mac,' said Harold Roy, 'you *stole* the book.'

'Up yours, Harold!'

It might have petered out there, just another slagging match between middle-aged prima donnas with nothing better to do on their lunch break, if Freeman Davis hadn't chosen that moment to unlock the door from the inside and poke his head out to see what all the commotion was about.

Harold barged past the younger man almost as if he weren't there. Only seconds later he was back in the corridor and bearing down on the producer.

'Couldn't wait, could you, Mac? Couldn't wait to let this jumped-up fuck-up start re-editing my footage. Cutting the fucking stuff to bits!'

If Resnick hadn't stepped in quickly, Harold Roy's fist might have done more damage this time than last. All those early years directing angry young men were coming home to roost.

'Uh-uh, Harold,' Resnick said, the fingers of his right hand tight around the director's wrist, his left closed around Harold's best punch, 'not a good idea in the circumstances. This time the provocation might be harder to prove.'

'Let him go,' said Mackenzie, but without a great deal of conviction. 'He won't catch me twice and get away with it.'

Resnick stared into Harold Roy's face until the latter looked away and the tension had seeped from his arm. 'We have to talk, Harold and I,' Resnick said to Mackenzie. 'If you could make somewhere available.'

'Sure,' Mackenzie said, backing off. 'Of course. You want anything? Anything else?'

Resnick shook his head. Down along the corridor, Diane was leaning against the wall, finishing her salad with her fingers. There was a smile in her eyes, brightening the corners of her mouth. How could she stand there dressed like a house-painter, thought Resnick, and be so sexy?

For herself, Diane Woolf was still thinking how quickly for a big man Resnick had moved, how fast. Maybe there was something about him after all; something more than those eyes that didn't want to let her go.

26

Harold Roy clenched his fists and stared at his knuckles until they were quite white. If ever there'd been any chance of salvaging his future with this particular company, the last half-hour had blown it. Once the rumours made their rounds, the usual vindictiveness, more than usual exaggeration – couldn't finish the series, couldn't keep to schedule, boozed up on the set, taking swings at the producer – he'd be lucky to get a job directing sixty-second promos for satellite TV. Some men in his situation might have somewhere warm and comforting to crawl; someone to hold their hands and pour their vodka, lick their wounds. What he had was a shrew of a wife who was in the process of rediscovering her sexuality in the company of a professional criminal with a semi-permanent hard-on. What he had was a blade-wielding drug dealer who would joyfully slice him down the middle at the first hint of betrayal.

Harold Roy was forty-nine years old and life could have been better. He felt around in his pockets, coming up with a used tissue and spirals of green-and-silver paper.

'Damn!'

'What's up?' Resnick asked.

'I'm out of mints.'

'Let's talk about it,' Resnick said, leaning forward, elbows on to the table, arms loosely folded.

Harold pulled at his tie, the idea being to free the knot, but all that happened was he tightened it instead. He looked more in need of a couple of valium than extra-strong peppermint.

Jesus, thought Harold, that's it. Why don't I do it? Why don't I say I'm going to the toilet, lock the cubicle door and hang my stupid self? Why don't I?

'How about it?' said Resnick.

'What?'

'Telling me what you know.'

Harold's shoulders slumped, a loud breath slid from his open mouth. There was something forbiddingly final about this man opposite him; the way he sat there, engaging him with his eyes, a big man, solid, something about him that said, it's all right, Harold. I know everything, know it all. All I want is for you to tell it back to me. Confess. Think how much better you'll feel once it's over – as if saying it lifted that weight from your back.

For a moment, Harold Roy could smell the sweetness of the incense, see the swing of the thurible. The shaded profile at the other side of the confessional, never clearly in focus.

Resnick hadn't moved, didn't move; enough to watch and wait.

'About all that,' Harold began, the words tumbling out. 'Out there just now, that and the other day, all that stuff with Mackenzie, the time I, time I hit him, that's it, that's what you want me to talk about. It is, all right? That's . . .'

Resnick carefully levered himself back on the chair. A muffled message sounded over the Tannoy. Sweat, only a little of it, slipped along Harold Roy's forehead, around his eyebrow and on to the side of his nose. Harold picked the crumpled tissue from the desk and dabbed it away. There would be more.

'That's not it?'

Resnick shook his head.

'Not what you want to talk about?'

'No, Harold.'

'Oh Christ.' His head went down into his hands, as though that was one last way of escaping. Pull the blankets up over your head and the frightening things will all go away. The pulse at his wrist was so fast he could feel it all along his arm.

'The burglary,' Resnick said evenly. 'Why don't you start there? Then, in your own time, you can get to the rest.'

'OK,' said Harold, almost thankfully. 'All right, I'll start there.'

When the phone first went, Maria was in the shower and didn't hear it until the tone was almost an afterthought; the second occasion, she was stretched out on the settee, midway through an article in *Good Housekeeping* about watching your weight while still being able to indulge in those little lip-smacking secrets. She should say! By the time she'd finished the sentence, got her feet inside her slippers, it had stopped. Ten rings: who the hell hung up after ten rings? Surely not Grabianski. He had a little more staying power than that.

Disgusting, all those bottles sitting there, waiting to be opened. Her hand shook at the wrong moment and gin ran over the rim of the glass down on to the front of her robe, her hand, the floor.

'God, Maria! You're becoming a sloppy drunk.'

She knew that what she should do was call a cab and go into the city, see a movie. There had to be something decent on, something with a taste of good old-fashioned adultery; Kirk Douglas leaving his architectural plans on the table to go pussy-footing after Kim Novak, forever dropping off her kid at the school bus-stop in a backless red dress and no bra. What was the name of that film?

Harold would know. She'd have to remember to ask Harold. One thing he was good for, any movie between, oh, '32 or '33 and the end of the sixties. Harold could tell you who starred, directed, the name of the studio, date, sometimes even the cinematographer. The only thing he wasn't so hot on, the writer. Even so, pretty impressive. The kind of mind *Trivial Pursuit* was made for. Just so long as everything stopped with *Easy Rider*. The pre-baby-boom period.

Pretty trivial, that was Harold. She dipped the tip of her tongue into the glass. That way it could last her as long as an hour, more. No, she was being unfair to the bastard. The way he'd handled bursting in and finding the two of them in the bath. Good as. Jerry jumping out, standing there, holding out . . . actually holding out his hand. *Let's go outside, we've got a lot to talk about.* Leaving her there, alone, trying not to wee into the bathwater.

When the phone went again, she half-stumbled, nearly lost her footing. 'Where've you been? Here I am, sitting around all day, worried sick, waiting for you to call. What's happening with you?'

'I did call,' Grabianski said. 'Twice.'

'That was you?'

'You were there? Why didn't you answer?'

'I tried.'

'Somebody was there with you?'

'Nobody. I've been going crazy all day.'

213

'You've been drinking.'

'So you're going to tell me I can't drink now?'

'I'm not saying anything.'

'You've been drinking, that's what you said.'

'I only said it, that's all. Not: look, don't do it; stay sober. Just a fact, that's all, you've been . . .'

'I know, I know, I've been drinking. What d'you expect me to do? Hanging round here since this morning. You told me you were going to call.'

'I did.'

'That was this afternoon.'

'I'm sorry. I was busy.'

'Planning another burglary?'

Grabianski didn't reply.

'Is that what you've been doing, getting ready to . . . Jerry, look, don't, you can't. I'm worried about you.'

'That's nice.'

'It's not nice. I wasn't made to sit at home, worrying.'

'Then don't.'

'I can't help it.'

Silence again. Maria tried to picture him, imagine what he was doing. Whether he was in a call-box or not. These days, modern phones, you couldn't tell the difference.

'The police were here,' she said.

'What did they want?' Trying to keep his voice calm, on the same level, and not quite making it.

'They know I lied.'

'How can they?'

'They know, that's all.'

'No way can they know.'

'He stood there and told me: the statement you made, we know you were lying.'

'That was what he said? I mean, exactly?'

'We have reason to believe that you falsified your statement on the whatever whatever, in particular as far as the identification of the two men were concerned.'

'What did you say?'

'Nothing.'

'Nothing?'

'I asked him how he thought he knew that.'

'And?'

'He sort of leered at me.'

'Jesus!'

'Exactly.'

'He didn't say you had to go to the station, make a fresh statement?'

'Not yet.'

'Not yet?'

'Not at this juncture.'

'He said that? Juncture?'

'It could have been junction.'

'You didn't go along with this? I mean, you didn't agree to change what you'd said?'

'Nooo.'

'Which means you did?'

'I said it was possible, looking back on it, I might have made a mistake.'

Grabianski swore.

'Jerry, I only said, might.'

'Yes, yes. This police officer, plainclothes? A detective?'

'Detective constable.'

'From which station?'

'How should I know? We didn't stand around exchanging addresses.'

'He wasn't the same one you saw before?'

'Before there was an inspector and two constables. He wasn't any of those.'

'And you say he didn't ask you to make a fresh statement?'

'He sort of invited me.'

'You declined?'

'Haven't I told you?'

'But you did say you might have been wrong?'

'Yes. Yes. Yes.'

'What did he say to that? I mean, at the end. How did he leave it?'

'He said, if those clever buggers were black, I'm a baboon's uncle.'

It wasn't immediately that Maria realized the connection had been broken. Almost as soon as she did, the phone rang again.

'Did you hang up?'

'It wasn't Harold, was it?'

'Did you just hang up on me?'

'It wasn't Harold?'

'What wasn't Harold?'

'Told them about this? Go round and lean on my wife. I think she's lying?'

'He spoke to Harold, yes.'

'He what?'

'But that was outside, before. Right before he came to the house.'

'Then Harold did tell him.'

'Why would he do that?'

'The fact that he found the pair of us . . .'

'Harold doesn't give a toss about us, whatever we were doing.'

'I wish you wouldn't say that.'

'What?'

'Give a toss.'

'I'm sorry. Not ladylike. I was forgetting you were the sweet, old-fashioned kind. Only liked women who said please first, thank you afterwards and refused to unbutton their blouses while the lights were on.'

'You know that isn't true.'

'I know.'

'Which doesn't alter the fact that Harold . . .'

'Harold has made a deal to fix you up with his drug-pusher. That doesn't come off, he's going to be walking round minus his balls. The last thing he wants is for the police to get on to you.'

Silence. Grabianski was thinking.

'Jerry?'

'Yes?'

'It'll be all right, won't it?'

'Yes, sure.'

'I mean, there's no other way they can get at you, is there?'

'They haven't so far. Not as much as a sniff.'

Maria sighed. 'I'm glad.'

'I'll call you,' Grabianski said. 'Tomorrow.'

'You're not coming round?'

'It's too late.'

'Tomorrow, then.'

'I don't know. I'll see.'

'You're not pulling out on me, are you?'

'No.' He said it quickly enough for Maria to believe him.

'Jerry . . .'

'Um?'

'Be careful, won't you?'

He made a kissing sound down the line and hung up again and this time he didn't ring back. Maria didn't know whether to have another gin or soak in the bath. In the end she found a dog-eared Jackie Collins that she'd read before and decided to do both.

By the time Harold Roy had stopped talking to Resnick he felt twenty pounds lighter and his head, instead of aching, was a whole lot clearer. Walking out at the back of the studios, the light was darkening to purple across the rooftops. The only things Resnick hadn't done, instructed him to make a perfect act of contrition, say five Our Fathers and ten Hail Marys, hear the final words of absolution.

Those would come.

27

'Lager, please,' Patel said.
  'Draught or bottle?'
  'Er, draught.'
  'Pint or half?'
  'Half.'
  'Didn't think your lot drank.'
  'Oh, yes, some of us do.'
  'Against your religion or something, alcohol.'
  Looking over his shoulder, Patel saw the man he had followed, Grice, feeding coins into a gambling-machine that flashed lights and emitted an electronic jingle. 'Thanks,' he said, collecting his change, picking his glass off the counter.
  Not exactly according to instructions, this, but, mild for the time of year or not, standing around was leaking the cold into his back and shoulders. Three times the elderly woman with the astrakhan collar had been back down to him, when was he going to go and arrest the man who kept looking into her bedroom with his binoculars? She didn't feel safe taking a bath, getting undressed.
  When Grice had come out, standing by one of the parked cars for a few moments, deciding whether to take it or walk, Patel had made up his mind. The target had moved off right and Patel had stayed down behind the phalanx of green bins, calling into the station, before following.
  Grice had walked fast, hands jammed into his topcoat pockets, not breaking stride until he reached the pedestrian lights at the head of Castle Boulevard. Behind them, the castle itself, the rebuilt seventeenth-century version of it, held its ground high on weathered rock. Patel followed over and almost immediately right, past the Irish Centre where they sold Dublin papers on a Sunday morning, where lines of mostly English students queued on a Saturday night, eager to dance and drink into the early hours.
  The pub itself was on the canal, seats outside where later in

218

the year you could watch the barges making their slow passage through the lock. Patel chose a table between the amusement-machines and the main door, the third point of a triangle. A copy of yesterday's *Post* had been bunched up against the seat nearby and he opened it out, folding the sports pages to read about the cricket being played in New Zealand. Richard Hadlee, now there was a competitor: Patel had been lucky enough to get a seat on the top deck at Trent Bridge several times during the last couple of seasons, and had watched Hadlee bowl from behind the arm. Patches when the ball was moving both ways, digging in, virtually unplayable.

His man came past him and Patel prepared to finish his lager, get up and leave, but all the target did was go to the bar and order another drink. Sitting back down, he glanced at his watch, not once, twice. All right, thought Patel, he's waiting for somebody. Good. The cricket report finished, he turned on to the classifieds. Now that house prices were stabilizing, maybe he should think more seriously about moving out from his couple of rooms, buying a place of his own, one of those terraced houses east of Derby Road, close enough so's he could still walk to work each morning.

Patel could see the knowing smile that would come to his mother's face, the studied look of approval on his father's: he was settling down, not a boy any more, marriage, he needed a good woman to look after him, children.

Patel felt his blood quicken as soon as the newcomer came through the door. Medium height, slight build, eyes that were a shade nervous as they picked out the person they were looking for. A low-alcohol lager carried behind Patel and into the corner. Quick shake of hands.

Patel's finger moved down the page. It was still possible to find something perfectly reasonable for less than forty thousand, and if his mortgage would stretch to a little more . . .

The new man was wearing a dark double-breasted suit, pale-yellow shirt and striped tie. Patel put him at thirty-three or four. He would have guessed somewhere along the range from car salesman to insurance; estate agent, even. But he didn't think the hushed conversation had anything to do with surveys or searches, nor that what was passed between them — a padded envelope, the size that would fit down into an inside pocket, a sheet of paper, folded three times – had anything to do with land deeds, options to purchase.

Grice stood abruptly, moving towards the gents. Patel waited, watching the man in the suit, a small dark moustache drawn across his face like a mistake. Suddenly the man's head turned and he was looking directly at Patel, eyes widening with interest; no, he was looking past him, a woman entering from the street, forties, short skirt and good legs. Grice almost collided with her on his way back.

The two men, both standing now, exchanged a few more sentences before Patel's target turned towards the door and his friend sat back down.

Options jumped through Patel's mind and he stayed put, letting Grice go. Initiative or stupidity, time would see. He went back to the property pages – Arnold, New Basford, Bulwell. The man in the suit was more relaxed now; he made a second trip to the bar and said something to the woman in the short skirt, who laughed. Sitting down again, he lit a cigarette and leaned back easily, and Patel thought he was in for a long wait. This time he would ask for a ginger ale. But no. The cigarette was pressed down into the glass ashtray, half-smoked, the glass drained as the man rose to his feet. He was out of the door and on to the pavement before Patel had nodded to the barman, crossed the floor.

Time to see him getting into a black Ford Escort, stabilizer at the rear, car phone, sun-roof, hardly a patch of dirt on the wheels. Unable to follow, Patel took out his notebook and wrote down the number.

Resnick was back in his office in time for Patel's call. No way of knowing whether Grice had gone back to the flat or if Grabianski had left in the meantime. There were other things to do, shifting priorities, and to keep Patel watching a potentially empty set of rooms was wasteful. Come back in and get together with Naylor over the VDU.

'Coffee,' Resnick called out into the CID room. 'Black and now.'

The adrenalin was pumping and he knew they were close; just unsure as yet exactly what they were close to, how big.

'Jeff,' he said into the phone. 'Charlie Resnick.'

'Thought you'd been avoiding me,' said Harrison, caustic yet wary.

'Snowed under.'

'You and me both.'

'Still game for that drink?'

'Seven suit you? Seven-thirty?'

'Difficult. You can't make it around nine?'

'You still go to the Partridge?'

Not since I was there with Rachel, Resnick thought. 'Yes. Nine o'clock, then.'

Harrison grunted and broke the connection. Resnick had the list underlined in his head: Skelton, Lennie Lawrence, Tom Parker, Norman Mann – and Graham Millington, else he'll feel left out, stepped over. He was dialling the first number when he saw Lynn Kellogg through the glass at the top half of the door, the expression on her face.

'I didn't know, sir.'

''Course you didn't. How could you?'

'Had no idea.'

'I know.' She sat there with elbows to her knees, head down, face resting against the palm of one hand. Unusually for Lynn, she didn't want to look at him. 'Even if you had . . .'

She shook her head.

'Her father . . .'

'Not here, sir. Not in the building. I don't know . . .'

'No.'

Resnick was on his feet, moving around the desk. Naylor appeared at the door with his coffee and Resnick waved him away. 'Sounds to me as if you did well . . .'

'No!'

'What you were there for.'

'But it wasn't, was it? Organized gangs, that's what I've been looking out for, wasting my time. Not one kid.'

'Lynn.'

'Yes.' She looked up at him, her cheeks more flushed even than was usual. 'Yes, sir?'

'Is she downstairs?'

Lynn nodded. 'I didn't know whether to send for her mother or not. The superintendent . . .'

'I'll go down.' Resnick opened the office door. 'You all right?'

'Thanks, sir. I'll be fine.'

'You'll write up your report?'

'Now, sir.'

'Naylor's got some coffee out there, have it with my compliments.'

He went out and left her sitting in his office, seemingly staring at the elaborate duty-rota fixed to the wall behind his desk. Before quitting the CID room he signalled to Naylor to take the coffee through.

He hadn't seen Kate in person since she was thirteen years old. Only the scrubbed face on the superintendent's desk, blank and smiling. Today he expected somebody much older, more mature, but the face that swung up at him from behind the white of the custody sergeant's shirt was every bit as young as he remembered it. Different, though. Eyes rubbed raw and cheeks swollen with crying.

'Hello, Kate.'

She blinked at him, another in a succession of police officers.

'You probably don't remember me . . .'

'No.'

'Let's go upstairs.' Shrugging, she stood. 'That OK?' he said to the sergeant.

'Help yourself.'

'Are you taking me to my dad?' Kate asked on the stairs.

'Not yet,' Resnick said. 'When he comes back.'

'He doesn't know yet?'

'No, I don't think so.'

'He'll kill me, won't he?'

Resnick found a smile in his eyes. 'I doubt that.' On the landing he said, 'Fancy a cup of tea, coffee?'

She shook her head.

'Come and watch me, then. I just gave mine away.'

They sat in the canteen. Kate relented and had a tea, spooning so much sugar into it, she couldn't stir it without the liquid swimming over the edge and running on to the edges of her jumper, but she didn't seem to care or even notice.

'Haven't got a cigarette, have you?'

Resnick shook his head. Did her father approve of her smoking, he wondered, before realizing what an asinine thought it was.

After twenty or so minutes of difficult silences and desultory conversation, most of it Resnick's, Lynn Kellogg waved at him from the doorway. Jack Skelton had returned.

Lynn waited outside with Kate while Resnick knocked and went in. Skelton had hung his suit jacket on the hanger behind the door and had yet to gain his desk.

'Charlie. What can I do for you?'

There was warning there already in the concern that sat on Resnick's face, the lack of any ready reply. Skelton eased back his chair and remained standing.

'Don't beat around the bush, Charlie.'

'It's your daughter, sir, Kate. She's . . .'

'She's all right?'

'She's outside.'

Skelton started towards the door, stopped close to where Resnick was standing. The two men looked at one another and it was Resnick who looked away.

'She's in trouble, then?'

'Yes, sir. She . . . DC Kellogg, she was on duty at the centre. Kate . . .'

'Christ,' breathed Skelton. 'She's been caught shoplifting.'

Resnick nodded. 'Yes.'

'She's here? Here now?'

'Outside.'

'God, Charlie.' Skelton's fingers rested on Resnick's arm as the life seemed to pass from his eyes. Turning back to his desk, the spring had gone from his step, his shoulders, ever straight, slumped forward.

'There's no question?'

'She's admitted the offence. On the way in.'

'I see.'

'Others, too. It seems . . . seems to have been going on some little time.' The occasions he had been forced to do this, parents called unknowing to the door, mistaking him for a Jehovah's Witness, some cowboy wanting to set slates back on the roof; their minds still swimming with whatever they'd been watching on TV. Slowly dawning: I'll kill the little bastard, what's he been up to now? Belligerence. Anger. Tears. My Terry, he's off t'youth club, I know for a fact. My Tracey . . . My Kate.

Skelton didn't say anything, sat there trying not to stare at the family photos, precise and particular on his desk.

'You'll want to see her, sir. Before she's interviewed. Makes a statement.'

'All right, Charlie.' He looked poleaxed. 'Just give me a couple of minutes, will you? Then ask DC Kellogg to bring her through.'

Resnick nodded and went towards the door. It seemed a strangely long way and all the time he was expecting the superintendent to call him back, say something more, though he didn't know what that should be. But there was nothing further. Resnick opened the office door and closed it again behind him.

'A couple of minutes,' he said to Lynn.

'Right, sir.'

When he looked at Kate, she turned her head away.

28

Graham Millington was feeling pretty chipper. His wife had agreed to take time off from her evening classes, one of the neighbours had promised to keep an eye on the kids, they had seats for the Royal Centre, third row centre. Petula Clark. As far as Millington was concerned you could take all your Elaine Pages and Barbara Dicksons, Shirley Basseys even, lump them all together and they still wouldn't rival Petula. God, she'd been going since before he could remember and that had to say something for her. And it wasn't just her voice that was in great shape. She wasn't page three, of course, never had been and wouldn't thank you for saying so, but at least what there was was all hers. No nipping and tucking there. None of your hormone transplants either. Fifty whatever she was and looking like that. Incredible!

Millington wandered across the CID room in happy reverie, whistling 'Downtown'.

'What is it with you, Graham?' Resnick asked.

'Sorry, sir?'

'Last year it was all I could do to keep you from murdering "Moonlight Serenade".'

Millington looked down at his feet and for one awful moment Resnick thought the sergeant was going to break into a soft-shoe shuffle. 'Your mother wasn't frightened by the Black-and-White Minstrels when she was carrying you, was she?'

Millington had been inside Resnick's house once; he'd seen the inspector's record collection. The sort he listened to, half of them snuffed it from sticking needles in their arms before they were thirty.

'Heard about the super's kid,' Millington said, changing the subject. 'How's he taking it?'

'How d'you think?' said Resnick sharply.

Millington had a clear vision of one of his own, the time he'd found him sitting down behind his bed getting too interested in a tube of Airfix glue.

'Anything new?' Resnick asked. 'Fossey, for instance.'

The sergeant recalled the other reason he'd been whistling happily. 'Patel, sir. The bloke our man Grice met in the pub, he put the number through Swansea. Car's licensed to an Andrew John Savage.'

'Fossey's friend.'

'And helper. Low-grade insurance broker. Lowest quotes, immediate and personal service guaranteed.'

It was Resnick's turn to smile. 'Fossey didn't get back in touch with his records, I suppose?'

Millington shook his head. 'Might be enough now to get a warrant.'

'Let's wait on that one. Push too hard and he might be tempted to do a runner. They both might. We'll have a little get-together first thing tomorrow, make sure the strategy's right. OK, Graham?'

'Yes, sir,' Millington nodded. But he didn't move away – and neither did he stop smiling.

'There's more?' Resnick asked. He hoped it wasn't going to be 'Don't Sleep in the Subway', even, heaven forbid, 'Winchester Cathedral'. 'Sailor!'

'Trevor Grice. We never ran a check on him till now.'

Resnick waited for the punchline.

'Two years for burglary back in '76.'

'Clean since then?'

'According to the computer.'

'Except we know better, eh, Graham?'

'Yes, sir.'

'Well done. Good piece of work. Tell Patel, if you haven't already. And Graham . . .'

Millington looked at him expectantly.

'Get yourself an early night. Next couple of days, I'd say we're liable to be pretty busy.'

Skelton and his daughter sat at either side of the superintendent's desk, avoiding each other's eyes, not speaking. When Lynn Kellogg had first shown her into the office, when the door had closed behind her and she had been left alone there with her father, Kate had cried. Tears she had thought used up already.

Her father had offered her a handkerchief and she had moved her head away, preferring a handful of tissues, pink and wet and torn.

'Sit down, Kate.'

She had sat, knowing the questions he must want to ask, the answers he was quickly learning to dread. After a while it was almost calm, almost pleasant. The hum of sound from other rooms, steps that moved closer, past and away. Their breathing. Telephones. Traffic changing gear before the traffic lights, the roundabout. Her mother – somewhere her mother was folding a school blouse after ironing, laying it down inside a drawer in Kate's room. Moving to the kitchen, perhaps, a glance towards the timer on the oven, a casserole to be tasted, salt and black pepper ground in and stirred. 'That child,' Kate had overheard one dismal evening, 'you give in to her too easily. Things she gets away with. In this house and out. The way you are with youngsters in your job – a pity a little of that hasn't rubbed off here. She might not be as wild as she is. Might show us both a little more respect.'

'Kate . . .'

'What?'

'Do you want to . . .?'

'No.'

'Do you want to go home?'

Right across the road from where Resnick was walking there had once been a mainline railway station. Now the original clock stood on its tower in front of one of the city's two shopping centres, this one with high-rise flats rising from inside it like concrete stalagmites. Up here on the left the Moulin Rouge: one and nine it had cost Resnick to see his first foreign film, patchy subtitles and imitations of carnality; barely remembered glimpses of Brigitte Bardot's breasts, somewhere that might have been St Tropez. Gone like most of the other fleapits where he had watched Jerry Lewis, Doris Day.

Resnick pushed open the door to the Partridge and walked into the left-hand room. Jeff Harrison was nursing a scotch at the end of the bar and he scarcely looked up when Resnick entered, but clearly knew he was there. Most of the bench seats

227

were taken; at one of the round tables four young men still wearing long overcoats smoked roll-ups and played dominoes. Resnick squeezed in alongside Jeff Harrison and ordered a Guinness and a bag of plain crisps.

'Bit late, Jeff. Sorry.'

'Overtime?'

Resnick shook his head. 'Feeding the cats.'

'Give them all the tit, do you, Charlie?'

Another shake of the head. 'Whiskas, as a rule.'

Harrison looked towards a couple of empty seats in the back corner. 'Want to sit down?'

'Suit yourself.'

Apparently it suited Harrison to stay as he was. They chatted sporadically, Resnick pacing himself down his glass, wondering how long it would take Harrison to get to the point.

'Anyone had asked me, Charlie, I might have said we were mates.'

Resnick looked at him along his shoulder. 'Not that exactly.'

'But not enemies.'

'No, not enemies.'

'Then why all this?'

'Come on, Jeff, there's no all about it.'

'Vendetta, that's what I'd call it.'

Resnick didn't answer. He'd known this was going to be difficult, one of the reasons he'd been putting it off as long as he had. Maybe he should have left it another forty-eight hours, or did he owe Harrison more than that, mate or no?

'You've had men going behind my back . . .'

'No.'

'I'm not stupid. Not a fool.'

'No one's been doing anything behind your back.'

'Like buggery!'

'Jeff, you know . . .'

'Yes?'

'There were reasons for pushing on the Roy investigations. You were told what they were.'

'This has gone further than that.'

'All through the DCI.'

'Pals, together, that it, Charlie? Scratch my balls, I'll scratch

228

yours. Or is it the trouser leg rolled up the knee, the funny handshake?'

'Pursuing an inquiry, that's what it is.'

'Yes?' Harrison stared at him. 'Into that burglary or into me?'

The woman behind the bar was trying so hard to listen she'd developed a serious list to one side.

'Not here, Jeff.'

'No? Why the hell not here? Or would you rather wait till the interview room, back at the station?'

Resnick's Guinness tasted sharper than usual. 'Is that where this is all leading?'

'Right. You're asking me. As if I know what's going on. I'm the last to know what's going on. Just ignore that fucker, waltz around him, make him dizzy. Don't tell him a thing.'

'Jeff . . .'

'You've had that Paki nudging away at my lads behind my back, seeing if they won't cough for some misdemeanour or other, own up to how far I tied their hands behind their backs. Questioning my evidence, my procedures. Going back to my witnesses . . .'

'I asked . . .'

'Once, once you came to me, face to face, and asked. This is something more, this is different.' He grabbed hold of Resnick's forearm and pressed it hard against the edge of the bar. 'Charlie, there's blokes in the force get a hard-on doing that kind of shit. Shafting their own. That's not you. Not without you've got a special reason.'

Resnick looked at Harrison, glanced down at the grip he had on his arm. Harrison released him and turned abruptly away. He might have been leaving and Resnick would have been glad to see him go, but all that happened was he went to the gents and came back.

'Promotion, Charlie – is that it?' Harrison signalled for another scotch and Resnick placed his hand down over the top of his own glass, not wanting more. 'Fed up with plain inspector?'

Resnick didn't answer. He could think of a great many places he would sooner be; not one that, right then, might be worse.

'You'll be all right there, Charlie. Oh, you might be an odd sort of a sod, not exactly by the book, but, I'll give you this, you get results. More than your fair share, I shouldn't be surprised. But then, you're still in the action. Nobody shunted you out to one side because your face didn't fit; you hadn't made the mistake to mouthing off a few home truths to the wrong suits, the wrong faces.' Harrison downed his scotch in one, wiped the back of a hand thoughtfully across his mouth. 'There's more to life out there than this, sitting back behind a desk and waiting for a pension. Open a little shop somewhere, move out to Mablethorpe and start up in a bed and breakfast. You know the way things are going, Charlie. Law enforcement. Private security. There's housing estates down in London pay for their own patrols, round the clock. Some bloke in a uniform, a guard dog and a flashlight. They don't care who it is, just so long as they can look out of their window of an evening and see somebody there. The less we do it, the more they want it; the more they'll pay. I don't want to wait until it's too late, until I retire.'

'You've got connections, then?' Resnick asked.

'Never you mind what I've got, just get off my back. That understood?'

Resnick lifted the glass to his mouth and Harrison grabbed him again, the elbow this time, the rim forced against the underside of his lip.

'Understood, Charlie?'

The pub noise went on around them. They both knew that Resnick was unlikely to do anything there and then.

'You don't know anything, Charlie,' Harrison said, turning back to the bar. 'If you did, you'd not be here now.'

''Night, Jeff. Finish the crisps, if you want.'

Resnick shouldered his way between customers and stood for several moments outside on the street. A city bus went slowly past, one woman sitting alone on the top deck, staring out. He wasn't sure where he wanted to go himself, what he wanted to do, except that, rare for him, he didn't want it to be alone.

Of course, the directory was missing from the phone booth and the young man fielding inquiries informed him that no Diane Woolf was listed. Resnick put the receiver back in place, lifted it back almost immediately and redialled. A different voice, a woman this time, gave him Claire Millinder's number. Resnick looked at it, written in biro on the back of his hand.

Charlie, we're not talking major commitment here.

He left the booth and headed back to where his car was parked, erasing her number with even movements of his thumb.

29

'There've got to be other ways,' said Grabianski, a touch wistfully.

'Of getting inside?'

'Of earning a living.'

Grice looked up from the rear window-catch in disbelief. Until he saw Grabianski's face clearly, it wasn't possible to tell if he was being serious or just winding him up.

'Funny,' Grice said. 'Can't see her hand, but it must be there.'

'Where? What hand? What are you on about?'

'Her. The one who's got you by the balls.'

'Nobody's got me by the balls.'

Grice's attention was back on the window. 'What's she after? Round-the-world cruise, is it? Then half a lifetime of happiness in Saffron Walden?'

'She isn't after anything. She's nothing to do with this.'

'Just your regular cold feet, then?'

Grabianski shook his head. 'Considering the options, that's all.'

The catch yielded enough for Grice to gain some real purchase. 'We did that a long time back, the pair of us.'

'No reason we can't think again.'

Grice smiled. 'When we're doing so well?' The window slowly lifted, only the slightest of squeaks from the sash.

'We can't go on getting dressed up and turning over other people's places for ever.'

Grice hoisted himself on to the sill. Inside the room he could see the outlines of heavy furniture, recently bought in sale-room auctions; hear the monotone of a grandfather clock. Small fortune passed over trying to reinvent an upstairs, downstairs sort of past. Stupid bastards!

He took a firm grip of Grabianski's hand and helped him through the open window, pushing it down behind them. 'You're right,' he said.

'About what?'

'We can't go on forever.'

Knowing Grice was being facetious, Grabianski waited for what was to follow.

'Every hundred extra we pay into those pension schemes now becomes around a thousand at sixty-five. Is that attractive or what?'

'Who've you been talking to?'

Grice grinned. 'You know very well. What's the point of having your own tame broker if you don't take advantage of professional advice?'

Grabianski was moving stealthily between two high-backed chairs with rolled arms. 'I'm going to check the other rooms before we start.'

'Don't worry,' said Grice, happier now they were inside. 'You're not about to strike lucky twice.'

High against the back of his skull, Grabianski was getting a headache. He went into each and every room, expecting to find someone sleeping, sitting up, insomniac, with cheese biscuits and a book. If he had found somebody, he might almost have felt easier. It would have explained this feeling he was getting, not just the one beginning to throb inside his head.

Grice whispered gleefully from the bathroom. In a plastic bag pushed back beneath a cluster of towels, close to £1,300 in twenties and tens. Mad money? Money to pay the interior decorator, cash in hand and forget about the VAT? Either way, it didn't matter: now it was their money, his and Grabianski's. Already, in a decorated cigar-box on the dressing-table of the master bedroom, they had found Eurocheques, sterling traveller's cheques, Spanish, US and German currency. Gold rings wrapped inside pink tissue and stuffed down inside a pair of tights. Grice did appreciate people who were careful – it made their task so much the easier.

'What's the story here?' asked Grabianski.

'Story?'

'The owners.'

'Moving up from Kent. House they had was going to be left standing, but the orchard and four acres were being ploughed under for the Channel Tunnel rail link. They've got a flat in the Barbican and now this. When he's not abroad, the bloke spends

233

most of his time in London. Wife and kids'll move in up here when they've got prep schools sorted out. Till then, nobody here save for the occasional weekend. Satisfied?'

Grabianski didn't answer.

'Relax.'

'I am relaxed.'

'You won't be relaxed till we're back in that cosy little flat of ours and you're whisking up your Horlicks.'

'Think that picture's worth anything?' Grabianski asked, nodding in the direction of a dusky portrait on the wall, a sallow-faced woman with her hands folded across her lap and eyes that seemed to be staring out of another painting altogether.

'Search me,' said Grice. 'You're the one with culture.'

'You make it sound like an incurable disease.'

Grice laughed, more a hiss than a real laugh, and before the sound faded they heard the key turn in the downstairs lock. As if by magic the throbbing in Grabianski's head ceased, to be replaced by a keen, knife-like pain. The front door opened and closed; one light went on, then another.

Neither Grice nor Grabianski moved, not as much as a muscle.

A radio was switched on and tuned between stations, voices, some low-grade pop music, more voices, a snatch of Haydn, silence again. Grice knew, in the semi-darkness of the upstairs landing, that Grabianski was staring at him. Knew that he was thinking whatever else, no way you could call this the occasional weekend.

What if, Grice wondered, it's another burglary? Someone with a copied set of keys, a skeleton? But then the man – the weight of his steps suggested that, yes, it was a man, went into where they knew the kitchen to be and they heard the faint click of a cupboard being closed.

Grabianski signalled towards Grice: while whoever had come in was making whatever it was in the kitchen, there was time for them to descend the stairs, get out the way they'd come in.

Now it was Grice who was indecisive, but a hand to his shoulder propelled him forwards and down. They were three rises from the foot of the stairs when Hugo Furlong, his plane rerouted to East Midlands Airport and within easy reach of a friendly bed for the night, wandered through from the kitchen.

234

He was spooning raspberry jam from a jar, just about the only edible thing he'd been able to fancy and find.

All three stared at one another.

Hugo Furlong stared at the two intruders, who, after looking hard and quizzically at each other, stared back at him.

'Don't . . .' Grabianski began to say.

The jar slid between Furlong's fingers and crashed on the parquet floor, raspberry juice and shattered glass. For some seconds the spoon stuck out from Furlong's mouth; anything less than silver, he would have bitten it right through.

Grice made a move towards him and Hugo Furlong turned fast and smacked his head against a raised wooden pillar, hard. He cried out and rocked on his heels, clutching at the pillar as he slid towards the ground.

'Move!' Grice shouted, grabbing at Grabianski's arm.

But Grabianski was leaning towards Hugo Furlong, drawn by the muffled sounds emerging from the crumpled body.

'Now!'

Grabianski shrugged him off. Down on one knee beside Furlong, careful not to kneel in raspberry jam, he took hold of him by the arms and turned him over. Blood ran freely from a cut alongside the right eyebrow, but it wasn't the blood that Grabianski was concerned with. More worrying was the sudden paleness of his face, his lack of consciousness.

'We're out!' called Grice. 'As of now.'

Grabianski struggled with the knot of Hugo Furlong's tie, fingers too fast and fumbling, forced himself to slow down, prise his fingernail beneath the silk.

'What the hell d'you think you're playing at?'

'He needs help,' Grabianski said. Even though his hands were less than steady, his voice was strangely calm.

'Help? We'll be the ones who need help.'

'He seems to be having some kind of heart attack.'

Grice pushed his arms around Grabianski from behind and hauled him to his feet, not easy with such a big man. 'Listen,' Grice said, the manner of explaining to a recalcitrant child, 'we are getting out of here this minute. We do not want to take any more risk than necessary. No fault of our own, we're already in trouble enough. Right?'

Grabianski seemed to nod.

'Good. We're going.'

'What about him?' Grabianski was glancing back over his shoulder.

'He's no concern of ours.'

'I think he's stopped breathing,' Grabianski said.

That morning, the fourth morning in a row, Hugo had sat down to what some restaurants still described as a traditional English breakfast. Right up to and including the fried bread. He had spent the previous two days – and most of the evenings – attending a sales conference in Glasgow. All the reasoning that dictated orange juice, bran flakes, at most a couple of slices of wholemeal toast, went out of the window as soon as he caught the familiar smell of bacon crisping at the edges, the spit and splutter of frying eggs. Besides, wasn't that what everyone else was having?

What Hugo Furlong was having, right now, on the polished wooden flooring of his not-yet-fully-occupied new house, was a heart attack.

'Come on,' said Grice.

Grabianski continued to unbutton the man's shirt, the pain in his head gone now, disappeared as he struggled to remember what he had read one damp afternoon, a magazine he had been leafing through while waiting to have a new exhaust fitted in a quick-fit garage in Walsall.

'Leave him.'

Clothes loosened, Grabianski began to search for a pulse; pressed his thumb as hard against the inside of the wrist as he dared and there was nothing. He shifted his position and felt alongside the neck. No pulse. Not even a whisper.

Grabianski got up and moved around the body, straightening the legs, pulling the arms back down to the sides.

'Call an ambulance,' he said.

'You're joking!'

Grabianski pointed down. 'Does this look like a joke?'

'Sure. It looks like a fucking joke to me. That's exactly what it looks like.'

'You're not going to call an ambulance,' Grabianski said, back on his knees, 'then get over here and give a hand.'

Grice watched as Grabianski took hold of the man's head – as carefully as if it were some vase that might crack, never mind the blood that was collecting there, smudging his hand – took hold of the head and tilted it back.

'A cushion!' Grabianski sang out.

'What about it?'

'Get me a cushion.' He wasn't sure if that was right, but took the one that Grice almost reluctantly handed him and squeezed it behind Hugo Furlong's shoulder blades, the back of his neck.

'Now what're you doing?' said Grice with a strange sort of fascination. Grabianski was opening the man's mouth like he was a dentist.

'Clearing the airway.'

To Grice it sounded like something to do with pirate radio.

'Shit!' Grabianski exclaimed.

'What's up?'

'He's got false teeth.'

'His age, what else d'you expect? Forty-five, fifty, you expect it. I've got an upper set, none of them mine. Don't you?'

There were a lot of fillings in Grabianski's head, but every tooth was his own. Brush with salt his grandmother had told him, salt and warm water, every day. These lower dentures had been jolted loose by Hugo's fall and were sideways across his mouth, pushing up against the palate. Finger and thumb, Grabianski eased them out and shook them a little before laying them aside.

'Jesus!' Grice complained. 'That's disgusting.'

'You'd rather he died?'

'Of course, I'd rather he died. He saw us, didn't he? He's not another one you can talk into calling us a couple of niggers. He's going to pull through this, help some police artist with a photofit, there we are flashed up all over the country on *Crimewatch*. He's dying, let him die.'

Grabianski wasn't listening.

Still on his knees, he straightened the rest of his body, brought both hands level with his face, the left locked around the wrist of the right, which was shaped into a fist.

'What the hell . . .?' Grice began. He was wondering if what he was watching was some kind of primitive Polish prayer.

Grabianski brought his fist down into the centre of Hugo's chest with all the force he could muster, striking a couple of inches to the left of the sacrum.

'Jesus!' Grice shouted again. 'I didn't mean kill him.'

Hugo's body, the upper half of it, had lifted forward with the impact of the blow, a bolt of air expelled from the lungs. But when Grabianski checked for a pulse, there was still nothing. He shifted closer to the head, pinched the nose tight and lowered his lips over Hugo's mouth.

'I'm going to throw up,' said Grice, as much to himself as either of them. The one on his back wasn't hearing too well, anyway.

'Pump his chest,' said Grabianski urgently.

'What?'

'Pump his chest.'

'Hey, you're Dr Kildare here, not me.'

'OK,' Grabianski swivelled on his knees, pushed himself to his feet, one hand going in that damned jam and picking up a splinter of glass for his troubles. 'Get round there, give him some mouth to mouth.'

'No way!'

Grabianski had his hands locked, one over the other, arms tensed straight; he leaned forward and began to pump hard against the man's heart. One, two, three, four . . . Glancing at Grice, threatening him with his eyes. Five, six, seven . . . Allowing himself a breather. There, eight, nine, ten and one for luck. Grice was still hovering, holding himself back. 'Are you going to do this or not?'

'Give myself a mouthful of whatever he's been chucking down all day? Forget it!'

'Give him mouth to nose, then?'

Grice looked disgusted. For a moment he thought, genuinely, that he was going to be sick. Grabianski elbowed him aside and repeated the mouth to mouth, twice, remembering to let the chest fall.

Move fast, more bumps to the heart. He could only keep this up so long, and without help what was the point? He would be losing him.

Grice was thinking the same things. 'Look,' he said, 'Jerry, I know what you're trying to do. Other circumstances, you know, it's the right thing to do. But here . . . we got to leave him.'

Grabianski jumped up from a couple more mouth-to-mouths and hit Grice across the face, more of a slap than a punch, not too hard but hard enough. 'You don't give a shit what happens to him, fine. Just think what kind of charge they'll give us if they find out. Eh? Think about that and get to the phone. Call emergency, tell them they've got about five minutes.' He glanced round at Hugo Furlong. 'Less.'

There wasn't time to see that Grice was doing as he was told. Grabianski checked the pulse again. Shit! Already his arms were beginning to weaken, muscles aching; his own breathing was becoming ragged. He thought it possible Grice might have left the house without phoning, left them both where they were. But then he heard the receiver being replaced. The hospital, the ambulance station, both were less than a mile away.

'Come on,' Grabianski yelled at the body below him, 'whoever the hell you are. Don't die on me now.'

As he pumped his mind continued to race. From somewhere he pulled the fact that the brain could last out three minutes after the blood had stopped flowing from it. He hoped that was right, fact and not fiction. He had no thought of still being there when the ambulance crew came barging in, all hi-tech trained, armed to the teeth with electric paddles, their – what was the word for it? – defibrillator.

In less than two minutes he heard the siren.

He covered Hugo Furlong's mouth with his own for the last time. Exhaled. Watched the chest rise and fall. 'Good luck,' he called, heading not for the rear window, but the front door, sliding the catch down on the lock so there was no way it could slam shut. The siren seemed to be only in the next street and as he ran he caught sight, reflecting off the buildings, of the swirl of blue light.

30

Jack Skelton had scarcely slept at all and when he had he had stirred restlessly, a ragged turning from one side to the other. Even so, it was his wife who woke first, alerted by the cautious opening of the door.

'Jack,' she said, hushed, her hand pushing at his back. 'Jack, wake up.'

With a small groan, Skelton rolled towards the centre of the bed, levering himself into a sitting position. Kate stood in shadow just inside the doorway, looking towards them. When Skelton spoke her name she turned and left the room, the door open behind her.

Standing, Skelton refastened his pyjamas and slipped on his dressing-gown. 'Go back to sleep.' He kissed his wife high on the cheek. It was a little after three in the morning.

Kate sat on one of the kitchen stools, dribbling honey from the blade of a knife down on to a slice of bread she had already smeared with peanut butter. Her skin was sallow; spots, small and white and without heads, clustered above and below the corners of her eyes and close to her hairline. When she had arrived back from the police station the previous afternoon, she had gone straight to her room and locked the door. Aside from visits to the bathroom, she had not emerged until now. Sandwiches and tea that had been left on a tray outside had remained untouched. She had not spoken a word to her parents, not to either of them.

Skelton watched the thin sweet line falling from his daughter's hand. In rather less than three hours there was a meeting at the station, the latest information to be appraised, final decisions to be taken, briefings to be given. All of that had to happen, regardless.

'They'll send me to prison, won't they?'

'No.'

''Course they will.'

'I shouldn't think it will even go to court.'

'Why not?'

'Because it won't.'

'Because of who I am, you mean?'

'No, that isn't what I mean.'

'Yes, it is. 'Cause I'm your daughter.'

'That won't have anything to do with it.'

'Yeah!' Kate laughed harshly, turning her head sharply away. 'Not much it won't.'

'You make it sound as though you want to be convicted.'

'They send some poor twenty-year-old with a baby to Holloway for not paying her TV licence, why not me?'

Skelton fidgeted on his stool, sighed. 'Because of your age, the lack of previous convictions, all manner of reasons.'

'Like my family.'

Skelton looked at her.

'That's right, isn't it? That's what the solicitor or whatever will say. Good home, caring parents. Good family. They'll say that, won't they?'

'Probably.'

He looked at her for a while and then asked: 'Would it be so far from the truth?'

Kate twisted the knife then put the end of the blade between her lips, licking it clean. 'Not what the papers will say, is it? If they get hold of it.'

Skelton wanted to make another cup of tea; he wanted to go to the bathroom and pee. He watched as Kate began to spread the honey here and there across the peanut butter, as though making a painting with a palette knife. He knew all too well what the newspapers would make of it, should it get out.

'Kate . . .'

He stopped himself, but not before she had followed where his eyes were pointing. Some of the honey had started to run across the surface of the table. 'That's it,' she said, 'your daughter's been done for shoplifting and all you're worried about is getting the kitchen in a mess.'

'I'm sorry,' Skelton said.

She jumped up and tore away several pieces of kitchen roll.

'Here,' pushing them into his hands, 'wipe it up. Clean and tidy before she comes down.'

'Kate . . .'

'There, go on. Every last little . . .'

Skelton threw the paper in her face, lunged forward with his arm and swept everything from the table. The knife clattered against the front of the microwave, the bread landed face down, the honey jar shattered and stuck where it fell. For the first time since she had been very small, Kate looked into the anger of her father's face and was frightened.

'Jack?' came the voice from the stairs. 'What happened?'

'Nothing. It's all right. Go back to bed.'

'I heard a crash.'

'It's all right.'

Slippered steps and the closing of the bedroom door.

Kate opened the cupboard beneath the sink to take out a dustpan and brush.

'Leave it,' Skelton said.

'It won't take a minute.'

'Kate. Kate. Please. Leave it be.' He reached out to take the dustpan from her hands and she flinched as if he were going to strike her. Skelton stepped back, shoulders slumped. When she looked at him, her face was still angled away.

'All right,' she said.

'What?'

She ran the tap and lifted a glass down from a cupboard, drank a little of the water before turning the glass on to the draining board, face down. 'Now this has happened,' she said, back to him, not looking at him, 'there's no way you can't find out the rest.'

'Is that the baby?' Kevin Naylor asked, struggling from sleep.

But, of course, Debbie was already awake.

'I thought I heard the baby.'

She was sitting more or less upright, her pillows flattened back behind her, the front of her nightdress buttoned to the neck. A paperback book, a guide to Greece, a country Debbie had never visited nor expressed any desire to visit, was folded open on the bedside table. It had been there for four nights, five, exactly the same position.

'I'll just go and check,' Kevin swung his legs around beneath the duvet.

'Stay there, I'll go.'

'It's all right . . .'

'Go back to bed.' He was on his feet but Debbie was already over by the door. Her face looked small and severe; her lips were slightly parted and the overbite at the front of her teeth was visible. 'Go to sleep.'

More definite this time, a half-whimper, half-cry from the next room.

'Maybe she was dreaming,' Kevin said.

Debbie laughed.

'Likely she'll turn over, go right off again.'

'No, Kevin. That's you. That's what you do, remember?'

'That's not fair.'

'It's true.'

'It's still not fair.'

'So you say.' She was glaring at him, the folds of her cotton nightdress clutched at her waist. The crying was becoming more insistent, higher-pitched. Kevin moved towards the bedroom door but she stood in his way.

'Come on, Debbie.'

'No.'

'Come on.'

'No!'

Kevin stepped back, looked at the carpet, the way Debbie's toes curled down into the pile. The noise was shrill and angry.

'You still think it's just a dream?'

'No. I don't know. A nightmare, perhaps. I don't know.'

'No, you don't. You don't. You can't.' With the insides of her bunched fists she was beating against him now, driving him back, slowly, across the room. 'You can't! You can't! You can't!'

Sometimes he caught at her wrists, her arms and held on until he felt whatever it was dissipate inside her; other times he backed off against the wall and allowed her to hit him, over and over, until her strength had gone and the tears came in its place. Tonight the noise from the cot was too urgent for either.

Kevin side-stepped around her, so that she was striking at air. She made a flailing grab for him, easily avoided.

'Kevin, come back here!'

He carried on through the bedroom, towards the baby's room, not looking back.

'Kevin! Don't you dare! Don't you dare!'

The baby had got herself all twisted round inside the cot; white lacy covers kicked into a corner, finally, one leg trapped inside the bars. Kevin reached carefully down and freed her, easing her up into his arms. Her face was plump and red from crying; he held her high against his chest, her head on his shoulder, patting her back softly, saying, 'Sshh, sshh.'

But she wouldn't shush: not yet.

He began to walk around the room with her, round and around the cot. Sometimes that worked, but not tonight. Once he thought it had happened; the noise cut off suddenly, but it was no more than punctuation, breath caught in the throat and held. This time when he walked he came face to face with Debbie standing in the doorway. She had been crying too, she was paler than before, her hair had a peculiar quality, seeming to have neither colour nor shape, to be just hair.

When Debbie held out her arms, Kevin placed the baby inside them and by the time he had lain back down in the bed she had stopped crying.

'Oh, God, Jack! She could have AIDS, anything!'

'Not this way, she couldn't.'

'Yes. All those teenagers living rough. You saw that programme. That's how they catch it.'

Skelton smoothed his hand along the inside of his wife's arm; her eyes widened and startled, as if caught in a sudden light. 'Not without injecting.'

She looked back at him, uncomprehending.

'You have to inject.'

'But you said drugs. You said Kate . . .'

'The HIV virus, you catch it from the needle, a dirty needle. It's not the drug itself.'

'What are you saying, then? She's just been smoking pot, cannabis?'

244

Skelton shook his head. 'LSD. Sometimes amphetamines. Mostly LSD.'

'And you believe that's all? You believe her?'

Skelton could still see his daughter's face and understood that talking to him downstairs, telling him all that she had in that neat and perfect kitchen, had been the most difficult thing in the world for her to do. There must have been times, he thought, when she had longed to throw it all in my face, like a fist. But this had not been one of those times.

'I believe her,' he said.

'What I don't understand, where did she get her hands on these drugs? It sounds as if she only has to walk in somewhere off the street and there it is. LSD. Whatever you said it was called.'

'Ecstasy.'

'What?'

'The particular drug Kate's been taking. Been buying. It's called Ecstasy. Apparently, the group she goes around with, it's pretty prevalent. The done thing.'

'But where . . .?'

'Where not? The clubs she goes, some of them. Coaches off to Sheffield, Manchester. Something to keep them going, keep them awake.'

'And that's why she was stealing?'

Skelton nodded. 'She could hardly come and ask us for an increase in her pocket-money, could she?'

'Jack.'

'I know.'

It was hard for them to look at one another; Skelton touched his wife's arm again; held, for little more than a moment, her hand.

'You're cold,' he said.

'What will happen?' she said.

Skelton didn't know. He couldn't be certain what would happen about the stealing, and anyway, that was the least of it. What he didn't know about was addiction, how possible or difficult it would be for her to stop, always supposing that was what she wanted. And other things. No matter what he had said to his wife, Skelton couldn't wipe his mind free of AIDS. All right, so she was unlikely to have caught it from using a dirty needle. But that didn't rule out other ways. No matter how hard he tried to close off his mind to those, it wasn't yet possible.

Kate.

'They'll crucify you, won't they?' his wife said, standing close beside where he was sitting on the edge of their bed. 'Not just the local ones. All of them. They'll love it.'

Skelton leaned his head against her hip. 'That doesn't matter,' he said. 'It's not important, what anyone says about me.' Wanting to mean it: knowing that it wasn't true.

31

By the time details had filtered back from the hospital, Resnick had left his house for the station. Millington greeted him at the entrance to the CID room with a concerned face and a strong tea. It took less than five minutes to convey everything that was known.

'He's going to pull through, Furlong?' Resnick asked.

'Looks like it, sir. Wouldn't have stood much chance if they'd just done a bunk, that's for certain.'

'No identification?'

Millington shifted his weight across on to his other foot. 'Too early for that. Still, I don't think there can be a lot of doubt, do you? All things considered.'

Resnick nodded agreement. The briefing was due to start in a quarter of an hour. Jack Skelton wasn't going to be too happy that he'd pulled Patel off watch and not replaced him, beyond asking one of the night patrol cars to report the presence of Grice's vehicle. Then that wasn't all the superintendent was going to be unhappy about. Poor bastard! Resnick wondered if he should try and take him to one side, say something; then, what did you say, situations like that?

'Sir.' It was Naylor, face like a bleached sheet in need of ironing. He was waving a piece of computer print-out close to Resnick's nose. 'Don't know why it didn't show before, probably asked the wrong questions; sorry, sir.'

'Come on, then.'

The DC stopped fanning the paper and held it across his chest like a shield. 'I was just checking burglaries, that's what it was, I suppose. Break-ins, security, that was the angle. I . . .'

'Kevin.'

'Yes, sir?'

'Stop fannying about.'

Naylor coughed, came close to blushing. He could hear Divine laughing at the far end of the CID room. 'What I missed, Fossey was in trouble four years back. Before Sergeant Millington interviewed him. Motor accident. Someone ran into the back of him at a roundabout. Came out that Fossey was driving without insurance. He was told to report next day, but no charge was made. All blown over.'

'And now,' said Resnick, seeing the smile beginning at the back of Naylor's eyes, 'you're going to get to the interesting part.'

'It was DI Harrison, sir. That Fossey saw.'

'Four years ago,' said Resnick. 'I wonder if that was when he met Andrew John Savage? Insurance broker of this parish.'

This morning Jack Skelton looked as though he was held together by fortitude and shaving soap. His early glance seemed to say to Resnick, all right, Charlie, I know what you're thinking, understood, but keep your distance. Resnick sat down between Norman Mann and Bill Prentiss from the Serious Crimes Squad. Tom Parker was there, exchanging pleasantries about DIY with Lennie Lawrence. Graham Millington kept opening his note book and closing it again, for all the world as if he were about to give evidence.

'Gentlemen,' Skelton said. His voice was pitched an octave lower and Resnick thought he'd aged ten years overnight. 'I think you all know Bill Prentiss. Bill's here because of some wider interest in our two rear-entry merchants. Bill?'

Prentiss was a Devonian who'd been promoted away from his home patch and kept inside his head a calendar on which he ticked off the years till he could retire back there. Little place overlooking the sea near Lynmouth: on a clear day you could see the refineries at the other side of the Bristol Channel.

'We've got a lot of unsolved burglaries,' Prentiss said, 'similar MO to your lads and stretching back, oh, six, seven years or more. Midlands, mainly, but moving up to the north-west. Nothing north of Manchester.'

'I'd always suspected that,' laughed Tom Parker.

'Bloody sight more than south of Watford,' said Lennie Lawrence.

'Never got very close to them,' Prentiss went on, 'never sure if that was down to their luck or whether they had themselves a good source.'

'You're not suggesting,' interrupted Skelton, 'that somehow

248

this pair have got people across half the country peddling them information?'

Prentiss shook his head, lit a cigarette. 'What seems to be the pattern, they move into an area, make connections, milk them for a year or two – not too greedy, never enough to let us get a good line on them – and then try somewhere else.'

'Last couple of years,' said Resnick, 'we've been the lucky ones.'

'Bit like fleas,' said Prentiss, 'they come and go.'

'Seasonal,' said Tom Parker.

'And we've got enough to tie them in with Fossey and Savage?' Skelton asked.

'Enough to bring them in and lean on them, sir,' said Millington. 'I think once one of them goes, the others'll cave in pretty sharpish.'

'What I'm still not happy about,' said Tom Parker, 'is trying to fit Jeff Harrison into this.'

Resnick passed on to the meeting Naylor's findings, Patel's suspicions, the conclusions he had drawn himself as a result of the meeting between them.

'What I don't see,' Lennie Lawrence leaning forward, uncrossing his legs, 'is what Jeff reckoned he was getting out of this, always supposing Charlie's right.'

They turned and looked at Resnick. 'It sounds a cliché, but I think he's disillusioned. Thinks any further promotion is blocked; considers he's been shunted aside, whatever reason, good or bad. He's been looking for a way out.'

'So he hooks up with this outfit for a few envelopes stuffed with fivers, that what you're saying?' Lennie Lawrence shook his head in disbelief.

'I don't think it's that at all,' Resnick replied. 'I doubt that he's had any contact with Grice or Grabianski. I hope he's never taken money from them. No, I think Fossey's what interested him. Whatever else Fossey is, he's a good talker. Eye very much on the main chance. If he saw the way things were going in the security business three years back, the spread of private police out into the general public, he could have got Jeff Harrison excited enough to want to keep him sweet.'

'What was he hoping to get from Fossey?' Tom Parker asked.

'Contacts. Names. Enough up-to-date information so that when he went in to talk to people he had it all at his fingertips. All his years in the force plus a good knowledge of state-of-the-art surveillance techniques.'

'In exchange for which,' said Prentiss, 'this Fossey wanted the occasional favour.'

'A blind eye.'

'An investigation that stalled before it got out of the drive.'

'Like the Roy burglary.'

'Exactly.'

'Jeff would do what he could, not much skin off his nose, all the time waiting for the right moment to jump ship.'

Skelton was on his feet and walking, stiff-backed. 'There's an awful lot of conjecture here, gentlemen.'

'We're not thinking of touching Harrison yet anyway, I presume,' said Tom Parker.

Resnick shook his head. 'Not until we've lifted Fossey and Savage.'

Graham Millington allowed himself a short laugh. 'See what happens when we shake their tree.'

'And Grice and Grabianski? If they find out we've moved in on their informants, they'll be gone.'

'Grice we'll take the moment he leaves his flat,' said Resnick.

'The other one? Grabianski.'

'Ah,' said Norman Mann, speaking for the first time, 'your DI and myself, we've got plans for Mr Grabianski.'

The unmarked car slowed to a halt fifty yards back from the Fossey house, the opposite side of the street. Millington leaned his elbows on the front seats and opened radio contact.

'In position?'

'Ready to go.'

'The back covered?'

'Three uniforms.'

Millington checked his watch, twenty minutes shy of seven o'clock. No indication that Fossey ever left the house before eight. The morning paper was still half in the letter-box, half out. Two pints of milk on the step. One of the advantages of living out here, Millington thought; we get ours in cartons and never till eleven.

Millington lifted the handset to check with Divine, on watch outside Savage's house. 'You're sure Savage is inside?'

Divine used his elbow to shift condensation from the car window. 'Far as we know.'

'How far's that?'

'His car's here.'

'Lights on in the house?'

'Nothing.'

'Jesus,' said Millington. 'What we don't need – one without the other.' He looked again at his watch. 'Unless he tries to leave, give it a couple of minutes.'

'Right, sir,' said Divine and signed off.

Savage had a maisonette down at the fashionable end of the canal; young executives with over-powered motors and small boats moored in the marina. Divine guessed the narrow brick buildings would have been described as individually designed, architecturally enlightened. Not enough room inside to hoist a sail. Mind you, they wouldn't hurt when you were trying to pull a bird. Waltz her straight out of happy hour in the Baltimore Exchange and on to the waterbed.

'What d'you think?' Lynn Kellogg asked, seated alongside him.

'Don't know if I could get used to all that squishing.'

'Eh?'

'Waterbeds.'

'Savage, you think he's in there?'

Divine cleared away a little more condensation; sixty seconds and they'd find out.

Graham Millington tapped Naylor briskly on the shoulder, nodded in the direction of the house.

'Sir?'

'Go.'

Naylor swung the car across to the other side of the road and brought it to a standstill at the end of the open path leading up towards the front door. As soon as the handbrake was set, he and Millington were smartly out and on their way. Less than five

251

yards on and the door opened and Fossey's wife was standing there, dressing-gown over baggy silk pyjamas, struggling to free the paper from the letter-box. She recognized Millington at the second glance and ran back inside, shouting her husband's name.

Naylor was faster than his sergeant and had the underside of one foot wedged inside the door while Mrs Fossey was still trying to push it shut.

'Lloyd, Lloyd! It's the police!'

From inside there came the sound of at least two radios playing, tuned to different stations; a banging of doors and feet heavy on the stairs.

Naylor pushed his warrant card around the edge of the door. 'I'm Detective Constable Naylor,' he said, 'and this is Sergeant Millington. We have a warrant . . .'

'Watch it!' shouted Millington and landed his left shoulder midway up the door so that it sprang inwards, knocking Fossey's young wife back to the foot of the stairs.

'Shit!' yelled Millington.

Fossey was on his way out through the French windows, still zipping up the front of his trousers. He had a briefcase under one arm, car keys in his hand and no shoes on his feet.

'Lloyd Fossey,' Millington began, but Fossey wasn't listening. So much the better. The sergeant wasn't as fast as five years ago, but over the length of your above-average suburban garden he was fast enough. One fist grabbed Fossey's collar and jerked him back hard. Case and keys tumbled towards the winter lawn and Millington's other arm tightened into a head-lock.

Kevin Naylor had finished helping Fossey's wife to her feet and guiding her in the direction of a box of multi-coloured tissues; as he came down the garden, the cuffs were ready in his hand.

'What d'you reckon?' Divine asked for the third time, sullen-faced.

Lynn Kellogg shrugged and looked towards the upstairs windows.

Divine used the knocker sharply, pounded on the woodwork with his fist. The back door had yielded nothing either.

'He can't have slept through this lot,' Divine said angrily.

'Doesn't mean he's not in there,' said Lynn, 'hoping we'll just go away.'

'Fat chance!'

He was giving serious thought to battering the door down when the black-and-white pulled up just ahead of the CID car and Andrew Savage got out.

'Look who's back from a night on the tiles,' said Divine softly, the smile returning to his face.

Savage had taken a few paces away from the curb before he realized what was going on. The cab had begun to pull clear and Savage jumped back at it, waving an arm and shouting. He landed one blow on the roof as the driver gave him the finger and accelerated away.

Savage made a run for it, sprinting towards the bridge that humped over the canal. Car headlights drew gold and silver lines along the boulevard beyond. Already there were two fishermen hunched beneath green tarpaulin alongside the water. Divine loved all this. It was Saturday afternoon again and Savage was the opposing wing forward, desperate to make the winning try. Divine's mouth was open in a full-throated roar as he dived, tackling Savage sideways into the railings of the bridge. No sooner were the pair of them down on the pavement than Divine was scrambling up again, knee hard in Savage's groin, foot on his forearm, fingers poking straight for his face – all good sporting stuff.

Savage cried out and tried to wave his arms, signalling enough.

Divine hauled him up and whirled him round, throwing him smack against the upper railing, bending him down over it, one hand firm to the base of his neck while he wrenched his arms behind his back.

'What kept you?' he grinned to Lynn Kellogg over his shoulder.

Lynn looked at him and shook her head. Divine's face was glowing. Once they were back at the station he'd sink two egg-sausage-and-bacon sandwiches and make the whole business sound like Twickenham or Cardiff Arms Park. Or South Africa.

By ten Grice was bored. The television was all men in corduroy jackets talking earnestly about amoeba or re-runs of documentaries about New Forest ponies. Not even *Playschool* or some such, with young women in short skirts who bent their knees just enough and talked baby talk. A walk into the city would clear his head and he could stop by the video shop and take out 9½ Weeks or that other one, where she walks away from the bandstand in that white skirt and it flaps open wide to her pants, the one where she's getting her lover to kill her husband. He'd recognize it from the box.

If he still felt like it, he could even wander back into the estate agent's and see if that woman was there, the one with the Aussie accent and the red heels. Grice wondered what it would cost to get her to pay a house call? He could provide the massage lotion and the towels. All she'd need to bring . . .

'Trevor Grice?'

Grice gave a little jump, hadn't seen the man coming. Turning fast he was staring into this slim face. Asian, apologetic almost. Tall for their kind, wiry most likely. Grice was reckoning his chances as he made the unmarked car opposite, saw a uniformed officer hovering at the far end of the street.

'Yes,' Grice said. 'What's up?'

'I'd like you to come with me to the station,' Patel said.

'All right,' said Grice, starting to walk with him towards the car, 'why not?'

As they drove off, Grice looked back through the rear window and saw an old woman in gym shoes, standing in the middle of the road and cackling her head off. Stupid cow!

32

'You sure you're all right?'

'Fine. I'm fine.'

'Only if something's wrong . . .'

'Jerry, I'm telling you.'

'OK, OK. It's just you seem a little . . .' He let his finger ends glide along the dimpled flesh inside her upper arm. 'It doesn't matter.'

'A little what?'

'Tense, I suppose.'

'Because I didn't come?'

'No, not that.'

'No?' Maria laughed.

'Well,' Grabianski elbowed his way lower and kissed between her breasts, below. 'That might have had something to do with it.'

'Listen,' she said, plucking at the thick hair at the back of his head; she liked the feel of it, strong, like wire almost, 'if you knew how long it had been . . . since I came with a man, anyone but myself, then you, you wouldn't be so worried.'

'I'm not worried.'

'Or so quick to notice.'

'Maria . . .'

'Hmm?'

'Nothing tense down there.' His face was pressed against her belly, tasting the residue of sweat down there, saltness of the skin in amongst where those fine dark hairs rose up like a half-opened fan.

Maria couldn't see, but she guessed that his eyes were closed and thought that now he might take a nap. Harold had gone out of the house this morning like a man who'd dreamed himself in the dock watching the judge reach for the black cap – then woke up and discovered he hadn't been dreaming at all. Whereas she had taken her second cup of coffee up to the bathroom and enjoyed a good soak while Simon Bates worked his way towards

'Our Tune'. Getting ready for Jerry Grabianski: lying there, pampered by bubbles and perfume and warm water; there, she could imagine it continuing forever. Even allowing herself to, encouraged it. Fantasies, too, not the kind with handcuffs and leather, but real Mills and Boon doctors-and-nurses stuff; the penniless artist who turns out to be the son of a rich laird and has a castle in the Western Isles. At her age. Her fantasy, and she didn't want to lose it too soon: you're not going to get your hands on a lot worth having at your age, Maria, so when you do . . .

Grabianski stirred and settled.

Maria smiled and glanced at the clock. If he dozed for another half an hour, she would get up and go downstairs, make them both hot chocolate, some of those nice biscuits she'd bought from Marks, maybe she could talk him into sharing yet another bath. Two or three a day she'd had since this had begun; Maria started to giggle but didn't want to wake him – what a psychiatrist would have to say about all that sudden desire for cleansing, her and Lady Macbeth both.

Grabianski wasn't sleeping. He kept seeing the face of that poor, overweight guy expiring in front of him. Near enough. Before getting a cab out here he had bluffed his way up to the ward and although they hadn't allowed him through the door, he had talked with the staff nurse. His condition was stable, all that could be expected; he'd had a lucky escape – change his lifestyle, he might live till he was an old man. Well, an older one.

'What in God's name did you do that for?' Grice had sniped at him, back in their rented flat.

How did you answer that kind of a question?

'You could have had us in all kinds of trouble. You could have had us nicked, five to ten, inside, that what you want?'

'He was dying,' Grabianski had said.

'I know he was fucking dying. Whose fault was that? He should never have been there in the first place.'

In the end it hadn't been worth arguing. Grabianski had left Grice to drink, his eyes closed, watching some middle-of-the-night TV movie with Angie Dickinson and Telly Savalas, and had leafed through some back issues of the RSPB magazine he'd come across in a second-hand shop on the Mansfield Road. Grice was right about one thing though, he'd thought, the man should never have been there, his property or no. Something about their luck, the quality of the information they were buying, something was changing.

Then – stirring, grazing the inside of his lips against Maria's pliant skin – all the luck he'd had hadn't been bad.

Neither of them heard the car, but there was no avoiding the peremptory knocking at the front door, the finger hard down on the bell. Maria's first thought was Harold again, but, as they knew, Harold was likely to use his own key. Grabianski's assumptions were of a different nature.

'We'd better get some clothes on,' he said, rising from the bed.

'Wait here,' Maria said, 'whoever it is, they'll go away.'

Grabianski, reaching for his trousers, bent down and kissed her softly on the mouth. 'I don't think so,' he said.

Resnick was standing alone on the doorstep. No other officers in attendance; even the car had been left out of sight on the street, rather than deliberately blocking the drive. Maria Roy stood back to let him in, causing Resnick to wonder whatever she would have worn if housecoats had not been invented.

Grabianski was in the kitchen, standing between sink and table, jacket already on and ready to go, if that was the way it was going to be.

'Inspector.'

Resnick nodded, fought back an impulse to shake the man's hand.

'Aren't we at least entitled to some kind of explanation for this?' Maria began, walking around the table to Grabianski's side.

'It's OK, Maria,' Grabianski said, patting his hand back against her arm.

'Like hell it is. This is my house. I . . .'

'Maria, hush.'

'You wouldn't like to make us some coffee,' Resnick said.

Grabianski caught himself wanting to smile – so that was the way it was going to be. 'D'you mind?' he said to Maria, who

257

glared at the pair of them but moved towards the coffee-maker all the same.

'Have a seat?' Grabianski said, for all the world as though it were his own house.

Resnick shrugged off his topcoat and folded it across the back of one chair before sitting on another. 'Your partner,' he said to Grabianski, making a point of checking his watch, 'Grice, he's been in police custody for the best part of an hour.'

Very little else was said before the coffee was brewed and in front of them. It wasn't strong enough for Resnick's palate but better than he might have expected.

'I don't know,' Grabianski said. 'The answers you want, I don't know them. Names or faces, connections. It was part of the deal. The less we were both involved the better.' He half-grinned at Resnick over his cup. 'In case of eventualities like this.'

But Resnick was already shaking his head. 'That's not what we want from you. Not what we need to know.' He drank some of the coffee. 'Most of it we have already, just a matter of corroboration.' He glanced across at Maria, who scowled and looked away. 'Asking a few people to reconsider statements they may have made a touch, er, rashly.'

Grabianski leaned back in his chair, one foot resting against a leg of the table; his cup was cradled in both hands. The inspector could have been stringing him along, though somehow he didn't think so. Which left him precisely where?

'It's the drugs then, isn't it?'

'What drugs?' exclaimed Maria, staring across at Grabianski; knowing, almost before the words had left her lips, knowing all too well which drugs they were talking about.

'On the button,' Resnick said.

'That's the name you're after. The bloke who's dealing.'

Resnick's turn to smile. 'Too late, Jerry. We know that, too.'

Grabianski's face showed that he was impressed. 'I can't see, then,' easing his chair back down, 'just what I can do to help.'

Still smiling, enjoying himself, Resnick took his time. 'Think about it some more. While we're enjoying the coffee – think about it.'

*   *   *

258

The room seemed airless, neither windows nor ventilation. Not wishing to take the chance of bumping into Grice, they had taken Grabianski to the central police station. Resnick and Norman Mann sat on the usual anonymous chairs, Grabianski with his elbows resting on the usual scarred table. As the day had progressed, his enjoyment of it had grown less.

'He's put you in for it, Grice.' Norman Mann tipped ash from the end of his cigarette on to the carpetless floor. 'Really putting you in for it. Time he's finished with you, all it'd need is an airmail stamp and you could send it straight to some studio. Sort of thing they love – stud who was a criminal mastermind. Climbing into his best suit to screw a few safes; out of 'em again to screw a few women. Stallone. What's his name? Schwarzenegger. Be fighting over it.'

Grabianski wasn't so keen on the idea of Schwarzenegger. That film where he played a Russian cop – he could picture him trying for some kind of Polish accent and missing by a mile. No, as he'd always thought, it was a shame Cary Grant grew old too soon.

'You hear what I'm saying to you?' Norman Mann asked.

'Yes.'

'You don't react.'

'Tell me how.'

'I don't know. A little anger, what do you think, Charlie? If it was me getting stiffed by my partner, I'd show a little anger, eh?'

Resnick was thinking about Jeff Harrison, not that they'd ever been partners or anything like, but all the same he couldn't help wondering how much Harrison had heard on the grapevine, whether or not he was showing a little heartfelt anger.

'You hungry, Jerry?' Norman Mann asked. 'Want something to eat?'

Grabianski shrugged. Anything that would break the relentlessness of the questioning would suit him fine. 'Yes,' he said. 'I would.'

'Later.'

Funny. Grabianski thought. Very funny.

'First I want to know if you're pissed off that your friend's stitching you up for as much of this as he can. Any more and he'll have it that all he did was drive the getaway car, keep watch. And that's not true, right?'

'You know it's not true.'

'So what are you going to do about it?'

'What can I do?'

'Maybe you don't believe us? What Grice is saying about you?'

Grabianski believed it: Grice would have had his grandmother boiled down for soup if he thought the time–profit ratio was favourable.

'What you can do,' Mann said, 'is make sure we put him inside for a long time. Tit for tat, right?'

'Yes,' Grabianski said. 'Sure. Right. Tit for tat.'

'OK!' Norman Mann scraped back his chair, clapped his hands. 'You're not saying this to get your choppers into the meat pie and mash? Three courses and then change your mind?'

Grabianski shook his head.

Anything ever goes wrong, Grice had said, really fucking wrong, it's every fucking man for himself, you remember that. Grabianski was remembering.

'Whatever you need,' Grabianski said. 'If I know the answers . . . if I can help, fine.'

'That's good. That's great. Eh, Charlie? Cause now we can go feed our faces knowing we've got that far along the line.' He rested a hand on Grabianski's shoulder, close to the neck, and squeezed. 'Then we can talk about the rest.' He squeezed harder. 'I've got to be honest, when I first heard this one, when Charlie tried it out on me, I never thought you'd go for it. Honest. Not that it isn't a good deal; for you, I mean. It is. What it was, I didn't think you'd have the bottle. Someone who gets his kicks turning places over like he's dressed for a Masonic dinner. But, no – ' He leaned his face close to Grabianski's ' – you've got the bottle, all right.' He straightened and stepped away. 'Bollocks like a bleedin' rhinoceros.'

33

Loscoe Miners' Welfare Silver Band: the bottom edge of the poster, yellow over-printed in black, curling away now, catching in the shrill wind. Last concert of the previous summer. The sun was out, January: warm for the time of year didn't have to mean warm, not when you were sitting on a bench facing the deserted bandstand, waiting for somebody who might never show.

It had taken forty-eight hours to set up the meeting and there hadn't been one of those in which Grabianski hadn't felt his mind changing, regretted what he'd agreed to do.

Wearing a wire, wasn't that what they called it?

He remembered a television programme, documentary, two detectives leaning on a prisoner to give them information, neither of them knowing of the hidden tape-recorder, evidence against them spooling unseen. A film, also, more than one, TV again, *Cagney and Lacey*, *Hill Street Blues*, the cop pretending to be the bad guy, going in with a microphone taped to his chest. Sometimes they were found out, sometimes got away with it. A .45 Magnum in the face or a citation from the commissioner, a medal – the way it went depended on status, who was playing you this time around. Whether you were needed for the next episode or not. Exactly who you were in this story: hero or villain.

Late morning and there weren't too many people around. An elderly man in a raincoat sitting, hands in pockets, at the other side of the circle, staring off into nothing that was there. Two girls from one of the nearby offices taking an early lunch, baked potatoes forked from pale plastic boxes. A ragged crocodile of primary-school kids was making its way along the steeply angled path towards the castle; pieces of paper flapped back from their hands, duplicated questions about Mortimer's Hole, a space to make a sketch plan of the moat and bailey. The teacher was hanging back, discouraging one of the boys from digging up the early crocuses with his foot.

Look at it this way, Resnick had said, people like Stafford, you don't want them out on the streets any more than we do.

'Look at it this way . . .' Resnick was standing behind the chair, hands in pockets, waiting until Grabianski did just that, looked at him at least. 'People like Stafford, they're as close to vermin as you can get; you don't want them out on the streets any more than we do.'

'Who's arguing?' Grabianski said. It was the same dim room, the same claustrophobia. Grey smoke collected beneath the low ceiling in coils: Norman Mann chain-smoking now, lighting one from the nub of the other. 'You're right. What you've told me, he should be put away . . .'

'He's a piece of shit,' put in Norman Mann.

'Arrest him,' Grabianski said. 'Lock him up.'

'We need your help.' Resnick lifted one leg, set his foot down on the seat of the chair, holding Grabianski with his eyes. Grabianski knew what he was trying to do, this Polish cop with the edges of an East Midlands accent; trying to make him feel guilty, that's what he was doing, wanting to get him involved. What was it to be? Solidarity? Poles apart?

'You've got the cocaine,' Grabianski said. 'Harold Roy, Maria, they'll testify Stafford was selling the stuff, that he'd been supplying them.' He looked from one detective to the other. 'I don't see your problem.'

'Problem is,' said Norman Mann, 'if we go that way, the only thing likely to stand up is letting this Harold have a few grams here and there and maybe, if we're lucky, possession of a kilo.'

'So?'

'So what've we got to sit on Stafford and squeeze him? Next to nothing. He comes across as strictly small time, pleads guilty and waits for his parole. What do we learn?'

The drugs-squad detective used his middle finger and thumb to make an emphatic zero. He ground his cigarette out beneath his shoe and headed for the door. 'I'm going for a piss,' he said.

Strange how one person saying it, thought Grabianski, makes you want to go yourself.

'The cocaine that comes into the country,' said Resnick, 'the shipments that matter, two to three hundred kilos at a time, they're broken down and spread out, city to city, broken down again. Someone like Stafford, in that process he's not major, but we think he is big enough to know names, contacts, procedures. Putting him away for a few years isn't enough. Nobody that matters will get touched. As far as they're concerned there's a hundred Staffords each way you turn; they'll sacrifice him as soon as spit on the street. They can trust him not to talk and as long as we've nothing more on him, they're right.'

Grabianski didn't like the way Resnick was looking at him, expecting some response; he wasn't comfortable with it. He'd look away, but whenever his head swung back again there was Resnick, staring, waiting.

'I don't see it,' Grabianski said. His hands should have been sweaty, but they were dry, the palms were dry circles, beginning to itch. 'Even if I wanted to, I don't see what I can do.'

'If we could help you with that . . .?'

'Help?'

'Find a way where you could help.'

'No.'

'No?'

'Forget it.'

Resnick moved close and Grabianski rose to his feet: two men, big men, tall. Less than an arm's length apart.

'All we need is proof that Stafford's part of something big. Not unwittingly, knowingly. That's all.'

'Proof?'

'A tape.'

'No.'

Resnick touched Grabianski on the arm. 'Jerry, you said you don't want him on the streets any more than we do. Vermin. Worse.'

'Next you'll be telling me it's my duty.'

'Isn't it?'

'As an honest citizen,' Grabianski laughed.

'Why not?'

Grabianski could feel Resnick's breath on his face, feel the inspector's hand on his arm, increasing the pressure. 'You're already helping us with a large number of previously unsolved crimes; if you were instrumental in a major drugs arrest . . .'

'I'd have my face razored before I'd been inside an hour.'

'Then we must do our best to make sure that doesn't happen.'

'Once I'm in there, there's nothing you can do.'

'I meant, to make sure time isn't what you do.'

Grabianski held a breath, turned slowly away, released it. From somewhere there was a dull humming in his ears, making it difficult to think.

'You're serious?'

Resnick didn't need to answer.

Still Grabianski shook his head. 'I'm not sure.'

'It's not just Stafford. There's people behind him making millions. You've got no more time for them than I have. You'd feel good, knowing they were locked away.'

'Stop accusing me of morality.'

'Why else jump in front of an axe for a woman you've never seen before? Why risk prison giving artificial respiration to a perfect stranger?'

'Because I didn't think about it. I was there, in the situation. I did what I did. What you're asking, it's different.' Grabianski looked past Resnick towards the door. 'I need the toilet,' he said.

'Right.' Resnick opened the door and nodded at the young constable standing there. He had escorted Grabianski out of sight when Mann came back in.

'He going to do it?'

'He hasn't said so yet, not definitely, but yes, I think he'll do it.'

''Course he will. He's banking on being convicted of nothing less than a public-service award. He's down there now, taking a slow piss, betting the judge is going to fall in love with his conscience.'

What Grabianski was hoping was that Stafford wouldn't keep him waiting much longer, stand him up altogether. What he was praying was that the whole business would get done without delay, without any trouble, without anyone getting hurt.

'Any sign?' Resnick asked.

Norman Mann shook his head. 'Nothing.'

Officers wearing dark blue overalls were stretched flat on the roof of People's College opposite; more were stationed behind the turrets of the Castle's East Terrace. Either side of the bandstand, where Grabianski was sitting, they were looking down through high-powered field-glasses, stills cameras on tripods, ready to catch anything and everything at a hundredth of a second.

Resnick and Norman Mann were hunched together in a temporary workman's hut beneath the bridge at the centre of the Castle grounds. Although they were less than a hundred metres away, their view of the scene came via a video camera, also on the terracing, played out to them on a twelve-inch black-and-white monitor. Whatever was picked up by the microphone beneath Grabianski's shirt was relayed to them through a single speaker: so far there had been a certain amount of rustling, a lot of strong breathing.

'Bloke's got the heart of an ox,' Norman Mann remarked.

'And the balls of a rhino?'

'The woman obviously thought so. Mary?'

'Maria.'

'Couldn't get enough.'

'You going to charge him? Harold?'

'You going after her? Obstructing the course of justice?'

Resnick shook his head. 'Not if this works out. Grice we've already got dead to rights. Savage is back-pedalling so fast we'll have to test him for steroids.'

'How about this Fossey?'

'Still claiming regular consultation work. Admits he may have let his tongue slip once or twice over a drink. Swears there were no kickbacks.'

'Can you break him?'

'Difficult. At least two of the most recent cases, he was on his honeymoon. Savage is the one who met with Grice, passed on whatever was passed on.'

Norman Mann shrugged. 'Either way, you come out of it smelling of roses. That's a lot of burglaries off the file.' He cracked his knuckles, grinned lopsidedly. 'Get this one, too, you're flavour of the month, no mistake.'

'Let's wait and see what happens.'

'He'll show.'

Resnick wished he could be as sure. Gazing at the monitor, Norman Mann pursed his lips into a slow whistle.

'Charlie?'

'Yes?'

'See that?'

'Uh-huh.'

'That I wouldn't mind a taste of. How 'bout you?'

A young black woman, Afro-Caribbean, wearing a smart dark suit, white blouse, black heels, walked in front of Grabianski and the camera panned with her, steadying as she sat down at one of the benches. Watching, Norman Mann whistled again as she crossed her legs; smiling, he blew on the screen as if to cool it down.

'No, Charlie? Expect me to believe that?'

'No.'

'You surprise me, Charlie. Never struck me as prejudiced before.'

Resnick straightened and arched his back; they'd been cooped up inside for too long.

'Shit,' murmured Mann. 'Why can't he keep the camera still?'

'Good reason,' Resnick said, bending forward again. 'Look.'

Taking his time, not a care in the world, Alan Stafford was strolling along the avenue of trees towards the glassed-in bandstand, hands in his blue car-coat pockets.

34

Grabianski had seen him coming too, had known him from the description he'd been given, been aware of the hardness of wood against his back as he pressed himself against the bench, the blue British Airways bag back on the ground between his feet. Stafford continued to take his time, sauntering, taking an interest in the trees, the coming flowers, the way the sun lit up the domed roof of the new Lace Hall beyond Weekday Cross. Of course, he was looking at none of those things; he was checking to see if this was a set-up, if he was being watched.

At first it seemed as if something might have spooked him, as though he might stroll right past Grabianski and only stop at the wall, maybe pause there to enjoy the view. The two soccer grounds, their floodlights poking up at either side of the Trent; the stoned windows of the empty British Waterways building, the pale-green paint of its doors flaking and fading away; low roofs of the Gunn and Moore factory just across the boulevard. Here it was, close to here, Albert Finney stood with Rachel Roberts filming *Saturday Night and Sunday Morning*. Was that really more than twenty years ago?

Stafford paused at the last moment, paused and sat.

'You Grabianski?' he asked.

'Stafford?'

Stafford nodded, eyes now firmly on the bag.

'I was just beginning . . .'

'Is it there?' Stafford interrupted him.

'The . . .'

'Shut it!'

Grabianski felt himself go tense, willed his muscles to relax. 'It's OK,' he said. 'It's all there, the cocaine.'

'Why don't you wave it around? Broadcast it?' Something wild was flying at the back of Stafford's eyes. Till the moment he'd sat down he had seemed really casual, but now, alongside Grabianski, close alongside the kilo of cocaine, it was as if something had him hyped up. As if he'd drunk down five strong coffees, continental roast, one after the other: that or something else.

'There's no one close,' Grabianski said, glancing right and left. 'Nobody can hear.'

'You sure it's all there?' Stafford was leaning back against the end of the bench, one arm stretched out along it, fingers fast-tapping the wooded edge. His eyes, when they settled at all, settled on the carry-on bag.

'Sure,' said Grabianski and reached down to pull back the zip.

'If it's been messed around, cut with something, anything . . .'

'Nothing. Look, it's the way it was. Aside from putting it in the bag, it hasn't been touched.'

'Aside from taking it from Harold Roy's safe.'

'Yes,' Grabianski agreed. 'Aside from that.'

'That bastard!' hissed Stafford. 'That stupid bastard!'

'It wasn't his fault,' Grabianski said. 'Bad luck.'

'Screw bad luck!' said Stafford with feeling.

Grabianski couldn't stop himself from glancing up, up towards the Castle, knowing that he shouldn't.

'What's that?' said Stafford sharply.

'What?'

'What the hell are you looking at?'

'Nothing. I was looking at nothing.'

'Suddenly you were looking round.'

'The Castle, I suppose. I don't know. Why does it matter?'

'If you're fucking me around, you know what that'd mean? For you? You got any idea?'

Grabianski nodded.

'You sure?'

'I think so.'

Stafford's hand was fast, fingers digging deep into the leg, each side of Grabianski's knee. 'You need to do more than think.'

'All right, I know.'

'Know what?'

'What you'd do.'

'If you were jerking me around.'

'Right.'

'What'd I do?'

Grabianski didn't answer. His leg was hurting, a nerve seemed to be trapped; he wanted to lean back and then slam a fist to the side of Stafford's head and make an end of it.

'I'll tell you what I'd fucking do,' said Stafford. 'I'd fucking kill you.'

'Yes,' Grabianski said, 'I know that.'

'Good.' Stafford pulled his hand away, leaving Grabianski wanting more than anything to rub his leg but not allowing himself to do it, not giving Stafford any more satisfaction than he could help. Resnick had been right, Stafford was vermin: he needed locking away for a long time, forever.

Grabianski picked up the bag and placed it on the seat between them.

'What d'you do that for?'

'We're going to exchange it, aren't we?'

Now Stafford was looking around, jumpy as a couple of men in muted grey suits walked around the circle, a woman talking baby-talk into a pram, two kids running across the grass and the teacher shouting at them to get back where they belonged.

'That's all you've got in there? The package?'

'What else?'

Stafford gave a nervous little laugh. 'How about a microphone? A tape-recorder? You got one of those in there? A little insurance on the side?'

'Look for yourself,' Grabianski said, moving to open the flight bag again. 'I promise you, there's no recorder in there. No mikes.'

Stafford pushed his hand down on the top of the bag, keeping the zip closed. 'You know what I'm doing here, don't you? Paying you for what's already mine.'

'We've been into that.'

'Yes. Right.' He reached inside his coat, going for an inside pocket and Grabianski held himself tense, watching. It was a white envelope, five by seven, some such size. Not very fat; fat enough.

'You don't want to count it,' Stafford said.

'Yes.'

'Like fuck you do!'

'That's right.'

Stafford slapped the envelope down into Grabianski's out-stretched hand and watched while the flap was torn aside, the notes flicked through still out of general sight.

'OK,' Grabianski said, placing the envelope in the inside pocket of his own jacket. 'Here.' He slid the British Airways bag further along the bench towards Stafford, who took both handles into his left hand.

Grabianski held out his right hand for Stafford to shake.

Ignoring it, Stafford stood up quickly now, one curt nod and he was standing, turning away.

'Shit!' whispered Norman Mann at the monitor.

'Wait,' said Resnick, continuing to watch and listen.

'Hey!' Grabianski called. And as Stafford's head swung back towards him, 'What's the hurry?'

'What d'you think . . .?'

'I've got an idea.'

Alan Stafford hesitated, seconds from going, walking clear.

'A proposition.'

Stafford with the words on his lips, telling this jumped-up sneak-thief where he could stuff his proposition.

'How many kilos could you put me in touch with, regular?' Grabianski had him, thought he had him, close enough to try a smile: his winning smile. 'Anything close to five, six, we could be in a lot of business.' Stafford heading back towards him, sitting back on the bench. 'A lot of money.'

'I already make a lot of money.'

'Yes. But there's always room for more.'

'You're a burglar. A house burglar, for Christ's sake.'

'Hitler was a house painter; that didn't mean he was in the same trade all his life.'

'What the fuck's Hitler got to do with anything?'

'Nothing.'

Stafford was staring at him; a nerve beside his right eye was doing somersaults.

'Moving stuff around,' Grabianski explained, 'I meet a lot of people. I know they're in the market for other things. Your kind of thing. But regular. It would have to be regular. You understand?'

'Think I'm fucking stupid?'

'I mean, if this . . .' pointing at the bag, '. . . if this is just a one-off thing, we can forget it.'

'Don't you worry about that.'

'I mean, I could go elsewhere . . .'

'I told you. As much as you want, I can get.'

'Cocaine?'

'Of course, cocaine. You think I'm talking . . .'

Suddenly Stafford wasn't talking any longer. The sun slipped out from beneath a cloud and a reflection leaped from the college roof right into Alan Stafford's eyes. Binoculars, telephoto lens, it didn't matter. Whatever it was, it shouldn't have been there.

'Wait . . .'

But Stafford was on his feet, arching away from Grabianski, turning and then having second thoughts, swinging back; his hand came out from his car-coat pocket and something else bright flickered in the sun. Grabianski saw and dived back fast but never fast enough. The tip of the blade broke the skin at the wrist beneath the arm; broke and sliced across the ball of the thumb, the palm, through the webbing taut between centre fingers. Grabianski screamed and pulled his hand away, flinching as the knife arced away before flying in again for his face.

Resnick was already up and running, Norman Mann behind him, shouting orders through the microphone.

Something splashed across Grabianski's eyes and he blinked it away; when he touched it with his fingers, then he knew that it was blood.

Alan Stafford was running full-tilt towards the bandstand, swerving left between German visitors complete with guide books, nearly colliding with an elderly man who had stooped to replace his shoe. Resnick changed his direction on the slope, veering towards the exit, keeping it between Stafford and himself. Stafford charging at him now, airline bag in one hand, knife in the other.

Belatedly, somebody along the avenue of benches pointed a hand and began to shout a warning.

Resnick, stitch sharp in his side, breathing heavily, stood his ground. The knife, he told himself, whatever else, watch the knife. It was the bag that struck him, low and to the left of his stomach, doubling him forward. Resnick felt his knees going, a

271

blur of movement racing past him, a shrieked curse; he threw himself sideways as he fell and grabbed at whatever he could.

Stafford's leg.

The thin material of the trousers slithered through his hands and Resnick's fingers caught ankle and heel. Stafford swore and yelled as he struck the path and kicked his other foot viciously at Resnick's body. The first blow connected with the collar bone, sending him numb. The second hit the jaw below the ear and the third never landed because Grabianski had Stafford by the hair and collar and was dragging him back, grazing his face along the surface till it bled.

'Right,' said Norman Mann, loud to be certain he was heard. 'You can let him go.'

Grabianski, blood running from a four-inch cut across his own forehead, released his hold and stepped back. On his knees, face to the ground, Stafford allowed his arms to be held behind his back while he was handcuffed.

'You OK?' Grabianski watched as Resnick, still breathing unevenly, got to his feet.

'Better than you,' Resnick said, looking not just at the wound to Grabianski's head, more the freedom with which he was losing blood from the cut across his hand.

There were police officers around them everywhere: uniform, overalls, plainclothes. What they wanted were nurses, surgeons, an ambulance.

'Did you get it all on the tape?' Grabianski asked.

Resnick nodded. 'Yes,' he said. 'Every word.' He wanted to go forward and shake Grabianski's hand but wasn't certain that if he did that one of them might not fall over. 'Thanks,' Resnick said instead. 'Thanks.'

Bleeding, Grabianski grinned.

35

They were sitting in Mackenzie's office on the upper floor of Midlands Television. The company retained to service the rubber plants had gone into liquidation and the specimen behind the producer's desk was drooping dangerously and beginning to brown around the edges. Mackenzie was at his most businesslike, tenting his fingers together over a sheaf of faxes and the current copy of *Broadcast*. Seated discreetly to one side, Freeman Davis sipped Perrier from a plastic cup and looked cool.

'What you have to realize, Harold,' Mackenzie said, 'we wouldn't be doing this if we didn't think it was right. For the series. That's what we're all concerned about, after all. The series. *Dividends.*'

Harold Roy didn't say a thing. After what had been happening he was numb; in his mind, numb. The police had intimated that he might not be charged, at least not with anything major, but they still weren't making promises. Not until he had given them everything they needed: on the dotted line. 'Keep your nose clean,' the drugs-squad detective had said, tapping one nostril. 'We'll be in touch.' Maria had packed and unpacked her suitcases a half-dozen times, whether for a holiday or a divorce was uncertain.

'Harold,' Mackenzie said.

'Um?'

'You heard what I said?'

'Um.'

'You know I've talked with your agent.'

Harold nodded.

'Your name stays on as long as you want it that way. Beneath Freeman's.'

'Be . . .' Harold swallowed it back. Freeman Davis looked smugger than usual, if that were possible. When you were in the catbird seat, the only things were to get fat and smile.

'. . . so there'll be no problems with residuals,' Mackenzie was saying. He may have said more, but if so Harold had missed it.

There had been a letter that morning from the insurance company: since they understood the updating of security measures they had advocated had not been carried out, the level of cover was in doubt. Harold tugged at his trousers, just above the knees. Mackenzie was staring at him; Freeman Davis at the rubber plant. Had he missed something else?

Executive-like, Mackenzie strode around the desk and lifted Harold's coat from the black ash-and-chrome stand. He held it out and waited for Harold to get up and step into it.

"Bye, Harold,' Mackenzie said, pushing the door to behind him. 'You can find your own way out.'

Grinning, Freeman Davis made his two first fingers and thumb into a gun, set it against his temple and pulled the trigger.

Resnick knocked on Skelton's door and waited. The superintendent called him in, seeming sprucer than at any time in the past few days. When he'd walked into the station that morning, much of the snap had been back in his stride.

'How're the bruises, Charlie?'

'Deep purple, sir.'

'Picture in the *Post* makes it look as if you've gone three rounds with Mike Tyson.'

POLICE BREAK CITY DRUG RING the headline had read. *Inspector makes dramatic arrest in shadow of Robin Hood.* There had been a paragraph about a police informer, suitably vague; Grabianski had not been named. In a column on page two, Norman Mann of the Drugs Squad was quoted as saying the arrest had come about as the result of months of undercover work and coordinated investigation.

'Sooner me than you, sir,' Resnick said.

There had been no mention anywhere in the press, local radio or television about the arrest of Skelton's daughter. The DCI had agreed that in view of her lack of any previous record, no charges would be brought. Restitution and apologies had been made to the firms concerned, along with a promise that extra policing would be maintained.

'Tom Parker was on the phone earlier,' Skelton said, 'the Chief Constable's received Jeff Harrison's resignation. Apparently he's off to head up a new security agency in south London; specialize in anti-burglary work, uniformed neighbourhood patrols, ex-forces personnel.'

Skelton offered Resnick a chair. 'Grice's been charged?'

'Thirty-seven counts of burglary. Grabianski gave us a list half a yard long. Photographic memory.'

'Fossey?'

Resnick made a face. 'He'll go into court screaming not guilty.'

'You do think he'll go to trial?'

'I'd like to be certain.'

The superintendent prodded papers on his desk. 'We'll have to get something stronger than this.'

'We'll keep trying.'

Skelton nodded. 'I know what I've been meaning to ask you, Charlie? How's the house sale going?'

'Sounds as if someone's made an offer. Matter of fact, I'm off to look at a new place this evening, just in case.'

'Another house?'

Resnick shook his head. 'Flat.'

'Better, Charlie. More sensible. What d'you need a whole house for?'

The cats? Resnick thought. He didn't say it.

The CID room was like Gatwick in the middle of a security alert. Above the movement of bodies and the spiral of voices, Resnick heard Patel's shout and saw him pointing towards one of the phones. He pushed his way across and picked the receiver from the pile of pink forms where it had been laid.

'Resnick.'

'Inspector Resnick?'

'Yes. Who's this?'

'Diane Woolf.'

'Diane . . .'

'Don't tell me you've forgotten me already?'

'No.' He could hear the smile in her voice and see the shades of red as she moved her head. 'I was just surprised.'

'You're a star now, you know.'

'I see,' said Resnick, and then, when she didn't respond, 'Five-minute wonder.'

'Well, I'm impressed.'

'Thanks, but you shouldn't be.'

'Modest with it.'

What was she phoning for, Resnick wanted to know. What was this all about? The sound was still swilling about him and he had to keep the earpiece pressed hard against his head to hear her clearly.

'Anyway, congratulations.'

'Thanks.'

For Christ's sake, thought Resnick, ask her to meet you for a drink. What's wrong with dinner?

'Maybe we'll bump into one another again,' Diane Woolf said. ''Bye.'

Resnick stared at the phone for a few moments before setting it back down.

'It'll look a lot better when there's furniture,' Claire Millinder was saying.

The walls were the not-quite-white of toilet tissue. Passing through the kitchen she switched on the extractor fan to prove that it worked; dropped paper into the sink and ran the tap to test the waste disposal.

'Twin power-points in every room,' she said.

If Resnick stood up on his toes he could leave finger marks on the ceiling.

'So what do you think?' Claire asked.

They were standing by the double-glazed window, rustproof aluminium frame. Resnick couldn't be certain if what he was seeing was a reflection of this flat in the glass or another one opposite, different but exactly the same.

'I think I'd go mad inside a month,' he said.

'Let's go and have a drink,' Claire Millinder said. 'Spend some of my commission.'

'Spend what you're getting from me, we'll be lucky to drink water.'

'What I get from you,' Claire grinning her broken-toothed grin, 'I might as well be in the desert.'

'Thanks.'

'For nothing, Charlie. Come on, we'll find some good New Zealand wine and first thing in the morning I'll phone those people and tell them we're sorry, but the deal's off.' She locked the flat door behind them and slipped her arm through Resnick's on the way to her car. 'The vendor's changed his mind.'

'You know I'm not going to stay in for ever, don't you?'

Kate looked at her parents across the breadth of the living room. Wendy Craig was doing something in a conservatory but nobody was watching.

'We know that, Kate,' Skelton said.

His wife got up and left the room.

'I can't sit around here like a vegetable.'

'Nobody's suggesting you should.'

'She is,' said Kate, nodding towards the sound of crockery from the kitchen.

'That's not true.'

'Isn't it?'

'Kate, when you do go out, we'll want to know where.'

'I'd have told you before if you'd asked.'

'Told us the truth?'

She gazed for a moment at the television set where happy families were being created to the sound of studio laughter. 'Probably not.'

'And now?'

'Yes. All right, I'll try.'

'More than that.'

'All right. I'll tell you where I'm going. The complete itinerary. Satisfied?'

Skelton looked at her carefully. 'And the rest?'

She swung her legs from beneath her and headed for the stairs, back up to her own room. 'You're going to have to trust me, aren't you?'

Claire stopped the car outside Resnick's house but kept the engine running. 'That was nice, thanks.'

'Yes, it was,' Resnick agreed.

'See what a good time you can have when you relax?'

He set a hand to the catch and opened the door. Dizzy was already running along the wall to greet him, his tail with that old familiar crook.

277

'Here,' Claire said, fishing in her bag. 'You'd better have these.' She dropped the keys in his hand, the agency tag still attached. 'I'll get someone round tomorrow, take the board down.'

'Thanks.'

He stood a shade anxiously on the pavement, looking down.

''Night,' Claire said, raising her hand. She leaned across the front seat and watched him walk towards the door, the cat fish-tailing in and out between his legs.

'I'll give you a ring some time,' Claire called.

'Do that.' Resnick waved back, unlocked the door and let Dizzy into the house. Just before she drove off, Claire saw him stoop towards the mat and pick something up, an envelope. The way he looked at it, she hoped it wasn't unwelcome news. She turned the car around and headed back towards the main road, towards the city, and by then Resnick's door was closed and he was back inside his house.